MALFUNCTION

THE NEW AGE SERIES
BOOK 6

NICOLETTE FULLER

NEW AGE SERIES

New Age

Rebirth

Meridiana

Crisis

Sacrifice

Malfunction

Resurrection

New Dawn

Retribution

Lost Years (A New Age prequel)

I dedicate this book to the dreamers.
To the romantics and to the rebels.
To the non-believers, who can now believe. To the believers (and beta readers) whom I thank.
To all those who inspired me. From main characters to the secondary ones.
The Rebel Commander's, Dorian's, Adam's, and Amara's.
To my husband James Fuller who I'm sure wanted to throw a thesaurus at me many times. Who encouraged me to write and do something with this story.
This is for you.

MALFUNCTION

HOKURA NERVOUSLY LICKED HER lips as she stood in the medical facility. Had she waited too long? There was a possibility. This morning's coughing fit had been a bad one, and she had regretted not doing this sooner. She picked up the phone and dialed the number she had etched in her memory, even though she had never dialed it before. Until today, there wasn't a need to do so. She put the phone back from the receiver and waited for a moment. The phone rang, and she picked it up.

"Dorian..." Her voice was listless.

"Hokura? You've never paged me before. What is it?" Worry struck him, she always just sought him out, and lately, she knew exactly where to find him.

"I need you to meet me in the medical facility. It's urgent." With that, she hung up the phone. It had been three weeks since his operation had been deemed successful. She couldn't hold out any longer. Things were getting worse, and she feared she might be too late as is. She waited and watched as he walked up the hallway towards her when her throat caught.

She tried to steady herself but couldn't help it. Maybe this was for the best. He could see it for himself as she doubled over and started coughing violently to the point that she was grasping at her chest as pain burned through her.

He ran to her, worry etched upon his face. "Hokura!"

When she was finally done and could finally catch her breath, she was shaking as she looked up at him as blood oozed from her mouth. "I'm dying."

"What do you mean you're dying?" He brought her into his arms and cradled her. Fear washed over him.

She closed her eyes. "I'm not healing. My system is shutting down. Something is happening, and I'm not getting better."

He trembled at the thought. "How long?"

"Since you rescued me...I think..." She coughed again. This time the taste of blood filled her mouth, as her chest tightened. "This was the final trial...Dr. Richter injected me with something before you rescued me. It's attacking and weakening the regenerated cells."

"Why didn't you tell me?" His voice was hard as he shook her. "Dammit, why didn't you tell me right away if you suspected something?"

"I needed to make sure you were going to be alright." She smiled lightly at him. "I'm sorry, I guess I was in denial, but now you know...I need you, Dorian."

He faltered. "We're going straight to the medical labs." He looked at her in worry, he knew the answer, but he needed to hear it from her. "Have you told Gavin?"

"No..."

He shook his head as they walked. He couldn't conclude anything yet. He didn't even know what to say. Anger boiled inside of him that she would keep this from him. Even more so, that he *knew* she was keeping something from him, and this had been it. The anger wafted into rage. If there was anything wrong with her system, it had been going on for over four months already when he could have been on top of things. He glowered; she hadn't told him because she had been worried about his wellbeing. He took a deep breath. He was hoping this would possibly be nothing. Still, with what he had just witnessed, he couldn't help but feel like he had missed some key facts. She had been continuously exhausted, something he figured had to do with all the trauma she had encountered, plus he knew that dealing with him in the state he had been in would exhaust the strongest of people. They walked to a large medical room as Dorian opened the door and held it for her. What could he possibly say? He needed to remain calm and keep the storm brewing inside of him from spilling out. She sat on the gurney and looked at him expectantly as he set his jaw. "I'll need to draw blood, and you're going to tell me absolutely everything. Do not leave out any details, no matter how minuscule you think they are. I need to know *everything,* Hokura."

She shrank back; his voice was stern, but she knew this was to be expected. She knew he wasn't going to be happy about the situation. She had only hoped that he would be able to find out what was happening and hopefully cure her. "I'm just so tired Dorian, even when I sleep, I haven't woken up actually feeling rested in weeks. I've been getting the sweats, my heart races..." she looked at him. "Not like that...it physically hurts. My vision starts to blur, and everything spins around me. I feel like I can't breathe. I'm bruising..." She lowered her pants to her hip. "I walked into the kitchen table three days ago..."

Dorian took in the dark bruise. It horrified him; it looked like high-impact damage. "Did you break the table?" he asked.

She shook her head. "No, I simply scuffed against it with my hip. The bruise from when I fell off the bike is still there."

He felt himself go pale as a whitewash of sickness flooded over him. "We'll need to get you into X-rays. I want to look at your chest, as well as a CT scan. I want to make sure I don't miss anything." His head lowered. What on earth could Dr. Richter have injected her with that could be destroying her cells like this? How was it possible that something was killing her? He didn't want to think of that yet. He couldn't. "Does Gavin even know you're down here?"

She shook her head.

His world turned red, the negligence, unto herself, unto the person most precious to him. She had allowed this to happen to herself, and it had been happening right under his nose for the last few months. He had to turn from her. He walked away, needing his distance. "Damn you, Hokura," he seethed. It hurt to be upset with her, to feel this kind of anger towards her. He looked back at her. "How could you be so damn careless?"

Her body slumped on the gurney as she lay back on it. She didn't have the strength to fight him. She simply lay there.

"You will answer me! You owe me an explanation!" Dorian's tone was hard as he walked up to her again.

Hokura closed her eyes for a second. "I knew only you could save me, but you needed to be whole and in the right mindset to do so. I knew you were struggling with the setbacks, that you needed to have your full concentration on getting your arm back, so I waited. I was going to tell you, but it never came out. I had lost the chance. Whenever I was around, your body fought harder. You couldn't even be around me. You were my priority. Either way, I knew you would be successful. It wasn't until a few weeks ago that it had gotten noticeably worse." She wasn't going to be sorry for this as she looked up at him. "And now that everything is in place for you, you can work on fixing me."

His brows furrowed in sorrow as he took her hand. "I swear I will. I will make this right again, but dammit, you should have told me! If you had, then maybe things would have been different!" His voice softened. "I thought we were done keeping secrets..."

She hadn't said anything. There had been many secrets, like what had truly transpired on the roof. Those raw feelings that if he would have ended it, she would have been beside him in death. She didn't want to think of that now. She simply lay on the gurney with a shameful expression on her face when he looked at her again.

"Before I begin, you are going to tell Gavin. This instant!"

"What?" Hokura cried in horror.

Dorian pointed at her. "You owe him that much! I can't be doing blood tests when you bruise like that without your husband knowing that's going on here." He picked up the phone and dialed the governor's office. "Gavin. I need you down to the medical facility. Room 101A, it's urgent." He hung up the phone before he could say another word as he stared at Hokura's worried expression.

"You're not being fair! I have no idea what to even tell him!" she cried, sitting up on the bed.

"Fair?" Dorian asked as he gave her a dark smirk and shook his head. "This isn't about fair anymore, Hokura. You'd best figure out what you're going to tell him because he's on his way."

With that, Dorian left the medical room and waited in the hallway. He needed to compose himself. His hands were shaking. He quickly put them in his pockets as he tried to breathe. His nightmare, his greatest fear, was unraveling in front of him. She couldn't be dying, he would fix this, but first, he needed to do the right thing. Gavin... had he noticed a change in her? Or had he brushed it off as everyone else did? That she was just healing, and it had been a slow process due to her physical and emotional trauma. Either way, he needed Gavin to know before he went any further. He took another deep breath, trying to steady himself. He couldn't be in the room with her right now. He couldn't look upon her without feeling angry, so he would bide his time and wait for the governor.

Gavin walked down the hallway and gave him a questioning glance. "What is it?" His eyes narrowed.

"It's your wife," Dorian said in a low tone. "She has something she needs to tell you."

Gavin's eyes widened; he gave Dorian a look which the professor knew right away what the accusation was.

Dorian huffed. "It's nothing like that, governor." He placed a hand on his shoulder. "But you need to brace yourself for what she's about to tell you, and you need to know that we will do everything we possibly can."

Gavin couldn't help but feel confused. "Why aren't you telling me?"

"Because you deserve to hear it from her, she *just* told me. She's been hiding this for a while." He opened the door and let Gavin slip into the room. He didn't dare follow; this was something that needed to be private between the two of them.

Gavin walked into the room. His eyes met hers. She looked frightened as she licked her lips and took a deep breath but didn't say anything. He had no idea what he was about to hear, but he knew he needed to remain calm with her. "Dorian said you have something to tell me." He ran his hand nervously through his hair as he sat beside her and took her hand. "Whatever it is...we'll work it through. It'll be okay."

"I don't know if it will, Gavin..." Her voice was small. "Ever since I came back from being rescued... my system, it's been shutting down." Her eyes met his in full sincerity. "Gavin, I'm dying."

"What? No..." Gavin cried as he threw his arms around her. "This whole time? Since you've been back? You knew?

You knew, and you didn't tell me." Why did this feel like such a large betrayal as his lips trembled? "How could you?"

"Gavin," she cried. "I'm so sorry...I...for a while... I was just in denial, but then things started changing. I thought I had more time. I thought there would be a way to fix this, or that I would just simply grow old as my system stopped working. I didn't think this would happen so fast, but I know that I'm running out of time."

"So what? You thought you would just be some regular human and age out and die?" His voice hitched. "Is that what you've wanted, Hokura? To simply be a regular human being and die? To be just like *him*? Is that what this is about? You're done, and you want to die so part of you can return to James?" He grabbed hold of her arms as tears started to stream down his face. "Is that why you're leaving me?" He didn't know what to say or do, but maybe if he were physically holding onto her and didn't let her go, this wouldn't happen.

"That's not at all what this is about, Gavin. It was never about that." Tears fell from her eyes. "I didn't think it would end like this. I thought it was just another issue, just another thing that I had to overcome, and that Dorian would fix this."

"He can fix this!" Gavin trembled. "Of course, he can fix this. He just needs some time. We have the means to help you, to fix you, to keep you alive. We'll get everyone on this, every doctor, every technician, every scientist. I'm the governor, dammit! We will save you if it's the last damn thing that I ever do in this life!"

Her face held nothing but sorrow. "You need to be prepared if they can't, Gavin."

Shock filled his face. As if she had just shot an arrow through his heart and ripped it out of his chest...to say such a thing. "No," Gavin stated. "I will not prepare myself for such a thing Hokura, how can you ask me for such a thing? How dare you!" He shook her. "I just got you back! And if you have already accepted this, already accepted that you're going to die, then you've already given up without even fighting. What about your children, think about me, about Dorian! Dammit, Hokura, have you given this any thought? You can't simply tell us to prepare for this and to possibly accept it!" He couldn't think...he couldn't get his thoughts straight. "What does Dorian think of all this? You told him first, why him!" He couldn't even be mad with her about that. He couldn't be upset that he would be the first person she would tell. What fueled his anger was that she had told him to prepare. "What did Dorian think when you told him?"

She trembled. "That's why you're here. I just told him, and he said that I needed to tell you before he did anything."

"Don't you trust him? Don't you know that he will do whatever he can to save you?" He needed to know that she did. "He would die himself to save you, Hokura! You know that! I know that! Please tell me that you have faith in him and that you know he's going to save you from this!"

"I..." She faltered.

"Don't *do* that," Gavin cried as he brought her to him and embraced her. "Don't you dare doubt for even one second that he's not going to save you! I won't allow it! I won't allow you to accept that you're dying! That's not how it is! That's not how it's going to be! Dammit, you're going to live forever, and you're going to stay by my side forever." He looked down at her. "Dammit, I don't even care if you stay by my side. I don't care... I can't care... all I can care about it that you live on and that you don't leave us!"

"Gavin!" she cried. The sentiment broke her heart even more that her husband suddenly didn't care if she stayed by his side, whether she was with him or not. "Gavin, I made a vow to you, and I love you ...this has to do with the facts that I might not see..."

He didn't want to hear it as he held her, as the world around him broke apart. "No more... please... Please no more," he sobbed. "What will I do if I lose you? What would my life be without you in it, Hokura? I would be nothing. This compound would be nothing. Life wouldn't be worth living, and I have an extended one. I wouldn't want to live it without you." He felt like he was begging. He *was* begging, begging her not to be telling him this. At that moment, he wished he could go back in time, that he would have paid a little more attention to what she had been hiding from him. "We're going to figure this out. I am going to be by your side through all of this. I'll step back from being governor until I see you through this and you're deemed okay. Adam can take over my duties. He's been learning the ropes." He looked at her. "I swear to you with all that I am that you are going to continue on for a very long time Hokura, that this wasn't all in vain." Why did it hurt so bad? Why was he going through this again? Already the grief had set in, and he had wanted to deny the reality that there would ever be a time where she wouldn't exist at his side. And then, at that very moment, he couldn't help but understand her more than ever. She had gone through this with the rebel commander. She had these exact thoughts of denial and not wanting to accept the fact that he was a mere human and that she was genetic perfection and would go on living forever.

"Gavin, I promise I'm not going to give up on you, that I'm not going to give up on anyone, but I needed to wait on this. Please, you need to understand that I needed to make sure that Dorian was of sound mind before I told him. That I *do* believe in him, that I want to believe that he's going to save me but first I needed him to deal with what happened. I needed him to be whole again before he could put me back together."

"You could have said something earlier, dammit! Spindler and Lucien would have worked at his side to see to you. He would have done something...he would have even possibly taken off that damn bionic arm that was killing him if you would have told him," Gavin seethed through the tears. "You just allotted more time to pass when we could have already been on this."

Dorian walked through the door; he had heard enough. "I have told her as much, but we're not going to sit and play the blame game here." He looked at Gavin. "I am going to need to administer a number of tests. You need to be prepared for how her body reacts to them. She's been bruising at apparent simple bumps." His eyes went to hers. "There will most likely be light bruising from the array of samples that I'm going to need from her, blood tests especially."

Gavin's grip on her softened. "Do whatever you can... please, Dorian."

"You don't have to tell me twice, governor. This is going to be a delicate project, I am unsure what we're dealing with, but my hopes are we can get to the bottom with this." He stared hard at Hokura. "You are not to accept this for one second. We have the technology and medical know-how to create peace-keepers. We certainly have the knowledge of how to keep them alive. You will not give up on us."

Hokura nodded as she bit her bottom lip.

Dorian's tone was stern. He had reverted to being the professor with her. He was now a mentor who was very upset with her. "If there is anything further. Anything at all that you have left out from this or from the past, you are to tell me right now."

She faltered. She was already in this too deep. What was a little deeper when it came to finally telling them the truth?

"The bike accident." She took a breath. "It wasn't a miscalculation. It was this."

"You lied to me." Dorian's voice darkened. "I directly asked you if there was anything more, and you said it was a mere slip-up, that you were pushing too hard and made a mistake! Were those not your *exact* words to me?"

She winced as Gavin held her. His voice was soft. "You need to be honest with us, Hokura. Your life depends on it!"

Dorian's fists clenched to the point he was sure he was cutting off the circulation in his hands. Gavin was mourning and being sympathetic. His own emotions had swung the other way. He was furious with her. He needed to calm down before he said something he would regret before his tone became too hard. He couldn't control what was rising inside of him. "I need a moment. Please excuse me." With that, he walked out of the room and down the hallway.

Hokura was about to go after him, but Gavin's grip on her tightened. "Give him a few minutes." His voice was a soft whisper. "He needs to work through his emotions before he comes back... until then, just sit here with me and talk with me," he soothed. He wondered where the professor was going and where he would be calling maintenance to next.

Dorian strode angrily down the hallways. By the look that he wore, everyone passing him gave him a wide girth as he passed. His jaw was clenched as his knuckles were turning white. How could she be so careless? How dare she put him before herself. Did she not understand that her life was worth more than his? That her very being was more important than the entire compound or city? He seethed as he entered the training facilities boxing area. There were a few people in the room as he entered. He glared coldly at them as he walked up to a bag and threw his fist in a heated rage. It swung with force.

"Damn her," he seethed as it swung back. He brought his fist of his good hand back again as he released everything he had inside of him into his punch as he yelled even louder as he made impact with the bag causing it to fly back with such force that the chain snapped and sent it flying into the far wall. He glared furiously at it as he breathed hard. This would do for now. He knew he would find himself in the RTC Simulator later that night. That he would exhaust himself and his temper fully once he had dealt with Hokura and getting her tests done. This was a good enough physical distraction for the moment. It was better than destroying any of his offices. He breathed deeply... he needed to calm himself. Scolding her and being cold towards her wouldn't help. So many emotions were battering him at the moment. He wanted to shake her, to scream at her, to swear at her. Another part of him wanted to hold onto her for dear life.

"Idiot..." he murmured as those inside the room cast wary glances towards him. He straightened himself, cracked his knuckles, and composed himself. He felt slightly better. He needed to get back on this.

The professor strode back to the hallway. He needed to breathe, needed to remain composed and in complete control. Something he hadn't been in for months. He needed to remember who *he* was and that he indeed had the technology and know-how to fix this. If he could create a peacekeeper, if he could clone and re-attach his arm, he could deal with her ailments.

Dorian entered the room to see that Gavin hadn't left his spot. He was still holding her as she had her head resting on his shoulder. Dorian cleared his throat. "We will need to see to some blood tests. Hokura, I also want to get some full scans as well as X-rays. We need to be thorough with this. The symptoms that you listed and what I saw in the hallway are cause for concern, but at the same time, they're ailments that can be dealt with." He walked over to the far drawer and grabbed a syringe. His mind reeled. Several things can easily cause bruising. Coughing up blood, however... he wouldn't make any deductions yet as he walked back towards her.

He gently took her arm and inserted the syringe as she sucked in air through her teeth and winced. That right there told him something. "Pain?" he asked, narrowing his eyes.

"Yes," Hokura breathed as her eyebrows furrowed in worry. She had blood tests done more times than she could possibly count. This wasn't the first time she had flinched while getting blood drawn. She had done so when she had been a peacekeeper, but ever since receiving the super-soldier vaccine, she hadn't observed pain having a test administered.

The professor pursed his lips. The peacekeepers and soldiers all had incredibly high pain tolerances. If a small prick from a syringe was causing her pain, it was definitely something to do with her system. He wanted to take a few vials from her but was now concerned about what would happen if he took more than her frail body could handle. He would take three, and hopefully, between himself, Spindler, and Lucien, they would be able to conclude something.

Hokura lightly shook as Gavin held her. "It's never felt like this before."

"It'll be over soon," Gavin coaxed. He looked at the professor and didn't like the look of worry etched across the man's face as he took the samples. This was a man who knew her system better than anyone, who had created and perfected it. He could only imagine what was going through Dorian's mind.

The professor collected the samples, placed them in a holding tray, and picked up the phone. "Spindler, I need you and Lucien to halt whatever you're doing and get down to room 101A stat." He placed the phone back on the receiver. He didn't want to turn and face them. He didn't want Hokura to know how deep his concern ran with this. If her cells were weak and weren't replenishing themselves, he could see about trying injections with her again, that in itself could be fatal. It could result like the last batch of children from so long ago. Children that he had once seen as merely test subjects, the three that had survived, had become so much more to him. *She* had been so much more to him. He couldn't lose her. He brought his hand to his forehead and kneaded it before turning. His eyes were closed as he continued the motion so he wouldn't have to look at them. "I will not make any deductions until I am one hundred percent sure of what we're dealing with." He took a deep breath as finally his eyes met hers. "I will not entertain the idea that you are at all dying." His voice was tight.

At that moment, Dr. Spindler and Dr. Lucien walked into the medical room. They took in the scene and waited for the professor to brief them on the situation.

The professor took the three vials and transferred them over to Lucien and Spindler as he eyed the doctors. "Spindler, every medical test you can possibly run, I don't care if it takes you all day. I want you to be thorough." The doctor nodded silently. Dorian then turned to Lucien. "Run every cell test you can on this. I will release her files to you, and you will run those tests as well. We need to figure out what is happening with her system." The men stood tensely. "Yes, sir!" They both nodded as they took the samples. Dorian cleared his throat. "We will brief on this situation at eighteen hundred hours in my private laboratory office. I want to know everything you uncover."

With that, the two doctors hurriedly took their leave. The professor's attention went back to Hokura as he turned to her. "You need a CT scan." His face was devoid of any emotion, as was his voice as he had reverted from being Dorian.

Gavin and Hokura followed him in silence to the room

where he set her up in the machine making no conversation other than giving her instructions. "This will be a full scan, so it'll take about thirty minutes to complete," he stated as she nodded, and he turned the machine on. His face had shown no hint of emotion as Dorian turned and sat as he crossed his arms.

Gavin walked up to him nervously. "Do you want to take this to the hallway and talk about it?" His voice was soft.

"Lucius Annaeus Seneca once said, the best remedy for anger is delay," Dorian said as he closed his eyes and tilted his head back.

"You're allowed to be angry, Dorian. Just because you love her doesn't mean you can't be upset with her. Believe me, I'm feeling it myself," Gavin confessed.

The professor opened his eyes as he sighed and got up. He would oblige the governor and speak to him in the hallway. He would make sure to keep his temper in check. The two left the room as Gavin leaned his back against the wall. He didn't know what to say as he eyed Dorian and his blank expression. "You don't have to do that..." Gavin stated.

"Do what?" Dorian's voice was even.

"Revert and turn it all off because you're hurting." Gavin brushed his hand through his hair. "I've seen it before, Dorian. I remember how you were when I first came to power. You were cold and calculated. You didn't converse, you merely existed as an empty vessel, and it took years for you to slowly wear down. Don't start doing that now, not to her...."

"It might be best for everyone involved if I become this way again, governor."

Gavin shook his head. He pitied the man in front of him as his lips slightly curved. "You don't have to put up the walls. You should know that better than anyone because the second those walls crack and come down, you'll feel everything you were avoiding and then some. Just like you did when she returned."

His eyes narrowed. "I don't know what to feel right now. We've been through so much. I didn't think she would keep something like this from me. I thought she told me everything. I never imagined her lying to me like this."

"She had her reasons." Gavin's voice was small. Somedays, he honestly wondered what it would be like to understand his wife, to feel things and rationalize them the way she did. He doubted he ever would.

"She *always* has her reasons," Dorian groaned, raking his hand over his forehead and through his hair. "And I was those reasons... she did this because of me... she knew if she told me that I would have flown off the deep end even further." But maybe if he would have known sooner, he *would* have taken off the damn arm which harbored so much pain within him. Maybe looking after her would have been enough to keep himself sane while waiting for the clone to be completed. It didn't matter. "What's done it done."

Gavin nodded. "What do you think this is?"

"I don't know..." The words caught in his throat. Her words echoed in his thoughts, the final trial. That Richter had injected her with something before he had rescued her and that it was attacking her system. His eyes widened. The pain trials, the regenerative tests, was it that the man had been trying to unravel everything that she was in order to figure out all the pieces to what she had truly been? He faltered.

"What is it?" Gavin asked in earnest.

The professor opened his mouth. He was trying to articulate the words. "The final test..." he whispered. "It's attacking and destroying her from the inside. The cells she's regenerating were weakening. Her body wasn't repairing itself. It was fighting to survive."

Gavin gave him a look as horror etched over his face.

The professor pursed his lips. "I can fix this." His mind was racing. It had already been four months. He had already lost so much precious time. "I'm *going* to fix this."

Gavin was at a loss for words. He didn't want to think about the possibilities of her dying. He needed to hang onto hope. He looked at the man who had been so many things to him, so many things to her. He had seen the professor as a rival, as the other man Hokura would always love. He knew the emotions that still lingered between them. He wasn't blind, nor was he stupid, but she had chosen to be with him. "I know you can."

Dorian stood, his mind racing, making lists of tests, going over possibilities. If only he had a sample of what was injected into her. If only he had an idea of its compounds and what was causing this. It could have been anything from some kind of virus to radiation poisoning. Some sort of chemical warfare that had been injected. Was it a kind of cancer? That had been cured well before the war. He thought about the symptoms of radiation poisoning and looked at Gavin. "Has she been experiencing headaches?"

The governor's brows furrowed. "She has, but she's been under a lot of stress as well with everything that happened. She's been fatiguing easily ever since she came back."

"What about vomiting? Blood? Hair loss? Dizziness?"

Gavin's eyes widened as the professor continued. "I...I don't know...." he stammered and mentally kicked himself as she shook his head and slid down the wall into a crouching position. He placed his head in his hands. "I didn't think she'd hide something like this from me. How could I be so blind and not notice?" He looked to Dorian. "You must think I'm a neglectful jerk for not noticing."

The professor gave a huff and placed a hand on Gavin's shoulder. "No, I don't. I know how well Hokura is at hiding things. She's become very adept at lying and covering things up over the years. Too adept apparently because, like fools, we believed her when she said she was simply tired or gave us excuses." He squeezed Gavin's shoulder. "I'm just as much to blame. She's been by my side constantly for the past four months. I should have paid more attention, but I was so caught up with things even though I should have seen the signs, but instead, I brushed them off." He thought about how many times she had simply shut down and slept in his arms or next to him. How easily she tired. The bike accident. How many opportunities had there been that she was going to tell him but didn't because he was falling apart? "Either way. We're moving forward now. I'm going to go over the diagnosis and see what the results are. With all the medical and scientific knowledge we have, we'll be able to come up with something."

Gavin merely nodded.

"Once the scan is done, I'll have her come back to the room and give her a checklist of symptoms. In her state, it's possible that she's missing things. Simple things that she may have brushed off and not thought of." His mood darkened, or things that she was still hiding because of her pride. He couldn't fault her for being prideful. He had been a horrible influence on her when it came to allowing such a thing to get in the way. "If you'll excuse me, I'm going to grab that now."

Still, Gavin didn't say a word.

Dorian pushed away from the wall and made his way to the office. He could have easily waited until the scan was done, but he didn't know how much more he could take standing in the hallway offering sympathy to Gavin when he didn't know what more could be said. Medical checklists weren't even needed in the compound anymore, but he knew where he could still find one. There had always been copies kept in her file. He went to his main office and closed the door, taking in the peace, one of his sanctuaries, which she seemed to frequent. He walked over to his desk, retrieved the keys, and then went to the large cabinet, unlocked it, and grabbed a copy of her files. Forty years ago, there had only been one copy, along with several forgeries. It wasn't until she came back that he had offered her a copy of them. With that, he made a secondary copy for his office. The originals were still safely tucked away in his suite.

He grabbed the manilla folder and stared at the paperwork. His heart panged at the though. His life's work that had flourished that had been everything, that had been the image of perfection, was now crumbling before him. He wanted to hold her, to swear to her that he would do anything for her and make her believe it. He took out the page he needed and quickly scanned and copied it. He took a moment and stared at it: bleeding. He had already seen that. Fatigues easily. Headaches. Dizziness. Blurring Vision. The list went on. He closed his eyes and wondered how much she had suffered. She had done so alone because while she was supporting him, she was keeping this to herself. He couldn't imagine the fear she had kept locked up inside her as her system slowly started depleting. The loneliness she must have felt while harboring such a secret. "I'm so sorry, Hokura. I promised I would make it all up to you, and now I will."

He returned to see Gavin still on the floor, his eyes closed with his head resting against the wall. "The scan will be finishing soon." When Gavin didn't move, the professor narrowed his eyes. "Get up. You need to be strong right now. *She* needs you to be strong right now."

Gavin angrily stood, glaring at the man. "You really don't get it, do you? Do you have no empathy? The love of my life might be dying, and you're telling me to be strong?" he shot back. The words were out before he could stop himself. He caught the professor's demeanor as he winced at the words. "I'm sorry," Gavin sputtered. "I shouldn't have said that."

"It was spoken out of anger. You're going through a lot of emotions right now. It's alright." Dorian straightened, his eyes boring into Gavin's. "Whatever you do, don't take this out on her. If you need to be angry, if you need to yell and take your anger out on someone, you can come to me."

Gavin shook his head and ran his hand through his hair. "You don't deserve my anger either."

"No," he said. "I don't, but I'll take it." He turned as the two went back into the CT room.

Hokura sat up as Gavin took her hand. "We have a few more things to go over yet." His voice was soft as he looked down at her with a solemn expression.

She nodded. "I feel guilty. I shouldn't be keeping you from work right now. If you want, I can finish up, and we can talk about this later..."

"No!" Gavin jolted. "I'm here. I'm going to be by your side through this. *All* of this." He bent down in front of her. A look of desperation on his face. "Please. Let me stay by your side."

Her heart ached as she got him to his feet. "Of course, you can stay by my side." She couldn't help but feel remorse weighing on her. It's because she had kept this from him. She had wanted to struggle through this alone. No... she had been disillusioned in thinking she could go to Dorian with this and keep it from Gavin. That she would just silently go through the motions until he cured her.

"We'll get through this together as a unit," Dorian offered. "For now, Hokura, I have a checklist that I would like you to go over."

She raised an eyebrow at him. "What about more tests? What about the X-rays?"

He took a breath as he kneaded his forehead. "We can see to X-rays in the next few days or so. For now, we'll focus on the samples along with what shows up on the CT scan. There's no need to start going overboard on things until I get a clearer picture of what we're dealing with."

She nodded as she and Gavin followed the professor back to the medical room.

Upon sitting back on the gurney, the professor handed her a clipboard. Hokura sat looking over the extensive checklist of symptoms as she slowly and guiltily checked things off.

Gavin's breathing hitched as she did so. "You've been having difficulty breathing?"

She sorrowfully looked at the array of symptoms to come that she needed to check off. "Among many other things." Her voice was barely audible. She marked off another and another.

"Hokura..." Gavin's voice was tight. How on earth was she capable of hiding all this. He needed to know. "Was I just not seeing it?"

She took a deep breath as her eyes met Dorian's, who had kept his distance and was leaning against the far wall with his arms crossed, with a blank expression. "No," she admitted. "I was hiding it and lying about it constantly. There were a few times I started coughing in front of you, and I brushed it off as something else. For the most part, I hid it. I would get dizzy in the shower and simply sit down and wait for the spell to pass. My hair started falling out..." Her eyes held Dorian's in desperation. "That's never happened before! I know the human head is supposed to shed, but it scared me! I've never lost my hair before!"

The professor sighed helplessly as his brows furrowed. "Several things can cause that, even non-medical, something as simple as your body not being able to combat the stress." He hated seeing her like this. Still, he needed to keep his distance. He needed to keep his demeanor in front of her while he was breaking apart inside.

Hokura continued checking. Every time she marked something off, Gavin seemed to internally wince, as if he was wondering if it was something he had overlooked. After a few agonizing minutes, Hokura held the paper out to Dorian. "I think that's all of them."

He took it from her and scanned it over. There was so much, and yet anything could be causing these. He had witnessed her coughing up blood. That was one minor symptom that might help narrow things down. Why wasn't anything coming to him? He was a medical genius, he should have been able to look at this and have an idea, yet he was stumped as he glared at the piece of paper. Then it hit him. With all the advancements, this could be something he had never seen before. His grip tightened as he fought to keep his expression blank. "Very well, this will be enough for today. Spindler and Lucien are running tests on your samples. I'll take a look at your CT scan and will get back to you."

"When?" Gavin's voice was urgent.

The professor huffed. "When I get whatever it is I need to deduce what we're dealing with. That or we'll need to run some more tests." He saw that he hadn't given Gavin the answer he had wanted. "Later tonight or tomorrow morning."

Hokura nodded as she took Gavin's hand and stood. "Thank you, Dorian."

He looked at her. There had been so much more he had wanted to say, wanted to do, and yet he couldn't. "We'll get you well again. I promise."

"Yes," Gavin said as he turned to her. "This is just another bump in the road. Everything will be just fine. You can rest for the rest of the day, I can have some work brought up, and we can go back to the suite and relax together."

She nodded solemnly. She was hoping it would be just that. She didn't want to spend the day stewing about this. "Maybe tonight we can walk the garden," she offered, hoping he would allow it.

"Sounds nice," Gavin said as they left the room and were on their way.

Dorian watched as they left. He stood perfectly still with his stiff demeanor until they were down the hall. He slumped and exhaled deeply as he raked his hand through his hair. He wanted to talk to her further in private, he should have waited on calling Gavin down, but his instincts drove him to pick up the phone. Nonetheless, there would be time to talk to her later. Until then, he had much to see to.

Gavin and Hokura walked in silence through the compound hallways. She nervously chewed on her bottom lip when she could take it anymore. "Gavin... I'm sorry."

He glanced at her as he squeezed her hand. "You don't need to be sorry." His tone was solemn. "I just wish you would have said something... that you wouldn't have kept this from me." The reality of the situation was slowly starting to come down on him. It made sense how she seemed to be deteriorating in front of him. How the once-proud peacekeeper who had more energy than anyone he knew suddenly tired after walking the gardens, how her appetite was non-existent, even the light in her eyes, which shone brightly, seemed to have dimmed. They got into the elevator, his hand still tightly holding hers. "We'll figure this out." He swallowed hard. "Dorian will figure this out. He won't let anything happen to you."

She nodded at him. "Are you sure you don't need to be back at work?"

Gavin grimaced. "After all this... no... I need some time... I doubt I'd be able to concentrate on work today." He grabbed her and held her. "Do you think so little of me?"

The elevator dinged as the doors opened. Still, he held her to him, not moving. She didn't know what to say. "Gavin..."

"Do you think this wouldn't affect me, Hokura? That I would simply get the news and go back to work like it was nothing?" The doors closed.

"The elevator..." Hokura stuttered.

He hit a button on the keypad as the doors opened and stayed open as he gave her a stern look. "Answer me... do you really think I could go back to work after getting such news? Don't you know that you're my everything? Or do I need to prove it the way Dorian has?"

She didn't understand. "This isn't about...."

"I feel like it is." His tone was sharp. "I feel like you wanted to hide this from me and entrust everything to the professor that you couldn't trust me with this. That it wouldn't mean anything to me."

She stepped from his arms. "That's not what this is at all! I didn't want you to worry about me!"

"Worry about you?" Gavin raked his hands through his hair and pulled at it. "Dammit, Hokura, of course I'll worry. I've *been* worried ever since you were kidnapped!"

"And you don't deserve to keep worrying!" she countered.

His brows creased. "You have a real skewed way of thinking. Like you weigh these things and keep a tally of them. Something is happening to you... my wife..."

"Don't you trust him?" Her brows furrowed in desperation. "He can fix this!"

Gavin grabbed her wrist and extended her arm as he took in the large bruise which had formed from the blood samples that had been taken. "Tell me this isn't something worth worrying about! In the past fourteen years, you've taken bullets, and I've never seen you bruise like this before, and this is from a simple syringe!"

Hokura wrenched her wrist away from him.

He stood, giving her a look she couldn't quite decipher. "For the time being, I am worried. Until Dorian can come up with an answer, I have the means to be worried. It's done so out of love and devotion. You have no idea what I went through while Tobias had you. I don't know what I would do if I lost you again."

She faltered. "How many times do I have to apologize?"

"You don't have to apologize..." Gavin took her hand. "You just need to stay by my side and let me be there for you." Not ask whether or not he was going back to his office for the afternoon after finding out the news... not brushing off her own well-being and not allowing him to worry or dote on her. He brought the back of her hand to his lips. "That's, of course, if my lady would have me...."

Her heart broke. "Of course, I would have you... there's nobody else." The words caught in her throat, they were spoken automatically, but they felt like a lie, just another lie that pulled at her heart. She knew she loved Gavin more than anything, but why was Dorian always in the back of her mind when she said such things? Maybe it's because of what she had said on her wedding day... that he had created her so part of her would always belong to him. She shook her head. She didn't want to confuse herself further. Right now, the only person who mattered was standing in front of her, his own heart bleeding for her. "Let's go home and be together," she stated. "We can have lunch and then just be together however you want."

A slight smile came to Gavin's lips. "Let's."

The professor had made his way to the medical labs where Spindler and Lucien were running tests on the samples. He paced nervously. "Have either of you found anything?"

Dr. Spindler's voice was tense. "I don't believe this is radiation poisoning... however." He shook his head.

Dr. Lucien looked up from his spot. "There's definitely something happening."

"Of course, something is happening. We need to determine what!" Dorian paced. "We need to figure out the what and how. I need something more than "something is happening!" He moved over to where Lucien was working and grabbed the microscope as he peered into it. What he saw perplexed him. "This is all wrong! Why the hell does it look like she's anemic?"

Dr. Lucien sat back and crossed his arms. "My deduction would be because she is, sir."

"That's impossible! She's a peacekeeper!" He bristled. "This doesn't even look like a peacekeeper's sample... let alone Hokura's!" He stopped... it was as if a piece of ice went through him as he stood. His eyes widened in horror. What had made her a peacekeeper was no longer there. Sickening chills went up his spine. "How is it possible?" His voice was a whisper.

Dr. Spindler shook his head. "It doesn't mean she's no longer a peacekeeper, sir. It seems that whatever is happening to her system, it's all slowly disintegrating. It's no longer replenishing itself, or rather if it is, the rate is so incredibly slow that we can't track it."

"There must be something attacking her cells, but what?" the professor mused. "What could Richter have injected her with that's causing this?"

Both men shook their heads as Dr. Spindler stood as he placed a hand on the professor's shoulder. "Maybe instead of looking for the "what," we focus on the "how we can change this."

The professor gave him a questioning look. "In theory, we can dose her again, just as we did when the peacekeepers awakened."

"I would suggest you spend some time testing that theory first," Lucien said as he eyed the professor. "There's a possibility of her cells being too weak for such things."

Dorian pursed his lips. Why did he feel like he was suddenly being backed into a corner? "I'm going to take a small blood sample back to my labs along with the CT scan... I need to be alone." He grabbed half a vial from where Lucien had been set up and quickly left the room. His mind was reeling. There was so much, and yet nothing pointed to one direct thing. He left the medical part of the compound and down to his personal lab. He noted the stares as he strode, how people noted his hand that was once again one of flesh. He wondered how long it would take for rumors to start circulating about Hokura being ill... that a peacekeeper's system was possibly failing. Would they start wondering about their own systems? No... he wouldn't worry about that now.

He entered his lab and sat as he grabbed her files and stared at them. He knew her components by heart, knew exactly how things should appear on her samples, knew what normal looked like. Dorian eyed the CT scan, his heart dropping. There was so much to go over. His hand shook as he looked over what he had, his jaw trembling. Why were these scans showing so much internal trauma and damage? He knew there was damage when she came back when she was in the medical facility, he had seen the scans himself, but they hadn't looked like this. Had he missed something while she was being tested on during those two weeks? He moved quickly as he went to his filing cabinet and grabbed another file, everything that he had overseen after she was rescued. He flopped the files down on his desk and started meticulously comparing the two as his brows furrowed. How on earth was he going to break the news to her? Her system was indeed weakening in a way that, if not taken care of, could... no... he wouldn't think of that. He needed to remain optimistic. This was only the first day. He concluded that she was deteriorating but needed to know more. They didn't have a timeline. He wondered at that moment if her cells were regenerating at all. He let out a deep sigh. The only way to do this would be to start from the bottom and work his way up, just as he had done when he had first started the stem cell project. He had her sample. Now, it was time to treat it as a puzzle and find what pieces were missing or damaged. "Hokura... what on earth is happening to you?"

It had been later in the day. Gavin had so much on his mind but had kept it to himself as he eyed her sitting on the couch reading. It was as if the morning had barely phased her. She had stated that she wanted no more talk about things at lunch and had been agreeable with him when they had lay down for an afternoon nap. He paced as he noted the book she was reading. "Finally got to the second one?" He wanted to keep things light before this discussion.

Hokura made a face. "The boy with the bread... and the boy who taught her so much... she went through so much in the first book, and now she has to go on a victory tour. Her whole life has already been set for her." She marked the book. "Seems like the author had a thing for torturing her characters and playing with their hearts."

Gavin raised his eyebrows. "It seems like everyone's read it. Maybe I should pick it up."

She gave a small chuckle. "I don't know if it's worth you reading. It's not exactly your taste in books."

He sat next to her, leaning against her. "Doesn't mean I wouldn't read it, especially if you're enjoying it."

Hokura nibbled her bottom lip. "Enjoying might be a stretch. I guess I'm curious how it ends, how she overcomes everything, and who she ends up with."

Gavin could see the distance in her eyes. Was that something she was wondering herself? "I know you don't want to talk about this, but there is one matter we haven't discussed, which we need to."

She placed the book on the coffee table and rubbed her face. "We haven't even heard back from Dorian yet. I can't keep worrying about this when it's in his hands."

"That's fine," Gavin said. Did she feel that passing this off to Dorian suddenly didn't make it her problem? Their problem? "The kids, we need to..."

"No!" Hokura stiffened as she took Gavin's hands. "Not a word to them yet, not a word to anyone about this yet, Gavin," she said in earnest. "This may not be anything that anyone needs to worry about. The last thing I want is to cause them more worry. Please, Gavin."

She was begging. That was something he never wanted from her. It made him feel sick, considering what she had told him about her experience with Tobias. He sighed as he squeezed her hand "alright... we'll give it some time." He didn't know if it had already become obvious to the children that their mother wasn't doing well. Perhaps it was because it had already been so many months of steady decline that they hadn't caught it. Or if they had, but they had stayed quiet about it.

"There's one more thing," Hokura added. She looked up at Gavin will full sincerity. "I understand that you want to be by my side through all of this..."

He was about to protest when she brought her hand up.

"You owe it to the people of the city and the people of the compound to continue as their leader. I want you by my side Gavin, but I'm sure there will be days where I'm just waiting or simply getting tests." She tried to ease the blow to him as she gently took his hand and gave him a small smile. "Be there for me on the hard days."

He couldn't help but feel like he was being dismissed. How could she ask for such a thing? Then again, he needed to understand where she was coming from as well. She was still fully capable of doing things on her own. She still needed her independence. He would bend for her. "As long as you're honest with me, I will be there whenever you need me." He took in the time. "The children will be home soon. Let's do up a nice meal together tonight. We can try and get our mind off of things and spend it relaxing as a family, maybe play some cards or something." He faked a smile.

Hokura chuckled. "Because you want to see Cass and I go head-to-head again?"

A boyish grin set on Gavin's lips. "It was rather entertaining..."

***

Dinner had been light as the kids conversed about their days. "I don't understand why math is so important for us to learn."

Cassandra scowled. "Especially algebra. I'm not planning on becoming a scientist, so why do I need it?"

"It helps with figuring out unknown variables," Cyrus muttered.

The girl gave her brother an annoyed look. "I know what it's for. I just don't know why I need to learn it."

Gavin cleared his throat, looking over at his daughter. "I thought you were doing well with all your lessons. Are you struggling with math?"

She slunk as she pouted. "I've been doing fine. I just hate it."

"She's gotten one hundred percent on all her tests. She just likes to whine," Cyrus added.

Hokura smiled at her daughter. "That's excellent, Cass!"

Still, Cassandra crossed her arms. "That's not the point." She looked desperately at her mother. "With the higher education system, aren't we supposed to learn and train in the things we're actually interested in?"

Gavin chuckled. "There are still fundamentals that everyone learns before they enter the higher education program. In any case, you're still young. You have all the time to learn and change your mind."

Hokura nodded. "Besides, it seems like you and Cyrus are ahead of the game with such things. You're doing your training, and he's been down in the labs alongside the scientists. We're both very proud of you two." She took in her daughter, who was still pouting. "Don't be in such a rush to grow up. You have all the time in the world."

Gavin nodded but pursed his lips. He wondered if his wife would be there to watch their children as they grew. He closed his eyes. He wouldn't allow those thoughts to assault him. He needed to remain positive as he felt Hokura's hand close around his.

"How about I help with the dishes, and then we can enjoy a bit of a game night." She smiled.

Gavin had appeased her by letting her dry the dishes. The children helped clear the table and made their lunches before the family sat around for a few rounds of cards. There was laughter from Hokura and Cassandra as Cyrus frustratedly put his hand down and said their luck was barely even scientifically plausible. His father couldn't help but chuckle at the boy as they played a few more hands. The kids excused themselves to wash up and relax for the remainder of the evening as Hokura picked her book back up and rested comfortably on the couch as Gavin showered.

It wasn't until half past twenty hundred hours that the phone rang, and Dorian asked for the two to come down to his office.

Hokura and Gavin stood in front of him, their hands clutching so hard that their knuckles were almost turning white.

Dorian sat at his desk, tired, listless, running over what on earth he was going to say as he cleared his throat. "Why don't you two actually take a seat instead of just standing there."

"Was it good news?" Hokura's voice was just above a whisper as she sat down, her hand not straying from her husband's.

The professor licked his lips. He couldn't even meet her eyes. "No, however, with that said, it's been rather inconclusive of what is happening with your system. We've been able to determine that it is indeed weakening. We have yet to find the source that is causing such a thing." He brought his hand to his forehead. He hadn't wanted to tell them tonight but knew they had been waiting for some kind of answer. "The medical team will need a few days. We're exploring different options on how to treat this, but there will be more tests that ensue."

Gavin faltered. "Is there anything that can slow this down? Or even make her better right away?"

Dorian sighed as he glanced briefly at Hokura and stared at them both. "As per usual, resting when needed, fueling her body, taking it easy." His eyes shot up and held hers. "Not pushing herself in *any* way." His words were terse. He was giving her a direct order. He watched as she slightly trembled, just enough for him to catch it. "I know this news has been daunting on all of us, but I have no reason to believe that we can't move forward and repair her system."

Gavin nodded. "You're optimistic."

"I need to be," Dorian stated. "However, this is going to take some time on the medical end of things. The only answer we have today is her system is not holding up..."

Hokura's brows furrowed as she swallowed hard. She needed to know. "With being a peacekeeper, though, aren't my cells still regenerating?"

The professor felt chills run through him. The question had caught him off guard as he studied her. He already said there would be no more secrets, and yet this wasn't something he had wanted to put into words. Something he wasn't ready to admit yet... and still. "What made you a peacekeeper is no longer in your system, Hokura."

Her eyes widened. "How can that be?"

"I don't know... but I'm going to find out, and I'll find a way to fix things," Dorian answered. He took her in. Why did this seem to be more of a shock than finding out that she was possibly dying?

Hokura turned to Gavin and was quickly in his arms. A small sob escaped her.

"It'll be okay." Gavin tried to ease her. "We can get this back..."

Dorian stared at his hands steepled in front of him. "Indeed, if I can create a peacekeeper, I can certainly put your system back to what it once was. I just need some time." His mind was spinning. He wanted to talk to her. Wanted to comfort her, and yet there was Gavin doing just that.

The governor looked up at him. "Thank you for this, Dorian. I'm sure you've been working on this nonstop throughout the day. Your efforts are commendable." It didn't need to be said. He knew that the second Hokura would have gone to him about this, the man would be exhausting himself to make things right again.

The professor nodded. "It's been a very long day for everyone. I suggest we all get some rest, so we're able to continue tomorrow. I have some different theories already running, which will hopefully conclude how we can stabilize things. Dr. Spindler and Lucien are also on this, but some tests take time. I'll be in touch if anything comes up."

Gavin gave a slight nod as he looked down at his wife, who had buried her face in his chest. He couldn't imagine what was running through her mind. "Hey, it'll be okay." His voice was soft as he gently rubbed her back. "Come on. You've had a long day. Let's have an easy evening and tuck in. I'll even give you a back massage." He merely felt her nod against him.

Dorian stared at the two as they got up. Hokura didn't even look at him. He had wanted to say something, had wanted to assure her, why hadn't she said anything more to him, dammit? He gave an inward sigh. He would find a way to talk to her tomorrow. He knew this would affect her in ways he couldn't understand, in ways nobody would. It had been beyond decades since anyone within the city walls had passed from any kind of sickness. The idea that the peacekeepers should never have to worry about. After the two left, he felt the need to move.

He made his way down to the training facility to the RTC simulator and got changed. He would physically exhaust himself before retiring for the night. He went into the viewing room and set the simulator to the hardest mode. Taking his frustration out on the simulations was better than anyone else facing his wrath, especially Hokura. She didn't deserve his anguish. He walked from the viewing room to the simulation room after he strapped on his sensors. The world around him transformed as bullets started whizzing by him. He ducked and maneuvered successfully, avoiding them as he shot with precision.

A bullet merely missed him as he dove into an alley panting hard. He hadn't expected to be bombarded so quickly as he took a quick moment to adjust his clip. An assailant came from behind him but not fast enough for the professor as his knuckles met the simulation's face as his fists rained down on it. "Damn you," he seethed. The simulation below him disappeared as others were on him just as quickly. He rolled, taking one with him and throwing it into the other as their bodies smashed against the alley wall. This wasn't doing it. He felt like his rage was only growing as he fought them. He walked to the one he had thrown and wrapped his hands around its neck as he slowly added pressure to it. The sensation of crushing its neck had felt so real against his hands. His attention had been solely on what he was doing that he hadn't heard the simulation coming up behind him. A flash of pain shot through his shoulder as he turned, his eyes narrowing. He stalked the simulation as he grabbed the scruff of its neck and disarmed it. The figure turned and warped in his mind as it took on the form of Tobias.

The professor smiled maliciously as he grabbed its arm and

tore it from its socket. There was no screaming from the assailant as he ripped into it, bloodying his hands as he tore it to shreds. "If it weren't for you..." he seethed. "If only I could have tortured you..." He brought his hand into the simulation's stomach as it penetrated its guts as the form disappeared. Dorian turned to see more simulations coming upon him. They all wore Tobias's face. "If only I had killed you that night I saw you touching her in the library!" he screamed in torment as he unleashed a killing spree of gore, forgetting the simulated bullet which pulsed in his shoulder. He would never falter again.

<hr />

Hokura and Gavin had made their way back to their suite. Her reservation had been grating at his nerves as she simply stood looking out the large bay window. Her silence was thick as it weighed on him until he could no longer take it. He walked up to her, placing his arms around her. "Don't leave me while you're still here." His voice was a whisper.

She turned to him in desperation. "I don't want to... but I don't know how to..."

His lips were on hers passionately as he brought her in closer. He needed to feel her, to pour himself into her, and make her believe that he would do anything for her.

"Gavin..." she stepped away.

"No... whatever you have to say can wait." He was back on her. He didn't care. The kids were in their rooms. He picked her up and quietly took her to their room, where he laid her on their bed as he continued gently kissing her, covering her. He noted the bruise on her arm from the tests as his lips avoided it. He gently lifted her shirt as his eyes went to the large bruise on her hip and side as he sucked in his breath. He couldn't help but stutter. "Wha?"

"The kitchen table... I smacked it..." she groaned.

His lips were at her neck as he came up to her ear. "You need to be more careful." His tongue teased her earlobe as her hands ran through his hair.

She brought her face to his as she cupped his cheeks. "Gavin." She sighed. "I love you... I'm sorr..."

"Enough," he whispered as his hands took hers, and he went back to kissing her.

It had been some time since they had been so thoroughly passionate with one another, into the night until they had exhausted themselves and were entangled in one another's arms as Hokura slept soundly against him. He dared not move. His body wouldn't let him as he kissed her forehead. He idly looked down at her and wondered if he had at all marred her skin from holding her and touching her during their lovemaking. The idea wore a pit inside his stomach. His hands causing her harm was the last thing he ever wanted. He wouldn't think of it as he drifted off to sleep to the sound of her light breathing.

It was well past midnight by the time Dorian heaved himself up the training facility hallway. He had gotten so caught up in his rage and the simulations that he had lost track of time. His body burned as he felt exhausted. He had screamed to the point his throat was as raw as his emotions. He couldn't even keep track of how many Tobias's and Richter's he had killed in cold blood. It would never be enough. He deeply wished he had tortured Tobias when he had a chance, that he would have been able to see the fear in the man's eyes as he re-enacted every act on the man that he had allowed to happen to Hokura. Instead, he had died by a bullet to the brain. Richter had been another one who had gotten off too easy. The fury burned deep enough that the professor would have driven back to Michigan himself to destroy the compound. No... Hokura needed him here. Yet, he wondered if it would be worth doing so in order to find out any information about what Richter had injected her with.

As the professor made his way down the hallway towards his suite, he needed to remind himself that today was only day one. It had taken years to put together the stem cell project. He wasn't going to be able to crack the code in less than a day when he didn't even know what he was looking for yet. He was putting too much pressure on himself to think he could do this with a snap of his fingers. No, the genetic makeup of the peace-keepers was all unique unto themselves. He needed to start at the beginning. Dorian went into his suite and slowly made his way to his bathroom. His mind had felt sluggish, it had all been too much that day, and he simply wanted to shut it off. He undressed and slipped into the shower, allowing the water to bounce off his body as he examined his left arm. The scarring was fully healed, the pigment was perfect. He flexed it out of habit, taking it in, and sighed. The time he had spent being obsessed over regaining his arm he could have spent looking into her. Maybe he would be on his way to solving this if she would have said something. He shook his head, regretting his actions. It was futile to wish he could go back. All the wishing in the world wouldn't change things. "This is partially my fault," he groaned. "If only I hadn't been so obsessed with getting my arm back, maybe I would have seen it."

Brooding in the shower wouldn't get him anywhere. He needed his sleep. He needed a good night of rest so he would be able to be back on things tomorrow morning. He dried off as he went to his kitchen, wrapping his towel around his waist as he grabbed a drink and stared out at the city. The city she thought was beautiful as he tried desperately to see it as she did. Alas, there were parts of her even he would never understand as he called it a night and found his way to his bed. He would talk to her tomorrow...

Gavin stirred as his alarm clock awakened him. He moaned as he stiffly turned and placed his hand over it, silencing the chime. Grumbling because he had forgotten to turn it off the night before. He then snuggled back next to Hokura, who was still lying close to him.

"Aren't you going to work?" Hokura asked as she slowly opened her eyes.

"I wasn't planning on it," he stated dryly. She had been fitful through the night, and although she didn't wake up screaming from nightmares, she was obviously still having them.

"We talked about this..." she replied. "You still have a responsibility to your people as governor."

"I have a responsibility to you as a husband as well," he retorted.

She gave him a playful shove. "Is that how it's going to be?" She gave him a smirk as he kissed his forehead. "I doubt anything is going to happen today, see to your work, and if anything comes up, I promise I'll get ahold of you."

He grunted at her. "I'll get ready in a few minutes then. It's not like anyone is keeping watch over when I get to my office." He grabbed hold of her and wouldn't allow her to escape his grasps as he snuggled against her. "Do me the kindness of giving me a bit more time."

She caught the undertone to what he had said. She had already felt guilty about the way things had played out. She shook her head. She couldn't keep feeling remorseful. After last night Gavin wouldn't dare doubt her love for him, but as much as she needed him, she needed some time to figure out how she felt about things.

It was twenty minutes later that the governor begrudgingly got out of bed as Hokura followed him. He drank his coffee across from her as the kids went about getting ready for lessons and saw themselves quickly out the door before Cassandra commented about the skies.

"Looks like we might be in for some weather," the girl stated, staring at the darkening clouds in the distance.

Hokura noted the sky and inwardly smiled. It matched her underlying mood. "Have a good day at lessons, you two."

"Love you, Mom!" Cyrus called as he was out the door.

Cassandra smiled at them and followed in her brother's wake.

"You haven't eaten anything," Gavin noted, staring at his wife. "I can make you breakfast before I head out. Remember what Dorian said."

Hokura rolled her eyes. "I just don't have the stomach for it right now. It's still early." She gave her husband a small smile. "I'll make myself something, or I'll head to the cafeteria. Besides, you haven't eaten anything either."

Gavin winced. He hadn't exactly had an appetite this morning. Even after the night they had spent together, he was feeling unsure about leaving her side. "Honestly, my stomach is in knots this morning. I don't like the idea of leaving your side."

She gave him a sympathetic look. "I promise if anything comes up, I'll phone you." She figured if she didn't, Dorian definitely would. It seemed like the professor was dead set against there being secrets between any of them. Her heart panged.

Things would change. They already were, she was going to be his test subject, and he was reverting to the professor. She had already felt it yesterday. Hokura felt Gavin's hand meet hers as he leaned in.

"I'll take your word on that." He glanced out at the unsettling skies. Why did they seem to match his mood? "I'll finish my coffee and be on my way then... if you need anything, you know where to find me."

She nodded lightly as she stared out the window, transfixed on the sky, which almost seemed to hold an electric pulse to it. She knew exactly where she wanted to be once Gavin left.

After a decent sleep, the professor was back to his labs early that morning. He had sat in his main office after grabbing Hokura's files as he aimlessly went through them. Her genetic structure that once was versus what he was looking at was so different as he mused over her charts. Was it possible that she was now aging? That her body's internal clock was recognizing how old it truly was? He brought his hand to his chin as he leaned back in his chair. No, that wasn't it. She didn't physically look any older. She looked fatigued, but there hadn't been any noticeable physical changes that said she was aging. No gray hairs, no fine lines, he was perplexed. It was hard to start at ground zero when she already had the perfected system. Now it was seeing what was missing and deteriorating and figuring out how to reverse the effect, but where to start when everything was declining at such a steady rate? Especially when he missed so much when this had first started months ago.

There was only one thing that would fix all of this. He needed to get healthy regenerative cells back into her body.

Dorian left his office, noting the time. He wanted to speak to her, but still, there was something he needed to see to as he went back towards his private lab. He still had samples from before she had been kidnapped, samples he had taken from her after the war to see how the super soldier gene was counteracting with her system. He had been pleased with the outcome. He came to the room and grabbed one of the old samples from a small freezer. Indeed, this should hold an answer if he could see about extracting the cells and testing them on her newest samples. If he was successful, he might be able to inject her with them. He couldn't say whether or not this was a sure thing, but it was better than nothing.

It would take some time to properly thaw the samples as he moved them to the fridge. He didn't dare think about rapid thawing. In doing so, there was a possibility of decomposition if not done correctly. He would have to wait until at least this afternoon to double-check his theory. He wouldn't waste his time with anything else. Doing so would only cause more hassle when this was the more direct route to take. Either way, both Spindler and Lucien were seeing to the task as well. He was sure all three of them would converge later with any further findings.

It was now mid-morning. The professor couldn't hold back any longer as he decided to seek her out. He went to her suite and knocked on the door, strangely nobody answered. He thought it was odd since she should have been resting and that at the very least, even if she were sleeping that Gavin would be home. After a moment, he double-checked the library, which was empty. Dorian gave an irritated huff as he turned. He had wanted to talk to her and to see how she was doing. He wondered if Gavin had taken to his office to get some work done. The notion perplexed him. He figured Gavin would surely be constantly by her side. Then again, he knew Hokura well enough, she originally didn't want her husband even knowing about her condition, so it was possible that she had told him that she would be fine and told him to see to his own business. Still, that didn't answer where *she* was... He went to the governing office and found the door closed as curiosity got the best of him. He knocked, hoping he had been wrong, when he heard Gavin's voice.

"Come in."

Dorian walked in and gave him a questioning look. "You're here..."

He sighed slightly. "Yes, I'm here. Hokura made it clear that she didn't want me continuously brooding by her side. That she needed a little space, so I came down here for a few hours. There are some pressing matters that I need to see to. What can I help you with?"

"I wanted to talk to her about things and see how's she's doing. You haven't seen her, have you? Do you know where she is?"

Gavin's brows furrowed. "No, I haven't seen her since this morning." He wondered where she might have wandered off to if the professor was looking for her. "I've been in my office. Haven't you looked outside? It's raining out!"

Dorian narrowed his eyes at the governor. Was this the pressing matter he needed to see to? "So?"

"We haven't seen this amount of precipitation in as long as I can remember. Should I call in an emergency? Should I alert the city?" he stammered.

The professor gave him an odd look. "A little rain never hurt anyone. If anything, the civilians can enjoy it. I'm sure it'll be over soon enough. Besides, the gardens could use it after the heat we've been going through. Now stop making a big deal about this and use your head. I asked you a question."

Gavin drummed his fingers irritably. "It seems like you know her just as well as I do."

Dorian closed his eyes and kneaded his forehead. He didn't want to do this. "Are we going to have issues about this again? I'm not in the mood for a pissing match right now, Gavin."

"No," the governor sighed. "There won't be any issues. I should know by now." If the night before hadn't been a testament of her love for him, then nothing would ever be enough. He knew the feelings she felt for Dorian, but the reality was that, indeed, she wasn't sleeping with him.

"Very well, I think I might have an idea where she is." He turned to leave but stopped. "And don't waste your time worrying about the weather. Like everything, it'll pass." With that, he left. He was certain he knew where he might find her and felt slightly foolish that he hadn't checked there first.

Dorian found her on the roof, head tilted back, eyes closed, arms out to her sides, standing in the rain. He cleared his throat. "Being a little melodramatic?"

She looked back at him and smirked. "Haven't you ever stood in the rain wishing it would wash away all your problems?"

He walked up to her. "No, I don't exactly care for being wet while outside." He gave her a cool glance. He didn't want to be this way with her. "Hokura, please, come inside."

"If you don't want to get wet, then go back in. I'm fine."

Dorian bristled. "Will you stop with that already?" He grabbed her wrist and turned her to face him fully. She didn't. Instead, she lowered her head, refusing to meet his eyes. "Will you stop with the lies? Since when did you become so damn good at lying to everyone?"

A dark chuckle came from her. "I've been lying for decades, Dorian." Her face rose. "I've been lying since before I first escaped here. I must have learned it from my *mentor*." Her words were sharp.

He stepped back, unimpressed. "Stop it." He looked away from her and clicked his tongue as he took a deep breath. "I know you're not "fine." Are you angry with me about the results? Because if you are, you have full right to be. Part of this is my doing because of the state I was in when we returned." He glared at her. "But you cannot fully fault me."

She faltered as her voice softened. "I don't."

His eyes narrowed as they stood in the rain, silently staring at one another. "Then what is it?"

"I feel like things are going to change between us again. Don't say they haven't because they have. I feel it." Her expression turned to one of sorrow.

He swallowed hard. "Maybe it would be best if they changed Hokura."

"Why? Because I'm not a peacekeeper anymore?" she snapped angrily. "Because I'm a test subject again? If I'm dying, shouldn't I get whatever I want? If these are my last days, shouldn't I spend them feeling content and loved?"

His emotions rocked over him. "You'll always be a peacekeeper! It doesn't matter what runs through your veins! Besides, we haven't been able to conclude that you're going to..." He couldn't say the words. "You know better than that."

"You said it was different between us. We've drawn the lines!" she yelled at him.

"We've danced on those lines and overstepped them, maybe not physically, but emotionally we did," he countered angrily. Lightning lit up the sky as thunder echoed, drawing their attention to the horizon. Could he really be upset like this? Was it fair to her? "You *know* you're loved."

She wrapped her arms around herself and turned away from him. Why was she doing this? Because she was afraid, of dying, of death, and of losing what they had before she died. "I'm scared, Dorian." She shook as a chill came over her even though it was humid out. "Even if things change, my feelings won't. Why should we deny them?" Tears came to her eyes. It hurt. "I don't want to lose you in any way!"

His arms wrapped around her back as she cried. "How can you say that? If anything, I'm the one losing *you*." His voice was a whisper.

The lightning crackled in the distance again as she solemnly looked off to the horizon. "If only you had been awake to hold me like this last time I stood in the rain," she breathed, closing her eyes.

"I'm here now..." She had him in a vice... as much as he wanted to step back, this wasn't the time to do so. "Those lines... they need to stay solidly stay in place, but I won't let you go."

Hokura looked up at the sky. Maybe the rain *had* washed away some of the pain. No, it wasn't the rain. It was him. She breathed deeply, becoming intoxicated with his scent. She was soaked, as was he as he was braced against her holding her. "Odd weather we're having."

"So it seems." He stood still, holding her, trying to understand how she felt so content to stand outside in the rain. Wishing he could somehow tap the emotions she was feeling at that moment to better understand her. Lightning lit up the sky again, closer to the city as the thunder rolled loudly and boomed echoing through the barren city streets. "Are you ready to come in and dry off now? You shouldn't be on the roof during a storm like this."

She turned to him. Her expression was unreadable.

He took her in. Her system was weakening. She was becoming so fragile, so breakable, and yet she was still the most beautiful thing he had ever seen. Even soaking in the rain with red eyes and a tear-streaked face. "Come, if you don't want to be alone, we can go back to my suite. I can get us some towels and get us dried off. After, I can make us some tea if you wish, and we can talk." He couldn't help but notice the goosebumps on her arms. He automatically touched it to find her skin was cold. Odd despite the rain, it was still warm out. "I don't want you to catch a chill." He took off his jacket, placing it around her, and placed an arm around her shoulder, leading her back inside.

They were in front of his suite when he asked. "Do you want to go to your place and dry off and grab some extra clothes?"

She shrugged, taking off his jacket and handing it to him.

This mood of hers was starting to get to him as he licked his lips and stared at the ceiling. "Or you can just come in. I did offer." He opened the door for her as they walked in, and he hurriedly went to fetch a few towels and change his clothes as she walked over to the kitchen and stared out the bay window. She stood silently, lost in the moment. She had done this before, so long ago as she traced her fingers over the glass. A towel dropped on her head as another went over her shoulders.

"Dry yourself off. I'll make some tea," Dorian said as he set to work behind her.

Hokura turned and idly dried her hair as she stared at him. He grabbed a kettle, filled it, and plugged it in. He then grabbed a teapot and started scooping some leaves and herbs into a diffuser. It was strange watching him move around his kitchen as he set to work grabbing two cups. Even stranger to see him in a regular black t-shirt along with casual slacks.

"Have you had breakfast?" he asked, still busying himself. "You need to eat."

The was taken back by the question... "no... I haven't...."

"Then I'll make you something," he stated, going to his fridge, and grabbing some supplies as he started on another task. "You should go back to your suite and get some dry clothes..." He turned to meet her stare and gave her a questioning look. "What is it?"

"I've never seen you in the kitchen before," she stated.

Dorian stopped. "If that's what has you so enamored, I'll wait until you get changed to start on breakfast for you." He sighed, hoping that would be enough to get her to agree. He was relieved when she finally nodded.

"I'll be back in a few minutes then," Hokura said as she slowly moved to the door. She gave him one last look before she left.

Dorian shook his head. He didn't know what had gotten into her, why she was suddenly so taken back by the basic idea of him cooking. He didn't understand, but he would wait. The kettle had since heated up enough to pour the hot water into the teapot and add the diffuser. At least she would have something to warm herself when she got back.

It was a few moments later that she walked back into his suite. He raised an eyebrow. "Didn't you dry yourself before changing?" He noted the drips of water still on her collarbone. That's when he noticed that it had become more defined than usual. He was taken off guard as he stared at her further. Why hadn't he seen it before? Or was it because he had seen her nearly every day that he hadn't noticed the gradual change until now. She looked like she had at the river when they had bathed together. No, not quite as emaciated. His heart broke. He swore he would get her well again. "I'm going to make you a big breakfast." He quickly turned as she followed him to the kitchen. "You can sit and simply watch," he stated.

She sat beside the bay window at his small table. "Afraid I'll make a mess?"

"No..." He grabbed the tea and poured some in a cup for her. "I have a system for being the only person in my kitchen." He placed the tea in front of her and a cup of sugar that held a small spoon.

She watched in awe as he moved about. His steps were fluid and graceful as ever. Her eyes never left his form as he grabbed pans and utensils. "How's the arm?"

He stopped for a second and looked back at her as she scooped a bit of sugar into her cup. "It's doing well, it doesn't quite have the same amount of strength yet, but the transition has gone rather seamlessly. I'm still doing exercises with it. I must admit I didn't think it would take as easily as it did." He looked down, flexing his left hand and opening it. It was a miracle that between himself, Spindler, and Lucien, they were able to crack the code of syncing the arms stem cells to the ones in his body, that the medical team had done such a stand-up job on the operation itself. He went back to work. "How do you like your eggs?"

She chuckled. "How about you at least let me cook the eggs? If you like scrambled, that's supposedly one thing I'm good at." She stirred her tea and took a sip of it, allowing the sweet aroma to wrap around her.

"Fine," Dorian groaned. "You're just determined to help me in my kitchen, aren't you?"

Hokura grinned, satisfied that he would allow it. "Let me know when you're around four minutes away from everything."

He shook his head. "If you want to help, you can help with the dishes afterward..." He wondered if that was a wise idea in itself.

"Fair enough," she replied as she continued to sip her tea and stared out the window at the rain. Another flash of lightning caught her attention as the thunder boomed loudly, causing her to shudder. "It's close to Meridiana... do you think there's a need to worry?"

"You sound like your husband. It's just a thunderstorm and some rain," Dorian retorted as he diced up a few potatoes into small cubes and placed them on the pan, which was already heating on the stove. "Technically, we're in monsoon season. The fact that the weather is actually doing what it used to might mean that the globe is finally regulating again."

She licked her lips. "It rained quite often in White Rock. It was something that I came to enjoy. It wasn't like this, though. It was refreshing. This is just hot and heavy. It's going to feel sticky and humid afterward instead of cooling everything off."

"It tended to rain a lot on the north coast," Dorian offered, adding a few sausages to another pan as he spiced the potatoes. He usually opted for something simple in the mornings, toast and an egg, a muffin, something quick and easy, but he wasn't about to let this opportunity slip past him. He doubted Gavin was at all strict with her consumption. She still needed to fuel herself, or she'd slip even further than she already was. He then turned, grabbed his cup, and filled it with tea. He brought the pot to the table and sat across from Hokura. "You still have a few minutes before you destroy my stove."

She sat back with a smile. "Just you wait, professor. I'm going to surprise you yet."

Dorian chuckled. "You're still one of the few people who can elude me. I'll happily take surprise over a kitchen fire." He sipped his tea and stared out the window. The sky had darkened quite a bit as the rain still fell. It matched his ominous mood. He enjoyed a few moments of simply sitting as the two looked out the window. It was peaceful. He took a deep breath. "You ready to scramble some eggs?"

Hokura nodded and got up. As she took a step forward, a blinding flash pierced through the sky, followed immediately by a bellowing crash as she cried out. Dorian's arms were immediately around her as she trembled. "What on earth was that?"

"Lightning striking the lightning rod on the roof." He looked down at her and patted her head. "Another reason why we don't stand on the roof during a lightning storm." He steadied her and walked over to the phone. "I'm surprised the lights didn't even flicker. It means the setup was obviously successful all those years ago when this place was first being converted." He picked up the phone and dialed. "Governor... yes... it hit the rod. There shouldn't be any damage." There was talk on the other end as he glanced over at Hokura. "Yes, I found her. She was on the roof." A smirk came to his mouth. "No, she's with me now. She's perfectly fine. Would you like to speak to her?"

Hokura raised an eyebrow at him as he offered her the phone. She licked her lips and took it. She wondered exactly what Gavin would think of her being in Dorian's suite. "I'm about to destroy Dorian's kitchen. He's letting me cook." A wide smile came across her lips.

"Oh?" Gavin choked. "What did he do to deserve that?"

"He says I need to eat since I didn't have breakfast, so he offered to cook. The compromise was that I get to cook the eggs."

There was a small chuckle on the other side. "Then there won't be that big of a mess. I just wanted to make sure you were alright."

She shrank slightly. "I'm fine... I'll see you when you get off work." She handed the phone back to Dorian.

"There you go," Dorian said. "I suggest you get electrical

maintenance out after the storm passes to check out the roof, just as a precaution."

"Thank you, Dorian, and thank you for looking out for her."

"Of course." He hung up the phone and was quickly at Hokura's side as she entered his kitchen. "What do you need?"

"Eggs would help," she said, opening his fridge as she stared at its contents. Everything seemed to be in a perfect systemized order. Nothing was touching, and everything was where it could be easily seen and reached for. It was the exact opposite from hers.

"Here," he said, grabbing the eggs and handing them to her. "I have oil too."

"Not oil. I need butter," Hokura stated. He gave her a look as she crossed her arms and huffed. "I'm making them my way!"

Dorian rolled his eyes and produced the butter as he handed her a pan and allowed her to set to work. He stood next to her at the stove as he double-checked his potato cubes and sausages, watching as she allowed the butter to melt, cracked the eggs, and started folding them as they hit the pan. A small painful smile crossed his lips. This could have been them... no, he didn't want to ruin the moment. His smile grew. Only she could make something as mundane as cooking interesting. He watched her work as she concentrated on her task at hand.

He plated the cubes and sausages. He had also done up some toast on the side as Hokura finished the scrambled eggs. "I think you went a little overboard..." she commented as she sat at the table, and he placed her plate in front of her.

"It's coming up on lunch. This is a decent midday meal since you skipped breakfast and most likely won't eat until dinner." He went back towards the kitchen and brought her a glass of iced tea.

She took it, her heart panged. Of course, after all these years, he would remember her favorite as he sat across from her and went straight for the eggs. She held her breath, staring at his serious expression, watching him as he tasted them. His eyebrows rose as he took another bite. Hokura leaned forward in anticipation. "Well?"

He nodded with a smile and looked up at her. "These are indeed the best scrambled eggs I've ever tasted."

She chuckled slightly, which grew as she burst out laughing. "See, I said I'd surprise you." It felt good to laugh again. Something about it felt freeing. Everything that was happening right now just felt right to her in a way she couldn't explain.

Her laugh was infectious as Dorian let out a chuckle himself. "You did, and without destroying my kitchen."

Hokura wiped a tear away from her eye as she composed herself. "Thank you. This is nice. I needed this." Her eyes met his. "I still need you, Dorian. Not just to save me but for things like this... when it seems like you're the only one who can pick me up and dust me off."

He took another bite of breakfast. "And I'll be here."

She nodded as she continued to eat. She glanced outside to see that the rain was starting to ease up and couldn't help but feel at peace despite everything that was happening as she glanced up at him. Maybe everything was going to be okay? She took a bite of her meal. "This is really good. I guess you surprised me as well."

"Oh?" Dorian raised an eyebrow as he sat up and sipped his tea.

"It's interesting to see you doing domestic tasks. It always catches me off guard." A smirk came to her mouth. "To think of you cooking, cleaning, of doing... normal everyday things."

"I'll remind you that I'm human as well." He understood where she was coming from. He had his demeanor of being the professor outside of his suite. He had created a façade over the years, and there were very few people who got a rare glance at this side of him. He mused for a moment. "You're the first person I've ever cooked for."

Hokura busied herself chewing. The statement didn't surprise her. Other than Spindler and Lucien, she doubted anyone else had ever been inside his suite either. She was going to say he should open up to others but knew better. He was who he was; he had solidified himself over the decades, and there was no changing him. Finally, she looked up at him. "I'm honored, although I still think you went overboard."

Dorian grunted at her. He was fine with the accusation. He gazed up at her happily eating as she looked out the window and then stared at him. He wondered if or when she would tell the others. She'd have to, eventually. There was no hiding what was happening to her. He didn't want to spoil the mood by bringing it up. "Are you feeling a little more content now?"

She bit her bottom lip. "I am now, thanks to you."

"I'm glad to hear that. I'll need to get back to the labs this afternoon." He wanted to keep things light. "Maybe we can do this again sometime. I'll cook for you again."

"Can I help?" she chimed.

He grimaced. She had gotten lucky with the eggs. "Maybe..." His voice was tight. "We'll see how well you do with the clean-up." He gave her a wink.

The two ate a leisurely meal as Dorian's attention was entirely on her. They made small talk until Hokura brought up the education project. The professor's eyes narrowed. "There are more important things at hand right now than the project, if you wish to make some notes here and there, that's fine, but I don't suggest you start tiring yourself over this. We still have plenty of time to perfect it."

"I know, but it's important...."

"*You* take priority," Dorian stated clearly. "If you tire your-self out with this, neither your husband nor I would be too impressed." He let out a huff. "Why don't you do something relaxing like painting or drawing?" Would that be enough? No, he needed to give her a better outlet, an easy project. He cleared his throat. "I, for one, would appreciate another art piece."

Hokura's eyes widened. He had never asked her for anything like this before. She was taken back by the gesture. "Another canvas?" She looked over at the only piece of artwork hanging in his suite, the one she never quite finished and had spent in storage for nearly forty years. "I... I can make one that compliments the original one I created for you if you wish."

He smiled in satisfaction that she took the bait. "Whatever you think I would enjoy, I'll leave the creative process in your hands."

She nodded as he finished and grabbed his dish, walking it to the sink as he started clearing up the few pans they had used. "I said I was going to help!" she cried.

"Finish your meal. You can help me dry," he stated. He didn't want to tire her out, and he definitely didn't want her to feel like she was expected to help with the clean-up and that he was only joking with her beforehand.

Hokura continued eating as she watched the weather outside. The rain had slowed and became a drizzle as drops slowly ran down the windowpane. Her eyes followed as they slid down the glass, hitting others as their descent quickened. She couldn't help but feel at ease as she sat and watched as if something inside of her calmed as the storm outside did. She idly wondered why as she gazed out, transfixed as the warmth of being in Dorian's suite washed over her, the way his scent lingered on everything he touched. It had been so different from Gavin's light breath of fresh air. Dorian's was always masculine, spicy, almost woodsy. She wondered if it was the soap blend he used or if it was something more like a cologne. Either way, it always seemed to comfort her.

Dorian glanced towards her. She was looking out the window, her eyes seemingly staring blankly off into the distance as she appeared to be deep in thought. He noted how she was casually and comfortably sitting in the chair with one leg up as her foot rested underneath her. He wondered if that's how she sat at home while staring out her own bay window. He had seen intimate glimpses of her life every so often throughout the years. When she was pregnant, she had entertained him a number of times in hers and Gavin's suite as she taught him different card games. They had worked closely together through so much, had *been* through so much... his heart ached. The idea of her time being limited was too much for him to bear. He shook his head. He wouldn't let such thoughts batter him as he gazed at her form. She seemed so at peace that he didn't want to disturb her as he slowly dried the few dishes that were left. Finally, when she seemed to be done, he walked to her side. "Let me take your plate if you're finished."

Hokura snapped back to reality. "Oh..." Her eyes met his and then went to the kitchen. "I was going to help with the dishes!"

"No need." He lifted her plate. "You were lost in your private thoughts. I saw to the dishes myself because I didn't want to disturb you." He took in her disdain as if she had felt guilty about not helping as she had said she would. "You can help next time." He added with a kind smile.

"There will be a next time..." Her voice was soft.

It sounded like a question to him. Was she asking because she didn't know how much time she had left? Or because she was unsure whether they would get a chance to? "There will be a next time," he confirmed "I'll make you whatever you want."

A smile came to her face. She couldn't explain how she was feeling. It was something different as he took her plate.

"At least now I can rest at ease knowing that you've eaten a substantial meal today," Dorian grunted, narrowing his eyes at her. "You're well past your prime. Eating three square meals a day should be part of your daily schedule, and yet you seem to wrestle with doing so. Don't be so negligent with yourself."

It was the professor scolding her as she bit her bottom lip and looked away, her cheeks reddening. The scoldings were because he cared for her, and she knew it. "Yes, sir."

He placed the plate in the sink and smirked at her slightly as he turned on the water. "No arguments?"

"No." Hokura sighed, tilting her head upwards. "I know better. You've told me, Gavin's told me, I need to look after myself."

"That's definitely part of this," Dorian said. "This is going to be a team effort. As much as the medical team can do, we need you to be on board as well, which means doing what I've been preaching to you over the past how many months now." He shook his head as he finished washing the plate and walked over to her. "I need to get down to my lab. You've had a full morning. I want you to go back to your suite and rest a bit. Read, start a new painting, do something relaxing."

She nodded solemnly. "Thank you for looking after me."

"I will *always* look after you." He offered her his hand as she stood. He couldn't help his actions as he embraced her. "Please, from now on, just be honest with me and take care of yourself." He didn't know what he would ever do if he lost her again. There had been too many times already. She couldn't leave him now.

Hokura closed her eyes, enjoying the feeling. As much as he loved her, he was still her mentor. "I promise, Dorian."

His arms came to her shoulders as he looked down at her. "I need to get going. If anything comes up, I'll let you know."

She took him in. He looked tired. She wondered how much he had exhausted himself yesterday when he found out the news and how many hours he spent in the labs and the simulator. Did she dare say that he needed his rest as well? No, that would be a slight against him and what he was doing. She knew saying such a thing would be fruitless. He would stop at nothing to get the answers he needed. He would rest when all this was done. "Thank you again for everything." She excused herself and made her way back to her suite. She had no doubt that the professor would quickly finish cleaning up before he changed into his official black suit and lab coat before heading back down to the medical facility.

Hokura went to her suite. Upon opening the door, she saw that her phone was blinking with a message. She played it as she grimaced. It was Amara… someone she had been avoiding for the past week. She frowned as she deleted the message. She wasn't ready to tell the others. Hokura went into her bedroom and pulled out some art supplies from her closet, along with a large canvas, as she mused about what to paint. Dorian had stated he would let her have creative reins. That's when the idea came to her. He never understood what he saw in the city's beauty… she would show him.

She made her way to the kitchen and set up as she slowly started. The emotions flooded over her, the years looking over the city, the memories were still fresh in her mind. The first time she saw it was from the executive dining room when he had taken her for lunch. The awe of seeing it in the sunlight and wondering if she would ever be allowed to walk in it during the day. Looking over it again when she came back through the same windows which had been turned into the grand library. Staring out over it as she rubbed her pregnant stomach… and now looking over it again as it rained as she ate lunch with Dorian. Her brushstrokes were steady as her bottom lip trembled, tears slowly came to her eyes, an overwhelming feeling rocked through her as she started with the background color. Maybe this would make him understand.

Dorian made his way down to Gavin's office. He figured he would update the governor before heading into the labs. He curtly knocked and allowed him in to see Gavin on the phone as he sat at his desk.

Gavin raised a finger as he continued his conversation. "Thank you for looking into it. If there's anything else, please let me know." He hung up the phone and turned to the professor. "The lightning rod held up, minimal damage." He licked his lips. "How is she?"

The professor shrugged slightly, crossing his arms. "Other than being slightly melodramatic on the roof, she's okay." He sighed as he ran his hand through his hair. He needed to be honest as well. "She's going through motions none of us can understand. Even when she's being honest, there's so much underneath the surface. She's scared."

"Of course, she's scared. We're all scared!" Gavin retorted. "How can I be there for her when she's pushing me away like this, though? She didn't want me around this morning..."

Dorian's eyes met Gavin's. "Give her some time. She needs to work through some things on her own. She's struggling with some inner turmoil that only she can get through. I gave her a project to take her mind off things. Hopefully, being creative will distract her, or it'll be therapeutic. Either way, it'll be helpful."

Gavin nodded with a sad sigh. Again, the professor was solving her problems. He felt like he had barely anything to offer her, he wanted to be so much more, to be the person she ran to, and yet... no... last night was a testament. He couldn't help it if Dorian still knew her well enough to distract her and help her. He cleared his throat. "I'm grateful that you found her and that you were there for her."

"And I always will be governor, and that isn't a slight against you. As I told her, this is going to be a team effort for everyone involved. That means you as well and keeping on top of her when she slips up. She needs you."

He knew the words were meant to comfort him. "Has there been any further progress in determining what this is or how it can be stopped?" Gavin's words were tense.

"I'm going down to my labs now to see to things. Unfortunately, some of these things can't be rushed. The process can be meticulous." He watched Gavin's expression turn as he sighed and settled into his seat, leaning into it. "She told me a while ago that she told you everything that happened to her...."

The governor nodded. "Yeah, she did... I wish I had gone with you. Instead of working against you, we could have worked together, and I could have been there for her too."

Dorian shook his head. "It happened the way it did. Besides, if you were with us, who knows what would have happened to you? It could have been worse. You could have been killed, and then what?" He pursed his lips. "You're not a fighter Gavin."

"Neither was Cassandra."

"No... not until that point, but she is her mother's child and has the peacekeeper genes that flow through Hokura's veins. She didn't falter when she was needed. She took action and took the responsibility that came with those actions," Dorian continued.

Gavin raised an eyebrow. "Could Cass's DNA help at all in this?"

The professor shook his head. "No, Hokura's genetic make-up is unique. Everything I use to put her back together has to be hers. Either way, as I was saying... in a way, I'm glad you weren't there to witness what I had, governor, and I mean that wholeheartedly."

"Why do you say that?" Gavin's throat was dry. "I'm sure you've heard the gossip of what I went through while she was gone. Without her, I'm less of everything."

Dorian's expression turned jaded. "Because, Gavin, I know exactly how strong she is. When I found her, I thought she was dead. After rescuing her, the damage done to her body would have turned you. You would have been afraid to even touch her when she needed medical attention. Do you think you could have helped her when your hands were causing her pain? Do you think you could have stood by and let me work on her while she cried out in agony?"

The man deflated. As much as Hokura had told him, there would always be things he didn't know because he hadn't witnessed them firsthand. His heart bled. He had doubted her, had wondered about what had truly unfolded between the two during the rescue. He couldn't ask her. Yet... "Dorian. I swear nothing will come of this but when you rescued her. In a way, I kind of figured, but I need to know... and I know I've asked before. Honestly, did *anything*..."

He knew the question. His insides recoiled. Those lines were danced upon. When he was going through his transition with the bionic arm, there were times he was unsure of what had transpired between them. The one thing that he was sure about was where his loyalties lay. "Nothing happened between us, Gavin. I tended to wounds that were over her entire body, I held her as she slept and screamed because of nightmares, I saw her through hell, but there was nothing sexual between us."

The governor nodded, and a smile came over his face that seemed like a weight had been lifted from him. He gave a huff as a small chuckle escaped him. "I said it didn't matter, and it really doesn't. I love her more than anyone, but still, it's a relief to hear that."

"And yet asking her that would have only caused more issues during this precarious time." His eyes held Gavin's. "Tread lightly with her as well. Her mental health has been a slippery slope since returning. Indeed, she's had times when she's been fine, and yet I can't help but wonder about all the demons she harbors within her. I was one of them."

Gavin's eyes widened. "Not anymore. You should know that."

A smirk came to Dorian's lips. "Every so often, though, I am reminded." He rose from his chair. It had been true. The way she had snapped at him on the roof had stuck with him. Every so often, when they had their spats, she would say something that threw him. It hurt, but he knew it was said in the moment. He wished the memory would fade from her mind, but indeed there would always be their rocky past which had been deeply ingrained in everything she had done after leaving the compound, which had pointed directly at him. "I'm going to be in my labs." He turned as he went for the door. "Make sure she eats a decent dinner. I'm sure she'll try to get out of it because she had a large lunch, but she still needs to stay on top of her intake." With that, he left the office.

Dorian made his way down to his lab, wondering if the sample would be slightly thawed. Even if there were a small amount that he could work with, that would be enough. He would set to work and see about extracting the healthy cells and introducing them to her newest samples. He would also see about dosing a sample with the original blank cells to see if he could come up with something. As he entered his lab, he noted the time. He couldn't be upset that Hokura had taken up his time that morning. He had wanted to talk to her and had gotten to do so. Beyond that, he was able to spend some precious time with her, taking care of her. The professor craned his neck back as he cracked it. "It's going to be a long day..."

Hokura sat in the kitchen, looking out the window as she dabbed the canvas with her paintbrush. The strokes had been sure as she gently glided it over her artwork. Dorian... he had never seen it the way she had. She didn't think anyone did. Then again, it always seemed to be the one thing that made her stand out from the others. She always felt things differently. Had it been her genetics? Her unique coding, which seemed to drive her emotions further and deeper? She had once decided to look it up, to try and understand. She was an empath, emotionally deep. Sometimes it felt like her heart held so much that it was going to break open.

That... that's what this felt like. Every time she looked at the city, her heart swelled with what was within it, with who and what she had done here. As much as White Rock had been her residence for forty years and held so many special memories, she never felt the same as she did here, looking out over the city of Meridiana. And yes... there were places that were more to her that she could never understand why. The ocean had held a special place in her heart and always would. A small smile came to her lips. Dorian was right. This had helped. Her mind drifted as her hands moved in a serene motion as she created.

There had been so many beautiful memories created here. She wanted to hold onto them and let the past ones that weren't so fond go. Meeting her love... coming back and the astonishment she had felt... walking the city with Gavin, taking lunches in the park with Dorian, riding her bike with the others, visiting the sweets shop with the children. All the people that she had brought back to the city from White Rock... everyone she loved. "I'm not ready to go," she whispered to herself.

———————

Gavin made his way up to their suite a couple of hours later. He had been too worried about her to concentrate on work. A few things had come up from the civilians regarding damage inside the city, pooling water, and a few leaks within some buildings, but nothing disastrous. Adam had helped him get city maintenance out quickly and in an orderly fashion to make sure his people were looked after. In doing so, he felt like he was neglecting the one person he should have been beside. He smiled as he walked in the door to see her set up at the window painting. It was as if, for a moment, everything was as it should be.

Hokura turned to him with a meek smile. "You're home early."

"There isn't much going on right now that needs my attention," he lied sweetly as he walked up to her and kissed her. "I can see your creative juices are flowing."

She turned back to her canvas "It's a work in progress. It'll take some time before it's done. Right now, is just the base." She took in the size of it, maybe she should have done something smaller, but she had wanted this to be a piece that she could pour her heart and soul into.

"How was your day? How did cooking in Dorian's kitchen go?" There was a slight chuckle to the question. He just wanted to communicate with her as he loosened the collar of his shirt and comfortably leaned against the kitchen counter.

A smirk came to her face. "His kitchen is still intact if that's what you're asking." She crossed her arms, still staring at the canvas. "It's strange to see him do menial tasks like cooking."

The statement puzzled him. "Why do you say that?"

Hokura chewed on her bottom lip. "Because he's always everywhere else, doing everything else... maybe it's because he still puts forth the façade of being the professor, which makes it hard to remember he's human." She looked back at Gavin. "I've never seen him cook before. Well... at least not in a kitchen... I guess when he came for me, he heated up rations..." A sarcastic smirk came to her lips.

Gavin raised an eyebrow. "What's that grin for?"

She let out a chuckle. "I guess he's come a long way. Before me, he had never left the compound, had never slept in a tent, or camped. I'm sure before me, he never used the woods as a bathroom either."

"Odd sentiment." Gavin shook his head. "I guess you do that to people, though. You bring them out of their shells." He took a step towards her as he cupped her face. "I had never been out of the city before you, had never dreamed of doing such things, and yet with you by my side, it was all so easy." He kissed her cheek and moved towards her mouth. His lips met hers as he pulled her closer, just wishing he could take this all away.

Hokura stepped back as the kiss ended. "I'm not gone yet, Gavin..."

"You *won't* be gone... you're not going *anywhere*. We're going to get this figured out, and once you're better, we're going to do more. Make more memories. Do things that we never dreamed of doing before because we'll have the rest of time together."

She smiled at him and kissed the tip of his nose. "We will... but for now, I guess I should clean up this mess before the kids come home."

Gavin watched as she went to work on washing and putting away her paints and brushes. He wished there was something he could do. That he could just hold onto her, and time could stop. His emotions were riding high, and yet for her, it seemed like she wasn't trying to overly think about it, or if she was, she wasn't letting anything on. He wondered what Dorian had encountered on the roof. He had stated that she was being melodramatic. What did that even mean? Even now, there were sides to his wife that only the professor saw that he very much wished she would share with him as well. "Do you need any help with anything?" He was reaching.

Hokura turned with a bright smile. Why was he being like this? "Nope, I'm good!"

He turned from her, not wanting her to see his disappointment. "I guess I'll freshen up, and we can start on figuring out dinner then." She would fight to stay independent as long as she could with him. She didn't want his help. Maybe that's what this was... Gavin walked towards the bedroom and changed. After hanging up his shirt, he couldn't help but sprawl out on the bed and stare at the ceiling. Was this his punishment? Was she pushing him away because he hadn't listened to Dorian about Tobias? Because he had allowed the man into the compound? Because he hadn't been the one to save her? Or was he reading too much into things?

"This is ridiculous. I'm literally making up scenarios in my mind..." Maybe he was torturing himself because he was partially to blame for what had happened, and he had yet to forgive himself. He doubted that he ever would. Gavin moved from the bed and made the conscious decision that he would spend as much time by Hokura's side as he could. Brooding wasn't going to get him anywhere as he changed his pants and quickly washed up. He left the bedroom to see Hokura had put everything away, and yet she was standing in front of the bay window again.

"The sky looks so ominous. It's absolutely beautiful," she breathed, taking in the orange of the sun mixing with the almost dark purple clouds.

Gavin walked up to her and brought his hand through her hair. "You're far more breathtaking." He kissed the top of her head.

"Gavin... please..." She groaned as she turned and hugged him. "Please don't let this change things."

"You're cruel to think that it wouldn't, Hokura," he growled, holding her.

"Well, what about what I want?" She scowled. "We're not telling the kids, and I want you to just go back to the way you used to be before...."

He took a deep breath. "Before you were kidnapped, and I thought I had lost you forever? You have no idea what it was like thinking I lost you."

She didn't want to hear it. Maybe she *was* being cruel but for him to say such a thing. She understood better than any of them what it was like to lose someone. Was she being selfish? She had been the one who had gone through hell, who had harbored this secret in order for Dorian to piece himself back together. "Let's get things figured out for dinner. I want a peaceful night. I don't want to think about this anymore today."

It was then Cassandra and Cyrus walked through the door. Hokura turned with a bright smile on her face. "Perfect timing. We were just figuring out our evening."

Gavin nodded. He would play along and do as his wife wished.

———————— ✦ ————————

The day had moved forward at an even pace. It was now late into the night. Dorian had exhausted himself to the point where he didn't know if he could physically stand upright a moment more. Once his vision began to blur, and he was continuously rubbing his eyes, he knew his day in the labs was over. There was nothing else he could see to for now as staring hard into a microscope all day hadn't gotten him where he wanted. As much as he didn't want to bring her back into the medical facility, he needed more samples. He had spent two hours in the RTC simulator, getting out whatever physical exertion he had to spare. Now he was slowly making his way down the hallway to his suite. He was so tired he hadn't even changed from his training gear.

He opened his door and kicked off his shoes as he slumped against the wall, the day had been a long one, and he hadn't been any closer to a solution. Tomorrow was another day as he walked to the shower, washed the sweat from his body, and fell, undressed, into his bed, not caring that he was only half-dried. He didn't have the energy to make his way to the kitchen for anything to drink, the only remaining energy he had was enough to click off his light and cover himself with his blanket. At least he wasn't becoming dependent on sleep aids. Before he was even able to slightly stir, he was asleep as his dreams took him.

He was standing on the roof, staring at her as the rain slowly bounced off her form. He took a moment to take in her beauty, the way the sun streamed off her silhouette. She looked otherworldly as he took a step towards her.

"Standing in the rain again?" he asked, his tone was light as a smile came across his face as he approached her. His smile turned to horror as she turned to him.

"Dorian..." Hokura's face was ashen and sunken in. As the rain fell upon her head, small chunks of her hair started to fall out, landing at her feet. "I'm dying..."

"No!" Dorian cried, trying to reach her. "I can save you."

She shook her head. "Nobody can save me now...."

"Don't say that!" he urged as his arms came around her to hold her. Her body shrank and withered in his grips as it turned to nothing but skin and bones as she deteriorated in his grasps. "No!" he cried in desperation. "Hokura... I can fix you... I can save you..." The light left her eyes as he shook her corpse, fear coursing through him. "No! Hokura, wake up... Hokura please! No..." Her body turned to dust as he screamed her name, trying to keep hold of her as she simply disappeared, and there had been nothing left but him, crouching in the rain, sobbing, on top of the roof. "Don't leave me..." he whispered.

Dorian awoke with a start as his eyes widened. His breathing hitched as it caught. "Just a dream..." he panted. "Just a damnable dream." He should know better, he *did* know better than to allow such a trivial thing to shake him, but still, his body trembled as he gasped. His body moved out of the bed. He needed a moment to collect his thoughts and clear his mind as he walked to the kitchen. He grabbed a glass and got some water. He couldn't stand to look out over the city tonight, so he made his way to his couch and sat on it as he tilted his head back. "Hokura," he whispered, wishing he could see her, wishing he could simply gaze upon her at that moment to confirm that she was okay. He took a deep breath. Of course, she was okay. She was in bed next to her husband, hopefully sleeping soundly.

He kneaded his forehead. He could spend the night regretting things, or he could do what was required, and at that moment, what he required was sleep so he could be well-rested and back in the labs. Dorian moved back to his bedroom and lay down on his bed, fighting to get comfortable. "Just sleep, damn you... stop thinking about it..." he groaned. How could he not think about it? How could she not be everything on his mind? He sighed. He didn't need setbacks, and right now, he was going to sabotage himself if he didn't rest. He finally got into a position that was comfortable enough that he could feel the effects of sleep starting to wash over him again. He hoped that some sweeter dreams would embrace him. Ones where she was going to be alright, ones where he could delve into her or simply enjoy being next to her... He rolled over and wished for anything but nightmares. He needed to simply clear his head. At least the rest of the night had been kind as he fell into a deep exhausted sleep.

The compound bustled to life as everyone started their days. Gavin asked his wife once again about staying home for the day. Hokura had stated she would be fine. "If anything comes up, I promise to call you," she groaned as she took in his displeasure. "Please, Gavin, I'm still well enough right now that I don't need to be under constant surveillance." She kissed him playfully. "How about I get up with you, and we have an easy breakfast together."

He had complied and was happy to see her eating.

Cassandra and Cyrus exited their rooms and joined their parents.

Hokura looked up at her son with a smile. "Where do they have you stationed today in the labs?"

The boy gave a grin. "Right now, Nathan and I have been standing in with the botanists. We've been keeping an eye on the way the weather has been changing lately, too, and how it's been impacting the gardens."

Gavin raised an eyebrow. "Oh?"

"There's been nothing conclusive yet, but they've changed the watering schedules slightly for certain fruits. They're hoping to avoid damage. Apparently, the cherries can split if they get wet and then don't dry properly, causing decomposition." Cyrus smiled. "They're pretty on top of things, though."

"Good to know," Gavin muttered. The professor had stated that there hadn't been anything to worry about weather-wise. Between the lightning strike and now this, he wondered if the man was just trying to brush it off or if there was any actual cause for concern. There had been some city maintenance but nothing too much. He could only hope that nothing more would come up.

Cassandra chimed in. "I've been running track. I absolutely love running!" She smiled proudly.

Hokura smiled at her daughter. "One of my favorite

training exercises as well. It's amazing how you can feel after a good sprint."

Cassandra eyed her mother, she didn't want to say anything, but she doubted her mother would be able to come close to any of her standing records in the shape she was in. It seemed like she was beginning to slow more and more lately. She had been worried but had hoped it was part of her continuous healing. Surely if there were anything to worry about, she would have said something.

Cyrus stood. "Well, we're out of here!" the boy chimed.

"What about breakfast?" Hokura asked. "You just sat down... you still have some time before lessons start."

Cassandra smiled. "We're going to grab some baked goods from the cafeteria and grab Nathan before hitting lessons."

Why did Hokura suddenly feel like she was grasping at straws? Her children were always out the door fairly quickly lately. She didn't want them to catch onto anything as she smiled up at them. "Fair enough. Maybe on break, we can do a family night and play some games or head into the city again," she offered. She wanted to spend some time with them before everything dropped and the truth finally came out.

"That sounds great!" Cassandra smiled.

"Oh, I know a good game we can pick up from the games room, we haven't played Yahtzee yet, and it's pretty much all luck!" Cyrus looked at both his mother and sister. "No manipulations or card counting."

Gavin chuckled. "Now, now. You need to give your mother and sister some credit with their educated deductions when it comes to games."

The boy only rolled his eyes. "We'll see you two this evening." With that, he and Cassandra left on their way, leaving their mother and father to finish their breakfast.

"I can clean up before heading in," Gavin offered, taking

his plate to the kitchen sink. It seemed that Hokura was taking her time enjoying her meal as he sat back across from her.

"Don't bother." She chewed. "It'll give me something to do."

His eyes narrowed at her. "Dorian has you painting. You still have your book series that you're slowly making your way through. You have enough to occupy your time."

She stared up at her husband with a raised eyebrow. "I'm not beyond doing a few dishes."

"I never said you were," Gavin offered. "Need I remind you a few weeks ago, you were fine with getting out of dishes? You don't need to start taking on tasks to prove yourself."

Hokura pouted. That's precisely what she was doing. She wanted to prove to everyone that she was still fully capable of doing everything she had done a few weeks ago, that this diagnosis hadn't changed anything. She was fighting it but knew it was her stubbornness that was going to end up being her downfall. No, she wasn't ready to fully accept things yet. "I'm not trying to prove anything," she lied as she smiled at him. "Just trying to be a dutiful wife, I haven't picked back up on the higher education project again. I'd like to get to that too."

"There are more important things." Gavin's voice was flat. He didn't want to start a fight with her. "I'll make sure to pick up some dinner tonight." Changing the subject was the best way to avoid what might erupt between them. "Maybe this evening, after a few games with the kids, we can walk the gardens if you have the energy."

"That sounds lovely," Hokura replied. She knew exactly what Gavin had done with steering the conversation in a different direction. She'd allow it. She could understand that he didn't want to fight with her and knew she was in a mood, so he wouldn't keep pushing.

Gavin sat for a few more moments, more so to make sure

she ate her breakfast in full. He casually went over to the sink and dumped out a bit of his coffee as he swiftly washed the cup along with his plate, hoping she wouldn't take notice. He had cleaned up most of the mess before kissing her temple. "Enjoy your day. If anything comes up, let me know, and I'll be there in a second."

She kissed him back tenderly. "I'm sure I'll be fine."

After Gavin left, Hokura stared at the sink and the pile of clean dishes drying beside it. She knew he had done it on purpose. At least this way, he could argue with her that she could dry them and put them away if she so wished. Hokura shook her head. Their relationship was sometimes an intricate dance, and it always seemed that Gavin was in pace with her or, like today, changed the dance entirely.

Hokura crashed on the couch and picked up her book, which she read for a few minutes until she got a few pages further. Of course, the main character was going back to the games. "She doesn't even get to say goodbye..." Hokura mumbled as she put the book down on the coffee table. Damn book series, and it feeling so relative to what she was feeling lately. She hated it. Suddenly, the phone caught her attention. She faltered slightly and allowed the answering machine to get it when she heard Dorian's voice and quickly picked up the receiver.

"Sorry!" she cried.

"Are you alright?" His voice was filled with concern.

She wasn't about to tell him she was screening her calls. "I'm fine, just a little slow to get to the phone. That's all. What's up?"

He cleared his throat. "I was hoping not to trouble you today, but if it's possible, I would like to get another blood sample from you and do a quick check-in." His voice sounded tense.

"Yes!" Hokura breathed. "Of course, I can come down whenever you want."

"There's no huge rush. Take your time. I'll be in my personal lab. How about you come and meet me down here when you're ready, and we can go from there."

It didn't seem too dire. She still needed to freshen up and get dressed. "Okay. I'll be there in a bit once I'm ready," Hokura answered and hung up the phone, and wondered whether she should report to Gavin or not. She shrugged. It was a simple blood test, something she had done hundreds of times before. She failed to see a reason to involve her husband and possibly worry him. She idly looked out the bay window. It had started to rain again lightly. She couldn't understand but watching it always seemed to lull her, the sound, the freshness, and before she knew it, her eyes were transfixed on the city. It wasn't until she realized how long she had been sitting that she snapped out of her mental fog and went about getting ready and made her way downstairs.

The professor had been sitting at his desk rubbing his eyes as he was going over her charts when there was a light knock at his door. He looked up in time to see Hokura walking through it.

He raised an eyebrow. "You could have taken your time if you were busy."

"I *did* take my time. I got lost in thought," Hokura remarked, crossing her arms. "I'm not doing much anyway. I thought the sooner we did this, the better." She stared at the clock. "It's past mid-morning."

"Indeed, it is." Dorian pushed away from his desk.

Hokura wondered how long he had been down here

already since the professor was usually up at dawn. She followed him at his side as they strode down the hallways towards the medical facilities. "Is there anything more that needs to happen today other than blood tests?"

"Nothing invasive," Dorian answered as he opened the door to a medical room.

Hokura sat on the gurney and readied herself as Dorian gave her a tired look. "I just want to go over a few things today and take a few samples."

She couldn't help but look up at him. "You're exhausting yourself... have you been sleeping?"

He gave her a solemn look. He wouldn't tell her about his nightly routine. That when his brain tired, he exhausted his body into the RTC simulator and then got a few hours of tormented sleep. That he was having nightmares about her when his dreams used to be of the life he *wished* he had with her. "I've been getting a few hours a night. We both know I don't need much sleep to function." He had avoided the conversation and brought up another. "May I ask to see your side with the bruise? I want to see how it's healing."

Hokura sighed. It was back to formalities as she nodded and showed him her hip.

His eyes narrowed as he examined it. "And you said that you had done that a few days before you told me about everything...."

"Yeah..." Her voice was unsteady. Had there been something more? "It's still a little sore but not as bad as it was...."

The professor bristled, pursing his lips. His body had gone tight. "It's still dark purple and blue, which means you're still in the second stage of healing." He shook his head. Even without having a perfected system, even if she were a regular human, the bruise should have lightened by now. The CT hadn't shown a break or anything. Her system was indeed slowing, and he wondered how long it would take for her skin to heal. It was never something peacekeepers or anyone ever worried about in the compound. Even years ago, when she had grabbed his wrist with enough force to cause a bruise, it had healed up in a matter of hours. A regular person's wrist would have shattered under the strength. "We'll keep an eye on that."

She nodded. She hated this feeling, how he reverted like this. She tried to make small talk. "It was raining again this morning."

"Indeed, it was." He turned around, grabbing at something. "I'm going to take your blood pressure."

"It's never rained like this before that I can remember," she continued. "I think it helps me sleep."

The professor took the sphygmomanometer. He gave a sorrowful expression as he noted the bruises still on her arm from taking the previous blood samples. He took her other arm and placed the cuff on her. "How have *you* been sleeping lately?"

"I've been taking my sleep aids still... the nightmares are still there every so often... some nights I sleep... others not so much. I think it's more luck of the draw at this point."

He nodded as he noted the device. "Slightly low." He scowled as he turned and noted it on her chart.

Her heart ached. "Dorian, please..."

He stopped and eyed her. "Hokura." He sighed. "I apologize. It's hard being in the labs, being in here and not being..." He didn't know whether he had the words. "I've been the father of science for so long now that it's ingrained in me. It's who I am. You need to remember that you're one of the very few people who see the other side of me. It's hard to switch off the professor side, especially when things are like this, but I'll try."

She nodded. That was all she could hope for. "Is it bad... am I truly dying?"

Dorian pursed his lips. "I don't like that word. I suggest it be avoided at all costs. Your system is indeed going through something. It's slowing and not regenerating." He shook his head. "I guess you can say you're ill, sick... if you may...."

"But the end result..."

"Is that I will fix this." His words were stern. He grabbed a syringe and took her one arm as he inwardly winced. His eyes held hers as his tone softened. "Hokura, I swear I will. Just give me some time." His hand gently caressed her skin. "Please believe me."

Her lips trembled. "I do, I'm just scared..." she leaned towards him. "This is going to hurt."

"I'll try to be as gentle as possible." He crooned as he stepped forward, allowing her to rest against him. His hands worked delicately to not cause her any pain. The least he could do was allow her to be close to him as he drew her samples. Even with his fluid, graceful movements, she still flinched slightly as the syringe pierced her skin. "I'm sorry," he whispered... forgive me.

Once he was done taking the samples, he steadied her. "Easy now, don't get up too fast, or you'll give yourself a head rush. Take a few moments." He walked the containers over to the counter and returned to her side, placing an arm around her. "Hopefully, I'll be able to conclude some theories from these today."

Hokura leaned her head against him and closed her eyes, merely nodding. His scent wrapped around her. For a moment, she was able to feel at peace. She would try to fill herself with the notion that once again, he would save her. "Dorian..." she whispered as her body slumped.

"I'll take care of you... *we'll* take care of you. I swear it." His words were light as he gently ran his hand through a few stray hairs, brushing them away from her face when he noticed the texture. It hadn't been as smooth as it once had been. He raised an eyebrow and noted that change as well. He wished he could do more for her but wondered if his actions would be for her sake or for his own. She had Gavin. She needed to stop dismissing her husband from her side. He took a long breath, trying to steady himself. "Come on. I'll walk you to your suite. You need some rest."

Hokura nodded as she opened her eyes, and he helped her down.

The two walked in silence as Dorian walked her up to her suite. He kept his eye on her as he did so. "Would you like me to make you some lunch? You really need to eat something after having blood drawn like that. Your blood pressure is already low. You need to rest and replenish. I'm surprised I didn't have to carry you up here."

Hokura shook her head. She was feeling low. As much as she wanted to be around Dorian, she also wanted to rest. She would have been content to simply rest against him in the medical facility, but apparently, the days of falling asleep next to him were now behind her. "I'll be fine. I'll have something to snack on in a bit."

He eyed her. "I'll check on you a little later then, after my meal." He wondered if he made some extra lunch if he'd be able to simply drop it off at her suite. He was sure she would see through the ruse, but did it really matter? Either way, he would make something. If she kept her word and ate, she could always eat it later.

"Thank you for everything again, Dorian," she said softly.

He leaned against the wall, hovering over her. He wanted to be closer to her, and yet in the labs, it seemed so restricted to do so. "We're working on this. I promise you'll be okay." His voice was soft.

She nodded, not knowing if she truly believed him as her throat caught and she began to cough. Right away, one of his hands was on her shoulder as the other was on her back, soothing her. The fit didn't last long. She was grateful she hadn't coughed up any blood. "I'm going to rest," she promised, looking up at him.

Dorian watched as she made her way into her suite. She had looked pale. He almost wanted to ask if she wanted to rest at his place for a while as he made lunch and took a bit of a break. She had been right in her statement that he was exhausting himself. He was feeling it and figured he would make himself some coffee and lunch before returning to the labs. He wanted to test his theory on the cells and the possibilities of dosing her again without there being any issues. He made his way to his suite and started on his menial tasks, which were becoming more enjoyable.

Hokura walked into her suite and found herself on the couch, too tired to move as the phone rang again. She shook her head. She didn't think she had the strength to walk over to it. It wouldn't be Dorian since they had just parted in the hallway. If it was Gavin, he could come up to the suite to talk to her. She eyed the clock. It wasn't quite lunch break yet. She was sure if he needed something, he would come up. The phone continued to ring as the answering machine hit, and the line went dead. Hokura rolled over on the couch as she clutched a pillow. If it were urgent, they would have left a message.

Amara bristled in annoyance as she hung up the phone and cursed loudly just as Adam walked into the suite for lunch.

He raised a worried eyebrow as he took in his wife. "Should I come back later?"

"No," she retorted, crossing her arms, and slunk on the couch. "She's been ignoring my calls for what seems like weeks now! She said it wasn't going to be like this once the professor had his arm back!" She looked up at Adam almost accusingly. "Has Gavin said anything?"

Adam winced. "No..." He thought about the governor. He had seemed off the past few days. He had been absent the one day, and then whenever he had brought in reports, Gavin's thoughts seemed to be elsewhere. As if there had been something wearing on his mind, but when asked, he said nothing. He chalked it up to the weather lately, which had been making him feel anxious. Adam sighed. "Why don't you just go see her?"

She huffed angrily. "Because I don't want to feel like I'm intruding and pushing." She gave her husband a sidelong glance. "Why does it have to be like this with her? Why do I feel like I have to push her to hang out with me? To answer the fucking phone!"

Adam pursed his lips, heading into the kitchen as he started making himself something for lunch. "I don't know, Amara... I don't know why she does the things she does. I don't know why, since we rescued her, it's been like pulling teeth to see her again lately." He wondered if there was something underlying that Hokura and Gavin were keeping to themselves. Possibly something about the professor? He didn't know.

"Here... I'll make your lunch. You go and relax," Amara said as she grabbed two plates and hustled Adam out of the way. "Since pretty much all the vehicles have been fixed, I have a few days off. We're waiting on parts, so I need something to do."

"Perfect opportunity to go visit her," Adam replied, taking a step back as Amara set to work on making sandwiches. "The kids are at lessons. You have a few hours after lunch. Maybe you two can go for a walk in the gardens or even just play a few rounds of cards. I'm sure there's an explanation for all of this."

Amara rolled her eyes. "Of course there is, there's always an explanation, and then I feel like shit or make her feel worse for avoiding me. Maybe I should ask Gavin... or you could ask him and relay the message back to me..."

Adam cleared his throat. "Or... you could face her head on and just go to her suite and see how she is." He didn't exactly want to be playing messenger. He knew it would only make Amara all the more anxious waiting for news. If it were nothing, she would blow her top accusing that there was something, that they weren't telling him the truth, and then she'd be in the same predicament.

She made a face. "Fine. I'll go after lunch." She looked at the phone. She wanted to try again... maybe Hokura had been in Gavin's office visiting him. Maybe she was in the cafeteria or with the professor. There were plenty of reasons for her not to be in her suite answering her calls. Amara glowered. She had left enough messages over the past few days but hadn't done so just now because they had gone ignored. Hokura could have called her back. It was the least she could have done or sought out her friend since Amara had added a few times that she wasn't doing much and was off work. Why was this all so complicated?

"You know she hasn't been working alongside us since her return. Maybe she needs more time," Adam commented, trying to ease his seething wife.

That didn't help. "It's been months since she was rescued. Shouldn't everything start going back to normal?"

"Dorian hasn't been back to work either since his arm was cloned. First, it was with rehabilitation and then double and triple-checking that his cells would continue to accept the arm," he added. "Perhaps she's just been at his side again. You know what they went through together and that they couldn't be together for a time."

Amara glowered. "Pretty sure I know better than anyone." She shook her head. "This is something else... the feeling I haven't been able to kick." She took a breath in resolve. That afternoon she would seek her friend out.

───────────⬩───────────

It was after lunch. Adam had kissed his wife goodbye and wished her luck with tracking down Hokura in hopes every-thing would be fine. Once he had left, Amara made her way to the cafeteria, hoping to see Hokura; she hadn't been there. Amara had kept her eyes open for the professor as well, but he had also been absent from her search. With a small huff, Amara took the elevator to the upper suites. She went to Hokura's door and promptly knocked. She heard shuffling from the other side and waited patiently. After a moment, Amara's eyes widened as the door opened, and she took her in. "You... you haven't been returning my calls," she stammered.

"Amara..." Hokura sighed. She didn't want to do this right now, but it was too late.

The second child couldn't understand what she saw, why her friend had looked so frail. She had looked almost as she did when she and Adam had first rescued her. Amara studied the bruises on her arms. She couldn't distinguish them. "Is this why?" Amara asked, meeting Hokura's eyes.

Hokura nodded slightly. "Yes... I didn't... I..." Why couldn't she find the words? She suddenly felt incredibly self-conscious standing in front of Amara as she shrank back slightly.

"I haven't seen you lately. You've been brushing me off and then started just ignoring my calls. What's going on with you?" Amara demanded.

"Something is wrong with me...." Hokura confessed. "I've been in the medical facility and the labs. Only Dorian and Gavin know..." she licked her lips as desperation flooded her face. "My cells aren't regenerating... I'm..." The words caught. Dorian didn't want to use these words, but they were true. "I'm dying."

Amara took a step back in horror. "What? What do you mean you're *dying*? How? Since when?"

She couldn't meet her friend's eyes as she looked away. "Since Dorian saved me."

"That was months ago." Amara's voice was curt as her eyes narrowed. "But you knew, *didn't you*? This is what you've been keeping from everyone, isn't it?" Her voice rose. "This has been that uneasy feeling I've been having! And you knew the entire time, didn't you?"

"Amara..."

"*Didn't you?*" Amara yelled, pointing her finger at Hokura.

"Yes." Hokura sighed, leaning up against the doorframe. "I knew...but I had to make sure Dorian was better before..."

"That's a bullshit excuse!" Amara yelled. "Dammit, Hokura, why are you like this? Why have you *always* been like this?" Amara screamed at her. "Gavin knows... Dorian knows... You've told everyone else that's important to you, but Adam and I are always the last ones to know!"

"Amara, please..."

"Don't! Don't you fucking dare *Amara, please* me! I knew something was up weeks ago. I went to you, and you still didn't say a damn word." She looked at her in desperation. "I've always been there for you, and yet you've always kept things from me! I thought we were friends! I thought you were my best friend, and still... and now you're doing this to me! How fucking dare you!"

Hokura didn't know what to say. She sagged as she held herself. "I'm sorry..."

"Fuck you and your apologies!" Amara screamed as she turned and ran down the hallway.

Dorian had just opened his suite door. He had heard Amara's screams and watched as the peacekeeper ran past him and to the stairs as he tried to figure out the situation.

"Amara," Hokura groaned. She was about to go after her friend when she faltered. Her head started spinning as she took a step forward. Her body protested as she went to her knees. "Amara... please... I'm sorry," she pleaded as her breathing hitched.

"Hokura!" He was at her side, bracing her.

"Go after her, please... she needs to know I didn't mean this... I need to talk to her," she cried as she clutched her chest.

"You need to rest," Dorian offered. "You're looking pale. Have you eaten anything yet?"

She shook her head tiredly. "I figured I would just relax on the couch after the tests. I was fine until I got up to answer the door. I had a major head rush."

The professor huffed. "I took blood samples. You need to get something into your system." He picked her up in his arms.

"I need to..."

"You *need* to listen, eat something, and rest." His tone was stern as he walked her into her suite and deposited her on her couch. "You won't be talking to anyone if you're passed out in the hallway." He then turned and went to the kitchen. He had made her something, but he figured it had now become his dinner. He didn't know if she could handle anything too heavy right now anyway.

Hokura could hear him rustling around as she closed her eyes in hopes the room would stop spinning. She opened them when she heard a clink on the coffee table in front of her as she stared at the plate that held a muffin along with some fruit and a glass of orange juice.

Dorian stared down at her with a look she couldn't quite distinguish. It looked to be one of annoyance crossed with worry. He let out a large breath as he glanced towards the door. "I'll go speak with Amara if you promise to actually listen to me and eat something and *rest*."

She was too tired to argue as she nodded. There was nothing to even argue about. She knew he was right.

"Good." His tone softened. "I'll let Gavin know that you're to relax for the rest of the day, and I'll let you know how things go with Amara."

Her eyes narrowed. "You're telling my husband on me?"

A vicious smile crossed his lips. "You're sending me after Amara. You can deal with your husband hovering over you after not listening to me and ending up on the floor." He waited for her to protest. When she said nothing, he turned. "I'm sure Gavin will be up soon once I talk to him. I suggest you don't do anything daft." With that, he left and made his way down the hallway. He figured he'd let Amara have some time to brood, scream, and get out whatever anger she was exhibiting. It was better to let her cool a little than fully face her hot temper head-on.

Dorian walked down to the governing office. He didn't bother with knocking as he left himself into Gavin's office.

The governor looked up at him as he was looking over reports.

Dorian sat down and steepled his fingers, waiting for the man to put them down and address him.

Gavin turned and gave him a tired look. "Do I even want to know?" he groaned.

"No." The professor shrugged. "But you're going to hear it anyway, and then you're going to pack up your work for the afternoon and see to your wife, whom I've told to eat and rest for the remainder of the day. You're going to take on your role as husband, and if she dares to get back up, you'll threaten that I will cart her down to the medical facility where she can spend a few days if she doesn't do as she's prescribed."

Gavin raised an eyebrow. "That good, hmmm? What happened?"

Dorian leaned back in his chair and crossed his arms. "I took some more blood samples today. I want to see about dosing them and how I can possibly unravel what's being done to her system. It left her feeling rather weak, so I brought her to your suite to rest and replenish. I can deduce that at that time, Amara decided to go check in on Hokura, most likely because she'd been avoiding the peacekeepers ever since she found out the news. A yelling match persisted, which ended up with Amara screaming and running down the hallway and Hokura on the floor because she was most likely having a head rush caused by lack of red blood cells."

Gavin lowered his head into his hands. "Dammit," he whispered. He took a moment and then looked back at Dorian. "I was really hoping things would simply just go back to normal after all this. Instead, it's just gotten worse." He shook his head. "I just have this sickening feeling like I can't trust her anymore after keeping this from me for four months. What else hasn't she told me?"

Dorian stood. "She's just being difficult. She had her reasons for not telling us about this. A word of advice, governor, don't allow that seed of doubt to take root because once it does, it's damn near impossible to destroy. I already told you my end of things. You have nothing more to worry about." He turned. "Now, if you'll excuse me, I have a pissed-off peacekeeper to see to." With that, he left the office and grimaced. He wondered where he might find Amara.

Dorian had checked the garage. Amara wasn't working, nor was her bike gone, which meant she was still somewhere inside the compound. He checked her suite to no avail and made his way down to the training facility. As he walked down the hall, he could hear her defined yelling and grunts as he came to the all too familiar room. He peered in as Amara swung back and made contact with the bag as she screamed in anger. He couldn't blame her. He had done the same thing just a few days prior and had been exhausting himself nightly in the RTC simulator.

"Damn you!" Amara screamed as he swung again, causing the bag to swing back even further.

Dorian wondered if anyone else had been using the boxing room when Amara arrived and if her tantrum had cleared it. Either way, he took a breath and walked in, assessing what he was going to say to her. "Your posture's incorrect. It'll off-balance you, so you won't be able to counter and hit as hard."

She glared at him as she fixed her position and threw her fist. "Did she send you down here instead of facing me herself?" She seethed, hitting the bag over and over again.

He put his hands in his pockets. "She can't face you right

now. She's under direct orders to be resting. She should have had her lunch and went straight to bed. Instead, she decided to relax on the couch and open the door."

"Always stepping in to save her," Amara sneered.

The professor took a breath. "Would you have it any other way? I am the only one who *can* save her. You know that just as well as she does, and that's why she waited to say anything."

Amara's temper flared. "She should have fucking told me!" She hit the bag again and turned to Dorian as she walked up to him. "She could have said something to *me!*"

"Why?" Dorian asked, narrowing his eyes. "You know Hokura. She didn't want to be seen as a burden. She didn't want to project her problems onto you or anyone else."

"She's never a burden!" Amara countered.

"I know that!" Dorian growled. He closed his eyes and took a breath, faltering as he pinched the bridge of his nose. "She went through so much. She put everyone before herself, myself included. I was just as upset as you are now when I found out. None of us knew. She hid it well until it was too late." His eyes met Amara's. "I'm going to do everything in my power to save her, Amara."

The peacekeeper took a step back. "I know you will," she huffed angrily. "All this time, though, ever since we went out to search for you three, I've had this horrible feeling that something was wrong. Even when we got back, it didn't fade. I should have suspected something was wrong."

"Did you ask her?"

"I did..." She tilted her head back in annoyance. "She always had an excuse..." Her eyes widened. "When she crashed her bike..."

"Yes. That was due to this," Dorian confirmed.

Tears started to form in Amara's eyes. "She said it was a miscalculation... she lied to me."

"She lied to me too." His voice was soft. "For what it's worth, she lied to all of us, but we can't fault her for it."

"And why not?"

"Because it does no good to do so... not for her... not for any of us." Dorian sighed as he sagged. "I was incredibly upset when I found out... more than upset, and I'm *still* angry about it. What good does it do taking it out on her? What good is it harboring feelings like that towards someone you love?"

Amara scrunched her face, fighting the tears from escaping. "You know her better than anyone. Why does she do this? Why does she alienate herself from us like this? She's one of us, and yet she's always been on the outside." With that, the tears escaped.

Dorian walked up to Amara and put his hand on her shoulder when she grabbed hold of him and hugged him. He stiffened as she cried into his shirt. He had never seen the second child in such a way and was taken aback by it. He allowed it as he gently put his hands on her back and comforted her as she sobbed. "Hokura's always been different in ways that even I can't explain. There's no science behind it. She feels things differently as if her emotions and thoughts are heightened and hardwired to her actions. I might know her better than anyone, but at the same time, I don't always understand her. I wish I did, but sometimes there are things that she says and feels that are beyond me, and no matter how hard she tries to explain them, I can't begin to process them in the same way."

Amara sniffled. "I guess it isn't just me then."

"No," Dorian breathed. "She's an anomaly." He rolled his eyes. "In absolutely everything she's ever done, she's never done it the easy way. She's always cut her own path and followed her heart."

Amara wiped her eyes as she stepped out of the professor's arms. She couldn't look him in the eye as she stared at the ground. "We're supposed to be immortal... how is this happening to her?"

"When she was kidnapped, it was because of what she was..." He watched as Amara's eyes widened in horror.

"It could have been any of us then... myself or Adam." She was shocked.

Dorian shook his head. "Tobias had his eyes on her from the start. He was able to create a slight bond with her and was able to manipulate her. That's how he kidnapped her. Either way, the doctor and head scientist in Michigan ran torture and pain tests on her to see how fast she regenerated. He tried to unravel her in order to figure out how her system worked. He injected something into her which is attacking her cells and weakening them." Dorian pursed his lips. "I haven't been able to conclude what he injected her with. Right now, we're just working on a way to stabilize her system and buy some time."

"Buy time? So, she's getting worse?" Amara trembled.

"Slowly, but if she stays on top of taking care of herself, we'll be able to move forward." He didn't want to admit that it was a touch-and-go situation. That there was a very bleak reality to things that he didn't even want to think about... that her time could simply be up at a moment's notice. The thought haunted him into the nights and nightmares ever since he had found out—another reason why he had been avoiding sleep.

"I should apologize," Amara said bleakly.

"That would be the right course of action."

She looked up at him. "What do you do when you're angry and upset with her? When you want to shake her and scream at her?"

A small smile came to his lips. "Exactly what you're doing now." He gently placed a hand on her shoulder. "I know it hurts and that you're upset, but she needs all the support she can get right now. You have full right to be angry. Put that anger into something physical; don't let it build up inside of you." ...Or it might explode in a way we're not ready to deal with... he hadn't said the words, but he had certainly thought them. He knew Amara's temper to be as explosive as his own and wondered how Adam had been able to diffuse his wife over the years whenever it came up. Maybe it was something he should forewarn him about.

"Thank you for coming after me and talking to me," Amara said. "I'll call her tonight."

Dorian nodded. "I'm glad I could help." With that, he left the gymnasium and made his way through the training facility. His mind was reeling once again about what he had said. If only there were a way to fully stabilize her, suspend things... if only he could stop time. That was an impossibility. There had to be something else. He needed to get back to the medical facility. Maybe Spindler and Lucien had discovered something. If not, he would mull over it until he had an answer. He was hoping the cells would work. That his hypothesis was correct and that she only had to endure a few more days before starting treatment.

Hokura pouted. Upon coming home, Gavin had allowed her to simply rest on the couch and doze. After napping for an hour, he was content to allow her to read but was constantly refilling her glass and beckoning her to drink and eat.

"If I eat any more, I'm going to be sick." She gave him a weary look. "My stomach can only take so much."

Worry etched over his face. "Are you feeling nauseous? Should I phone Dorian or Spindler?"

She took a breath, trying to ease her frustration. "I'm not nauseous. I'm *full*."

"That's good." Gavin smiled. "You need to fuel your system."

She rolled her eyes. She had heard it all before. Over the last four months, it had been drilled into her brain to the point every time someone told her that she wanted to snap at them. "I know..."

Desperation washed over him as his tone hardened. "Do you? Do you *know* Hokura? Because Dorian told me you ended up collapsing in the hallway because you *didn't*."

She closed her eyes as she swallowed hard, trying to keep her tears at bay. She didn't want this. The last thing she wanted was to fight with him... She knew Dorian was already upset with her. Having Amara yell at her was bad enough. "Please, Gavin..."

"Do not realize the situation we're in?" Gavin pleaded. "It seems like you have a team working on trying to keep you with us, and you're not taking this seriously!"

"I am taking this seriously!" she cried. "What do you want me to do, Gavin? I've eaten my fill. I'm resting! I am relaxing! If I were any more relaxed, I'd be dead!" She stopped as her eyes widened. "I..." She stuttered as she took in her husband, his heart breaking in front of her. "I'm sorry... I..." she needed to escape... needed to get out of this situation before she made things worse, but she couldn't go anywhere. "I think I need to lie down for a bit," she muttered as she rose from the couch.

Gavin gave a pained expression. "Do you want me to join you?"

"No." Her voice was light. "You have work to do. I'll be fine. I just need a little pick me up. Apparently, I'm cranky." She gave him a small smile and went to the bedroom.

Once she closed the door, she fell onto her bed and sobbed

into her pillow. She was trying, yet it felt like everything she was doing was wrong and that she was hurting everyone around her. "I'm sorry," she sobbed quietly. "I'm messing up again... I'm always messing up, and now I've screwed up big time, and I'm bringing everyone down because of it."

The door cracked open as Gavin walked in. He had heard her. "Hokura..." His voice was gentle as he took her into his arms. "My love, please, don't feel like you need to get away from me to cry like this. What is it?"

"I didn't mean for all this to happen," she sobbed. "I thought I was going to be okay, that I was still healing... and that even if it was something that it would be easy to fix. I didn't mean to upset everyone. Now Dorian's working himself to the bone, Amara's angry with me, even you're here taking care of me when you have a full city to take care of. I've alienated myself again from my friends, and it seems like nobody understands."

He didn't understand. He wanted to. "I know you didn't mean for this. What's done is done, and now we just need to focus on getting you better again." He kissed her temple.

"I'm sorry..." she whimpered.

Gavin gave her a gentle squeeze as he brushed his hands through her hair. "You don't have to keep being sorry. It's forgiven..." He stopped. "There's nothing *to* forgive. You had your reasons, you did what you thought was right, and you were looking out for the person you knew could save you."

She nodded as her tears slowed. She hated this in every way. She wanted to be strong, yet it felt like she was unable to muster any strength inside her. She was simply a mess, and everyone she loved was suffering because of her negligence.

"You don't have to hide in the bedroom. I'm sorry I got upset," Gavin soothed as he wiped away her tears. "I love you... come rest on the couch. I'll rub your feet as I read over my documents. Please?" The last thing he wanted was for her to be in here when she could be by his side. After a few moments, she nodded and agreed as he kissed her forehead in relief.

It had been a little later in the afternoon when there was a knock at the door. Gavin answered it as Hokura slunk on the couch. She was afraid it was Amara. She didn't want to face her friend yet but knew it was going to happen. That's when she heard Dorian's voice.

"How's she doing?"

"Slightly drained and emotional," Gavin's voice was low. "She's been eating."

Hokura turned on the couch and caught Dorian's eye as she slowly got up. Gavin moved as the professor entered their suite.

The professor's eyes fixed on her. "Don't get up on account of me. Sit and relax," he said. "I just came to check in with you and to let you know that I spoke to Amara...."

She automatically lowered herself to the couch as she grimaced slightly. "How did she take it?"

Dorian put his hands in his pocket as he rocked back slightly. "The way you would expect her to. She went and got out some frustration on the boxing bags before I confronted her. There was some yelling...."

"Of course there was," Hokura groaned. "Thank you for going after her."

"She understands," Dorian replied. "She's going through some emotions that I've never seen from the second child before."

Hokura's eyebrows rose as Gavin sat beside her.

"There were some tears and a very awkward hug." Dorian made a face. "She's going to call you this evening."

Hokura nodded without a word.

The professor regarded her. "A word of advice: the other two are just as much your family as your husband and children.

Don't alienate them because of your diagnosis. They want to be there for you as much as the rest of us do."

Gavin's hands found her shoulders and gently squeezed them. "He's right." His voice was soft in her ear.

Why did she suddenly feel like she was being ganged up on? She slouched as she couldn't meet Dorian's eyes. "I..." She didn't know what to say.

Dorian noted her demeanor. "I'm sure it's been a long day for everyone, but what happened with Amara turned out for the better. Don't take it to heart. She was simply worried about you." He turned.

Gavin stared at the man. He seemed slightly off. Tired even. "Thank you for checking in."

The professor nodded. "Now, if you'll excuse me, I still have work to do." With that, he made his way back down to his labs... indeed, there was still so much to see to.

———※———

It was getting later in the evening as Dorian hunched over the lab table. Lucien and Spindler hadn't been able to figure anything out. They were both working on small concoctions that might stabilize her. He felt like the life had been drained out of him as if his heart wasn't even beating, and if it were, it was doing so by force because he needed to figure this out. His hypothesis had been wrong. He locked his jaw and clenched his fists as furious tears came to his eyes. He had introduced the strong cells to her new samples and watched in dismay as the new cells died before they even had a chance. It was as if they simply disintegrated. How was it possible that super soldier genes were being destroyed at such a rapid rate? He had gone through the trial three times to make sure what he was seeing was correct.

"Dammit!" His voice caught. His mind spun in so many different directions as the world around him started to crumble. He had failed her before he even had a chance to try. No... he wouldn't give up. His hand shook as he took the petri dish of her newest sample, as he shakily added one last thing. The initial dose of upped cells that the peacekeepers had been given had been generic genetic cells. They had been blanks until introduced to their systems. They were seen as weaker because since then, Hokura's system had been introduced to the upped super soldier genes. Maybe that was it... he added a small sample and watched in anticipation. His throat closed as his eyes widened. "No!" he cried as his heart raced. The upped blank cells were absorbed into nothingness. "This doesn't make sense!" He got up and stalked over to the back. "So bloody be it then!" he seethed, grabbing a syringe, and plunging it into his arm as he took a sample from himself. He would make himself a test subject again if that's what it took. Maybe he was overlooking the blank cells. Maybe after so long, they had deteriorated. There had to be something. He collected two vials and went back to his table as he grabbed more dishes.

"Give me something, damn you! Anything!" He slowly added his blood sample to the dish and injected the blank cells as he watched intently. They did what they were supposed to. They were blanks. They had no weak cells to attach themselves to, so they simply floated and slowly merged with healthy cells. Exactly as they should. So why were they ineffective with Hokura's samples? The horrifying realization hit him. It was her blood... he shakily took one of her new samples and added it to his. A whitewash of cold sweat fell over his body as he trembled in absolute terror. Her cells attacked his. They destroyed everything that was healthy. The professor felt physically sick as he stumbled back. What had that madman Richter concocted and injected into her? This was a chemical weapon, and it was destroying her system, would destroy *anyone's* system. His breathing quickened as his chest tightened. He had never encountered something like this before.

Dorian hung his head as a feeling of hopelessness swept over him. Suddenly, he needed to be away from the labs. He was in the hallway... his footsteps were quickening. He needed to be out of the compound... away from everything... away from what he had just discovered. He went down the hallway, turning another corner, through another, and out the garage. Dorian walked without thinking as his motions became automatic. It wasn't until he was a block away from the compound that he realized the sky was darkening. He hadn't even figured the time, hadn't cared to check as he continued. There was nobody out and about in the city as his feet kept pace with his random wandering. After a while, he found himself at the memorial park, the first park he and Hokura had visited when she returned to the city. The park which held the raised plaque in the garden which he was now standing over. He looked at the raised letters, at how over time, she had brushed her fingers over them so often that the finish looked golden instead of bronze. Why did he come here? He was running. So why here? It was odd as his eyes narrowed. His fingers crossed over the raised name, not to memorialize the rebel commander she had loved. James. But to memorialize her actions of continuously running her fingers over the words. To do what *she* had done.

His breathing was unsteady as something inside of him broke. "You can't have her. Not yet. I will save her." Was he really threatening a dead man? No, he was making a promise to him, a promise to protect her just as Gavin had promised, to love her. Dorian scowled in frustration and rage. He had been the first to love her, to protect her. Before all the others, it was *him,* and he would be damned if he couldn't crack this and keep her alive. That's when he felt it, a cold splash on his neck, followed by another, and another as the sky above him seemed to share his sentiments, and it began to rain. "Hokura." His eyes watered as the rain blended with the tears that now ran down his face. "I will not rest until I know you will be okay." He would destroy himself if that's what it took. He would use his own body to test results if hers was too weak to do so. He would lay his life down on the line if that's what it took. He bit his lip in sorrow as he sobbed. If only it were that easy, he would sacrifice himself for her, but it wasn't. He needed to stay strong her for, to figure this out, she would go on, she was timeless, ageless, the world would crumble around them, and she would still be standing. He rolled his head back and enjoyed the downpour as his arms slowly came out from his sides. The notion had been odd as he thought about their confrontation on the roof, about how she smirked at him. So, this was what she meant about having the rain wash away one's worries. A feeling came over him as he stood in the silence, his black suit soaked as a calm reassurance washed over him. "I will save you," he whispered to the night. "I swear on everything that I am. I will save you." The raindrops felt cool against his lips as determination set over him. He brought his head forward with new resolve. He was the father of science. It would take more than a foolish madman of a scientist from Michigan to take away what was most precious to him. He turned and looked at the plaque. It wasn't her time yet. It would *never* be her time. James had forty years with her. Dorian would have the *rest* of time with her. A small smile came to his lips with new vigor. He wasn't beaten yet.

The professor stalked himself back to the compound as the rain continued to fall. His mind was working towards new possibilities. Her genetics were attacking everything. Her cells had become a predator while destroying everything inside her.

What would mankind do when faced with a predator? What had evolution taught him? It was about creating a bigger predator that would destroy or cleanse what Richter had injected her with. Cleanse... the idea stuck with him as he continued his walk... not paying attention to how hard it was raining or how the water was starting to pool in the streets. It wasn't until the sky lit up that he even noted that the storm had gotten worse.

Dinner had been relatively calm and quiet. Everyone had set into their evening routines when Cassandra and Cyrus both asked if they could go out for a while. Gavin was tidying up in the kitchen when he stared out the window and raised an eyebrow. "It's getting late, and it's raining out."

"Exactly!" Cyrus chimed. "When do we ever get a chance to be in the rain?"

Hokura licked her lips as she sat on the couch. The weather was matching her solemn mood lately. "Just stay off the roof. Make sure when you come in that you dry off." With that, both teens were excitedly out the door. She gave a small sigh.

"I don't imagine they're going to get up to too much." Gavin smiled lightly. "But they're right. It's not like this is something they get to experience often." He came up behind Hokura and kissed her temple. "You've been quiet tonight."

"I wonder if I should go see Amara." She winced as she didn't want to overly leave the suite. The idea of facing off with Amara was tiring just to think about. "I need to explain things to her."

"Dorian went after her. I'm sure he did a thorough job of

explaining the situation to her." He sat down beside her and slowly shifted as he opened his arms for her.

Hokura grimaced as she relaxed in them. "Amara and Dorian...a great team for flaring tempers. I'm surprised Amara hasn't been at the door yet."

Gavin chuckled as he gently brushed his fingers over her arm. "She and Adam were going to find out eventually." He pursed his lips. "It's not like you can exactly hide what's happening to you."

She stiffened. "Is it that noticeable?"

He took a moment as he breathed in deeply and closed his eyes. "The compound and those living in it and inside the city are all perfected beings." He traced down her arm to the crook of her elbow and stopped. "The last time I saw a bruise on anyone, it was on Dorian after you came back and grabbed his wrist."

Hokura couldn't help but suddenly feel self-conscious about her appearance. "It's gotten bad... hasn't it?" Her voice was small.

Gavin sighed. He remembered those of White Rock and how they looked... human... and yet she still had an air about her, as if no matter how far she deteriorated, it would never falter. She had always stood out among the rest. "It's just noticeable, I guess." He didn't want to delve too far into this conversation. She lay in silence as he traced over her arm and shoulder, avoiding where she had gotten her samples taken. He was thankful when the phone rang a few moments later. "I'll get it." He rose as he walked over and grabbed it. "Hello?... yes... she's here..."

He handed the phone over to Hokura, giving her a hopeful look. "It's Amara."

She trembled slightly as she took the phone... bracing

herself for her friend to start ripping into her when Amara started on the other line.

"I'm sorry," Amara blurted. "I shouldn't have lost it on you like that. I..."

"It's okay," Hokura soothed. "You were upset, I should have been honest with you, but I had my reasons."

"That's what Dorian said." There was a pause. "You're never a burden, Hokura. You know you can tell me anything... like this... and... I know I say that..." Amara was getting flustered with herself. "Dammit, I'm not good with this kind of thing!"

Hokura chuckled faintly. "I know. It's fine. All's forgiven. Are you okay?" Why was she asking Amara if she was okay? She wasn't the one who was having the medical issues. And yet the way she had acted...

"Yeah. I'm okay." Amara licked her lips. "I guess you're going to be spending a lot of time in the labs and whatnot..."

"Not if I can help it." Hokura adjusted herself on the couch as she looked behind her. Gavin had wandered to the kitchen and was busying himself. Most likely making her a small plate of food to snack on.

"If you need anything, please let me know," her friend spoke in an earnest tone.

"How about you..." Hokura licked her lips. This was more for Amara than anyone. She didn't want to entertain her friend. She wasn't feeling overly social but knew that she needed this. Between Dorian and Gavin, she had enough people looking after her. "Come over tomorrow for lunch."

"I can bring lunch!" Amara chimed. "I can pick our favorites from the cafeteria, and we can do something!"

"Sounds nice. I'd like that," Hokura said. "We can talk more tomorrow, okay?" After hearing her friend's agreement, she hung up the phone and groaned.

Gavin came with a plate of different fruits dipped in chocolate. "By the sounds of it, I take you're not happy with the arrangement you just made. I figured these would help your mood."

Hokura sighed. She knew Gavin was only trying to help as he sat beside her again, and she shifted so he could wrap an arm around her. "It's not that I don't want to see Amara. It's that I just don't want to deal with her being overbearing." She made a pained expression. "This is exactly why I didn't tell anyone. I didn't want the anger, the sadness, the whirlwind of emotions thrown my way when I can barely handle my own!"

"It's okay," he soothed but stopped... "no... it's not okay. I'm sorry." He chewed his bottom lip, trying to articulate the words as he took her in. She didn't want any of this, and yet upon telling Dorian, the professor had alerted him right away. They had suddenly borne down on her. "I guess, in a way, I can see it from your side."

She shifted and glanced up at him. "Don't let me win that easily." Her tone was dull.

"No," Gavin stated. "I know you don't like being fussed over, that you're independent and try to do things on your own. That you're not one for over-the-top attention, so I guess I can understand why you didn't want to say anything. Still though... I am your husband..."

"I know." She winced. "And it wasn't a slight to keep it from you... it's just that..."

"You thought Dorian would keep your secret." He sighed. He couldn't help but wonder how many secrets the professor kept for her. He mentally kicked himself. Dorian had stated already that nothing had happened, but he couldn't help but wonder... the professor had been loyal to only her; surely even before the war, there had been secrets. He shook his head. This wasn't the time to question him. He was sure the man was working around the clock trying to figure this out.

Hokura nodded. "Yeah." Her voice had an edge to it. "To be honest, I was hoping he *would* keep this a secret, but the professor hadn't seen it my way." Was she really angry? No... it had felt like a minor betrayal, but she couldn't fault Dorian for it. Suddenly, a flash of light lit up the suite even brighter as a dull roll of thunder was heard afterward. She stood and walked over to the bay window in the kitchen. "Another storm..." Her voice was light as she placed her hand on the glass.

Gavin followed in her wake as he stood behind her. "Hopefully, the kids are enjoying it. I'm sure if it gets too close, they'll come in."

"We told them to stay off the roof. They should be fine." She traced her finger over the glass, watching the rain hit it.

"And what about you?" His arms wrapped around her. He just wanted to feel close to her. Why did it seem like she was drifting from him even though she was physically in front of him?

"Dorian will save me." Her words were hollow as she watched the storm roll through the wastelands and towards the city.

Amara huffed as she paced frustratedly. Adam eyed her from the couch, raising an eyebrow. "Is this now about Hokura or the fact that Nathan is out enjoying the storm?"

"A little of column A, a little of column B," Amara muttered as she stopped and looked outside the window as another flash of lightning lit up the night sky. She was also annoyed with her husband, who had taken the news almost too casually when she told him about their friend. She glared at him and continued her pacing.

"What do you want me to do for you?" Adam asked in a serene tone, knowing that his wife's temper was just coming to a boil.

She snarled, grabbing at her hair, and tugging at it. "I don't *know*, Adam!" She shot him a look. "There's nothing you can do! Nothing *any* of us can do! Only the professor can do anything about this!" she yelled as her expression changed. "Her life is in his hands."

Adam rose from the couch, his face remaining calm as he placed his hands on her shoulders. "You've already seen how far he would go for her. You've witnessed it firsthand, and you know how deep this goes."

Amara looked at him with a pleading face. "Why aren't you as worried as I am?"

"Because what is the world for the professor if Hokura isn't in it?" Adam stated. "After thinking she was gone for forty years and getting her back, do you think anything will stand in his way when it comes to keeping her alive?" He shook his head as his lips curved slightly. "Or is it that you're still letting the past interfere with your rationale?"

She crossed her arms and turned from him, not saying another word. He was right, the professor would do everything in his power to keep Hokura alive. He would exhaust and destroy himself in the process. So why hadn't this uneasy feeling left her? Maybe it was because of the past, the idea of her system failing was an idea that haunted her upon awakening. No, she knew better than that. "I'm scared for her. For what she'll have to continue to endure... the what ifs..." Amara answered her temper cooling.

Adam sighed lightly. "I'm sure you'll get some more answers tomorrow at lunch," he offered.

Amara turned to him. "Do you want to join us?"

He shook his head. "I think this is something that you need to do on your own." He gave her a gentle smile. "Face her and get out what you need to say. We can all get together at a later date." Adam nudged her slightly. "Why don't you go have a bath and relax a bit? I can hold down the fort with Erica and Ryan. I'm sure Nathan won't be out too late. Besides, he's with Cass and Cyrus."

Amara chewed her bottom lip. "I wonder if she's told the kids..."

His eyes widened. "Something you had better ask her and not bring up around them."

"You're right," she sighed as she kissed his cheek. "Thank you."

"For what?" Adam chuckled.

"Defusing the bomb." Amara winked at him as she walked towards the bathroom. Maybe a good soak was just what she needed in order to take her mind off things.

Cassandra's eyes held the sky as she smiled. "Another one! It must be getting close!" she cried in delight as she, Cyrus, and Nathan sat in the small alcove taking shelter from the rain.

Cyrus smiled. "If you count the number of seconds between the flash of lightning and the sound of thunder and divide by five, you'll get the distance in miles of how close it is."

Nathan scowled at Cyrus. "You just have to take the fun out of everything by adding math to it." He playfully shoved his friend.

The boy let out a chuckle. "The scientists were talking

about it the other day when we mentioned the storms we've been getting lately."

"I was paying attention." Nathan rolled his eyes.

Cassandra shushed them. "I want to count." She waited in anticipation for the sky to light up. Every time it happened, she could feel the energy in the air as if it made her heartbeat extra fast. She silently counted until the loud boom echoed through the skies. "Eight seconds," she whispered.

Cyrus gave her a look. "A little over a mile and a half away."

The girl smiled. "This rain has been unreal lately! Has it been causing more issues for the botanists?" she asked. Cyrus had brought it up before at dinner. She had been genuinely curious.

"For the botanists, among others," Cyrus answered. "It's causing some erosion around the city like in the roads and side-walks. Just things like potholes and whatnot. They're actually now using rain barrels to collect it."

Nathan's brows furrowed. "Odd that we weren't doing that before."

Cyrus stretched out his hand, allowing the rain to hit it. "Because before now, we've never gotten this much. It wasn't worth the effort." He shrugged.

Another flash with a loud boom hit. The three could almost feel the vibrations in their bones as the storm raged. Nathan smirked. "With that, I should probably head in. It was already late when you guys grabbed me. If I stay out too long, my mom will ream me out. She's already been in a mood today. I don't need any more dirty looks from her."

Cassandra nodded.

Cyrus gave his friend a look. "We can grab you tomorrow for lessons. I think the labs are going to be taking samples from the barrels tomorrow to check the ph balance and the purity of what we've been collecting."

"I look forward to it!" Nathan beamed as he left the alcove and ran towards the compound.

Cassandra humphed as she crossed her arms. "Are we going to talk about it now?" Her voice held a dissatisfied tone to it.

"Do we have to?" Cyrus asked, looking down at his shoe as he scuffed it against the ground.

"You noticed them too, and you didn't say anything," she accused.

"They're kind of hard *not* to notice Cass, what are we supposed to say? It looks like she had her blood drawn," her brother quipped.

Cassandra's eyes narrowed. "Mom's had samples taken tons of times before. Ever since she came back from Michigan, she bruises like crazy! That shouldn't be happening anymore if she's healing. People in the compound don't bruise Cyrus! Peacekeepers especially!"

The boy licked his lips. "That's most likely why she and Dad have been so off lately. Maybe things are taking longer than they anticipated." He looked at his sister. "I don't know what to tell you."

She made a face as she looked up at the sky. The storm seemed to be slowing. "If there's anything wrong, you think she'd tell us, right?"

He took her in. "Of course she would." He didn't know what else to say. "If you're worried, then why don't you ask her? You two have gotten closer lately."

She brought her hand up to her mouth and nervously chewed on her thumbnail. "I don't know if she'd tell me... but if anyone would... maybe the professor..." She had thought about it. She hadn't seen him around too much lately. She had visited him after the surgery to attach the clone had been deemed successful. She had been relieved about that and had checked on him twice after that, but the past week he had simply vanished.

"Come on... we should get in. It's getting late." Cyrus interrupted her thoughts. "Stop worrying. You're going back to old habits again." He raised an eyebrow as she brought her hand down.

Maybe her brother was right. Still, she was going to make sure she paid extra attention to their mother over the next few days. She couldn't help but worry that something was up.

"Get ready to run so we don't get soaked," Cyrus chimed, readying himself. "Think you can beat me?"

Cassandra smiled. "I *know* I can beat you."

It was another night of exhausting himself as Dorian stepped out of the RTC simulator. Sweat drenched his black sleeveless shirt as it clung to his toned body. He had spent another few hours in his lab, and when it came to having to simply wait for results, he decided to pummel imaginary Tobias' and Richter's into bloody deaths. It would never be enough. No matter how many simulations he killed, it wasn't the same. There hadn't been real flesh beneath his hands. There had been no screams of agony nor looks of fear in their eyes. He couldn't understand why the idea of losing his revenge nagged at him the way it did, why his rage didn't seem to cool when it came to what happened. Even now, he was tempted to go back to Michigan and lay waste the compound there, but even then, the people there were innocent. What good would it do to kill everyone? Of killing Silas when the man had directed him to the doctor's lab and hadn't blown their cover? He wondered if there was a cure for whatever had been injected into her somewhere in the confines of the science labs. His mind reeled as he made his way up to his suite. The Michigan compound was nothing in comparison to Meridiana. It was merely the luck of the draw that the madman had created and injected her with something that had eluded him. That wouldn't be the case for long. He would crack this.

Upon entering his suite, he walked over to the kitchen, grabbed himself some water, and took a long drink as he avoided looking over the cityscape. He found it only drove the knife deeper every time he looked at it lately. That he didn't deserve to see it or to even try to understand the way Hokura felt about it until he saved her. He let out a sigh as he stretched his left arm and made a fist. He stared at the hand and couldn't help but feel a pang of guilt. "It wasn't worth it. I would give this clone to keep her safe and well. Even if I knew I could never get it back..." There had still been so many unanswered questions about what he had put her through, and yet she never faltered. He had gone off the deep end, blacked out, destroyed his labs, and still, she was by his side, aiding him through the process because he had been so reckless and had allowed himself to slip so far. "If I would have kept a level head about things, we wouldn't be in this mess," he growled at himself.

No matter... he couldn't go back. As much as he wished he could. As much as he wished he could re-write their past well before Tobias, before the war, before she fled... he would have done everything differently. He sadly mused for a moment as he thought of her when she first awakened, of the vibrant life she had been. Full of questions, smiles, young and free before he had soiled her with his manipulations. Who would she have been if it hadn't been for all the trauma she had gone through? So much of it had been caused by his hand.

The professor shook his head. He needed to shower and then sleep. His daily routine had become just that. Resting until rejuvenated enough to get out of bed just to exhaust himself to the point of falling into bed with the hopes of not having nightmares. He stepped in the shower and let the water hit him as he thought about sleep. It had been the first time in a long time that he had suffered from such vivid and horrific dreams on a daily basis. Usually, they didn't affect him, but lately, they were getting more. He could understand why she had fought so much with sleep in the past when she was having them continuously. Long ago, she used to dream of him, that after she fled, he was out to get her, to capture her and bring her back—nearly forty years of having them until she returned. The notion was exhausting just to think of as he got out of the shower, dried himself off, and walked over to his bed. "I don't want nightmares. I just want you," he groaned as he lowered himself onto his mattress. The way it embraced him as he laid himself down felt so comforting he didn't think he could move. "Goodnight first-child... sleep well..."

━━━━━━━⋆⋆⋆━━━━━━━

Dorian groaned as he turned his head to the side and looked around. He was in the RTC viewing room, sitting in the chair. He didn't recall how he had gotten there. His body felt heavy and sluggish. Was it possible that he was sleepwalking? The door opened as he glanced up to see Hokura entering the room. A smirk came across his lips. "Seeking me out?" He reached towards her in horror as he stared down at the bionic arm. He couldn't understand as she stood above him, a syringe in her hand as she brought it forward. His reflexes were too fast as he grabbed her wrist. His bionic hand coming up and crushing the syringe under its strength as he took in her shock. A malicious grin came across his face as he rose, and she backed away from him.

"Why are you doing this to yourself, Dorian?" she asked.

He didn't understand where this lust was coming from, why he was suddenly stalking her. He wouldn't do this to her. His mind raced as words tumbled from him. She was nearly sitting on the control panel. She needed space from him. Why was he still moving towards her when his mouth met her ear? "How about we try a new experiment then?" He came between her legs and leaned towards her. "How about we see how much of a spark I start inside you again." With that, he grabbed her thighs and brought her closer to him. The lines blurring. This wasn't right.

She tensed as her breathing hitched and her eyes widened.

"No, no, no, don't get the wrong ideas, my love." The words were automatic. Where had they come from? Why did they sound so familiar? "Even like this, I would never fully cross that line unless you offered. I just want to see how fast I can get that heart of yours racing again with some fond memories."

"Why?" Her voice quivered in such a way it made his heart bleed. "Why torture the both of us?"

No... he didn't know what he was saying or doing to her. "Because, as I said, it's an experiment. Let us suffer through it together." His voice was husky. This was wrong. He could feel the heat between them. He couldn't do this to her as he felt her body pulsing against his. He was talking. His lips were moving. His hands were caressing her thighs. This was too intimate, too much for both of them. He wasn't in control of his actions. This wasn't a fantasy... this wasn't how he did things in his dreams... not how she responded. He was luring her, confusing her. "You're enjoying this." The words came out as she whimpered and trembled under his bionic hand. "What else did I tell you to do when I was like this?"

He jolted from his sleep as his eyes widened. His heart was pounding as he breathed deeply. "That was no dream..." His voice was husky as fear swept over him. He had no recollection of what he had just seen, and yet he couldn't deny how real it felt, how it stirred him in a familiar way. "Was it real? Had it been a flashback?" He wanted to ask her. Had he come so close to her in such ways and crossed those lines without being aware of it? There had been so many holes in his memory when he had the arm attached to him. One of those memories was between swallowing a bottle of pills, scrolling a goodbye note to her, and waking up in the operating room with her hovering over top of him. The sad smile she had given him. "You won't remember anyway. Think of it as a gift for everything you've sacrificed."

The professor moved from his bed. He needed to move for a few moments. If he asked, would she even tell him? A growl escaped him. She would mar herself to protect him, to give him the illusion that everything was alright when it really wasn't. He sighed as he walked over to the painting she had done for him all those years ago and stared at it, at the blues and reds, the memory of the man he once was. The type of demon that still lived deep down within him. If what he had seen had been a flashback, why didn't she fight him? Why didn't she push him away? The syringe... she was supposed to subdue him, but that hadn't happened. What else had he told her to do when he was like that? His thoughts turned. She was supposed to run... and yet she hadn't. He made his way to his couch and sank into it. This was the last thing he needed on his mind as he groaned, stretching his neck. "Hokura... why is it that I always seem to be the bad guy no matter what I do..." she loved him, and yet, he would never be good enough for her. All he could do now is make sure none of their sacrifices had been in vain. He had to save her.

It had been a restless night for Hokura. Her body fought the sleep aids as she tried to allow herself to simply relax. She fought the need to move and get the drugs out of her system. She could feel them tugging at her, trying to bring her down into the dark abyss of sleep as she closed her eyes tightly and tried to steady her breathing. It wasn't until one hundred hours that her need for rest finally won over as she rolled over and dreamt.

She could feel the blinding light in her face as she squeezed her eyes tightly. This was all too familiar. She knew she was back in Michigan, in the hands of Tobias and the madman doctor, as she took a breath. She needed to remember to breathe as she moved her head to the side and slowly opened her eyes. It hadn't been Richter with his back to her but Dorian.

"Dorian..." she tried to cry out, but she was so weak.

He turned to her, a solemn look on his face. "I was hoping I could bring you back here and find a way to cure you."

"You can. I know you can!" she pleaded.

He slowly shook his head. "I can't. I've tried everything." His brows furrowed and rose in desperation. "There's nothing I can do."

As he brought his hand up to caress her cheek, her eyes widened to see the bionic counterpart.

"No!" she cried as she struggled to get up. "Dorian, this isn't right!"

"I'm so sorry, I failed... but at least we can be together in death..." he said.

The scene changed in a disorienting way as she shook her head. A chill ran through her as she opened her eyes and looked over the city. A hand grasped hers as she looked up at him, her heart racing.

Dorian gave her a sad smile. "I can't save either of us, Hokura..."

"But... I can save you..." she cried desperately. "Take the arm off Dorian, be rid of it! Please, then you can move forward. I know the clone will be successful! Please, do it for me."

He sighed as he kissed the top of her head. "The choice is yours." With that, he squeezed her hand and let go as she grappled forward, trying to reach for him as his body went over the edge of the roof. She followed in his wake.

***

Hokura shot up as she woke up in a start, her heart in her throat as Gavin rolled over and looked at her.

"Another nightmare?" he asked as he sat up and held her.

She was shaking. It was more than just a nightmare. It could have been the reality. She would have jumped, too if he had decided to end his life. "A bad dream..." she whispered.

His arms were around her holding her, trying to soothe her as she trembled. "It's okay. You're safe. I've got you."

She could never let anyone know what truly happened that day, what would have happened, that she would have indeed followed Dorian to his death and would have died beside him if she wouldn't have been able to reach him. "I'm okay Gavin, I'm sorry for waking you up. I'm okay now..." Just another secret.

Dorian had finally made his way back to his bed half an hour later. He felt like he had barely closed his eyes as the sun made its way up and dawn came upon the city. The professor couldn't let today be wasted. He needed to be down to the labs and have Spindler and Lucien report and findings. Maybe they had something because upon what he had found the day before; it hadn't been good. Coffee in hand, he went down to his office and started with the samples once more. How was it that her blood had become so lethal? What on earth had altered it in such a way? He sat at his desk as he took out her sample. He needed to go with what he knew. She was deteriorating. Her blood was killing off new cells that were introduced to it. Her blood would kill off anyone's blood cells. He shook his head with a grunt as he picked up his phone and dialed Spindler. "I need you and Lucien to meet me at nine hundred hours so we can go over whatever we've found. Unfortunately, I've come across something rather concerning."

It had been an hour and a half later that the three converged in the science boardroom as Dorian paced in front of them. "So, neither of you have found anything that you can describe? Anything of help?"

Dr. Lucien shifted. "This is something we've never seen before, sir. What have you been able to uncover?"

The professor kneaded his forehead as he stopped and looked up at both men. "I am almost at a loss to describe it, but whatever is introduced to her plasma is overtaken and dies. It's as if it simply attacks and kills everything..." His throat tightened. "Which is exactly what it's doing to her." He looked up at the two doctors in desperation, hoping they would say something. After a moment, he gave a frustrated sigh. "Well? Anything?"

Spindler lowered his head. "We looked into blood poisoning... that isn't this. It's almost as if whatever was injected into her altered her system and reversed what her cells were supposed to do." He cleared his throat. "The peacekeepers have continuous regenerating cells. This is the exact opposite. There's no regeneration... just death."

Dr. Lucien perked up. "With that said, however, upon looking deeper, it hasn't taken over fully yet. There are still healthy cells in her body. That's most likely why there's been a steady decline. Her system may have fought it for some time but was so weak upon what happened to her it couldn't. Whatever this was grew and took over gradually and became stronger."

Dorian sat in his chair. "We need to figure out a way to slow this. Sitting around putting a name to it isn't going to get us anywhere."

Spindler's brows furrowed. "Cellular aging and deterioration..." He stared at Dorian. "Her food and water consumption, rest, and sleep are another part of this."

The professor winced. "All things she's been struggling with since she was kidnapped."

Dr. Lucien licked his lips. "A diet packed full of nutrition and antioxidants." He knew the other two were staring at him. "I know our food here is already fully packed, but what about an overload? At this time, we can see about overloading her system with a health regimen and possibly doing blood transfusions." A smirk came to his lips. "Professor, you created the genetics of the peacekeepers. Can you not clone her original cells just as you did the arm?"

Dorian's eyes widened. "I genetically modified their cells through injections... but possibly..."

Spindler let out a low growl. "She wouldn't survive a full blood transfusion in the state she's in."

The professor looked at the man and slumped slightly. "No, but smaller ones might buy enough time to get her to that point. It's a shot in the dark."

"It's something," Lucien offered. "We have the technology. We might as well start right away, and then we can continue on other hypotheses as we work."

The two nodded. It was worth looking into as they all nodded. Dorian took a breath. "Let's assemble then and get this going. Anything else that you two can add to the table would be appreciated." He faltered slightly as he got up. "I'm afraid we're only beginning, and I'm already running out of ideas."

———————⋯✦⋯———————

It was half-past nine hundred hours. Adam had walked the kids to their lessons with Amara, he had wished her a good day, and that lunch would be successful. He found himself slowing his pace as he made his way to Gavin's office. The man had been off the last few days, and now he knew why. He couldn't help but feel slightly betrayed by this secret but had kept it to himself. He knocked and went into the governor's office, where he sat across from Gavin expectantly as he folded his arms and took the man in.

Gavin looked up at him tiredly. "Good morning, Adam."

The third child raised his eyebrow at the governor. "Opting for casual conversation now that the cat's out of the bag?"

Gavin gave a deep breath as he turned all his attention to the man sitting in front of him. Over the years, he and Adam had become good friends and great working partners. "For what it's worth, she wanted to keep this a secret, *had* kept this a secret for some time now."

Adam shook his head. "What about you? How are you doing with all of this? You've seemed slightly off the past few days."

What was there to say? Gavin didn't know as he gave a pained expression. "The idea of losing her is haunting me, so I'm simply trying not to overthink any of it. I have to have faith that Dorian will come up with a solution." He shook his head. "She doesn't want me brooding around her, so I've been coming in and what seems like simply handing everything off to you as I stare at the clock, trying to actively think about anything else."

It wasn't fair, in many ways, but Hokura had always been this way. No... not always. There had been some time when she had been open about everything, a time before the professor started in on her that she had been innocent. She had shared everything, had a constant need to be around others instead of pushing them away and carrying burdens on her own. That had been so long ago... "this is simply who she is. She doesn't want us worrying about her. She's stubborn that way," Adam remarked.

Gavin gave him a placid look. "The only thing I can do is simply listen to her right now and give her what she wants."

Adam narrowed his eyes. "But what do *you* want?"

A small chuckle escaped the governor's throat. "It seems that's irrelevant at the moment." He gave a solemn look. "All I want is for her to be okay. That'll be enough for me." With that, he grabbed a few documents. "I'm sure you'll get the full update from Amara this evening, but for now, I do have a few things I want to push through, so, if need be, I can spend some more time with her."

Adam merely nodded. If this was what Gavin needed to get his mind off things, he would happily oblige.

It had been later in the morning. Hokura sat on the couch, contemplating. She had wanted to paint some more but Amara was due at any time, so she had decided to simply sit and wait as her mind ran a million miles a second. She hoped Amara would be calm about things. She rolled her eyes at the notion. That wasn't going to happen. There was a sharp knock at the door as Hokura opened it and took in her friend. Amara's hands full with two large trays of food.

Right away, Hokura tried to grab a tray. "Let me help you with that before you spill it all over my floor."

"No... you don't have to do that!" Amara argued as Hokura took a tray.

"I still have two arms, and I'm perfectly capable of carrying some food," Hokura growled as she walked hers to the table in front of the bay window. She stared down at her lunch and raised an eyebrow. "Geez, Amara, did you clean out the cafeteria? There's no way I can eat all this!"

Her friend placed her tray down across from her and slumped on her chair. "I didn't know what you'd be in the mood for."

"By the looks of it, not cooking dinner and having leftovers." Hokura sat as she took in the array. There were wraps, sandwiches, fruits, cut-up vegetables... "This is a waste."

"Not if you can save it for dinner!" Amara protested.

"And you're taking some home too to feed your brood as

well." Hokura looked at her as she picked up a wrap and started eating.

Amara picked up a sandwich and took a bite as the two sat in silence. How on earth was she going to bring this up. It seemed like Hokura was genuinely enjoying her lunch when she could no longer take it. "So, how have you been lately?" Amara mentally kicked herself. "That was a stupid thing to ask," she mumbled.

Hokura looked up at her with a smirk. "Just a little, what do I say?" She shrugged. "My system is..." she didn't know if she wanted to say the words.

"But Dorian's on top of things," Amara stated. "He'll be able to fix you up again, I mean... if it's your cells, he's the one who created us. This shouldn't be too hard of a puzzle for the professor, right?"

"I have full faith in him." Hokura ate her wrap. She didn't want to delve into how bad things had gotten. The hacking fits where her lungs burned, and she could barely breathe. Coughing up blood... everything was just too much. She knew what she looked like. She knew her system was failing. The bruises on her arm were testament enough of that. "I just need to be patient and listen to him."

Amara couldn't help but look away. She had wanted to bring up the day before, had wanted to ask why she hadn't said anything, but the professor had already told her everything. Bringing it up would most likely cause her friend more unneeded stress. It was hard to look at her. Hokura appeared like she had when Adam and Amara had found the cargo van at the side of the road when they were searching for her and the professor.

Hokura smiled. "So, it seems the boys have really taken a shining to the science end of the compound. I know Cyrus can't get enough of it."

"Yeah. Nathan has been all about the weather changes lately, too." She made a face. "Any excuse to go out and play in the rain lately. You'd think we purposely deprived him of it his entire life."

There was a light bout of laughter. "C'mon Amara, you remember standing in the rain too and how amazing it felt in the old city. How we'd sit out and watch the storms roll in over the ocean and watch the lightning light up the sky."

It was nice to hear her laugh as Amara grinned. "Nothing like those dark, moody skies and storms, not like the typical weather you see here." She wanted to ask more... had wanted to ask how Gavin was taking things... there was one thing she needed to know. "Have you told the kids?"

Hokura pursed her lips. "No, I was honestly hoping I wouldn't need to. Cassandra has a slight idea of what happened with me. She's seen me at my worse. Cyrus is just going off what she's told him." She faltered. "I can't tell them yet. I'm holding onto hope that I won't have to."

Amara faltered. She understood and couldn't imagine ever having to break the devastating news to someone she loved, especially her children. Still, she wondered how long Hokura could hold up the façade. There had been physical signs. "For what it's worth, I'm truly sorry about how I acted yesterday. I was out of line."

"This wasn't meant to be a slight against anyone." Hokura's throat was dry. She had grown disinterested in the topic of why she hadn't said anything. She was tired of the looks, of the accusations. She grimaced. Maybe she should have just come out and said something after she realized she wasn't healing. She shook her head. It didn't make any difference now.

There was a slight sigh as Amara continued to eat. She hadn't meant to bring it up, and yet she had. She was hoping to make the conversation a little lighter, but what on earth did one day to someone who was ill and supposedly dying? With the others, death had just come and taken them. Barack, Annette, Allen, the rebel commander who one day didn't wake up. "If you need anything, you know I'm here." That was a comforting notion, wasn't it?

"I know." Hokura chewed. She glanced up at her friend and huffed. "What do you want from me, Amara? I'm just feeling emotionally done with it all. I've been tired for months, exhausted. I went through everything that happened with Tobias and the backlash of it. Through Dorian and his trials of cloning an arm. Now I have my own shit to deal with and... and..." She was lost for words.

"You just wish it was someone else's?" Amara asked. "That someone else could deal with it?"

"That makes me sound petty..."

"You've been through hell," Amara countered. "You're allowed to sound petty."

Hokura looked out the window and shook her head. "I wouldn't have wanted anyone else to go through what I did. I can't imagine what would have become of me if Dorian hadn't rescued me when he did, and looking back now, as much as I'm not one for bloodshed." Her tone darkened. "I can never say it to his face, but I wish Dorian *would* have killed Tobias the night he pursued me in the library."

Her friend lowered her eyes. "I just keep bringing up all the wrong subjects today."

"No. I'm sorry." A smirk came to her lip as Hokura chuckled. "It's just a downer situation. How about we forget it. Let's move to the couch and play a few rounds of cards or something while we finish up."

Amara nodded as she gave a solemn look. How on earth could she forget about it when there was a very stark reminder sitting in front of her. She wondered if Hokura knew how far she had fallen, that she physically looked drained. "Sure, let's play some cards... I'll even let you win," she joked, hoping to lighten the mood.

———— ⚓ ————

Dorian paced his lab. He was wondering how Hokura was fairing, how her lunch was going. He had hoped that Amara had enough sense in her to not guilt her any further than she had already felt. His heart ached for the situation.

His mind wandered. These changes happening to her system weren't something he had seen before. There was DNA fragmentation, cell shrinkage, cells dying altogether, and yet the way it was happening... he couldn't scientifically deduct what this was. Why wasn't any of this making any sense to him?

"Dammit, man, you've spent your entire life studying this! Why can't I pull anything up on what this is and how I can save her?" He turned back, thinking about the night before. He needed to go with what he knew. Her blood was tainted. There was something in it that was toxic. It had become a weapon against itself. He let out a frustrated sigh. This was all such a process, and yet he felt like he was running out of time. Even if they could do a blood transfusion, it would be incredibly draining on her, and there was the possibility that it would do no good anyway if whatever was working its way in her destroyed the new blood.

He crashed at his desk and kneaded his forehead. What was this? A virus? A disease? A mutation? If he had that answer, he could work from there, but even that was eluding him. The compound in Michigan had been an army base, who knew what kind of chemical warfare they had there. He shook his head. It was amazing mankind destroyed themselves the way they had back in the day. There had been viruses, vaccines, cures... maybe he needed to brush up on his medical diagnoses... no... even Lucien and Spindler were stumped. This was something they had never seen before.

"Dammit, Hokura, I'm trying, but..." He couldn't afford to start doubting himself. He wouldn't. She had saved him in order to save herself. He owed her everything. He needed to snap out of this and figure something out. Her life depended solely on him, and he was sitting in here sulking because he couldn't formulate a plan. It was time to think outside the box. The suggestion of cloning blood was something. It was a start. There could be hundreds of different avenues, he needed to start somewhere, and if he needed to branch off in another direction, he could do that too. He figured he might as well get the process started.

Gavin sighed as he looked up at the clock. Adam raised an eyebrow. "You've been sighing and staring at the clock for the past half an hour. Why not just call it a day?"

The governor lowered his head. "Because I don't want to impose on her." He looked up at Adam. "Amara obviously told you what happened the other day, right?"

The third child clicked his tongue as he couldn't exactly meet Gavin's eyes. "I had gotten the gist of it. It seems like Dorian helped smooth things over slightly."

"Amara and Dorian, not exactly two people who I figure would clash well when tempers rose," Gavin murmured, looking down at his paperwork.

Adam let out an airy chuckle. "No, but over the years, it hasn't been that bad. Ever since he helped us get pregnant all those years ago, there's been some peace. They get along well enough, but I understand where you're coming from. Both have explosive tempers." He shook his head. "At least Amara's never physically destroyed anything..." He quickly shut his mouth. "That was a lie..."

Gavin raised an eyebrow.

"It wasn't here... it was in the old city. It was the first time Hokura and James went off on their own to camp. Hokura felt a need to leave the city, and it was very quickly dropped on us that they were taking off and weren't too sure when they were going to be back. Amara smashed a plate in our kitchen, and upon finding the sound of shattering glass satisfying, I had to drag her to an old scrap yard so she could lay waste on what was there." He took a deep breath and exhaled slowly. "Not her finest hour, but with everything that had happened, between Hokura being manipulated by the professor, us escaping, and finding a new life, I'm sure there had been a lot of pent-up emotion. I merely sat and watched her as she destroyed things, and after two hours, she had tired herself out, and we went along our way as if it had never happened."

The governor nodded. He had heard stories but had never fully witnessed one of Amara's flare-ups. He knew she had butted heads with the professor a few times and that her awakening had been a violent one. Hokura had mentioned a few times that it very much matched her personality. He had to agree. Amara had always been loud, rash, and to the point. She was blunt and spoke her mind, the opposite of the first child. "We all have different ways of dealing with our emotions."

"Is brooding yours?" Adam asked, raising an eyebrow. "Because it seems that's what you do instead of getting things off your chest. You know you can talk to me about these things."

It had been something Gavin was grateful for. Over the years, Adam had become a solid friend. Someone he could trust. "I guess it's a very old habit of mine," Gavin confessed. "I was taught to keep it to myself. To solve my own problems, and when things got too tough to not let others see..."

"Is that why you go to the gardens at night?" the peacekeeper asked.

Caught. "I guess there are eyes everywhere in this place," he muttered. "The gardens hold a false sense of solitude. At least everyone knows not to bother me when I'm out there on a tangent." There, he had admitted it.

Adam smirked and placed a hand on Gavin's shoulder. "It was only Talon who told me. He watches over this place and its people just as the professor did."

"Makes sense." Gavin sighed as he looked up at the clock again and made a face.

His second rolled his eyes at him. "Be done for the day. The rest of the reports are only minor damage reports that have to do with last night's storm."

"Nothing too critical, I hope," Gavin asked.

Adam gave him a sympathetic look. "Nothing that I can't see to myself. Go home to your wife and spend some time with her, and don't feel like she's pushing you away on purpose."

Gavin walked into a quiet suite to see her form resting on the couch. He walked in tiredly and sat in the chair next to her, simply taking her in. Apparently, lunch had been exhausting because it seemed lately that he had to coax her into resting. He was content just to sit and watch her as he mulled over what Adam had said to him about his brooding. He steepled his fingers. What else was there for him to do? He wasn't strong, wasn't reckless, and yet his heart silently bled. The gardens were indeed his escape, his solace where he could yell and bargain with a dead man. It was an odd thought, he had never spoken to anyone else who had passed, and yet the rebel commander and he had shared many one-sided conversations.

Hokura stirred lightly as her eyes slowly opened. "You're home early," she said, her voice still heavy with sleep.

He smiled gently at her. "I didn't have much work left this afternoon, and I wanted to see you." He leaned over and brushed her hair from her forehead. He wanted to ask if she was exhausted if lunch had been too much for her, and yet he wanted to keep things light. He didn't want to bring up the idea that a simple get-together would tire her in such a way. "How was lunch?"

"Lunch is going to be dinner." A half-smirk came to her lips. "Amara went all out. She took a bunch home but still, we'll be good for tonight, and the kids can figure out from what's left what they want to take for lunch tomorrow."

Gavin let out a chuckle. "Did she go that overboard?"

"Yes." Hokura sat up as she stretched. "And it wasn't because I didn't eat. It's because Amara has no idea what proportions are. She also used the excuse that she didn't know what I would be in the mood for."

"Fair enough." He smiled. "Did things go well?"

She shrugged. "Well enough, I only had to explain myself once, and the subject was dropped. We played some card games, talked about the kids, about life, I guess..." She made a face. She had told Amara she was tired and needed rest or that she would have both Gavin and Dorian reaming her out. She hadn't actually meant to fall asleep on the couch afterward. Hokura had wanted to get onto her painting project again. Perhaps she was still feeling sluggish from having her samples drawn the day before.

Gavin looked down at the table which held the book series

she had been reading, along with another book. He raised an eyebrow. "Get any further in your reading?"

There was a dramatic sigh. "I might be so inclined to ask the kids what happens in the trilogy I'm fighting through. Whenever I pick it up, I can only get a few pages in before putting it down. The other one I finished in a little over a day."

He couldn't help but chuckle. "It's fine to admit certain books aren't for you." He had never known her not to finish a book. He was curious to pick it up himself.

Hokura rose off the couch. "I'll get it done eventually. With all this rest that I'm supposed to be getting, I have more than enough time to power through it." She walked over to the kitchen as Gavin rose and followed her. She walked to the fridge and suppressed a sigh. He was following like a shadow. Why? She had simply been tired. It's not like she was about to collapse to the floor. She winced. Isn't that precisely what had happened yesterday? Hokura turned and looked at him. "Will you pass me a glass?"

Gavin grabbed one and handed it to her. He knew she was feeling frustrated with him. Possibly with herself, too, considering the circumstances. He watched as she poured herself some iced tea and drank it. Was it for show? Was she doing this because she didn't want him on top of her telling her that she needed to rest, drink, and eat? He couldn't help but question her motives for everything now, and he was starting to hate it. A few weeks ago, he wouldn't have thought anything of her simple actions. Now he was observing every little thing she did, thinking there was something behind it. "I saw the cards were out. Want to play a few hands before the kids get home?"

She smiled at him. "I can do that, but I need to warn you, I'm on a winning streak today."

Dorian had worked tirelessly beside Spindler and Lucien through the day. They had set up everything for cloning her blood cells when Dorian had brought in a few vials from one of his personal labs. Spindler raised an eyebrow. "Do we dare ask how many vials of her blood you have?"

The professor eyed the man. "Enough that if something arose, I would be able to save her," he grunted.

Lucien glanced up his way. "We still have plenty of samples from when she gave birth."

Dorian sighed. "These are from after she had taken the super-soldier gene. After the war, I continued to take samples from everyone who took it to see if the gene would eventually depreciate or if it would remain constant. It remained enhanced within everyone, another reason why I'm failing to understand what's happening to her system. It should be able to ward off anything."

Lucien straightened himself, his voice mellow and serene as always. "How about we look at the possibilities of cloning those cells along with her original cells." He gave the professor a small grin. "Surely you still have original samples from her peacekeeping days as well."

The professor nodded. "It's possible we're looking at this the wrong way as well. Maybe it's the white cells... or even the red cells..." His mind was whirling.

Spindler nodded. "We'll filter the samples then and go from there. The more ground we cover, the better, but filtering will take some time. We can set up, but none of this will be done for a few hours." He gave a sigh. "We can set up, get everything moving, take an early dinner, and then break back here."

The other two nodded as they set to work as Dorian meticulously double-checked everything. There was so much going on in this lab that one thing could throw the whole system off. He had checked and double-checked everything when the other two stated they were going to grab something to eat and would be back in an hour or so.

Spindler stared at the professor for a moment. "Get some food into your system. This might take longer. There's only so much we can do at this rate. It might even take until tomorrow until we can start making further deductions."

Dorian nodded. "I'll be a few minutes before I get some food... go on ahead without me."

Dr. Spindler left the room and saw that Lucien was waiting for him a few steps further down the hall. "He'll be alright," Lucien stated, walking beside Spindler. "He knows he has to keep his wits about him with this."

The doctor narrowed his eyebrows. "Just a month ago, he was a madman who was tearing himself apart... it's hard to think that he suddenly has his wits."

"This is Hokura we're talking about. It's something entirely different, he could care less about his sanity for his sake, but now that she's involved, he'll do everything in his power to keep her alive."

Spindler knew the man was right.

Dorian washed his hands as he let out a sigh. Working with the others might open up doors for possibilities he wasn't thinking about, but it also meant more hands for potential missteps. That in itself worried him. He knew his team had been competent, but it was hard to allow others onto this project. Still, it needed to be done. He looked at the time. It was still indeed early, only half-past sixteen hundred hours. There was something else he would do before heading to the cafeteria. Something he had been too exhausted to see to before ending his night in the RTC Simulator, and once he had decided he needed to exert his energy, he didn't have the right mind to make any upgrades. So, he made his way to the training facility.

Talon sat in the viewing room watching Cassandra. Her mind had been sharp as her moves that day as she swiftly defended herself. Her throws and punches were improving at vast rates as her speeds continued to climb. He glanced over towards the door as it clicked open, and Dorian walked through.

"Talon." The professor nodded.

"Coming in to watch or something else?" The watch commander lifted an eyebrow.

"Upgrades," Dorian stated.

Talon shook his head. "Can't seem to beat the targets hard enough lately?" he asked, his eyes going back to the screen. He knew the professor was giving him a look. "Or am I supposed to pretend I don't know what you're doing in there every night? Screaming your head off while ripping simulations apart like some kind of wild animal."

Dorian shifted. "So, you've seen my work?"

The watched commander sighed as he sat back in his chair, stretching his legs. "I'm reminded to never piss you off." He licked his lips. "You can't let your rage consume you. What you're looking for will never be in that simulator."

"And what am I looking for?" His voice had a sharp edge to it.

"You can't extract revenge on dead men that no longer walk this earth. All you can do is move forward and make sure their plans never come to fruition," Talon stated cooly, watching Cassandra as she finished her round.

Dorian sat next to him. "And how is it that you know all this?"

Talon leaned forward and hit the intercom button. "Good round, take a drink break and cool down and stretch for a bit," he said as he watched the girl nod and exit the simulator. Talon's lips twitched. "I'm not an idiot, Dorian. Unless you walk around this place with your eyes closed and your ears plugged, news travels fast. Plus, I'm not beyond making my own deductions."

The professor was about to say something when the door opened. He turned to see Cassandra as her face lit up. "It's been a while. How's the arm?"

He couldn't keep his cold demeanor towards her as he gave the girl a gentle smile. "Indeed, I've been busy lately. The arm is working well."

Talon cleared his throat. "Remind me that I have some reports to give you afterward." He looked over at the professor, who nodded but was still taking in Cassandra.

"Your training has been going well. I can see you've been improving," Dorian stated. "Maybe in time, I'll try and look in on you a little more often."

Cassandra couldn't quite read his face. "You've been busy... and so has my mother." Her words were guarded as if asking a question.

He wouldn't take the bait. He knew Hokura hadn't said anything to her children about this. He would honor her wishes. "Yes, we've both been busy, plus she also needs her rest as she's been healing still."

Cassandra gave him a solemn look. "Is she actually healing, or are you just saying that to protect her?"

Caught. Why were Hokura's offspring so damn intuitive?

"Why are you making such an accusation?" He would turn this around on her. If it were a battle of words, he would play her game.

"If it's the truth, it isn't an accusation." Cassandra boldly defended herself. She gave him a solemn look. "I just... I don't think she's getting any better..."

The professor's eyebrows furrowed. "Why would you say that?"

Talon cleared his throat. Bringing both their attention his way as he looked up at Cassandra. "Are you done with your training today?"

His question caught her off guard. "No... I was just..."

The watch commander crossed his arms, raising his eyebrows. "I have to oversee some new watch guards in a bit. Unless you want to be running with the rookies."

"No!" Cassandra quickly retorted. Her eyes went up quickly to the professor. "If I needed to know something, you'd tell me, right?"

He gave a curt nod. "Myself or your mother when the time was right."

She nodded and turned to Talon. "Sorry for taking up your time..."

"It's alright." Talon regarded her. "Third set, get to it, and then we'll be done today." With that, the girl was out the door and off.

Dorian let out an exasperated sigh as he closed his eyes and kneaded his forehead. "Thank you..."

"For what?" Talon smirked.

"For the lie... you don't have any watch trainees coming in today." He didn't exactly understand why he had done it, but he was indeed grateful.

Talon shook his head. "For someone as busy as you are, you

still know exactly what's going on around here." He gave the professor a look. "I know it's none of my business, but I know Hokura isn't well... I can tell by your demeanor and your undertones. Besides, why else would you be in here all hours of the night?"

"You're right, Talon." The professor grimaced. "It's just another damnable secret. She's not well... and I..." Could he dare confess that he was running into a wall with how he was going to save her?

"You've got a lot going on. It's understandable," the commander stated as he sighed and sat back in his chair, watching Cassandra take her place back in the simulation room. "She has one more run-through, and then you can do whatever upgrades you want. You can sit in, or you can check back."

"I might as well sit in." Dorian sat and crossed his arms as his eyes went to the monitors. His interest piqued. It was like looking into the past, it had only been a few months, and yet it seemed that Cassandra had picked up training with no issues at all. His heart panged. Her mother should be alongside her, helping her with this, yet he doubted Hokura would have the strength to do any of it. "You mentioned reports."

Talon grabbed a few sheets of paper and idly handed them over to him. "Considering her age, she's improving at peace-keeper rates."

Dorian eyed the reports. "That's no surprise. I'm sure she'll only get better in time." He made a face. "Girls her age should be sitting around gossiping about boys... and yet here she is."

The watch commander cleared his throat. "She chooses to be here. Besides, being here is keeping her out of trouble. Well over a month back, she let loose on a classmate and broke her nose."

The professor's eyes widened. He hadn't heard anything about such an incident occurring.

There was a chuckle as Talon shook his head. "From what I heard, she got what she deserved, Gavin was ready to pull the plug on things, but I informed him that she could be disciplined through her training more efficiently."

Dorian took a deep breath. He knew Cassandra had issues in the past with bad influences. He recalled the day he had gotten the page asking for Hokura, who received the news that Cassandra had breached the wall. They had both confided in him in different ways, Hokura, who felt like her daughter was defying her at every chance she had. Cassandra, who was frustrated that she couldn't understand her mother because Hokura had been keeping quiet about her past. "Just as well, if this is how Cass wants to spend her time training isn't a bad thing. It's a good outlet for her."

Talon nodded silently as the two watched the girl go through her last simulation.

Dorian noted her movements. They had improved, although she was still unsure about herself with some of them. There was faltering. It still wasn't the smooth grace that her mother once had. The thought hurt. To know what Hokura had once been compared to what she was now, one of strength and stamina to now needing him to slow his pace so she could keep up with his strides. He watched as the simulation finished, and Cassandra grabbed her towel and water bottle.

"Good job!" Talon congratulated over the intercom before looking over to the professor. "The viewing room is all yours." He was about to leave when he placed a hand on Dorian's shoulder. "You know better. This will never fix things. It'll just exhaust you. If physical exertion is what you need, then fine but don't lie to yourself thinking you're going to find any resolution in there." With that, he left.

The professor knew that he needed something technical to fill his mind for a bit. He was sure Spindler and Lucien were sitting in the cafeteria enjoying a lighter conversation while he was trying to find a way to harden the simulator's hits and make the enemy's attacks more malicious. The thought brought a dark smile to his face. All he wanted at the end of the night was to be a shell, an exhausted vessel that didn't need to think. To simply crawl into bed for a few hours of depleted sleep where his body could only calculate the most basic functions to keep him alive until the following day when he started the agonizing process all over again.

Spindler and Lucien sat in the cafeteria quietly eating their early dinner until Spindler spoke up. "Maybe we need to treat this like a type of cancer."

Lucien looked up at the man. "Cancer had been cured before the great war. It was wiped clean off the earth when stem cell experiments finally got the nod. Before the cure, doctors used chemotherapy to rid the body of such a thing. I don't believe Hokura's system would survive such treatment. Even once it was perfected, it put patients through hell."

Spindler scowled as he took a sip of his soup. "It would be easier if this wasn't affecting every aspect of her."

"Indeed, doctor, cancer could spread, but there were still ways to attack cancerous cells. This is literally *all* her cells." Lucien shook his head, taking a bit of his salad. "Immunotherapy won't even work on this."

"No, it wouldn't. Her cells most likely saw whatever this was and fought against it for some time. Unfortunately, if we would have known this right away and found a way to catch it, we would have been able to gain some ground." He shook his head. "We were all so busy overseeing other things. She was busy overseeing Dorian, that in that time, we lost that ground. I don't know if we'll be able to get it back."

Lucien gave him a weary look. "If something happens, do you think the professor would attempt to clone her?"

It was a huge possibility that Spindler didn't want to think about. "Now that we know it's possible, I fear he might, but I want to say in all rationale, he would know that it wouldn't be her. Cloning an arm is one thing, a peacekeeper..." He winced. He didn't want to think about it, to think of the children lost to the project that had brought them where they were today. They had their immortality but at so many lives lost.

"We should keep an eye on him as well." Lucien's voice was low. "His arm nearly tipped him off the deep end. This might be the breaking point for him if anything happens to her."

That was another thing Spindler didn't want to think about. He remembered Dorian in his labs with bleeding feet from stepping on glass after having a physical tantrum and fishing the glass from his feet and good hand. The way the man had confided in him about Hokura. He remembered Dorian phoning him in absolute panic when he had destroyed his lab and the cooling system for his clone. The way the man could barely look him in the eye. "Indeed, there's not much that seems to hold the man to his sanity the way she does ever since she returned. We need to make sure that sanity stays intact."

Lucien nodded, noting the time. "We might as well bring him some dinner. He hasn't come up yet from the labs or to get anything from his suite. I've been keeping an eye out."

"We'll definitely do that. I want to sit for a bit after finishing. I want to clear my head a bit before diving into this abyss."

"You and me both, doctor."

The evening had continued as Dorian's hands moved eloquently over the devices as Lucien stood beside him as he was an extra set of hands double-checking everything. Spindler was setting up machines that would filter the blood as well once there had been enough produced.

"That seems to be about right," Spindler said. "Do you have the samples?"

Dorian straightened. "I have two that we are going to test—her original cells and the cells that have the super soldier gene in them. I want to compare how they filter. One might work better than the other for lab tests. If we require something pure, then her original samples will be what we need. If we need something dosed with active stronger cells, then we'll have the upped samples for that."

Lucien mused for a moment. "Even if her original cells are what we need, it's not like you don't have the super soldier serum still. Maybe I can take a look at it. There's a possibility there's an answer that lies within the serum. If it's to act as a super steroid, perhaps that could also be the answer to the larger question of what she needs."

Dorian raised an eyebrow. Steroids, something to boost her system, and yet what he had tried cellwise hadn't worked. "It's worth a try. At this time, anything is. I'll grab it for you." He quickly left the lab, rubbing his eyes. He had been grateful that his colleagues had seen through his ruse and had brought him dinner, which he had picked at as they quickly went over the setup process before proceeding. He walked down a few doors to the coolant room where he had kept the super-soldier samples among different serums. He grabbed the serum from the cooling unit and sighed. Maybe Lucien was onto something. He could only hope. He didn't care whether he was the one who harbored the answer or not. He just wanted someone, *anyone,* to find it and figure this out. He would be fine with admitting it wasn't him to unravel the solution to this puzzle, all he wanted was for her to be okay.

He left the room and returned to see that the doctors had already started the process. The samples had already been set up, and the machines already turned on. With a small smile, he handed Lucien the vial. "Hopefully, you can find an answer with this, do whatever you need. There are more in the coolant room if need be."

Lucien gave him a kind smile. "I'm well aware, professor, still it was your creation. It's only right I ask your permission to look into my hypothesis using the serum."

Dorian gave him a look. "When it comes to this and saving her, you don't need my permission." He looked over to Spindler. "That goes for you as well. I don't care what it takes. She is our top priority. She needs to make it out of this and be well again."

Spindler nodded. "We're doing all we possibly can, Dorian. I promise you that." He licked his lips. "This is going to take some time, especially to clone enough plasma to start any filtering process."

Dorian nodded. "Thank you, both of you, for all your hard work. I guess there's nothing else for us to do this evening. You both deserve some rest."

It was Spindler who spoke up. "You need your rest as well professor, you can't beat yourself into the ground over this, or you won't be of sound mind when we need you when she needs you. I suggest you take the evening and relax."

With that, Lucien and Spindler bid him goodnight and left

the lab. Dorian stood for a moment as he took a deep breath. Maybe he needed to relax. Maybe he needed to actually rest instead of exerting himself into a stupor. He was doing this all for her... and at that moment, he wanted to see her... to talk to her as she had played on his mind all day. He huffed. Nothing was stopping him from doing so.

He made his way to his suite and stopped in the hallway. He could go down an extra few dozen feet and knock on her door, and yet he stopped. What if she was tired? Or unavailable? He had wanted to know how lunch had gone with Amara. How she was feeling after what had happened the day before... still he went into his suite.

"Since when have you become such a coward?" He cursed himself as he walked over to the phone and dialed her number. To his surprise, it was her voice on the other end. "Hey."

"Dorian, hey." There was a silence. "Why are you phoning?" Her voice had a slight chuckle to it.

"Am I not allowed to phone you?" he asked in a perplexed tone.

"You live a few doors down from me. Why wouldn't you just come over? Or are you tired? Have you been exhausting yourself?"

A wide smile came to his lips, ever so concerned about him when she was the one in turmoil. "I was going to ask the same about you, which is why I chose to phone instead of coming over to see you."

"Do you want to see me?"

He couldn't help but chuckle as his voice softened. "I always want to see you." He kicked himself. The reply had been natural, but it sounded awkward coming from him over the phone, like some prepubescent child finally confessing his feelings.

"I want to see you too," she admitted. "How about I meet

you in the library? I have to return a book. Then we can talk for a bit."

He agreed as she hung up the phone. The library, a mutual ground, he would wait for her there. Upon entering, he strode past her paintings, taking them in. The series had grown over time. He yearned to see it continue as she evolved as an artist. There were sunsets over the ocean, meadows filled with flowers, the wastelands. His heart panged at the thought of her collection not growing as he made his way to the large bay windows and took in the city. It was evening, and people were still walking about, families, couples, things he knew he'd never have, and yet at the moment, he'd be content to simply have her by his side. A few moments later, he heard footsteps, slow, unsteady, as he turned and took her in.

"Sorry." Hokura blushed. "I'm being slow."

A sorrowful smile came across his face. She was basked in light from the window, yet the shadows that bounced off her face made her deterioration all the more noticeable. "You don't have to apologize." He walked up to her and noted the book in her hand. He had recognized the cover right away with the cat among the gravestones. "My, that's a change from your regular genres."

"He was a big-name author long ago. There's a huge section of his work, and yet I never picked any of his books up because I wasn't into scary stories, I guess." She shrugged as they walked towards the particular section in the library. "I needed something different from the series I've been reading..."

Dorian nodded as he watched her replace the book. His eyes darted to the bruises on her arms where he had taken the samples from her. "How are you feeling now that you've gotten some rest?"

She smirked. "What's rest when Amara's over?" Hokura

gave a small chuckle. "I'm feeling a little better now, though. I slept for a bit this afternoon." She turned to him. "How about we sit on the sofa and simply relax?"

He led the way to the couches that were by the windows and figured she was still tired if she wasn't suggesting walking the gardens. "How was lunch?" Dorian asked, leaning back, and taking her in as she rested next to him.

Hokura pursed her lips. "Just me explaining myself and feeling guilty." She looked down solemnly at her clasped hands when his came over the top of them.

"Enough guilt. You don't owe any more explanations to anyone."

"But everyone is still upset. Everyone is suffering because of me. Even you... you're still upset with me. You're working yourself into exhaustion now... Gavin's following me around because he feels like I'm just hiding more from him." Her voice cracked. "I'm sorry..." She stared him in the eyes. "If I could go back, I'd do it all over again, though!"

He couldn't help but feel perplexed. "Why? There were ways around this!"

She gave him a sad smile. "Because Dorian, I could never be that selfish with you. You needed to be whole before you looked into this. How could I have possibly put myself before you getting your arm back?"

He could feel his temper rising as he clenched his jaw. "Because I have the rest of time to clone a damn arm. *Your* days are now possibly limited." He stood up and walked to the window. Why was she like this with him? Why didn't she understand? Why was this always the dance between them? He yearned to understand her, and yet, some days, he thought she was just as thick-headed as him. That was the revelation. They were both the same but asinine in their own thoughts. He sighed as he placed his forehead against the window. "I'm seeing about cloning your blood now... there's a possibility of doing transfusions."

Her arms wrapped around him from behind as he felt her head rest against his back. "See, I knew you could do this and that you'd find an answer." Her voice was soft, her body against his as his heart raced. He couldn't help himself as he turned and embraced her in his arms, holding her to his chest.

"Why are you like this? Why can't you understand that you are my life and that I put you before absolutely everything and everyone, including myself," he seethed as he breathed her in. "What else do I have to do or say to get this through to you, Hokura?" He didn't want to feel this anger towards her, but he would embrace it just as he was doing her.

She didn't say a word. They had yet to talk about this, he had yet to show her how he actually felt, and so she would allow it. She wanted this. If anyone had any right to be upset with her, it was him because she had cost him so much already, and again, she was costing him.

"I love you so damn much that it hurts," Dorian breathed. "I have let so much go in the past because all I ever wanted was to see you happy but to be so reckless with yourself. To be so reckless with the one thing that I have ever loved... you might as well just stab me right through my heart."

"Dorian..." Her voice was soft as she wrapped her arms around him. She could understand. "Then how can you ask the same from me. I couldn't put this before what you were going through. You were slowly killing yourself. I needed you for this just as much as you needed me by your side. Can't you see Dorian?" She looked up at him. "We're so much the same."

"I know..." He breathed. He lowered his chin and kissed her forehead. "In a maddening way we are, I promise I'll save you, just as you saved me." He didn't want to let go of her since he didn't know when he'd have a chance to hold her like this again. "You know I'm doing everything I can..."

"Of course I do." She nodded against him. "I have full faith in you."

He wanted to tell her not to. That he was running on theories at best and that he had yet to figure anything out. He wanted to confess that he had felt powerless, that this was a puzzle beyond him, and yet, she remained optimistic. He couldn't spoil that for her. He *needed* to figure this out. "Thank you for seeing me... I..." He'd confess to her. "I've been having nightmares lately."

She could understand. "Me too... about you... about us... but..." She looked up at him with a slight smile. "We're going to be okay."

"Yes," he breathed. "We're going to be okay." He followed her back to the couch as he leaned against it, looking tired. He had wanted to bring up his dreams, his supposed flashbacks, but it didn't seem like right now was the right time. For now, he just wanted to sit beside her and be close to her as her head rested up against his shoulder.

"Things will go back to normal again someday," she stated.

"They will." He felt like it was a lie. What was normal anymore? Nightmares because she had been abducted? Gavin never being able to trust newcomers? Him achingly wondering if there was anything more that she was keeping from him? As much as he wanted to go down to the RTC Simulator, this was so much more as he looked over at her. "Hey..." His voice was low. "If you're tired, you should go back to your suite and get some more rest."

"Just a few more minutes..." Hokura smiled. "This feels so nice." She wanted to indulge for a little longer in his strong shoulder, the plushness of the couch, and the gentle waft of his cologne. No lines were being crossed, but she felt so close to him right now that she just wanted a few more selfish moments of peace before returning to her suite. She let out a soft sigh. "I don't know how to fix this with Gavin."

Dorian gently brought his arm around her and rubbed her shoulder, trying to offer some physical comfort. "You've told him why you kept it from him. There's nothing more you can do other than being honest with him. It's going to take some time on his part." He took a breath. "He's worried about you. He wants to be there for you. Don't push him away."

She couldn't help but feel sorry about the situation. She had done just as Dorian described. She had run that knife through his heart how many times now? It had been a constant in their relationship. There were some days she wished she could go back and fix things, but those private thoughts hurt, she loved Gavin, and yet it was the professor who understood her better than anyone. "I'll try." Her voice was small. She wanted to simply fall asleep next to him and awaken from this nightmare.

"Come on." His voice was above a whisper as he gently shook her. "Let's get you back to your suite. You're tired. I can only imagine how the second child can exhaust someone." He cracked a smile at her as she returned it.

"Amara isn't that bad... some days."

He couldn't help but laugh. "It must have been a good day then." He led her back to her suite. "You've heard this before. Do I need to repeat myself, or do you know what you need to do?"

Hokura gave him a tired look. "I'm going to bathe, have a light snack, relax on the couch and call it an early night." She smirked. "You should do the same."

He knew he should.

"Don't give me that look either," she countered.

"What look?" Her snappiness caught him off guard.

"That look which says you're listening, but you're not going to do it." She grabbed his arm. "You need to rest too, don't start putting yourself out and exhausting your body and mind. You already said you were having nightmares. You need your sleep, too."

Caught. Dorian licked his lips. "For this evening, then we'll make a pact to one another that we'll get the rest acquired of us."

She hugged him one last time. "It's a promise you'd better keep."

Right now, it felt like it was the only promise he could keep.

***

Amara walked beside Adam. She had been feeling restless that evening and needed out of the compound. Luckily, Olga was always nearby to watch the kids when needed. The second peacekeeper was hoping being away would help her clear her head, but, in a way, it was just a silent escape from what she had learned today.

Adam looked over at her. "You seem quiet. What's on your mind?" He knew it had to do with Hokura but asking was the best way to get his wife talking again. After her initial bout of anger, she had seemed reserved about the whole situation. She hadn't said a word about lunch that afternoon.

She blew out a small breath as she tried to collect her thoughts. "No peacekeeper should ever have to go through their system failing them like this. No *person* in Meridiana should have to go through it, and yet here we are, and it always seems that it has to be her."

Adam squeezed her hand. "Maybe it's always her because she's the strongest of us. Perhaps it's because if anyone can see such a thing through, it's Hokura."

Amara shook her head. "What did she ever do to deserve the fate that's come from her life? People talk about karma, and it seems that the person who deserves the best gets the worst."

"You know what happened was purely situational," Adam said. He didn't want to get into it too much that Hokura had been too trusting. Everyone knew why things had happened. They were all to blame because they didn't see what the professor had. Dorian had known the type of person Tobias had been, and his warnings had been dismissed. Adam inwardly kicked himself. He should have picked up on it as well while he was touring Tobias around the industrial part of the city. The man asked more questions about his fellow peacekeeper than anything else.

"We were too late," Amara muttered.

"No..." Adam's voice was soft. "Even Dorian was too late. There's no way anyone could have made it on time with what happened. The damage had already been done, maybe Hokura could have said something earlier, but we can't even begin to go down that route."

It was something that was still incredibly heavy on Amara's heart. If only Hokura had said something earlier, if she would have told Dorian, he would have put off his project with his arm. He would have most likely even taken the bionic one off sooner instead of emotionally destroying her further. It was their damn complicated emotional love affair that she could never understand. Something that still gnawed at her from time to time. As much as Dorian loved her, he didn't seem to see what he did to her as well. "This whole situation is fucked, and I hate it," Amara finally growled.

A small smile came to Adam's lips as he let out an airy breath.

"This isn't funny," she continued.

"No. Not at all," her husband mused. "It's just a relief to hear you let it out in such a way." He wrapped an arm around her. "As much as I'm worried about Hokura, I'm concerned how this is affecting you as well." He kissed her forehead.

"You don't need to worry about me," she muttered.

"Amara, how long have you and I been together?" He chuckled. "If I don't know you by now, then I never will. I know you're worried and stressed. I know you're trying to push this out of your mind and bury your emotions. I know you're mad, hurt, and that you're taking in a lot. That's reason enough to be worried."

She made a face when he stopped and looked down at her.

"I'm worried too." He brought his hand to her face and cupped it. "I'm worried about a lot of things."

They stood on the sidewalk gazing at one another—Amara's heartbeat heavily in her chest. Adam had been there through everything, had seen everything, every emotional fit, every breakdown. He had listened to her scream, rant, and rave about her frustrations. He never once faltered with her. She didn't want to ask, didn't want to think about it, but the words slipped out before she could even think of the emotional repercussions. "What do we do if something happens to her?"

He gave a sorrowful expression. "We move on, just like she did after James. That's all we can do." He took her in. "I know that's not what you want to hear, but I don't have a magical answer for you. This is beyond us. The only person who is remotely capable of saving her is spending every possible moment he can in finding a cure."

Amara looked up and clicked her tone. "You're right. You're always right."

"You're not feeling any better about things," Adam mused as he turned her, and they continued their walk. "And I know you won't until things smooth over, but for now, how about I take you down the street and let you indulge in your sweet tooth."

She gave a small smile. "But it's getting late."

"All the more reason to be quick about getting there."

He was by her side and would remain by her side for all of time as she couldn't help but wrap her arms around him as they walked. "Don't *you* dare go anywhere."

Adam laughed, trying to lighten the mood. "I don't think I could if I tried." He looked up towards the darkening sky and the way the clouds were rolling in. "We better make this quick, or we'll end up walking in the rain.

She squeezed his hand. "I don't mind a walk in the rain with you."

The rain poured over the city through the night as the compound's lights dimmed. The hallways were barren as even the professor kept good on his promise, and instead of finding himself in the RTC simulator, he found himself in his bed at a decent time. His dreams wracked over him as the thought of losing her, his nightmare, had become a reality, as he tossed and turned restlessly, trying to think of better days and times he had spent with her.

Amara slept soundly in Adam's arms. After coming home, she had confided in him about her fears of losing anyone, about her fears of being alone, that she would never be as strong as Hokura had been. He had kissed her, soothed her, and had reassured her in every way possible that she was safe. She would never be without him nor their children. As he finally fell asleep, his own mind drifted, grasping onto hope that, indeed, the professor would be able to save the first child. He couldn't imagine the compound being without Hokura. He sighed in hopes that the future looked brighter for all of them.

Gavin had snuggled with his wife, thankful that she didn't need to be overly coaxed into bed that night. Upon kissing him and rolling over, he took a deep breath. As much as everyone else was finding the rain soothing, he found it to be as chaotic and disruptive as the storms that were rolling through the wastelands and into the city. His emotions were making him feel all the more restless, but alas... she was sleeping beside him, so the only thing left for him to do was to close his eyes and join her in hopes no nightmares would wake her and that they would all sleep better that night.

It had been early the next morning. Adam sighed, the rain had cleared up slightly, but it had been leaving a path of destruction whenever it did so. He had made his way into the city to oversee some reports which had landed on the governor's desk before the man had arrived at work. He had called to city maintenance and was now overseeing some of the damage.

"There's been erosion noted in some roads. There have also been some issues with raised sidewalks," Adam noted, looking over the report as the maintenance team stood by him. He breathed in the air. It always smelled so much sweeter after the rain. Being out in the city in the morning was something he had taken delight in as he shifted. "Start on what we have here. I'm sure more reports will filter in through the day. The live wire is on if you need to be in contact with me and is hooked into all your frequencies," he instructed. With that, the men nodded and were on their way to the designated spots around the city.

One less thing for the governor to worry about, it was the least he could do knowing what Gavin was going through with Hokura as Adam started his way down the road. He figured he would walk a bit and see if he came across anything noteworthy that hadn't already been reported.

The old city of White Rock had always been under constant repair due to erosion issues, not only due to the rain but also being next to the ocean. To see such things in Meridiana had been strange. It wasn't often that the weather system turned the way it had this past while. Usually, storms kept to the wastelands. At least they hadn't had to deal with any sandstorms within the city. The wall protected them from dust kick up, although it was always a remarkable thing to see when the skies reddened.

The third child smiled. He could have breakfast at a small shop this morning. There had been a few specialty bakeries he frequented now, one especially that served a steamed brew that he favored. As he walked, he heard a familiar voice call his name. He turned to see Yvonne walking down the street towards him.

"Good morning," Adam chimed, still holding his clipboard. "How have you been, Yvonne?"

The woman gave him a bright look as she tucked a stray hair behind her ear. "Adam, it's nice to see you out and about so early. Seeing to the city and what this strange weather has been doing to it?"

He chuckled. "Come now. Surely a little rain can't bother you after years of it in White Rock."

She shrugged slightly as she turned and walked with Adam. "Honestly, I've gotten quite climatized to this place. Seeing rain again brings back some fond memories... and some not so fond... I think my old bones were starting to feel the weather too often back in the old city. The winters left much to be desired.'

Adam smiled. "But the view of those snowcap mountains was something to behold." He remembered the beauty of it, of simply staring at the mountain as the leaves changed. It had been something he had never seen before. Hokura had painted it from memory not long ago, and it still took his breath away whenever he gazed at the painting in the library.

Yvonne nodded. "It was a beautiful sight. I must admit that I do miss the ocean." The smile left her face. "But I would never venture from this place to see it again. I've heard too much about what goes on beyond the walls to care to ever witness it."

The peacekeeper raised his eyebrow as they continued towards his destination.

"Oh, don't give me that face. You know, the people of the city gossip. What else is there some days? I'm very well aware of the cannibals out there, about the *people* out there, and what their motives are." Her voice lowered. "I heard Hokura had been kidnapped by the group that had come into the city under the ruse of looking to better their own compound."

He pursed his lips. "News travels fast... but that was months ago."

"I haven't seen Hokura out since then." Yvonne gave him a worried look. "Is she alright?"

He didn't know what he could or should say about the

matter. This was a private affair between those involved. "She's busied herself in the compound overseeing the higher education project alongside Professor Dorian." It hadn't been a complete lie. They came up to the bakery as Adam stopped. "I'm going to grab something here. Do you care to join?"

She shook her head. "I was actually on my way to visit Frederich for morning tea and to play catch up. It was lovely to see you, though. Please tell Governor Gavin that I send my regards." With that said, she turned and was on her way again.

Adam took a deep breath. He couldn't imagine the possible pandemonium it could cause if people found out that there was something wrong with a peacekeeper, that their lesser systems could possibly be attacked. He swallowed hard as he entered the pastry shop. Something he'd rather not think about. The aroma hit him and washed that thought aside as he ordered and brought his food to a small table. As much as Adam enjoyed working in the hustle and bustle of the compound next to Gavin, it was moments like this that he truly enjoyed as he looked over his notes on his clipboard. He wondered when this rainy season would pass as he looked out the window. The sun was already shining brightly. The puddles from the night before had dissipated as it was already starting to warm.

He took a sip of foamed coffee as other patrons walked in and out of the shop. Others talked quietly among themselves at tables in whispered voices.

"Some storm last night again."

"It's amazing how quickly it can come on. I've never seen anything like this before."

"It's possible that we need the rain... maybe the climate is changing."

Adam shook his head. It was possible. Maybe the earth was healing after the devastation that was caused to it. Maybe the atmosphere was finally calming, and the weather systems were returning. He had thought that was the case well over fifty years ago before they escaped. It wasn't until they had left Meridiana that they saw the actual change of seasons. A slight smile came to his lips as he reminisced. Something he seemed to be doing more lately as life had taken some unexpected turns. Hokura... surely the professor would be able to cure her. He wondered if Gavin would ever have it in him again to open the gates to those in the wastelands searching for sanctuary.

Adam's livewire clicked on. "Sir, we have another job to add to the list."

He picked up the radio. "What is it?"

"There's been a few minor leaks on the roofs of apartment blocks 305 and 306."

Adam swallowed another sip of coffee. "Send a team over there. I'll make my way over there and meet them in a bit." He made a note on the clipboard. This was something he wouldn't keep from Gavin. Basic upkeep on the streets was one thing. This was another. The last thing they needed was damage being done to apartments. He finished his pastry and splashed down the rest of his drink as he rose from his chair, thankful that they were only minor leaks. He left the shop and headed down the street. At least this would keep his mind occupied for the day. It was exactly what he needed.

Gavin had arrived late to his office. He had noticed a lack of paperwork on his desk as he raised an eyebrow. There had been a note left by Adam stating that he had come in early and had taken care of the maintenance reports and would follow up with the governor later once everything was seen to. The governor smiled as he sat in his chair, kneading his forehead.

Thank goodness he had Adam. The peacekeeper had stepped up beyond his means in taking care of this. He had wanted to leave his office, but Hokura had been adamant that she was fine and wanted the day to rest and relax. He made a face. He didn't exactly know what her definition of resting and relaxing was these days.

He had felt restless sitting in his office with nothing to go over. Surely, there was something that needed his attention. A scowl came to his face. There was indeed something or rather someone who needed his attention, and yet she was seemingly turning him away. His fingers drummed on the desk. He had wanted to know more... he was about to pick up the phone and dial for the professor when he stopped. Would Dorian give him a straight answer? Most likely not. As much as he respected and trusted the man, he didn't know if he would be forthright with this. He was certain he could do something to cure her. He would fight until his last breath... or... hers. The thought sickened him as he picked up the phone and dialed. "Spindler... are you able to take some time and come to my office?"

It had been a few tense minutes later that the doctor was sitting in front of him. He wore a tired look. Gavin was confident that Dorian had been drilling him with helping to come up with either a diagnosis or a cure.

Gavin took a deep breath. "I asked you because I wanted the truth about things."

The doctor's eyebrows rose. "And you didn't think you would get the truth from the professor?"

The governor clicked his tongue. "I believe Dorian believes he needs to be overly optimistic with this because of it being Hokura."

"Mmmm," Spindler mused. "And you want my diagnosis and to know whether or not I believe something can be done?"

He stared at Gavin and knew that's exactly what he wanted. The doctor steepled his fingers and closed his eyes for a moment to gather his thoughts. "The ugly truth of the matter is that we've never encountered something like this before. It's like a poison that simply multiplies and has started attacking everything inside of her. We're trying desperately to figure out how to either combat it or flush it from her system."

Gavin could feel his desperation building. "Is there anything that looks like it might work? Have there been any breakthroughs? She's..." He didn't want to admit it. "She's not getting any better. Every time Dorian takes a blood sample from her, she bruises. She's not healing."

The doctor pursed his lips. "I'm sorry, governor, I wish there was more to tell you. However, I can tell you this." His eyes met and held Gavin's. "Dorian will do everything in his power to see this through. He is her lifeline more than any of us. If anyone is going to save her, it will be him because he will never give up on her."

He had already known this. He was hoping for something more, for a better answer, as Gavin's head drooped. This hadn't helped at all. Maybe calling the professor in to hear his optimism was better than having Spindler talk to him. "From your medical viewpoint..."

The doctor knew precisely where this was going now. "Every day is a step forward. No matter the dead ends we hit, we know we need to take a different avenue." He cleared his throat. "Think of this medical mystery as a maze governor. We know there's an end, even if we can't see it. If we make a wrong turn, we can backtrack and find another way."

The governor nodded. The truth was that this made had a timeline... and that timeline was running out. "Thank you for coming in and talking with me. If there's anything that's needed, please let me know, and I will see to it."

Spindler rose from his seat. "We've got a good group of people on this. I'm sure we'll figure something out. We're men of science. Breakthroughs happen every day for us. Back when we were first on the stem cell project, everything changed in a matter of days." He gave Gavin a kind smile and left. As he walked down the hall back towards the medical facility, he couldn't help but feel slightly guilty. He had offered false hope to the man, but wasn't that just what Dorian was doing with all of them?

The week had moved on slowly without any progression from the doctors or professor as Dorian drove himself deeper into trying to figure out a solution. He only allowed himself four hours of sleep a night and was back down to the labs before dawn, straining his eyes and mind as he tried to unwrap the puzzle that Richter had so meticulously put together. Time seemed to blur for him. How much time had it been? As much as Hokura danced in his mind, he hadn't seen her. Something that worried him, but at the same time, he felt a small relief. Gavin was obviously making sure she was resting, which was what she needed. Spindler had mentioned his conversation with the governor to the man, Dorian had shrugged it off. If Gavin wanted to talk to him, he merely had to page him. The governor wasn't a distraction he needed at the moment. His brows furrowed as he re-read over his files. What on earth was he missing? How could a madman elude him in such a way? "Dammit, there needs to be something," he groaned as he stared at the clock, he had already been up for hours, and those of the compound were just making their way down from their suites for the day. He rubbed his eyes. Maybe he could take samples from himself again and go from there. The cloning process has been slow, and he couldn't help but feel agitated. He needed to keep moving forward.

It was afternoon, and Hokura had felt restless. She hadn't left her suite in a few days as she decided to hole herself up and paint. Walking the hallways of the compound had gotten her more stares than she cared for, to the point where she had opted to start wearing a larger sweatshirt over her shrinking frame. She had slipped into the library a few times to get new books, but even that was starting to bore her. It seemed like nothing was keeping her attention lately. She had spoken to Amara on the phone, but when her friend had asked about getting together to play cards, Hokura told her that she wasn't feeling overly sociable, that the phone calls would have to be enough for now.

Gavin now had a regular schedule of checking in on her mid-morning and at lunch and was making a habit of coming home early from work, stating not much needed to be done. He was on her about resting which made her feel all the more anxious when night fell, and she couldn't sleep, even with the sleep aids, she had been restless, and when she did finally sleep, she dreamt of death and those she would be leaving behind.

"Dorian..." she whispered as she stared out the window. She had brought out her painting but had yet to even pour the paint or lift her brush. Saying his name offered her some comfort. "I miss you, out of everyone that I haven't seen lately... of course, it's you," she sighed. She had felt alone because nobody could possibly understand what she was going through. For whatever reason, she felt more comfortable confiding in her creator than her husband. Maybe it was because Gavin had always seen her in a way that perplexed her. He saw her as strong, whereas Dorian had seen the truth. Her creator and mentor had seen her at her worse. As much as she hated it, he had still embraced her even when her body was failing her. She had shied away from Gavin seeing it. She had started sleeping in more than just a slip. She had started locking the door when she bathed or showered. This body would scare him, the bruises, the slight discolorations. She wasn't who she used to be. There was no physical strength left in her.

"I want to see you..." Her heart panged. She didn't want to disturb him from what he was doing. The professor had been wracking his brain trying to figure this out. To call him away from his work because she was feeling lonely would be selfish. She grabbed a piece of paper and penned away her problems to him. It felt freeing, therapeutic as she did, and so she asked him...

After slipping the note under Dorian's suite door, the day progressed. Hokura had packed away the paints after writing the letter. She had decided to bathe in hopes it would refresh her. Instead, she was horrified with herself. She stared at her arm, where she had the blood samples collected from. She gently pushed down on her skin, testing it, and felt a pain shoot up from the bruise, which hadn't at all healed. The colors were grotesque as they marred her body. She had only bruised like this once before, and that had been when she and Amara had gone head-to-head in training when her system was fighting off the injected cells all those years ago. Still... when Dorian had awakened her from that coma, the bruising had been completely gone as her system had fully healed.

Upon washing and drying off, Gavin had come home and was sitting in the kitchen drinking a cup of coffee. She smiled meekly at him as he glanced her way. "You're looking a little more refreshed. I made extra in case you want some," he offered.

"Thank you." She poured herself a cup and sat across from him. "Another day of not much going on?"

His eyes roamed over her body. She was wearing one of his oversized shirts again. Something she had started doing more often. The larger and more concealing the clothes lately, the better. He knew exactly why she was doing it. He wanted to ask her why she thought he was an idiot and why she was hiding herself from him. He didn't want a fight, and yet her vanity around him scraped at him in ways he couldn't explain. He cleared his throat. "Not much of anything at the moment, minor city repairs which Adam has taken on seeing to."

"Due to the rain?" she asked, knowing well enough but wanted to try to converse a bit with her husband.

"Yeah." Gavin sat back, running his hand through his hair. Why did it feel like there was suddenly a wall between them? "What did you get up to today?"

A strangled chuckle came from her. "You asked that every time you checked in with me today." She shrugged. "Not much, rested, read a book, bathed... you know, all that typical stuff that I pretty much do every day now."

He took a breath. This jaded attitude of hers was getting to him. It was possible that she didn't mean it. "And what would you rather be doing?"

Hokura's mouth set in an annoyed line. "Not dying would be at the top of my list," she snapped back.

The answer shocked him as he dropped his cup, spilling it over the table as Gavin shot up.

Her eyes widened as it happened, standing quickly as well as she stared at him. "Gavin... I didn't mean... I mean..." Her heart was racing. "What else do you want me to say?"

He quickly wrapped his arms around her. He hadn't meant

to upset her. "It was a stupid question for me to ask. I'm sorry. I know you'd rather be doing anything other than this. That you'd rather be working on the higher education project, that you'd rather be watching Cass train or... literally anything." He was an idiot for saying it.

"The coffee..." Hokura struggled in his grips.

"I'll clean it up in a moment. Just let me hold you." His voice was soft. This was tearing him apart as if he didn't know how to act around her anymore. She didn't want him around, and yet he pushed. Of course, she would snap back at such a question. He couldn't blame her. "I'm sorry." He let go of her, grabbed a dishtowel, and mopped the coffee off the table.

After the incident, Hokura had been reserved. She found herself on the couch pretending to read the book she had picked up. She had gone back to her original series and read a few pages in only to grimace and put it back on the table. She had thought about simply reading the last chapter of the last book and being done with it. Maybe she should ask the kids how it ended. Her eyes glanced over the words on the page, not computing or interpreting them. She knew she could get away with this without Gavin interrupting her. She wanted space from him which made her yearn for that night even more.

After the children had come home, she dozed lightly on the couch after dinner. It wasn't until Gavin asked if she wanted to call it a night that she became restless. She tossed and turned, thinking about her note when his voice came up beside her.

"Not able to get comfortable?"

"I spend most of my day sleeping... at least during the day I don't have nightmares. I think I'll take a bit of a walk..."

He wanted to ask if she wanted him to accompany her but knew better.

Hokura sat silently in the garden; it was late, and the compound had been asleep, except for one other person. She couldn't quite understand the loneliness that had come over her or why she had felt like she was in such a state lately. She gave a small sigh as she raked her hands over the grass. The sensation of it against her fingers soothed her as she tried to find some inner peace within the situation. She didn't understand the need to push Gavin away when all he wanted to do was embrace her. He didn't understand... again, it felt like Dorian was the only one who understood her. She noted the sound of light footsteps coming from behind her.

"Not sleeping again?" His voice was husky.

She couldn't help but smirk. "What's sleep these days?"

A wicked smile came to his lips. "Sleep holds a break from the harsh realities and lets us delve into our fantasies."

She turned and looked up at him. His black dress shirt had been partially unbuttoned, allowing the breeze to hit his chest. As much as the night masked him, his blue eyes seemed to pierce through the darkness as they held hers. "You found my note..." Hokura stated.

"I did. You said you were feeling lonely, that you were feeling off about things." Dorian offered her his hand. "I guess you thought a midnight walk through the gardens together would make you feel better? Hopefully, afterward, you'll finally be able to get some rest."

She took his hand and stood. She wrapped her arms around his and enjoyed the warmth of being beside him. Why did this feel so much better? Why was it that he seemed to quiet her demons lately when she was struggling? "All I want is to forget everything. To pretend it never happened."

Dorian cocked an eyebrow at her. "I don't dare to even look into such a thing. Even with all the technology we have these days, altering one's memory would be a dangerous game." He looked down at her. "I can understand that you wish none of it happened. I wish the same, but we can't go back."

"Then again..." Her grip around him tightened. "These feelings, though, they've wrapped themselves around me, and now I can't let them go. No matter how hard I try, they seem to tighten their grips to the point where I feel like my heart is being squeezed." She looked at him in desperation. "But you..."

There was something odd with her tone as she halted. "What about me?" He stopped as she did and turned towards her.

"You've never faltered. You've always remained true to your cause."

His eyes held hers. "*You* are my cause; no matter what else happens, the world could crumble around us, and I would still stand for you."

"But what if...."

"Enough." His voice was stern. "We're not talking about that tonight. This time is for us, not the what-ifs, not for the doubts. You know better than to ever doubt me."

"I do." Her voice was soft. He had yet to fail. She knew he wouldn't fail her, that he would come up with a solution. "Why is it that you're not sleeping? You always ask me, but I rarely ask you." They both continued walking.

He gave a small huff. "You should know better than to ask that. I've been wracking my brains out over the new stem cell project and blood cloning, about the key components I'm missing. Cloning blood but making it stronger is a feat. It's just like my damn arm all over again."

Her hand grasped his left. "But you were successful. You're getting your strength back," she offered.

"Only thanks to you... and what you did... which is something else that has been haunting my sleep per se..."

She looked up at him questioningly.

"Every so often, I get glimpses of what happened, sometimes they come to me as dreams, and I can't exactly decipher whether they're exact flashbacks or not. I've wanted to know, but I've been afraid to ask..." Dorian said. His tone was light. "We promised there would be no more secrets between us."

She tensed. He felt it go all the way up his arm as she did so. Her demeanor changed as it seemed she was holding her breath.

"That right there tells me that there was more to everything. That I crossed lines, that I took something from you that was very precious, and that I can never fix what I've done. Nor can I ask for you to forgive me. I was a monster in that state, and what I did to you was wrong." He lowered his head as they continued to walk. He had hoped he hadn't crossed those lines, that she wouldn't have allowed it... and yet it was true... as she told him before, he had the capabilities of still controlling her, something he never wanted to do again.

"I'll always forgive you. Besides, those lines were only crossed because I allowed it. In fact..." she looked up at the sky, another secret between them. "I couldn't help those feelings myself. I knew what was happening. I could have run, but instead, I made a conscious choice to stay every time." She trembled as she stopped and looked at him. "I'm absolutely guilty of it, Dorian... and I feel guilty for it... but I could never tell Gavin about these feelings, about what happened, or about what I initiated..."

His hand met her chin. "You should have run... but you weren't to blame."

"I was... I stayed, and I enjoyed what was happening, even if it was wrong. That... and there was something else, you never asked about what happened that day. I know that you wanted to know, but I kept quiet about it."

He wanted a straight answer as he brought her face to look at him. "You said no more secrets, no more lies. Tell me, Hokura. What happened that day? I have no memory of it other than a badly written note."

Her bottom lip trembled. "I found you on the roof. You were going to end it. I asked you to take me with you... I would have jumped right after you."

Dorian's eyes widened. "No..." sorrow etched over his face. "I would have never wanted that." He had remembered those suicidal thoughts, hence why he had taken an entire bottle of pills, but that hadn't been enough to take him out.

His hand was still gently holding her chin, but her eyes couldn't meet his. "I needed to lead you away from the ledge and buy some time. You said you never recalled what happened during your blackouts, so I told you I wanted one last kiss, and when our lips met and parted, that's when I ripped the arm off of you."

He took a moment, he saw it wearing on her face, had she enjoyed it? He was sure she now regretted it, regretted all of it. "Gavin doesn't need to know... he doesn't need to know any of this if you so choose. The choice is yours, but know that I will stand in your corner, and I will take the full blame for every-thing that's happened." She was about to protest when he cupped her chin a little tighter as he looked deep into her eyes. "You love him, and I will not allow you to ruin what you have because of what happened."

She forcefully turned away from him. "Why do you always do this? I'm at fault for what I did. I knew it was wrong." Her voice was terse.

A sympathetic look came over Dorian's face. "You did it out of love and out of your natural instincts. Survival of the fittest, you needed me so you could save yourself. Besides, do you want there to be tension between Gavin and yourself? Do you want him to doubt? Does he have reason to doubt now?"

Hokura pursed her lips as she faltered. There was reason to doubt. In her heart, she had loved both of them in two entirely different ways... she needed Dorian in ways she never could with Gavin... "No..."

He wondered if she was telling him the truth or if it was merely to save face. Either way, the lines were drawn. He wouldn't allow any faltering. There were bigger things at hand. "Then trust me. As much as I hate to admit it, as much as it makes me a hypocrite for saying so, sometimes things like this are best left unsaid. You love him... you want to be with him, why complicate things?"

A wiry smirk came to her face. "Because that's what I do, Dorian... that's what I've done since the beginning, and it doesn't seem like I'm living unless things are complicated in one way or another."

"That's not true..."

"Isn't it?" Her voice hitched. "Isn't that the definition of our relationship Dorian? Isn't that how we feel for one another?"

He shook his head. "The definition of our relationship and my feelings are two very different things. How I feel for you isn't complicated at all. In fact, the feelings I have for you are something that I'm absolutely sure about. There's no question to them, no faltering, no denying." He looked at her through the corner of his eyes. "It may be *your* feelings towards *me* that are complicated but not the other way around."

She huffed. "Can I tell you something?"

"You can tell me anything."

A small smile crossed her lips. "I..." Could she dare say it?

He took in her hesitation. "It'll stay between us. You know that."

Hokura licked her lips. She knew better. It was something she thought about often, but whenever she did, it felt like a betrayal, and yet she couldn't help it. "I always wonder... what could have been... and sometimes I can't help but feel that I went off track."

Dorian stopped and stared at her. "Your destiny and your life were not one for me to decide."

"Maybe it should have been!" She brought her arms around herself. "Maybe if it had been, none of this would have happened; I would have stayed safe in the compound; you always loved me, and you would have continued to do so...."

"Don't." His voice held an edge to it as he again hugged her. It then softened. "It's human nature to wonder about how life could have been, but don't start regretting what you have. Gavin loves you. You have two beautiful children. You have so much."

She wondered about what she could have had with Dorian as he held her, the way her heart still beat for him. The way she warmed at his touch and simply wanted to be wrapped in it. She couldn't deny her feelings, which still lingered. How she still thought about the kiss on the rooftop. "I'm just horribly selfish."

"No." His hand came through her hair as he brushed it. "You're human, and you have two people to who you are deeply tied to." He knew there was more to this. Everything for her was so much deeper; it was who she was and how she felt things. It's what made her so intriguing in ways he doubted anyone would understand. "It's getting late, though. You still need your rest." He kissed the top of her head. "We both do."

She looked up at him. "Will you actually sleep tonight?"

He closed his eyes for a moment, enjoying that she was in

his arms as he breathed her in. "I hope so. Are you feeling a little less lonely?"

"With you by my side, I do," she answered, wishing she could merely fall asleep as he held her. Why was it that she always felt so at ease when she was with him? As though she could simply be in his arms and close her eyes and drift. Because he was her protector...

"I'll always be by your side Hokura." His voice was soft in her ear. "But you're already starting to drift. Let's get you up to your suite and back into bed next to Gavin."

Hokura nodded automatically as he shifted, his arm wrapped around her shoulder as he seemed to be leading her back into the compound. She leaned against him. Was it so selfish that she still needed him? That they could never be more but that she couldn't let him go.

"You need your rest. Fatiguing yourself like this isn't going to help your cause," his voice stated from above.

"Yes, professor." The words barely left her lips. She drooped as she felt him stop beside her. "I think I'm finally tired..."

With a gentle and fluid motion, he scooped her up into his arms as she cradled her head against his chest. "I'll carry you back to your suite, but you need to get from your door to your bed." He stared down at her, at her closed eyelids. "To the couch will be a feat enough," he muttered.

"You're the best." A light smile came to her lips.

He had carried her through the compound, gotten her to the elevator, and managed to press the button before getting on. He looked down at her. Was she truly asleep in his arms? Had she exhausted herself that much as they walked? Worry etched over his face as he wondered if he should take her to the medical facility instead. He got off the elevator and walked her to her suite. "Hokura." His voice was a whisper as he tried to stir her... "You're home." She didn't even stir.

The professor huffed slightly as he quietly opened the door to her suite, gently deposited her on the couch, and wrapped a blanket around her. He couldn't just leave her like this as he kneeled beside her and gently lifted her arm, placing his index and middle finger to her wrist, checking her pulse. His attention went to her bedroom as a light turned on, and Gavin exited the room in a daze bringing his hand through his hair.

"What are you doing here?" His voice was heavy with sleep.

"She was up wandering because she couldn't sleep, so we walked the gardens. It seems exhaustion hit her pretty hard, and she ended up asleep. I didn't know whether or not I should bring her here or take her to the medical facility," Dorian confessed, still kneeling beside her.

Gavin walked up to her and bent down. Of course, she went to Dorian... it didn't surprise him, and yet he couldn't fault her either. "She's getting weaker, isn't she?"

The professor shook his head. "I won't make that deduction on her simply falling asleep while she was out. She told me she hasn't been sleeping well lately. This might be her sleep aids finally kicking in and getting the best of her." He stood. He knew it was a lie. "She's breathing normally. Her pulse is regular. I suggest you take her to bed and keep an eye on her tomorrow. I'm sure she'll be tired. If you feel as though something has changed, then please page me, and get her down to the medical facility."

The governor let out a sigh. He bent down and picked her up off the couch. "Thank you for bringing her back. You should get some sleep too. We all need a good rest."

Dorian nodded and made his way to his own suite. Indeed, they all did.

A few hours later, Hokura stirred. She woke up disorientated as she rolled over and realized she was in her own bed.

Gavin had felt her shift and rolled to face her. "Are you alright?" His voice was soft.

"I was in the gardens..." she puzzled for a moment. "I was coming back inside with Dorian. How did I end up here?"

He let out a light breath. "I'm guessing you crashed pretty hard during your walk, so he carried you up here."

"I did..." she confirmed. "The sleep aids must have finally kicked in."

"Is everything okay? Is there anything you need to tell me?"

She shook her head. "No, I'm okay... honestly, it felt good to get out and wander a little bit."

Gavin pursed his lips, *wander*... with the professor no less. Most likely for her to confide in him because it seemed that Dorian was still her anchor. He kept her grounded in ways he couldn't understand. Her husband was sure after their quip this afternoon, she had wanted to see him even more. "The professor suggested that I keep an eye on you tomorrow. If you contest, I can haul him in here, and you can hear it from him."

If Dorian suggested that Gavin keep an eye on her tomorrow, that meant he was worried about her and wanted to have her husband keeping a watchful eye on her. "That's fine. I have a feeling I'll need to catch up on my sleep anyway."

Gavin leaned over and kissed her forehead. "Sleep well, my love."

With that, she gave a small smile... Dorian... she rolled over in her sleep and caught a whiff of his cologne as it wafted from her body. He had brought her up to her suite and had gotten her to bed. The sheets had felt so warm and comfortable against her body.

Dorian... his name played in her mind. In her thoughts as she snuggled deeper. What would life with him have been like? She shifted again, the sheets. They felt different... the scent on them was far too pronounced as she rolled over again into a body. It startled her for a moment as her hands ran over it. It was larger than Gavin's... more defined... her eyes opened.

What on earth was she doing in his bed? She had distinctly recalled being next to Gavin as she slowly got up.

He felt her shift as his eyes opened and stared casually at her. "Can't sleep?" His voice was husky as his arm came forward and wrapped around her, bringing her closer.

"I...I..." she stammered as he let out a low chuckle.

"It was a simple question, don't overthink it."

A dream... but it felt so real to her senses as her fingers traced over his abdomen and her head rested on his chest. "Why would I want to sleep when I'm next to you?" She smiled dreamily.

Dorian raised an eyebrow. "Because it's a necessity that our bodies require rest."

"Are you getting scientific with me, professor?" She rose from her spot and stared at him. The scene was all too familiar from the past. He was just as beautiful in her dreams, except here, he held a serene, sleepy smile. He wasn't exhausting himself in the labs, not harboring regret or any other emotion but his love for her.

He rolled his eyes at her. "I'm with someone that seems to need constant reminders about the basics." He rose beside her as his hand came up and gently caressed her cheek. "Or perhaps you're no longer tired. That's something I can indeed help with."

Hokura felt her body tremble as his lips were on hers. Her mouth opened as her body warmed. His hands caressed her.

He kissed her hungrily. "I'm sure I can rise to the occasion and tire you out," a smirk came to his face. "Or if you wish, I can give you a lesson in anatomy."

"Dorian..."

He was on her, kissing her, touching her in ways that it seemed only he knew how. He was controlling her as she brought her hands through his hair. How was it that even after this long, he was the only one who made her feel this way? She felt as if her body was melting with ecstasy as he drove her further. Even in her dreams, it felt different when she was with him.

She cried his name over and over. She couldn't deny what she was feeling; it had been wrong, but at least here in her subconscious, she could... his words played into her mind "delve into fantasies." That's what this was, so she would delve as deep as she could while she was in the professor's arm, and he was driving her to heights she couldn't explain. "Dorian," she moaned as he rose above her.

"More?" He smirked, looking down at her.

Her eyes were wild. "Show me everything..."

As he came down on her again, her chest tightened. She opened her mouth as a cough erupted from her. Hokura rolled over, trying to gain her breath as she wheezed again, hacking, and fighting for breath.

She awoke to her coughs, gasping as her hand shakily went to the glass on her nightstand.

Gavin had woken and turned on the light as she rolled over and drank greedily. "Are you okay?" His tone sounded desperate as she sputtered into the glass, trying to swallow.

"I'll...be...okay..." Hokura coughed between words. "Just a tickle that led to this." She took a deep breath and slowly exhaled as she tried to control her breathing.

Her husband's hand was on her back, slowly rubbing it, trying to soothe her. "Is there anything I can do?"

Hokura cleared her throat as she took another breath, thankful that the coughing fit had been a small one, that there had been no blood or real cause for concern. "I'm okay." She slipped back down onto the bed, turning to her husband. "Honest Gavin, it wasn't that bad... who knows, maybe I just sucked some air in the wrong way in my sleep." She caught herself. Was it possible she had been moaning in her sleep? Thoughts of the dream assaulted her as she quickly leaned over and kissed her husband sweetly on the cheek. "Goodnight, my love." She brought the blanket back up around her and scowled. She couldn't even escape her illness in her sweetest, most sinful dreams.

Dorian had barely slept the night before. There was too much on his mind to get a peaceful sleep as he tossed and turned. He had been up at the crack of dawn and down to his labs, his mind reeling with the project. He had taken samples of the cloned blood and started running tests on them.

It was mid-morning as the professor paced in frustration. The morning had been filled with setback after setback.

"Dammit, it's like all those years ago!" he seethed. So many lives were lost to the stem cell experiment. They would all be in vain if he couldn't get things figured out with the first child. "Why is this happening again?" he growled as he went over to the microscope, clotting... the cloned blood was clotting. He didn't care. He added a drop of her tainted blood into it. Maybe this would still work. It was instant as the tainted blood attacked everything and killed off everything in the small petri dish.

"Dammit!" Dorian raged as he grabbed the microscope and threw it angrily against the wall. "Dammit!" He winced as it shattered and the blood from the dish splattered. "Shit." He closed his eyes. The last thing he needed was Gavin getting on him about destroying another lab or more equipment. He took a large breath as he stared at the damage he had done to the wall. He could easily cover it up with something. He had been thankful that it hadn't gone through.

At that moment, Spindler popped his head in. "Are you alright? I heard a crash!" His eyes went to the wall and the mess that was now on the floor. He pursed his lips.

Dorian looked up at the man with an annoyed expression. "Shouldn't you be in the labs trying to crack this?"

The doctor sighed. He knew he was walking on thin ice. The professor was obviously agitated and in a mood. He didn't exactly know if he had wanted to tell the professor about the discovery now, considering what he had walked into. "I was actually on my way down here to report. Lucien has been working on her samples. He had been able to unravel things in a way..." He cleared his throat. "What he found... wasn't good."

The professor's eyes widened. "What is it?"

"It's almost the exact opposite to what you had created with the peacekeepers. It's a cell that reproduces and takes over, almost like a parasite in a way, except it's toxic." Spindler couldn't meet his eyes.

Dorian's eyes narrowed. "We have ways of dealing with parasites and toxins." It hit him then. Cells that reproduce in order to kill. It was very possible that her system fought them off for as long as it possibly could before these cells started taking over if it was reproducing, though... From what he had seen, these cells had been incredibly intrusive with their takeover of others. He paled as he looked at Spindler.

The doctor wore a grave look. "It's already damaging her DNA, Dorian. She's going to start shutting down... she already is. We're running out of time."

"We need to suspend it! We need to buy time, doctor!" Dorian urged. "What about antibiotics? Anything?" He was grasping, and he knew it.

Spindler shook his head. "Her organs are already damaged. Any type of harsh medication might cause further damage. If the toxic cells see it as a threat, they may regenerate even faster, which will kill her quicker."

"Chemotherapy? Targeted at the cells?" He knew it wouldn't work. He wanted to hear it from the doctor.

"You know better, Dorian. It's spread throughout her body." He could see the man was desperate. "Lucien is testing to see if these toxins have any type of weakness. We'll keep in touch if we find anything else." He turned. He could see that the professor was falling apart at the seams. The look of loss had spread over his face. "Maybe you should get out of the labs for a bit, spend some time with her. Maybe something will come to your mind once you're away from everything."

"I can't just ignore this. I need to be on top of things. I need to save her," the professor muttered. He closed his eyes and rubbed them. There was a tension mounting in his skull.

"Banging your head off the wall and exhausting yourself

isn't going to help," Spindler said as he turned towards the door. "We have plenty of people on this. Spend some time with her." He knew of the connection the professor had with the first child. Maybe she could calm him down. If she were by his side, he would refrain from doing anything reckless. The doctor walked out of the lab.

"Dammit!" Dorian yelled as his anger surged, causing him to flip his desk. "Dammit!" He tilted his head back. "Get it together, man." He cursed again as he took a deep breath. He had ordered Gavin to stay with her and keep an eye on her. The way he was feeling right now, he'd destroy another lab if he didn't find a way to calm himself. He needed her, but first... he righted the desk and picked up the files and pieces of equipment that had now scattered along the floor. He thought of having maintenance come in. "No... you can clean up your own damn mess, you idiot." He cleaned the blood from the wall and winced at the hole. It was simply aesthetic.

Upon picking up the phone and dialing her suite, Gavin answered as Dorian cleared his throat. "How is she?"

"She had a slight coughing fit last night, but she slept in this morning. We're just having a late breakfast," Gavin said, looking over at Hokura, who was sitting at the table eating contently. "Is there anything I can do for you?"

"There is," the professor admitted. "If you could possibly send her down to my labs after breakfast. There's something I would like to discuss with her."

Gavin could hear the desperation in the man's voice. He wanted to ask if he needed to join but knew better. He had heard that tone before and wondered if maintenance was going to need to be called in before the professor had once again lost his temper. "I'll send her in a bit after breakfast." He stopped for a moment. "Are there going to be any issues?"

Dorian knew what he was asking. "No, there won't be any issues."

With that, Gavin hung up the phone and walked over to his wife. She was looking a little more awake today. There was almost a sense that she was well-rested despite the slight discoloration under her eyes. "Dorian has requested your presence in his lab once you're done."

Hokura gave him a confused look. "More tests?"

"None that he mentioned." He would be truthful with her. "To be honest, I think he may have hit a wall and needs you there to center him."

Her thoughts reeled. There had been times with his bionic arm that he had relied on her, where he had destroyed labs and himself in his madness.

"I should get going then." She rose from the table.

"No," Gavin stated quickly. "He knows you're in the middle of breakfast. He would want you to finish up. He can keep himself together a little bit longer so you can get a full meal in."

She nodded as she sat. She had just seen him the night before. What on earth could have changed so quickly?

<hr />

Hokura knocked on the lab door. Upon hearing his voice, she entered and looked to the side to see a prominent hole in the wall.

"Don't ask," the professor sighed as he sat at his desk.

"I don't need to..." she had seen this before and was impressed his lab hadn't been in shambles. A simple indent in the wall was much better than a chair that had gone *through* the wall and was sitting out in the hallway. "What do you need me to do?"

"Just sit for a few moments..."

She did as he asked and sat across from him, silently waiting for him to address her. She could see something had been wearing on him.

Dorian sat back in defeat; he wanted to break down, but he needed to keep it together for her. He couldn't let her know that he had no clue. That everything had come to a dead-end, and the project he was hoping to start had just died in front of him mere hours before. He needed her to continue to trust him and believe that he would save her. She had been waiting patiently for him to speak when he finally did. "It's been over a century, but I could sure go for a drink."

Hokura raised an eyebrow, not saying anything.

Dorian looked over at her and mustered a smirk. "Interestingly enough, when Meridiana was created, the government decided against continuing production of things such as alcohol. They didn't want to create vices for the new age of man."

She gave a small chuckle. This is what he needed: a distraction. "It's been a long time since I've heard of such things. The rebels tried to make moonshine every so often. James had foraged a few bottles of whiskey from long ago, which he drank every so often." She made a face. "I couldn't understand why anyone would want to drink something that tasted so foul."

The professor took a breath, glad that the conversation was on the lighter side, and that she had picked up on what he needed. Of course, she did. "It all depends on who's drinking it. It's an acquired taste. It's the effects that are desired."

"And you desire its effects right now?"

He did... did he ever. "It loosens one up in a way and gives you a false sense of freedom and confidence, I guess." He shook his head. "I was never one for indulging, but there was one night after I learned that my parent's experiment on me was a success, that the trials were at an end and that I was free, that I may have celebrated a little too hard."

Hokura felt a tug at her lips. "Now, you'll have to indulge me in that story."

Dorian chuckled, happy to do so. This was exactly why he needed her. He could never account such a story to anyone else. "I decided to have a few drinks of some very well-aged whiskey that I had set aside for the occasion. The idea of being my parent's science project really damaged my pride when I had my own works that I had wanted to experiment with. After a few too many drinks, I felt like I was on top of the world. I was free and could create whatever it was I wished. I had all these dreams and aspirations and suddenly the confidence that I was going to save the world. I had never felt as exhilarated as I did that night." He grimaced. "Unfortunately, it was a blur, and I awoke the next morning next to the toilet covered in my own vomit and a ringing headache. It didn't help that my father wasn't exactly pleased with my celebrations and was lecturing me about my poor choices." He hid a smile behind his palm. "Smartest being on the planet and decided to kill my brain cells by overindulging, which made me the biggest idiot alive at that moment. I'll never forget that scolding and what it did to me." He looked up at her. "That was the beginning and the end of my so-called rebellious stage. I nursed a hangover from hell and set to work the day after studying stem cells and regeneration."

"Not much of a story," Hokura mused.

"My life was not one for adventures or much for stories... it was science, tests, experiments, and being an outstanding student." He shrugged.

She could feel his mellowed, somber mood. "Nobody else holds your title. You helped create all this and an advanced version of mankind. Your life surely has some stories, Dorian."

He gave her a look. "Those were more so reserved for when you awakened, and the times spent with you."

"You got to see the ocean when you went back to White Rock with me." She gave him a solemn look. The memory was a double-edged sword for both of them.

He made a face. "Slept miserably in a tent as well... but indeed, the trip was a definite learning experience. Something I could never forget, something that held many firsts for me, such as leaving the walled city since I had come here all those decades ago. In your time here, you seemed to have taught your mentor as many things as I taught you."

A sly smile came to her lips. "Such as teaching you to ride a bike?"

His eyebrows narrowed. "That can be considered one of them. May I remind you that I never had a need to be on a bike, let alone drive one? I'm fine with taking up the role as a peace-keeper and soldier... however, I wasn't exactly ready for the adrenaline rush. Might I remind you that I didn't have the bike crash into the garage wall, unlike the second child."

Hokura let out a cackle. "Her pride that day! If there's one thing I never want her to live down, it was that! Good thing she picked it up quickly." She took a breath. "You did, too."

He gave her a look. "I did. However, I did find it more enjoyable when you were driving, and I was merely along for the ride."

A solemn expression came to her face. "I can't do it anymore...."

"You'll ride again, I promise."

Hokura made a dissatisfied noise. "In a sidecar, if Amara has anything to do with it." She shook her head. "There are more important things to see to right now."

"Indeed." Dorian rose from his seat. "We need to stay positive and move forward in this. We can't let our morale sink."

The words were a lie... his morale was sinking by the day. He had been beyond frustrated that everything he tried led to a dead end. He gave her a look. "How's the painting coming along?"

She gave a wistful look. "It's coming along. It'll be beautiful once it's complete if I can get what I want on the canvas."

"I know you will." He smiled at her. "Thank you for this."

"For what?"

"For this, for coming down and talking to me. I needed to get my mind off things and reset, and that's precisely what happened."

Hokura leaned back in her chair as she brought her feet up under her. "I'm always here for that."

He didn't want her to leave just yet. "I'm glad to hear that you got some decent rest last night. It's most likely not the best idea to go wandering after taking sleep aids, though."

She casually shrugged. "You were there... you took care of me." She thought of the dream as she swore she could feel her cheeks reddening.

Dorian took a deep breath. He couldn't fault her logic. He would always take care of her. "You need to know I'm working on this."

"I know." She did. Why was he telling her this? Perhaps because he had felt guilty for needing a break? For calling her down to make idle chit-chat. Or...

He had studied her from the moment she walked in the door. She was wearing a long-sleeved shirt to hide her bruises, but the effects of what was happening to her were becoming more visible. She had dark smudges under her eyes. Her hair had lost its shine. Even her fingernails looked slightly brittle. Hokura... he needed to figure something out. "I should let you get some more rest. Do you need me to escort you back up to your suite?"

She shook her head. "No, I can make it just fine. If you walk me up, it'll just give Gavin more reason to worry about me." With that said, she shifted from her seat. "I think I'll take out the painting if I have the energy today and put some more time into it."

Dorian watched as she left and sat back in his chair, drumming his fingers against his desk as he mused. She was getting worse, and there was nothing he could do to suspend time in order to figure this out. Time... he had all the time in the world, and yet hers was running out. That's when the idea hit him. He needed a backup plan. As much as the thought made him sick, if something happened, he still had that one option. One he had never wanted to fall back on. He wondered if it was even possible. Then again, it was a bigger possibility than what he was working with now.

He couldn't stop time, but there was a possibility to pause it for her if things came down to that. The thought made him tremble. It could only be done after she was technically clinically dead. He knew there had been chambers collecting dust in the compound, locked away in the lower labs that had been forgotten about over the decades. Why would they have to worry about cryogenics when everyone in the compound was seemingly immortal? The founders had wanted to keep every possible part of scientific technology they could possibly collect in the compound as they scavenged to keep science alive and moving forward, even after the war.

The professor groaned. He didn't want to walk down this path. He didn't even want to consider it but knew he would absolutely hate himself if something were to happen, and he didn't have a backup plan. He had sworn to her he would save her. He shook his head as he exited his lab and started towards the lower level. He didn't even know if the chamber would fire up, let alone be successful in being able to keep a steady temperature. His jaw clenched. What he needed was a system reset on Hokura's cell structure. His mind went in every direction possible. Maybe a full blood transfusion? Again, there was worry. He doubted she would survive such a thing... plus, he had altered the peacekeeper's DNA in ways that didn't exist in any others. They were all unique. It would have to be her blood, which he couldn't seemingly replicate without clots. He made haste from the science facility and towards the hallway, which held the door that looked more like a janitorial closet. He opened it and descended the stairs.

The lower half always seemed dimly lit in comparison to the upper levels of the compound. It was massive in size, with more hallways and board rooms imaginable. Still, there was a large number of people who worked down here. He strode past a few workers who merely nodded at him. Even down here, everyone knew who he was and wouldn't question what he was doing. He walked towards the North-East end, knowing precisely where he was going. It had been decades, if not more, since he had been down this way. In fact, he thought of where he was venturing to as more of a graveyard for medical equipment. Then again, once the fertility rate rose, Olga had sent a team to extract another ultrasound machine, so there were always two going in the civilian hospital.

Dorian reached his destination and opened the door. Plastic tarps laid upon odd-looking shapes as the lights flickered to life. There were extra gurneys and medical beds that were pulled from the civilian hospital long ago as it shrank in size, and the beds were no longer needed. The professor gave a sigh. It was almost disheartening to see all this equipment sitting and doing nothing, but it was a reminder of his achievements and how far they had come. There were dialysis machines, kidney machines, oxygen ventilators... all the basics. He scowled. It could be that the cryogenic chambers were in another room. He sifted through rows of equipment and machines as he tried to think. The chambers had been brought in, but he didn't recall them ever being used. He walked to the furthest corner when something large caught his eye. He walked over to the large piece of machinery and held his breath as he took the plastic from it. Indeed, it had been a chamber. The sight of it had been overwhelming as he started to tremble. "This is the last resort." He reminded himself. "It's always best to have a backup plan. Cryopreservation can work!"

Dorian stepped back for a moment eyeing the piece of machinery. The components for it seemed simple enough. He knew there would be manuals and textbooks located somewhere in the lower part of the compound about this particular piece. It hadn't been something he had studied, although a few decades before the war, the practice of cryopreservation and reanimation had been deemed successful in several cases. He sighed as his body sagged. He had his work cut out for him. Not only with getting the machine out from the basement and onto the main level and into a lab but also studying how this miraculous piece of equipment worked. "Nothing's ever easy," he groaned as he set to work, he could have asked for help, but he didn't exactly want Gavin to know about this plan yet. Guilt flooded over him. It was as if by having this fallback that he already doubted he could save her. No, he would save her, even if it came to this. Even if something happened, he would bring her back. That was the objective. He figured once he cleared a better path for the machine, he would bring it up to the main part of the compound later that evening when no one was around and set up a sectioned lab to have it in, and so the professor started the arduous task.

Upon coming home, Gavin asked how things had gone.

Hokura shrugged. "He merely wanted to clear his head for a bit; sometimes, just talking helps get one's mind off things."

"Do I need to be worried?" He raised an eyebrow.

She shook her head. "No, it seems like things are fine." She gave him a puzzled look. He had changed from his comfortable clothes into a suit. "Did something happen?"

He let out a hard sigh. "I can get Adam on it if need be, but I feel like I need to be there too..." He hung his head in annoyance. "There needs to be some major maintenance done to one of the apartment buildings, one of the older ones... the people on the top floor have been displaced due to leaks and so they'll be going over to another building temporarily until the roof is fixed."

Her brows furrowed as he gave him a look. "Gavin, you're the governor. You need to be there for your people." She smiled at him lightly. "I'm fine, my love."

"I don't want to leave you..." He scowled.

Hokura stood on the tips of her toes and kissed his cheek as she wrapped her arms around him. His arms automatically encircled her.

"I promise I won't be too long."

"And I promise I'll be fine," she stated. "I'll stay in the suite and relax."

The governor begrudgingly winced. He was ready to step down from his mantle and simply be by her side and see her through this. He had felt incredibly guilty about everything that happened, and that guilt only seemed to grow by the day. "I'll try to make this quick," he said again.

Hokura kissed him one last time and ushered him out the door ensuring him that she was going to be perfectly fine, that she would rest and eat when needed.

Upon leaving, her mind started up... she didn't want to be left alone with her thoughts. What on earth could have set Dorian off in such a way? Did he hit a snag in things? She needed to keep her mind off of it. Stay busy... Hokura paced. She looked around the room at the book that sat on the coffee table and grimaced. She didn't want to know the ending anymore. Any ending she came up with was surely better than what had been written. Maybe she would reimagine all of it in her mind: Gale, Peeta. They would all survive. They would all be happy and live happily together. The girl would be able to pick. She wouldn't have to feel trapped in her uncertainty. The capital would fall, and everyone would live equally.

"Maybe I should take up writing," Hokura mused distastefully. She thought about Dorian and the painting and made a weary face. Why was it so difficult to paint for him? She could paint at any time, and yet the emotion behind the painting was so deep. She wished she could simply pour her emotions onto a palette and brush them onto the canvas. She sighed and grabbed the canvas as she stared at it. It was the city at night, the beautiful colors she saw, yet the feeling behind it wasn't quite right yet.

Hokura brought out her tools, set herself up at the window, and started on it. The professor had never viewed it the way she did. To him, it was buildings of bricks and stone. To her, it was alive. It was colors that nobody else could see. It was home. It was a sanctuary that held her heart, her life, and her love. Even when she stared out over the city when she had arrived back so many years ago in the library, and he had approached her, she had been so broken, and yet looking at the city below filled her with hope as the lights bounced off the streets almost like stars that protected the people of Meridiana. "Nobody has ever understood. Maybe with this, you'll be able to." Her voice was soft as she added to her masterpiece. As if she bled into her work of art, it was a piece of her that she had created for him in hopes he could understand her better.

Dorian had told her that sometimes he had trouble doing so. Didn't everyone? Even the other peacekeepers, even her own husband. When she stated the city was beautiful, the professor had told her that it was... "never the city..." He had stared at her that night. She felt his eyes on her, she could almost feel his desperation. She had fallen asleep under the large bay window in the library. He had taken her back to her room and waited for her to awaken the next day. Why did her heart hurt like this? The tears flowed down her cheeks even though she didn't know why she was crying. "You're just like me... can you please understand me?" Could someone just please understand...

Maybe that's why, no matter what, she would always feel what she did for him. Not only because he had created her but because they were cut from the same tapestry. They had been alike, and they had been... the thought never crossed her mind before. The professor had already lived a decent life span when she had awakened, had endured a life before her... had she been his first just as he had been hers? Maybe she hadn't been... the notion hurt more than she expected to, thinking of him ever loving someone else. Maybe she could ask him... but then again, would confirming change anything? What if it hurt even more? She placed the brush down. "You need to stop destroying yourself over your own decisions and life choices already." She scowled at herself. Was she feeling this way because she was possibly at the end of her life, that soon she would no longer be able to make any further choices?

There would be a world without her... and yet she mourned that she would be without those she loved. With Gavin, her children, Dorian, the city...

"That's what this is..." She sniffled to herself as she picked the brush back up. It was what the feeling that the painting had been missing, and so for the rest of the day, Hokura delved into every emotion she had ever felt in the streets of this city, the love, the loss, every drop of pain and happiness. That's what made this place so beautiful, all of them. Yet the emotions as she finished were too much. They overwhelmed her as the truth seemed to sink further into her. She was dying. She was going to be leaving this place and leaving everyone she loved. It was too much as she placed her last brushstroke; the painting was almost finished, but she was bleeding too much to complete it. She needed to be away, where nobody would find her, and so she cleaned up and left to where she could be alone with her bleeding thoughts and misery. Nobody deserved to be around her when she felt like this when all she wanted to do was mourn everyone she would miss.

Dorian had cleared a path for the machine and retired for a bit after checking in with Spindler and Lucien. Still, they hadn't moved forward. Lucien was seeing what he could possibly extract from the cord samples collected over a decade ago from when she had given birth while Spindler was drafting up new avenues. They had both looked exhausted during their meeting. The professor wondered if he should bring up the possibility of using cryogenics. Then again, he knew Lucien and

Spindler would be open about it with Gavin. He didn't think he could trust the governor to go through with it if everything had come down to that. He would be alone with this, so he gathered up all the manuals he could on the chamber and sat in his suite reading them over.

He rubbed his eyes. The machine would have to be set at a bone-chilling -320F. He wondered exactly how much power it would need to have continuously flowing to it to keep it at such a temperature. He would also need to fill the chamber with cryoprotectant to ensure there was no damage done to her as the freezing process occurred. If not done properly, he would risk this procedure being all for nothing. This practice had been viewed as "quackery" centuries ago, but well before the Great War, it had been perfected. Still, the professor had never taken an interest in the theories. The idea of her being suspended in death sent chills down Dorian's spine. She would forever be moments after death. He would make sure her body didn't deteriorate any further. In this time, he would be able to figure this out. He would be able to bring her body from the chamber, cure her, and bring her back.

He winced as he read over the documentation. It seemed to be a meticulous procedure of making sure ice crystals didn't form, but once the first stage was completed and the body was frozen, that was all there was to it. He scanned over the large sets of documents of bringing a body out of the cryogenic state... "I'll worry about that later," he muttered to himself as he rubbed his forehead. Once she was cryogenically suspended, he had all the time in the world. Dorian grimaced. That wasn't the point of this. He wanted to be successful in finding a cure *now*, not once she was dead. The word hung in his mind. It was thick and ugly and full of failure.

Gavin had come home to an empty suite. He had puzzled over it as at least Hokura should have been there. He was exhausted after meeting with the city's civilians and setting up a slow move to a new apartment building. Adam had worked diligently beside him and even called in Amara to help with moving everyone. She had been incredibly helpful. He could see the questions wearing on her, and yet she failed to bring up the first child. Gavin's mind had been on Hokura ever since he left her. Coming home without her being there had thrown him off.

He was about to go looking for her when Cassandra walked in the door and greeted him. "By the way, Mom's in the library." Her voice was light. "She said she would be a few minutes."

Gavin nodded. At least he didn't have to seek her out. "How was training today?"

"Good." Cass smiled at him. "Talon's been running more accuracy drills with me. I've been loving the circuit workouts."

"And lessons?" Her father raised an eyebrow. "Any issues with classmates?"

She knew precisely what he was getting at. "No issues. Becca won't even look at me anymore, which is a relief. She's been leaving Cyrus, Nathan, and I alone."

At least that was some good news.

Cyrus came through the door a moment later. He caught the look his father gave. "Mom will be on her way in a bit. She's looking at art books."

"I'm sorry." Gavin withered. "Good day in the labs?"

The boy shrugged. "This rain seemed to be causing some issues. Have you come across any?"

"Yeah, there's been some issues with roofs leaking in the city. We haven't come across any issues in the compound as far as I know of... and if there has been, then they haven't been brought to my attention." He wondered if Adam had overseen anything, knowing that Gavin had been stressed enough with what was happening to Hokura. "What have you come across?"

Cyrus shrugged. "Just erosion issues, the plants have gotten used to their environment, and now it's been changed, so we've noticed that some crops have been having issues. Nothing huge. The botanists are on top of it. Just trying to balance things out."

Hokura walked through the door as everyone turned and stared at her. She felt incredibly subconscious with all eyes on her. "Sorry," she wilted. "I wanted to spend some time looking at art. I guess I got lost in immersing myself in all the old-world artists."

Gavin smiled widely at her. "It's okay." He kissed her, taking the stack of books from her arms. "I was worried."

She grimaced. Being away from him caused him such worry when before, he didn't even bat an eye at it. She could come and go as she pleased without so much as Gavin raising an eyebrow at her. Now it seemed like he had wanted to have her under constant surveillance. "We have so many beautiful books filled with artwork from hundreds of years ago... artists that I've never even heard of." She was hoping to lighten the mood. "There was one named Vincent Van Goh. He lived all the way back in the 1800s!" She saw that she was losing them. "Even after he died, they had museums dedicated to his artworks. They were absolutely beautiful; his style was so unique!"

Her husband gave her a look. "I'm so glad you were able to

spend your afternoon doing something enjoyable. I know how much you love art."

Cassandra gave an automatic nod, another thing she never understood about her mother. She had such a talent for art and a passion for learning about it. The girl had dabbled in sketching a few times but became quickly disheartened when she couldn't come close to replicating what her mother did. It was as if she could have a picture in her mind and easily bring it to life on a piece of paper or canvas. The girl envied her mother with how she was able to reproduce such beautiful images.

Gavin smiled at her lovingly. "How about we all have a restful evening, and I can phone down for dinner. We can pick at whatever we want, and you can go through your books and relax?" All he wanted to do was simply appease her.

Cyrus gave her a boyish grin. "Maybe we can all look through what you have."

Hokura knew what they were doing. She would allow it. "I'm sure that would be nice. Maybe you two might learn a thing or two about old-world art."

<hr>

The evening had been a casual one as everyone had their fill of dinner. Cass and Cyrus had entertained their mother by looking through the books and asking about the infamous painter. Hokura had begun to tire and had gone for a shower as they had retired to do their own thing. The phone had rung later that night as Gavin picked it up. It had been Adam.

"Everyone has been successfully moved to their new apartment block. Maintenance will start first thing tomorrow morning, and I have a few teams inspecting the other roofs of the city to make sure we're not overlooking anything," Adam said.

"Thank you, it's appreciated." The governor sighed. "I know I've been..."

"You've been busy. It's understandable. There hasn't been anything that's come up that's beyond me. IF there's ever anything that needs your direct attention, I'll bring it up."

Gavin wondered if there had been anything come up that Adam oversaw. Perhaps there were repairs that needed to be done to the compound that his right-hand man had simply signed off on. "Thanks..."

Adam cleared his throat. "Amara was wondering if Hokura was around if she could speak to her."

"I'll check..." Gavin looked over at her and covered the phone. "Amara was wondering if you can talk."

Hokura shrank into the couch with her book. "Tell her I'll call her tomorrow or something..." She didn't feel like being overly sociable. The other day had been enough. The morning with Dorian and painting had left her feeling emotionally raw. Beyond that, she had put on a brave face for her children, and that alone seemed to have drained her for the evening.

Gavin relayed the message.

"Fair enough." Adam sighed. "Maybe in the next day or so, just let her know we're worried about her."

The governor nodded and bid Adam a goodnight. He turned to his wife and took her in. "You've been quiet since the children turned in. Is there anything on your mind?"

She didn't want to talk to him about how she was feeling. He wouldn't understand anyway. Nobody would understand this loneliness that seemed to be taking over her. As much as she could fight it, she didn't. She knew she had people around her who loved her, that she wasn't at all alone in this, and yet... being alone almost felt better. "I'm fine, just lost in my own little world," she lied.

"Don't get too lost." He gave her a solemn look. He didn't

want her to feel as though she was alone in this, and yet it seemed the more he tried to push to be by her side, the more she pushed back and distanced herself.

✦

That night Hokura tossed and turned in her sleep. The nightmares had assaulted her violently until she could take it no more as she put on a robe and tiptoed out of the bedroom, being careful not to wake Gavin. By this time, her nighttime wanderings had become a thing again. He would know exactly what was up if he awoke without her there.

She strode down the hallway and peered under Dorian's suite door. The lights hadn't been on, which meant he was sleeping, or he was working tirelessly. She didn't want to disturb him. This was something she wanted to be alone for. She yearned to sit by the blueberry bush... to brood... to cry... to do whatever it was that she needed. After taking the elevator downstairs and walking through the compound, she idly hoped the professor had found some time to rest.

Upon coming to the garden, Hokura went straight to the plaque. She silently ran her fingers over it and took a breath... "my love... did you know when your time was up, or did it just happen?" He hadn't said anything the night before he never woke again. She had remembered it so vividly. She had kissed him goodnight and asked him to simply hold her in his strong arms... his arms which had grown frail over the years but still had a decent amount of bulk and muscle to them. The arms that swore to always protect her even though she was stronger than him. Hokura remembered every line on his face, his rough stubble, which had peppered over the years along with his long hair. His image would forever be etched into her memory.

"James..." Her leg felt weak as she sat on the grass and brought her hands through the dirt beneath the bush. "I can't tell the others... but I'm scared." She simply wanted to sit and be close to the plaque since it was the closest she felt she would ever be to him again.

It was late. As the rest of the compound slept, Dorian had made his way back to the lower level. He had successfully cleared a path for the chamber out of the room it had been stored in. He silently moved it from the room to the large service elevator towards the west end of the compound. He was thankful the vat had been one of the newest designs, so it wasn't overly bulky. Moving it had been a one-man job as he rolled it into the elevator and gave a sigh. It would bring him to the hospital part of the compound. From there, he would need to get it to one of his labs. He figured it would be best suited to be in the one by his office. If need be and things came down to this, he could quarter off a section of laboratories easily enough to work on this. Again, something he didn't want to think about. Getting the chamber to a room was going to be the easy part. He then needed to fill it with the fluid and set the temperature appropriately. It would take a few days for it to properly regulate.

The doors opened as Dorian pressed the locking button to the elevator as he maneuvered the chamber. He would need to make a second trip to retrieve the fluids which had been stored downstairs as well. Once he finally got the device into the hall, he started his way down towards the science labs. He wondered exactly how he was going to power such a piece of equipment, surely for the first few days, it would need to harness a decent amount of power to accelerate the cooling system. He needed

MALFUNCTION

the vat to get to at least -150 degrees Celsius. The sooner he could do so, the better. The last thing he wanted was to have something happen and not be ready for this process. Again, the thoughts assaulted him. As if bringing this machine up and putting it into play meant he was already expecting to fail.

"No," he seethed as he continued down the hallway. "This is the right thing to do. This doesn't mean failure." He knew he was lying to himself. Hokura would have to be medically dead before being immersed into the chamber. However, it would buy him precious time if he still hadn't been able to figure out what was wrong with her system. She would be suspended for as long as he needed to save her, only minutes after death. It panged him in ways he couldn't understand as he opened up his laboratory door and huffed. He would need to shuffle things around. The chamber needed to be along the back wall where he could power it up. He mentally kicked himself. He should have already seen to this during the day but had busied himself with everything else that was happening. At least this was something to occupy him physically. He cleared the lab and rolled the chamber in, tucking it in the back. He had hoped he never had to use it, that he could cure her and simply forget that the idea of cryogenically suspending her ever existed.

If only things could go back to normal. He was tired, and to think only a few months ago, he and Hokura were talking about the higher education project. They had secured a potential classroom and started making a list of courses... and then everything fell to shit. He would give anything to have those light conversations again, to have her healthy and working by his side again. He growled. The rage would forever simmer under the surface, the anger of allowing Tobias to live, that he had let the man go when he had known better. Under any other circumstance, he would have at least broken the man's hand after seeing him touch her the way he had that night in the library.

He should have ripped Gavin from his bed that night and had Tobias confess everything to the governor. Dorian shook his head. It hadn't happened; as much as he could regret it, there was nothing more he could do about the past. She had suffered because of their neglect, and now...

Dorian tilted his head back and rolled his shoulders. He would need to get a dolly in the lower part of the compound to get the boxes of fluid to the lab. It was going to be a long and tedious night, and he wanted to get this done now. He *needed* to get it done now. He didn't know how much time Hokura had left. "Don't think about it," the professor sneered to himself. All he needed to think about was the task at hand and getting it done and set up. Once he was done, he would grab a few hours of sleep before finding himself back in the medical facility the following morning. He needed to keep going. Her future depended on it.

<hr />

Hokura had woken up feeling groggier than usual. Had the walk to the garden the night before truly exhausted her that much? She puzzled over it. Over the days, which seemed to become a blur as she raised an eyebrow. Gavin wasn't next to her, most likely already at work. That's when the aroma of food wafted into her bedroom and hit her. It smelled delicious as her stomach growled. Staring at the clock again, she tried to piece things together as she finally moved from the bed to find Cassandra in the kitchen. She gave her daughter a puzzled look. "Aren't you supposed to be at lessons?"

The girl gave her mother an odd look. "It's a rest day... Dad had to go check in with some things, though, in the city. Cyrus is off in the labs..."

"You're not training?" Hokura asked, walking into the kitchen, her stomach panging at the smell.

Cassandra smiled slightly. "I thought this would be a good opportunity to spend some time with you." She poured some coffee and handed the cup to her mother, who had sat beside the bay window. "I told Talon I would be in this afternoon." She sat across from her mother. "Breakfast will be ready in a few minutes." She eyed her, her tired eyes, which seemed to have lost their shine. Her body seemed to be getting frailer by the day. "Mom... what's happening to you?"

Hokura tried hard to swallow. This wasn't the conversation she wanted to have this morning. Her mind was still foggy as she worked through the details about the night before. She had been restless again; it seemed like the dreams never stopped. She eyed her fingernails. They had dirt under them, which told her she had indeed been at the blueberry bush, that part in the night hadn't been a dream, and yet she swore that she had spoken to her long-lost love as well. All rationale told her that she had found her way back to bed and had dreamt of him afterward. Her thoughts were still muddled.

"Mom?" Cassandra's voice interrupted her thoughts as Hokura looked up at her. "You're not saying something, but obviously, something is going on with you!"

She shook her head. "I'm sick, Cass..." Her words were barely audible as she solemnly looked down at her coffee. "I didn't want to say anything because Dorian's working on a cure."

Panic flooded the girl's expression. "What do you mean you're sick?" she cried as she rose from her seat and threw her arms around her mother.

Hokura closed her eyes and embraced her daughter as she squeezed her. "It's okay... I didn't say anything because I didn't want to worry you or your brother. It'll all be okay, I promise." She tried to comfort her.

"What's happening to you? I didn't want to say anything, but you look like you did when we first rescued you..." Cass's voice was a whisper as she grasped her mother. She didn't understand the fear that was creeping over her. Dorian was working on a cure... that meant that he knew... she remembered their conversation. When the time was right... this is what he had meant.

"It's okay." Hokura stroked Cassandra's hair. "There's something wrong with my cells. I was injected with something, and it's been slowly eating away at my system. It's been a gradual slide, but..."

The girl bristled. "Why didn't you say anything? Has it been this *whole* time?"

Hokura sat back, her arms coming from Cassandra as she held her daughter at arm's length. "You're going to burn break-fast. Finish up what you're doing, and we'll have a talk about this like adults."

"Adults?" Cassandra fired back. "I'm thirteen! I'm not an adult at all!"

Her mother spoke firmly. "No, you're not, but you've matured enough to take things into your own hands and have made adult decisions. You asked an adult question, and so you'll get the adult answer." She raised an eyebrow. "Or are you not ready for such a thing?"

Cass took a deep breath.

"You didn't know what you were getting into when you got into the back of that cargo van and ventured out with Dorian. You didn't know what you were getting into when he taught you to shoot, nor did you know what you were getting into when you pulled the trigger. Are you sure you're ready for the answer, Cassandra? If I tell you the truth, are you sure you can handle it?" Hokura's words were firm.

Her daughter's eyes narrowed. "I knew I was getting into a rescue mission, and I was prepared to take on anything that came from it."

A smile came to Hokura's lips as a small chuckle escaped her. "That's because of who and what you are. You're indeed mature enough to know the truth." She rose from her chair. "Don't burn breakfast." She walked towards the stove and flipped the potato cubes.

Cassandra grabbed the bacon and the waffles and plated them, silently waiting for her mother to continue. It wasn't until they were both back at the table that Hokura steepled her fingers and gave her a knowing look.

"Are you ready to continue? I won't sugarcoat it if you can handle the truth, Cassandra."

The girl nodded.

"Whatever is happening to my system, it's killing it. I'm no longer a peacekeeper. My cells are no longer regenerating. My organs are starting to fail... I'm slowly dying." Her eyes held her daughter's. "Dorian is going to save me."

Cassandra's eyes widened as she swallowed hard. She didn't know what to say. "Of course he's going to save you!" she stated desperately.

"And that's why I kept quiet. As I said, I didn't want you or your brother to worry about me. I know what it looks like right now, but you need to put your faith in the professor. He's working every day and night on trying to crack whatever is happening to me. He won't fail me."

Her brows furrowed. She was too young to lose her mother. Nobody in the city or compound aged or died or ever had to deal with illnesses. "This isn't fair!" she stated.

Hokura licked her lips as she took a bite of her breakfast.

"Life isn't always fair, my child. It's an important lesson to learn."

"One that you learned many times," she countered. "That's why I wanted to know more about you, Mom: That's why I wanted to find out about your past. Dorian told me about it partially, that you ran away from the compound, that you spent forty years away from this place, that you loved the rebel commander and witnessed so much while you were out on your own. That it's something that'll always be there, and I want to know all about it."

Hokura didn't want to have that talk. She was still exhausted from the night before. She hadn't readied herself for disclosing the truth to her children. "That's a conversation for another day, Cassandra, but I promise we'll have it eventually. I promise I'll answer every question you have about my past honestly when the time is right." She stretched tiredly. "But right now, I'm just so tired..."

Cassandra couldn't help but feel slightly guilty about how things had gone. "I'm sorry... I knew something was up, and I bombarded and cornered you like this..."

Hokura shrugged as she continued eating. "I guess it was going to come out eventually. It isn't exactly something I can keep hiding. I'll tell your brother this evening... we can have a family sit down if need be..." She wasn't exactly looking forward to broaching the subject with Cyrus.

The girl sighed. "I didn't mean to cause more trouble..."

A hand came across the table and squeezed hers as Hokura gave her a gentle look. "You're not causing trouble, Cass. If anything, I just simply wanted to avoid talking about it. It isn't an easy subject for me to talk about. I don't want anyone to worry about me." Her eyes held her daughters. "Dorian created me. He'll be able to figure this out. It might take some time, I might get worse, but he *will* come up with something, and that's something you need to remember."

The girl nodded as she quietly continued her breakfast. She would forewarn her brother about this. "You're looking tired... how about you finish up, and I can clean up everything," she offered.

Hokura gave an exhausted smile. "I would appreciate that very much. I couldn't sleep last night, so I went for a walk in the gardens. Apparently, I overdid it." She tried to stifle a yawn. "Thank you for breakfast; it was delicious. I promise we'll have that talk eventually." With that, Hokura stiffly got up and made her way back to the bedroom. She was no longer hungry, but her body felt like lead as she moved. She just wanted to get herself back into bed and sleep until she was content.

As she hit the mattress and pulled the covers over herself, her thoughts roamed. *Dorian... how are things coming along? Are you moving forward?* She grimaced. She didn't want to tell Cyrus about what was happening. She didn't want to have another conversation about her well-being. This was all too much for her; she just wanted to sleep... and wished this was all a bad dream.

Cassandra found herself outside of the science facility. She wasn't exactly sure where her brother was stationed or where he would even be as she wandered. She stopped and sighed as she heard a familiar pair of footsteps approach her. She turned to see the professor giving her a tired look.

"Cassandra, what brings you down here?" he asked listlessly.

The girl licked her lips. "She told me... she told me she was dying." Suddenly her eyes couldn't meet his as she stared at the ground. "And that you were working on a way to save her."

The professor took a breath as his hand met her shoulder. "I am doing everything that I possibly can to save her."

"You didn't tell me," she continued. Why had it suddenly felt like a betrayal? He had known, and yet he had said nothing to her.

"It wasn't my place to tell you..."

Cassandra scowled angrily. "You told me other things... you told me about her past! You said yourself there were things you shouldn't have said about her, and yet you didn't tell me this!" Where was this anger coming from? "I thought we were friends!" she yelled.

He moved quickly and brought his hands to her shoulders as he bent down and faced her. "Yes, and my loyalties to your mother will still outweigh my loyalties to you any day of the week, Cassandra!" His voice was stern until it softened. "But for what it's worth, now that you know, I will answer any questions you might have."

Something inside of her broke as the tears welled in her eyes and spilled over as she grabbed onto him, clutching his black coat. "I'm so scared of what's happening to her! I knew she wasn't okay... she's just getting worse!"

Dorian took a deep breath as he comforted her. Why did it seem like he was doing this more often lately? He wasn't an empathetic being at all, yet it always seemed those attached to Hokura could bring such emotions out of him. "Cass," he coaxed the crying child. "Don't doubt for a minute that I won't save her. I promise you I will." More promises that he couldn't keep, and yet promises that he had damn well *better* keep. His mind drifted back to the chamber that had been cooling in his marked-off laboratory. The secret he felt he couldn't reveal to anyone.

"I was coming down here to warn Cyrus... to give him a heads up... she told me this morning," she sniffled. "Actually, I think I forced it out of her. She didn't want to tell me."

He pursed his lips as he rubbed Cassandra's back. Oh, Hokura, he couldn't imagine the grief she had to endure telling her children such a thing. He could understand why she had wanted to hold out for as long as she had. To have to tell someone you loved such a thing. He closed his eyes. "It'll be okay." His words were soothing. "Do you want me to come with you to find Cyrus?"

Cassandra came away from him, wiping her eyes, and nodded as she grabbed onto his arm.

It was a kindness, the least he could do for all of them. Hokura had endured all this while waiting for him to become whole again as he had struggled with cloning his arm. He would go with Cassandra and find her brother and explain the situation to him. "I believe I know where Cyrus is..."

The professor had led her to the Ecco greenhouse and down towards where the botanists were working. The scientists all stopped and paid him mind the moment he walked in with the girl. "I'm looking for Cyrus," Dorian stated as the scientists then quickly hustled to fetch the boy.

"You're known everywhere..." Cassandra whispered as she watched everyone and how they had quickly come to the professor's attention.

"Yes, I am." He folded his arms and waited briefly as a scientist hurried their way with Cyrus in tow.

The boy gave them a questioning look. "Cass? Professor? What are you two doing here?"

Dorian cleared his throat. "There is something that you need to be aware of... let's go someplace private to talk..."

Cyrus sat in Dorian's office with Cassandra next to him... he had been perplexed about what he had just heard as he shook his head. "I guess it makes sense..." His eyes went up towards the professor, the father of science, the man who was his idol. "That's why she hasn't been healing, why she's been getting weaker. If her cells aren't regenerating..." Desperation flooded him. "Is she aging?"

Dorian winced as he sat across from them. "No, not aging in a typical sense from what I've seen. However, her system is weakening at an alarming rate, and it seems that things are progressing faster now."

The boy hung his head as he stifled a sob. "Mom... what's going to become of her?"

"Cyrus." The professor's voice was commanding. "I have told Cassandra the same thing that I am going to tell you. We are working on this. We will save her. I will not have you two grow up without a mother." Dammit, why couldn't he just keep his mouth shut? Maybe it's because the more people he promised this to, the more pressure there was to not fail at this.

Cassandra placed a hand on her brother's and squeezed it. "We have to be strong, Cy, for Mom *and* Dad."

Dorian's brows furrowed. "How *has* your father been fairing?"

The girl chewed on her bottom lip. She had noticed the shift in her father as well but was unsure exactly what it was. "He's been off. I guess he didn't know about this from the start either..." she clammed up. "Everything has been so strange ever since..."

Dorian's eyes came up and held hers. "How have you been

since then, Cassandra? I know you dropped your therapy sessions, but maybe this is the perfect time to go back and have someone to talk to."

She pouted as she looked towards her brother and then back to the professor. "Can't I just talk to you? I know you're busy... but still..."

A small smile came to his lips. "I've been very busy lately, but if you want to talk and can track me down, we can always do so, although, mind you, I may not be the best person for the job. I don't exactly have my Ph.D. in being a psychiatrist."

"But you were there!" she countered. "Don't you ever feel like you need to talk to someone about it?"

Cyrus gave his sister a look.

Dorian straightened. "I have the genetics of a super soldier, I am usually one of sound mind, and I went into the situation knowing full well that I would do whatever it took to get her out. There was no hesitation when it came to the reality of things. I knew of the outside world, Cassandra. I have lived a long life and have seen the ugliness of mankind. You, on the other hand, had not. Besides, with this all coming up now with your mother, it might help you process things." His eyes went to Cyrus. "Both of you."

Cyrus swallowed hard as he slightly shrank in his chair. He wasn't one for talking about his feelings to anyone other than his sister. He was more reserved, whereas she seemed to share her business with everyone and anyone. "Thank you for the suggestion, sir."

Cassandra was still sitting with a melancholic look on her face as she stewed over things. "Are you close to finding a cure for her?"

It was a fair question, and yet the professor felt like answering it honestly would plant the seed of doubt. "We're going through a number of different avenues to ensure that we figure something out. Dr. Spindler and Lucien are working on this as well. I'm sure we'll have something to work with soon enough."

The girl noticed how he dodged the straightforward answer. He obviously didn't have anything as of yet, so why not just say it? Because he didn't want to let her down, she had guessed she could understand and didn't want her to start worrying. "Thank you for doing this with me, Dorian..."

Cyrus sat silently beside her, still processing the news. Still not knowing exactly what to think. His mother had been so much to him. It was odd having the professor break the news to him, so he merely nodded.

The professor had hoped this had lessened the blow, that it would be easier on Hokura having to tell her son the news as well. He had given them the scientific deductions but had also offered them both some hope. That he wasn't going to allow a bleak future without their mother fall upon them without a fight. "I hope I've cleared some things up for the both of you. If you have any further questions or want to talk, you can seek me out, but for today I should really get back to the labs." His eyes went up to Cassandra.

She nodded. "Thanks again..." With that, she rose from her chair, Cyrus following in her wake as she left the office.

Dorian took a deep breath and exhaled slowly as he rubbed his temples. He was making promises he might not be able to keep. He shook his head. No, even if it came down to not being able to save her, he still had the chamber. There was a backup plan, and as much as he didn't want to use it, he had it in place for a reason. He rubbed his forehead. He needed to check in with it and make sure it was regulating, and then he was going to check in with Spindler and Lucien. "Hokura, I hope I made things a little easier on you..."

Cassandra walked through the hallways with her brother beside her. "You're quiet," she stated, glancing over at him. She had been worried about how he took the news. There had been no tears, no outburst, no nothing. It was as if he was taking in word and calculating its worth.

"Just processing, I guess." Cyrus's voice was low. "I..." He didn't want to admit it. "I had a feeling something was happening with her, that she wasn't getting better." He put his hands awkwardly in his pockets. "The bruises, how she's resting or sleeping all the time... I figured she wasn't getting any better."

Her brows furrowed. "And you didn't say anything?"

He shrugged. "I was hoping that I was wrong."

Cassandra stepped in front of her brother and abruptly stopped. "You know you can tell me these things, Cyrus! You can tell me *anything!*"

The boy pursed his lips, still not knowing how to feel about things. "How about you and I go for a walk... just hang out for a while before heading up to our suite... unless..." He didn't exactly want to be alone at the moment. He wanted to have Cassandra beside him. He gave her a solemn look. "Do you have training today?"

She hugged him. "No, you idiot, I don't. I wouldn't just leave you like this and go to training... come on, let's get some fresh air."

Amara was sitting in the gardens watching Ryan play when she spotted the two. She raised an eyebrow as she let out a shrilled whistle catching their attention. Cassandra and Cyrus walked up towards her. "It's been a while." Amara smiled at them but took in their solemn mood. "And something has come up..."

Cassandra chewed her bottom lip. "Mom told me everything this morning."

"Ah." Amara nodded. "Yeah..." She rubbed the back of her head. "She didn't want anyone to know. She's been keeping quiet about this for some time. I found out not that long ago, too..." Why did this feel so awkward? "You two seem to be taking the news better than I did."

Cassandra's eyebrows rose. "Why, what did you do?" She knew Amara's temper was explosive.

The peacekeeper chuckled. "I blew up. I screamed, I swore, I went down to the training facility and beat a punching bag until the professor found me..." she shrugged. "Then I yelled and screamed and swore a bit more." She recalled how he had come to calm her down, how she yelled at him and fell crying into his arms. "Not one of my finest moments." She looked at Cyrus and couldn't help but feel her heart break for the kid. "Hey, she's gonna be okay... Dorian's on this."

He nodded quietly.

His sister put a reassuring hand on his shoulder. "Dorian actually just helped me let him in with what was happening... she told me this morning, but I wanted to give Cy the heads up."

A half-smirk came to Amara's face. "Always the professor to the rescue, hmmm?" She looked upwards to the sky. She didn't want to face them. "He cares for all of us. He wants what's best for you all... I'm sure his explanation was helpful. That he was trying to lighten the blow and offer you guys some comfort." An airy breath escaped her. "Father of science..."

Cassandra nodded. "More like the father of the compound some days." She wondered if he had ever wanted children of his own. He seemed like he would have been a decent biological father if it ever happened. Then again, he had only loved their mother, and that relationship obviously never happened.

Cyrus cleared his throat. "For what it's worth, I'm glad you gave me a heads up and that he took us to his office to talk to us. He looked towards the blueberry bush. "How about we grab a small bucket and bring some berries back for Mom I know she doesn't like the idea of picking flowers, but she's fine with the berries."

Amara smiled and nodded. "I know your mom would love that." She made a mental note. She would call Hokura later that evening and see how she was fairing. Maybe she would be feeling a little more social and be up for getting together.

———————— ✦ ————————

Gavin had come home to see Hokura sitting beside the bay window, sipping at a glass of orange juice.

"I'm sorry I was gone for so long..." He loosened his tie. "I couldn't just let Adam deal with everything, and there were things that I needed to be there to oversee."

"That's fine," Hokura said, not turning to him as she took another sip of juice. After falling asleep, she had endured another coughing fit. She had been relieved that Cassandra had already left. Her heart ached. "I told Cass."

Gavin walked up to her quickly. "You didn't have to do that alone. I could have been here when you told the kids..." He bent over and hugged her from behind.

She leaned her head against his and brushed his hair with her fingertips. "You know our daughter and how she is about things. She pushed for the truth, so I gave her the truth." She shook her head. "I was so exhausted that it just came out. She seemed to take it well... I went for a nap afterward, and she was gone."

"I'm so sorry." Her husband's voice was a soft whisper. "We can talk to them later tonight if need be."

Hokura licked her lips as she took a breath. "I haven't told Cyrus... he doesn't know yet. I'm sure Cass went to training to work off some steam, but he's still been left in the dark. I feel so guilty."

"We can tell him together. We can sit everyone down together and have a family talk once they all get home." Gavin kissed her cheek. "We can have a nice easy afternoon and day and try to keep things light afterward. We can grab some finger foods from the cafeteria and play some board games if you wish."

She had felt tired. If anything, she wanted to avoid everyone and simply sleep the day away in the comfortable darkness of her bedroom. That's what she had initially wanted. Now it didn't seem like that was going to happen.

He caught the way her body wilted. "How about for now you get some rest? If you wish, you can nap on the couch, and I can wake you when they come home?"

Finally, she nodded. "I'd like that."

Hokura awoke to hear the front door opening as Hokura sat up from the couch to see both Cassandra and Cyrus walking in. Her eyes went directly to her son. "Cyrus, we need to have a talk, my love..."

The boy gave her a weak smile. He kicked off his shoes and

was quickly across the room, hugging his mother on the couch. "Mom... it's okay... you don't have to worry about telling me. Cass and the professor filled me in." He squeezed her. "The professor said he was working on this and that everything will be okay."

Gavin, who had been sitting in the chair next to the couch, rose with a questioning glance. He looked over to Cassandra, who was slowly making her way to the sitting area.

The girl made a face. "I had to warn him... can you really blame me?"

Hokura shifted as Cyrus's arms were still tightly locked around her. "You warned him by going to Dorian? Let me guess. He pretty much explained everything to the both of you?" She shook her head. It was most likely that Cass had gone in search of her brother in the labs and had run across Dorian. Being who he is, he most likely knew exactly where Cyrus was and extracted him from what he was doing to sit down and have the talk.

Cyrus loosened his grip. "Don't blame her or the professor, Mom It was easier coming from them than coming from you.'

Her son... she could understand his complex emotions, how he tried to keep things together, how this may have lessened the blow to him to hear it from his twin sister and the superior who was looking after their mother's health. She silently thanked Dorian for what he had done. "Is there anything else you two need to know?"

Cyrus shook his head. "Just that you'll be okay." His voice was soft as his mother tousled his hair.

Hokura gave a small smile. She couldn't guarantee such a thing since she knew her health was slowly declining. She was tired, so incredibly tired since everything had happened. "I promise," she lied. She wanted to tell them if there was anything they needed to talk about to come to her, but there were conversations with Cassandra that she wasn't ready to have. As much as the girl had learned about her past, there were parts that even Dorian didn't know about. Her interest piqued. "Dorian assured you both that I was going to be okay…"

Cassandra nodded. "He did."

Gavin smiled slightly. He was grateful that the professor had stepped up and explained things to them. He and Cassandra had created an interesting bond over the past few months. As much as she trained with Talon, Dorian oversaw her progress. He sent down reports to the watch commander on what training and exercises she should be doing. Gavin wondered if it had been because Cassandra had been a carbon copy of her mother or if Dorian had felt guilty for what she had endured during her mother's rescue.

The afternoon broke into evening. The mood had been kept light as they had played some games and shared some laughs. Dinner had been spent in the family room as they quietly conversed. Hokura told a few old stories about being a peacekeeper and training with the others.

"The look on her face was priceless," Hokura laughed. "Her bike literally sailed across the garage and into the closed garage door! Talon was ready to have an absolute fit! I think even the professor was having a hard time keeping it together." She remembered the expression on Dorian's face as Amara swore and ended up flat on her butt after her bike crashed. It was that of a parent who had bitten off more than they could chew.

Cassandra laughed. "Hard to think of Amara being in such a position. Maybe one day you can teach me to ride."

Gavin paled as he looked at his wife.

"Maybe once you're old enough, I'll teach you." Hokura smiled.

It was later that Hokura said she just wanted to unwind

and have a bath. As she submerged herself, she heard the phone ring. The last thing she wanted was to deal with more people... as it was today had already been too much for her. All she wanted to do was be on her own. She couldn't do that, not to her family, not to her children who needed their mother's comfort more than anything that day. She needed some space, some time to think, some peace for her own mental health.

Amara sighed as she hung up the phone. "She's in the bath... let it go..." the peacekeeper mumbled to herself. She was being pushy... after having to tell her children, Hokura most likely wanted a night of peace anyway. Amara walked solemnly to the couch and plopped down next to Adam.

"Did you really expect her to want to get together right now?" he asked, cracking his neck. "After everything you told me, you should know better by now."

Amara scowled at her husband. "Is it so wrong to want to be there for my best friend?"

He gave her a look. "If that best friend was anyone other than Hokura." He shook his head. "You just spoke to her the other day...'

"On the phone!" his wife spat back.

He cleared his throat. It was going to be like this... he needed to be logical with her. "Do you really think she wants to be out and about right now in her physical state? We've all heard the whispered gossip about her lately. Hokura was especially sensitive to those whispers when she became pregnant. How do you think she feels now when she's bruised and looking ill? I don't blame her for wanting to avoid everyone."

Amara crossed her arms. "I already know what she looks like."

"Maybe she's getting worse... just give her a few days before bombarding her," Adam suggested, hoping that she'd take a hint.

His wife chewed her cheek as she pouted. "I just don't want to miss any time with her..." Her heart panged at the idea. "If something does happen... this is time that I've missed... and I don't want to think about it, but if she's getting worse, how much time does she have left? What if Dorian can't..."

"Enough." Adam's voice was gentle as he took her into his arms. "Getting all weepy like this isn't like you. I know you're worried, we're all worried, but we need to put some trust into the professor and what her medical team is doing."

She was about to say something when their youngest abruptly walked up to them and sat down pouting on the floor.

Adam looked at his son. "What is it, kiddo?"

Ryan's bottom lip trembled. "Erika won't let me play, and Nathan is busy doing schoolwork."

Amara grinned as she nudged her husband. She smiled down at the boy and brought her arms out for a hug which he ran into to snuggle his mother. "Is it that, or is someone getting hangry?"

"I ate all my dinner!" The young boy pouted.

His father tousled his hair. "I think your mother means dessert, boyo."

The boy's eyes lit up as his pout turned into a wide grin. "And Erika and Nathan can't have any!"

Adam rolled his eyes. Oh, to have siblings that were of different ages. Something he was thankful he never had to go through. His "siblings" had all been the same age as him, had been given the same destiny, and had been by his side through all the squabbles. "Now, now. We do need to share, but how about you get to be first to pick?"

The boy let out an agreeable cheer as he hopped from his mother's arms and ran into the kitchen. Amara watched as Adam rose from the couch. He kissed her sweetly. "Don't brood over it. Come on; maybe you just need dessert too." He coyishly winked at her as she laughed.

At least this would never change.

When Hokura had finished her bath, Gavin told her about Amara phoning. She stated it was too late to return the call and that she was tired. That had been three days ago as she had been successful in continuously avoiding everyone. She didn't want to see them... any of them... even Dorian. She moped in her room. Gavin had already checked in earlier that morning. She had a few more hours to herself before he came back for lunch.

Hokura sat on her bedroom floor with the box of shells as she picked through her memories of her old life. She stared at every shell as her fingers traced over the lines and ridges. What if things had been different? She dug a little deeper into the box and lifted a small piece of driftwood that James had carved into a heart. He had etched their names into each side of the heart. He had loved her so much. "I should have married you." Her voice caught. "It meant nothing to me, but it meant something to you... I had no idea what that even was... but I guess... in a way, we were like a married couple." Her thumb ran over the smooth wood, over both their names, as she brought it to her lips and kissed it.

What was this mood? This emptiness? Was this what it felt

like when one had lost all hope? She sat thinking about it. She thought she had lost all hope when James had died... when she would go wandering aimlessly at night because there was nobody there to hold her. She had become a shell of a person because she had lost him. Yet that feeling wasn't this... even as she left the others and ventured back here. She recalled the nights of restless sleep, of staring at her fire, feeling nothing. She didn't know what the future held for her back then either, but at least she knew there *was* a future.

Hokura took a breath, so many treasures... so many memories... all of them precious. All of them hers... and yet what would happen when she was no longer alive? Those memories would no longer exist. There would be no rebel commander, no peacekeeper to hold them. Tears pricked her eyes. Is that what mankind was made for? To live, to make beautiful memories, and to simply die? What was the meaning of all this if it was all for nothing? The pain spread through her chest. She was different. She was supposed to live forever. Dorian had given mankind a purpose, to continue on, to gain knowledge, and to last forever. To die now seemed like such a slight against him and his work. That hurt even worse as if she was letting him down. It was as if she was letting everyone down by doing this. Why wasn't this in her hands? She sobbed miserably. How many lives had she taken? How many lives were snuffed out by her hands because she had been a killer? No... that was different... that was self-defense to keep those she loved alive. To keep Meridiana thriving. To keep the professor's sanctuary and age of man alive and doing what he had destined them to do.

"I don't want this!" Hokura cried as she clutched her chest. "I don't want to die, dammit!" She took a deep breath. "Why? Is this my fate because of the blood that's on my hands? For every person I killed, I saved another! It isn't fair!" She took a deep breath. "It isn't fair!" she screamed through her sobs. She still had so much to do. She was supposed to teach Cassandra to ride a bike, to watch Cyrus thrive in the science department... to watch her children grow to the age of majority and become whatever it was they had dreamed of being... peacekeepers... scientists... governors... what about Gavin? She was supposed to be his wife... to be his partner, and to work at his side with all the projects to better the compound and the city. He would be alone.

Her mind went to Dorian. They were supposed to push this damn project through... he needed her. Not only for the higher education project but to keep ties with who he truly was. She feared that if she weren't around, he wouldn't have anyone to open up to. His smile would fade... he would become who he was when she fled the compound. He would become cold to others again and merely exist without any joy. "Dorian..." She rasped through her sobs. "I need you more than ever to fix me..." Why did it seem like the success of that happening was dwindling by the day? She hadn't heard anything. Hadn't been down to the medical labs to do any more tests. Was this indeed the end?

She wondered... what was it like to die? Would she simply go to sleep and stop existing? Was there an afterlife? Was her love waiting for her on a higher plain? There were so many old-world theories, and yet all of them scared her. Even the thought of being in James' arms again was a double-edged sword. She would be with her love, and yet she wouldn't be with those here. She wouldn't be there for her children, her husband... her friends. She shook her head. James was mortal, and that wound would never heal, but she shouldn't have to mourn her own death. The notion was odd. Once she was gone, there would be no more mourning... or would there be?

Hokura tilted her head back. She wanted to disappear, to simply not exist. Not to die but to have never been born. It was a dark feeling as she wiped her eyes. The phone rang, snapping her attention from her thoughts. The answering machine hit as Amara's voice came over it. Hokura could feel the pressure building in her heart. She didn't want to be here. She didn't want to be *anywhere*. Gavin would be home and ask why her eyes were red. He would be concerned. Amara would see her and worry about her and how sickly she looked. Even if she called her friend, she would pick up on the raspy voice from crying and would most likely be on her doorstep in a matter of minutes. Her panic rose. She needed to be out... away... alone... her body moved.

Gavin walked into Dorian's office in earnest. He didn't bother knocking to see Dorian reading over a thick document that looked like a manual. The professor looked up at him and casually put it in his drawer as he rubbed his eyes, hoping the governor hadn't seen that it had been on cryogenics. "Gavin... what is it?" he asked tiredly.

"I can't find her!" Gavin cried.

The professor gave him a perplexed look. "You can't find her? There's only so far she can go in her state right now." Worry etched over him. What if she had collapsed somewhere? He stood. "Where have you looked? Is her jeep here?"

Gavin ran his hands through his hair. "Her jeep and bike are here."

"Then she's still here in the compound. Get Adam and Amara on this at once as well. Alert Talon too." Dorian's mind reeled as his anxiety rose. What if she was in medical distress? "She didn't tell you anything?"

"No," the governor deflated. "She's been off again the past

few days. She's been avoiding the others. She's been spending her time painting and brooding over some books. I went to check in on her at lunch, and she was gone. Her box of shells was open, but she wasn't anywhere! I checked all the usual spots, but I still couldn't find her... I don't know what I'm missing!"

Dorian sighed. He knew that she was spiraling, that she was becoming depressed and possibly trying to detach herself from everyone. "Get the others. I'll start in the gardens."

Hokura sat, hidden on the far side of the roof. The emotions were too much. She was lonely, but it was better to be alone. Maybe she could just turn it all off. These feelings were horrible and overwhelming. She wanted to forget all the feelings and not feel anymore, just as Dorian had done long ago. Her eyes watered. Dorian... "How could you turn it all off and forget me?" Why did it suddenly matter? She knew why. It had been survival of the fittest, and that was exactly what he needed to do to survive. He had told her he was ready to die, to go to his suite and merely stop existing when he stopped searching for her. "I can't do it... I'm not strong enough."

She sobbed again in anguish. In despair, it felt like everything was breaking apart as she started coughing. Her throat ached as her chest burned, blood covered her hand. "I'm not supposed to die, dammit!" she screamed, which only started another coughing fit. Maybe this was it. Maybe she would die up here alone in her breaking emotion, away from everyone she was avoiding. Hokura tried to steady herself as she calmed her body and wiped the bit of blood away from her mouth. She was simply feeling sorry for herself. "I'm pathetic," she whispered.

She didn't want to die alone… didn't want to push everyone away or stop feeling… and yet she couldn't bring herself to leave her spot. She simply wanted to sit and brood a while longer.

The professor had combed through the gardens. "Hokura?" he called out as those around him stared. He had checked by the blueberry bush, the alcoves, the waterfall, under every tree. He figured Gavin had already looked, it was possible that he had missed her or that she hadn't come to the gardens yet. Panic started to flood over him. "Where on earth are you?" Was she hiding? Perhaps she didn't want to be found. Dammit, she could be anywhere then. Why was she doing this? She knew she could talk to him, that he would always be there for her. Surely, she knew the same about Gavin, so why feel the need to lock them out?

He doubled back and stopped by the blueberry bush again. If she were mourning, she would most likely be here. He stared at the plaque as he rubbed his fingers over it just as she had done. "Hokura… please… where are you?" Who had he truly been asking as he stared down at the risen name? It was imperative that he find her and make sure she was okay. He figured he would check the training facility next since that was closest. Was she possibly in the RTC viewing room? If so, then Talon would have confirmed so. He figured if she had been found that someone would have paged him by now. He clenched his jaw. He knew her better than anyone else. Surely, he could find her somewhere within the confines of the compound.

They had searched for over an hour as Dorian made his way upstairs to the library to see Gavin with Adam and Amara. The professor gave them a wary glance. "I take none of you have found her?"

Amara shook her head. "Is this what I get for trying to connect with her?"

Dorian looked up at her. "No, this isn't what you get for trying to connect with her. She's being like this with everyone. She's going through some heavy emotions right now." He lowered his head. "She's been avoiding *me* as well these past few days."

Adam tilted his head back. "This place is massive, and she could literally be anywhere. Should we just wait her out?"

The professor winced. "The problem with that is we don't know if she's in medical distress. She's become so weak and frail that it's hard to know if she's actually okay." He looked up at Gavin. "You checked the roof?"

The man gave him an irritated look. "Of course, I checked the roof."

Dorian didn't need that kind of tone from him as he gave the governor a cool look. "The *entire* roof?" Why hadn't he thought of it before now?

Gavin gave him a quizzical look.

"Dammit," Dorian huffed. "I know where she is..."

The three faltered as the professor rolled his eyes at them and cracked his neck.

Dorian turned. "Aren't you coming?"

Gavin stepped up, his head lowered as he didn't want to admit his mistake. "I think it would be best suited if you went for her... she needs her mentor right now. She'll listen to you," he stated in a defeated tone. If anyone could talk to her, it would be him. Besides, the professor had a knack for showing Hokura tough love when she needed it. Something he had faltered with in the past.

Dorian nodded. "I'll talk to her then and send her back to your suite."

Amara lowered her head. Of course. the professor knew where to find her. "I guess we'll go back to our suite then and, hopefully, she'll call me in a day or so."

Gavin could see that she had been upset as he placed a reassuring hand on her shoulder. "I'll have her call you once I talk to her. I'm sure there's an explanation for all of this."

Dorian sighed as he took in the scene. Did Hokura simply not understand what she was doing to all of them? He pursed his lips. She didn't want to be a bother to anyone, and in doing things like this, she was unknowingly hurting those she loved. "I'll get to the bottom of this." With that said, he started on his way to find her.

Dorian found her on the far side of the roof. It was the perfect place for her to hide from everyone, considering they had always spent their time looking out over the city instead of over the barren wastelands. He approached her as he cleared his throat, trying to keep himself in check. "You've been avoiding me." His voice was dark.

"I've been avoiding everyone." She sighed.

"Everyone's been looking for you. Everyone is worried." He studied her. "You've been crying..."

"I've been crying all day..." Hokura looked down, not

wanting to meet his eyes. "I was tired of all these horrible feelings. I thought maybe if I turned it all off that it wouldn't hurt so much... that maybe all this would just go away."

His brows furrowed in sorrow. "That's not how this works."

"I know," she confessed. "It was a stupid idea... and I failed anyway. I'm a bigger mess now than before."

Her response piqued his interest. "How so?"

"Because I figured if I didn't see you, then I would be able to escape all those feelings. That's an impossibility, though. I can't be indifferent to you." She craned her neck up. "I can't give up on feeling things. No matter how hard I try, I can't turn it off and stop caring."

"Nobody said you had to Hokura."

Desperation filled her face. "But isn't that what you did? Wasn't that how you were able to survive? I left, and you went cold. You were able to go on for forty years that way. If it worked for you, then why can't it work for me?"

He pursed his lips as he sat down beside her. "Because as much as you and I are similar, we're both also very different. You feel things differently than I do. You're a person who is fueled by your emotions. I try to be one fueled by rationale... although..." He took a breath. "When it comes to you, that isn't always the case." He looked forward since he couldn't meet her eyes. "When you left, I had an emotional breakdown, I became raw, I was hurt and grieved, I mourned and cried, and it wasn't until I was done that I was able to go cold and turn off my emotions."

"I can't escape my emotions, Dorian!" she cried. "I don't want to die!"

His arms wrapped around her. "And you won't! I swear to you that you won't, Hokura! We just need some time. Every day everyone is working on this! We will find a way to stabilize your system! I promise you!"

She grasped onto him, holding onto him for dear life. "And what if you fail?"

"I won't!" His voice cracked as he brought her away from him. "Don't you trust me?"

"This goes beyond trust, Dorian. There are some things that you can't change. Some things that even you have no control over!"

"Don't say that!" His voice was harsh. "I will succeed." His look softened. "You are going to go on for hundreds of years, you are timeless and ageless, and you will continue to be that way forever."

She gave him a solemn look.

"And if I fail, I swear on all that I am, on my name, on my honor, that I will find a way to bring you back. Please, believe me."

She nodded. She wanted to believe him, had wanted to hold onto whatever faith she had in him that he would save her. He always did, but this time it felt like things were different. That even the father of science didn't have all the answers. "I'll try..."

"And don't shut yourself out from me. Ever... please." He was begging because, in the back of his mind, even he was unsure of things. However, if her time was limited,the last thing he wanted was for her to avoid him. After everything they had been through, they had become each other's lifeline, and he felt like he was losing his grasp on hers. "Have you been this way with Gavin as well?"

She nodded slightly. "I feel like I've been pushing everyone away lately, but won't it be easier that way?"

"It's never easy, not for anyone involved. Something else you should know. There's no avoiding the motions. You can push away your loved ones all you want, you may not live to regret it, but they will." Dorian said.

"I'm being an idiot."

"Your words, not mine." A slight smirk came across his face. His arm was around her shoulder as she leaned into him. "Don't shut out the ones you love because it looks like the end Hokura, whether it's the end or not, they still love you, and you still love them. Why torment yourself and everyone else because of this diagnosis. There's still time, and tomorrow everything can change."

She let out a breath as she stared over the wall. "Nobody deserves this. Not you, not Gavin, not Adam or Amara... I just..." She licked her lips. "I don't know how to feel about things."

"That's a very human way to feel," he offered as he gave her a light nudge. "Stop looking at the what-ifs. If you can't put your faith in the doctors and me, then put your energy into something positive. Your children, your husband, they love you, and they want to spend time with you."

"You're right." Hokura bit her bottom lip. "I guess I'm just feeling sorry for myself. I apologize, Dorian. This isn't like me." She shook her head. "Ever since Tobias, I haven't been the same."

"And we're working on getting you back to the way you used to be. We're working on it," he urged.

She turned and wrapped her arms around him as his arms gently held her. "I promise I won't do this again."

"And if you do, I'll make sure to have Amara give you a subtle reminder." He smirked.

"It isn't nice to threaten me," she grumbled.

He let out a laugh. "I remember saying those exact words to you when you threatened to put me on teenage babysitting duty." His chuckles died down as he rose and offered her a hand. "Gavin is worried, everyone is worried. Come on, you need to go home. "

She took his hand and nodded. "I guess they'll be waiting for me. Did they send you out here to find me?"

"Gavin did," he confessed.

"Sending in the cavalry," Hokura muttered, giving a disdained look.

"As I said, he's worried about you. He's going through the motions as well. He thought he had lost you when Tobias had kidnapped you, and now this... he doesn't want to push or pry, but when you do things like this, it worries him even more," Dorian said as he turned to lead her back off the roof and to her suite.

She couldn't help but feel upset; she was putting up walls, and even her own husband felt like he couldn't penetrate them enough, so he had sent Dorian after her. She knew that notion obviously hurt Gavin's pride. "I'll talk to him... I'll be honest with him," she said, following him towards the stairway.

"Good. You need to call Amara, then you can spend the evening with your family, and you can be back to the medical facility tomorrow at ten hundred hours." Dorian smiled slightly, relieved that there had been some resolve.

Hokura rolled her eyes. "My favorite place."

"I'm hoping you won't have to spend much more time in there after this round of scans," he answered curtly. They walked down the hallway towards their suites in silence until they were in front of her door. "Have a good evening, Hokura."

Her arms were quickly around him as she hugged him tightly. "Thank you for everything."

"Nonsense, that's why I'm here." He placed a hand lovingly on top of her head. "Go on and enjoy your night. I'll see you tomorrow."

She nodded and opened her suite door to see Gavin had been anxiously waiting for her. She gave him a meek smile as she entered.

Dorian turned from her door and walked past his own suite. He needed to get on things. He knew time wasn't something they could afford. There had to be something that he was missing, something that the scans weren't picking up. He would find it. He would keep his word, and he would save her, but he was running out of precious time to crack the code. "Why do the cells keep dying off no matter what I try? What am I missing from this? What combination haven't I tried?" he muttered. He had taken more samples from her than he had when he was creating her. He wasn't sure how long her system could hold off. If there was anything he was sure of, it was that he would be spending the remainder of the day in the labs.

Hokura timidly walked into her suite to see her husband waiting for her. "I'm sorry," she said in a low tone. Her eyes met Gavin's. "I'm sorry you felt like you needed to send Dorian after me instead of coming yourself." Her eyebrow furrowed. "Am I that far gone?"

Gavin licked his lips. "You've been avoiding everyone again, not just Adam and Amara but myself, *Dorian* as well. That's not like you. We were all worried, and we were all looking for you. I'm just relieved that Dorian knew where to find you."

Tears came to her eyes. "I'm scared, Gavin! I can feel it every day. I'm not as strong as I once was. I'm so tired. I physically hurt." She shook her head. "All these things that peacekeepers were never supposed to go through, the pain was always possible, but it was a minimal thing, and our bodies heal so quickly that if anything it was a nuisance. I can feel my body shutting down around me, and it's terrifying!"

He grabbed onto her and held onto her for dear life. "Hokura." His voice was a soft whisper in her ear. "We're going to get through this. You aren't going anywhere, my love. We've all promised you. You're going to be alright. Dorian is going to fix this." His heart ached. He was putting this all on the professor. Was it possible for him to save her? He was starting to wonder; he didn't want to doubt him, but at the same time, he had also watched her slowly slip from him as her body betrayed her. "Everyone was so worried about you."

She gave a tired sigh. "That's the last thing I want. I don't want to worry or stress everyone out."

"It's okay," he soothed her. "Amara would really appreciate it if you got a hold of her. She's worried about you. She doesn't want to pry Hokura, but she's scared for you as well."

Hokura nodded... Amara... fellow peacekeeper, ally, non-biological sister, and her best female friend. She had been driving her away on purpose and knew she was hurting her all the more. "I'll see about getting together with the others in a few days. I'll call her tonight. Tomorrow, I need to get some scans done." The idea of seeing the others seemed exhausting in itself, but she was doing them a disservice in avoiding them.

He kissed the top of her head and held her as they stood in silence. Why did it feel like she was leaving them when she was still here? Why did it feel like she wanted to put a distance between herself and everyone who loved her? Possibly because it would be easier that way. "Do you want me to escort you to your scans tomorrow?"

She chewed her bottom lip. After what happened today, she knew better. Gavin needed this... "That's fine..." she let out a breath. "I think I'm going to take a bath and relax, then I'll give Adam and Amara a call, and we'll set something up so we can have some time together."

Gavin gave a sorrowful look. After being with her for four-teen years, he could catch her emotions when she slipped. She didn't want to see the others, didn't want him accompanying her, but she was giving in and doing it for them. "Let's put this afternoon behind us and have a nice evening. Go for your bath, give the others a call, and then we can do whatever it is you want."

Give and take, that's what held her relationship together with Gavin. That's exactly what this was, and she recognized it. She nodded, tomorrow was going to be another busy day, and she silently wondered how she would mentally make it through. She would phone the others tonight. She would go down tomorrow for her scans with Gavin at her side... she closed her eyes; she was just so tired of trying to be strong.

It was the following day, Hokura sat at the table picking at her breakfast. She knew she needed her strength but was having a hard time with her appetite as Gavin stared at her. "You didn't have to do everything today, you know. You could have waited a few days to get together with Adam and Amara."

She swallowed hard. The truth had been she didn't know how much time she had left before she physically crumbled and needed to stay in the medical facility. Something she didn't dare tell her husband. "I have the energy to do so. Why not live in the present?" Her voice was low as she fought to concentrate on the food in front of her.

"Would you like me to make you something else?" Gavin asked, concern coming across his face. She seemed to be having a hard time eating this morning.

"No." Hokura shook her head. "Just nerves, I guess. I'm not exactly thrilled about running more tests. It seems whenever we do that, the news is never good."

He could understand. "Hey, each day is a step forward. We need to keep a positive mindset on things." He was reaching and hated that it felt that way, that he felt like he needed to grasp at straws with her to simply be at her side.

Hokura took a breath as she wiped her mouth. "You're absolutely right. We have no reason to doubt. What was the old saying again? It's always the darkest before dawn."

A small smile came to his lips. "That's right, it is. We just need to hold onto that."

She nodded but wondered how much darker things would get or if she was doomed to fall into forever night and leave this place. As much as nobody wanted to think of it, her death hadn't been ruled out. There was no guarantee that Dorian was going to save her. Everyone was simply putting faith in something that might not be possible. She stared at the clock. "We should get ready. It's nearly time."

Gavin had been relieved to accompany her, but her quiet mood was putting him off as they entered the elevator. He had held her hand and refused to let it go. "Did Dorian tell you what kind of scans and tests he wanted to run on you today?"

She shrugged. "I'm not totally sure... I guess I didn't ask."

He squeezed her hand. "I guess we'll find out soon enough..."

The two came up to the medical facility to see the professor waiting for them at the entrance. "Good morning," Dorian stated. He had looked exhausted, and Hokura wondered if he had spent the night in the RTC simulator. "Today's test isn't invasive at all, no more syringes." He didn't know if he could take giving her more bruises.

A small smile came to Hokura's lips. "That's a relief."

Dorian nodded. "If you two would follow me." He turned

and started down the hallway past the CT room. "I actually want to check Hokura's blood flow. I'll be checking for clots, how her valves are functioning, circulation, etcetera."

She was perplexed. "What about the blood cloning?"

He winced. "There have been setbacks, it's been clotting, and for whatever reason, the process is taking longer than we had anticipated. This is another reason why I want to double-check things. I want to see if whatever is flowing through your system is having an effect on your circulation."

Upon coming to the room, Hokura raised an eyebrow.

Dorian cleared his throat. "We're going to use a Doppler ultrasound."

She sucked in her breath as she tensed, squeezing Gavin's hand.

"What is it?" Gavin asked, his voice low as he took in her expression.

Dorian turned and took her in. "It's nothing invasive, Hokura. You'll be just fine. We just need to run the transducer over your body. Just like when you were pregnant."

She couldn't help herself as she clammed up. "My body... it's... it's worse now..." She didn't want Gavin nor Dorian to see it as her bottom lip trembled.

The professor's eyes narrowed. "Would you rather I call in someone else for this? Perhaps Olga, Spindler, or Lucien..."

The idea of others seeing her state was even worse. "No!" she cried.

"Hokura." Gavin's voice was tense. "I've never known you to be so vain that you wouldn't accept the help being offered to you. I remember what you looked like when you returned to Meridiana after being captured."

Dorian cleared his throat. "We've both seen you at your worst. This is nothing to be so superficial over." He took in the oversized shirt she had been wearing. She had been donning clothes that fully concealed her more often lately. "Please, first child... we need to see how things are progressing. I need to make sure your arteries are healthy and that there won't be any further complications possibly having to do with your heart."

Her bottom lip trembled as she fought back the tears. She turned to Dorian. He needed to understand why she was hesitating. "Remember when you found me..." she looked up as her eyes bore into his. "When I said I don't want anyone to see me like this... my body is hideous like this..."

He knew precisely what she was talking about but couldn't say in front of her husband. These were her exact words when they had bathed together in the river. He nodded, his eyes not leaving hers. He sighed. "And I will remind you of our conversation. The body is merely a vessel that holds the greatness." He wouldn't say the last part. "Hokura, whatever I see, I won't falter if it's as bad as it was when I rescued you," his heart ached, "then I already know what I'm dealing with." He wouldn't turn from her.

She nodded slightly as they entered the room. Dorian shut the door as she went over to the bed and winced as she looked over her shoulder. Gavin had been standing there taking her in as well. She slowly brought the shirt over her head and heard her husband suck air through his teeth. She lowered her pants as well as she grimaced.

The professor spoke up. "You can leave your undergarments on. Please lay down on the gurney." His tone and expression had stayed neutral as he took her in. Indeed, she was worse than from when she had been rescued. Her body was incredibly malnourished, yet he knew she had been eating. The bruises on her side were still grotesquely colored and weren't healing. How had it gotten to this? He shook his head as he turned on the machine.

Gavin sat beside her, holding her hand. His brows furrowed as his lips pursed. He didn't know what to say to her.

Dorian took the man in. Did he not know what she looked like? Was she hiding herself from even him? He had been curious. Perhaps that's why she had been so nervous. As much as the professor had seen, her husband hadn't witnessed the initial damage that had been done to her. "Just like when you were pregnant, I'm going to administer this jelly on you. The soundwaves will reflect off your red blood cells and will show us how your blood is flowing. It'll also let us know if you have any blocked arteries or if there are any clots forming. I'm also going to check your heart. This will be a full assessment."

Hokura nodded as he slowly started with her arm. His touch had been warm and tender, especially over her bruises. It seemed he was going slowly, paying extra attention to what he was doing.

The professor made a face. "Unfortunately, there needs to be a slight pressure under the doppler, not much mind you. If you at all feel discomfort, please let me know."

Again, Hokura nodded and looked over to Gavin, who seemed to be elsewhere, as she squeezed his hand. "Is it that bad?" she asked. It seemed like he couldn't even look at her.

Gavin let out a breath. "No... it's not that bad. It's just..." He shook his head. "I knew you were wearing my clothes to cover yourself. Even at night, you've been sleeping in more. I just didn't realize how much you had depleted." Why did it look like she was half-starved? Why did her skin look so pale? He could pretty much see her ribs. Her muscle definition was gone. It pained him to see her in such a way. "I'm just worried."

Hokura chewed on her bottom lip, not knowing what to say.

Dorian slowly brought the transducer over her skin, paying attention to the screen. Her blood flow was normal. That in itself puzzled and troubled him. That meant this toxin that had been injected into her was easily flowing all the way through her. Affecting every part of her, every organ as her heart pumped it through her body. He tried to lighten the tension as the device went into the crook of her arm, causing her to tense. He stopped immediately.

"I'm fine," Hokura gasped. "It was just a little tender. Honest, you can continue."

The professor grimaced. He hated causing her pain like this. It was just like when he had rescued her and had to work on her back. At least she wasn't crying out in agony. He brought the transducer to her forearm, glancing over to the monitor. Nothing... He wiped the gel away from her arm.

Gavin perked up. "Did you find anything yet?"

Dorian sighed. He didn't want to say anything yet. "I still have a ways to go... I can't deduct anything just yet."

Hokura closed her eyes as the uncomfortable sensation ran over her. She shivered slightly as the professor applied gel to the other arm.

He noted it as he grabbed a thin sheet. "Here, we don't want you getting cold during this process." He placed it gently over the rest of her as he continued to work. It was a tedious task. He didn't want to miss anything as his jaw clenched. He looked over to the screen and took in what was happening to her. Her circulation wasn't what it should be. Her valves seemed to be functioning poorly. He was almost afraid to check her heart as he finished with her legs and went back upwards. "There's one last thing," he stated. His throat had felt dry. "I need to check your heart as well." He looked over at the man and could see that he was anxious.

Gavin nodded.

Hokura brought the sheet to cover her legs. "That gel makes me feel cold after you wipe it off." She shivered.

Dorian's brows furrowed. "Your circulation is being sluggish as well." That explained why she had been cold on the roof while she stood in the humid rain, why she was comfortable in the larger shirts.

She sucked on her bottom lip. "I guess that would explain why I've been so chilly lately. I guess I just chalked it up to the weather."

The professor closed his eyes and pinched the bridge of his nose. "No, it's been a symptom of what's been happening to your system." He couldn't be upset. They were in too deep for him to be upset with her now. He leaned over her. "This will be the last of this examination," he stated, taking the gel, and rubbing it over her chest. He could feel her heart pulsing under his hand. At that moment, her heartbeat was the most precious thing he could feel, but even as it beat beneath his fingers, he could determine it wasn't as strong as it should be. He couldn't help but hope he was wrong as he brought the transducer to her chest and held his breath.

Gavin's stared up at the professor. He swore he saw the light leave Dorian's eyes as he stared at the monitor. His steady hand faltered as he glided the mechanism over her skin and stopped. "Dorian." Gavin's voice was terse.

The professor brought his fist to his mouth and held it there as he tried to steady himself. He needed to breathe... he needed to keep it together. He wanted to fight with himself, to tell himself he wasn't reading the monitor properly, but he knew better.

"Dorian!"

It was Hokura's voice calling his name that brought him back as he looked down on her. He swallowed hard, trying to articulate the words.

She gave him a look that told him she already knew. "It's not good, is it?"

He cleared his throat. "None of your results since this started have been good. From what I observed, you don't have any blockages or clots. However, your flow circulation isn't what it should be."

Gavin couldn't take it anymore. "There's something else... what was it?" He needed to hear it from the man.

Dorian opened his mouth and closed it again. He let out a huff as he stared down at her as if admitting it to her was easier. "Whatever this is, it's also affecting your heart. Your heart muscles seem to be weakening." He wiped the gel from her chest.

Gavin shot up from where he was sitting. "What can be done?"

"Gavin," Hokura moaned beside him as her hand went to Dorian's, who was still leaning over her. "This gives you more to work with, though, right? From here, you might be able to get some answers." She wanted to be optimistic.

The professor nodded. "The more I know about how your system is depleting, the further we can work to understand what this is and how to stabilize you." He needed to know. "How are you feeling today?"

Gavin sat back down and interrupted. "Maybe you should call off the whole idea of getting together with the others."

Hokura gave him an annoyed look. "I'm actually feeling a bit better this morning. Some days are better than others. I want to see the others. I think spending some time with them today will help my morale."

"Morale is important," Dorian said, straightening. "However, you need to remember to take it easy and continue to rest. Nothing too physically strenuous. With this said, I don't want you to think your heart isn't working. We can still come back from this. The damage seems to be minimal at the moment." He didn't want to worry her any further. She didn't need any heavier burdens to carry when he was hoping to lighten them. He turned to Gavin. "Simply keep an eye on her. After she spends some time with the others, be there and make sure she rests." He smirked at Hokura. "Don't let Amara drain you."

She chuckled. "You're talking about the second child, right?" She sat up. "I promise to do as the professor and doctors have prescribed."

Gavin nodded. It had been a relief to hear it from her, but he wondered whether she was going to keep her word on this or not.

"I expect you to look after yourself," Dorian said, handing Hokura her top as she dressed. "I'm going to run these results to the others and look over them again myself. There's much to be done still."

Hokura and Gavin nodded at the man.

"If anything comes up on either end, we can page one another. Do either of you have any questions?"

Hokura shook her head. "I guess I'll shower and then meet up with the others. We're just going to meet on the roof for a light lunch."

The professor nodded. He wished they could have some time together to merely sit and converse, but he had an array of new findings that he needed to get to Spindler and Lucien. "Enjoy your time with them. I'm sure I'll check in with you later." He stared at Gavin. "Take care of her."

Gavin nodded. "I will. Thank you for everything, professor." He put an arm around his wife and gently squeezed her as they turned and made their way out of the medical facility and towards the elevator.

Hokura made a face as she thought about what she had just learned. She was getting tired of bad news lately. It seemed like with every test, there had yet to be any solid answers. If anything, they were posing more questions.

Her husband noticed her quiet demeanor as they got on the elevator. "How about you shower, and afterward, you can tell me what you need on the roof? I'll help you carry everything up."

A smile finally came to her face. "I'd like that."

"And afterward, you can just rest for the afternoon. We can keep things light." He was grasping, but after seeing that rare smile that came across her lips, he would do anything to see it again.

Hokura nibbled on her lip. At least if they were on the roof, nobody else would see her. After this morning, she had felt more self-conscious than ever. She waited patiently, looking at the food. Her stomach turned. She wasn't at all hungry but knew she needed to make amends with the other two. Her eyes went up to the door as Adam and Amara walked through it. Hokura stood as she tugged at her long-sleeved shirt. It had been bad enough with what Dorian had witnessed. She hadn't wanted the others to witness her further deterioration.

Adam threw open his arms as she rose and walked into them. Amara joined in their silent hug as the three stood simply embracing.

Hokura closed her eyes. She couldn't crack. She couldn't start crying in front of them. To do so would most likely cause Amara to go off. She sucked her bottom lip and took a steady breath. She had loved them so much, and yet she had pushed them away time and time again.

Adam loosened his grips first. "It's good to see you." His tone was light. He didn't want to give away the fact that it had been quite some time since he *had* seen her or that she had looked *completely* different. Amara had said she looked like when they had first rescued her; however, that was a while ago. It was more than just her physical appearance. Even the air that the first child had held around her had felt different, duller...

"I'm sorry," Hokura said, not meeting their eyes. "This has been one of the hardest things I've gone through..." She shook her head as she walked towards the blanket she had laid out for them. "Like I've been in a nightmare for months, and it just won't end."

Amara sat next to her, her eyes roaming over the first child's body, taking inventory of everything that had changed. "Thanks for seeing us." The statement had been guarded. She couldn't slip up or say anything that might upset her. Who knew when the next visit would happen. She had been worried, and by the looks of things, it had been rightfully so. "We just want a bit of your time. If you get tired, let us know, and we can help pack up."

Hokura nodded as she lay back and looked up at the sky as the others sat and stared at her. She noted their gaze as he raised an eyebrow. "Eat up. I already had a large breakfast and lunch. I figured that's why we'd have some finger food."

Adam gave her a worried look. He wondered if she was doing this just to appease them. "How did things go this morning?"

She rolled over and faced them but didn't meet their eyes. "Not well..." she made a face. "It's interesting. My body is slowly deteriorating like this, but it's not at all natural."

Amara gave her a look. "Of course, it isn't natural. Our bodies weren't meant to go through something like this."

Hokura shook her head. "I figured if something like this were to happen that I'd age..." she looked back up at the sky. "Like Barack had, like Annette, Allen..." She licked her lips. "I know it was a bit of a shock when Allen found out they were susceptible to getting sick, that their bodies had started aging again. I can't even remember how many times I asked him if he could take something of me and replicate what Dorian had done here." She shook her head. "Yet he had accepted his fate. I'll never forget his smile when he told me death was the natural order of things."

Adam looked over towards Amara. His wife was wearing a grave expression. Most likely due to Hokura's cryptic mood. He cleared his throat. "Allen was always one for natural order. Being Dorian's second went against his grain, and yet he was of a brilliant mind."

Hokura's brows furrowed as her expression grew dark. "Fuck the natural order of things."

Amara's eyes widened at what she just heard.

The first child scowled. "The natural order makes no sense anyway. Are you telling me mankind was born to simply live a few measly years and then die? For what purpose?" She rose and gave the two a hard stare. "What's the point of living then if we just die and fade away from existence? For what? To make memories that we can't bring with us? To hold sorrow for the ones we've lost? Because it seems that's what life is about lately... suffering!"

Amara's eyes held her friend's. "Whoah! Maybe that's what life used to be, but that's not what it's meant to be anymore..."

Hokura turned away from them. "We were all originally born mortals."

Adam piped in. "Yes, but might I remind you that and our parents knew about this project and were devoted to giving us a better life! A purpose which we've all lived up to."

Amara took her husband's hand. "Adam's right. You've had a fulfilling life and a huge purpose. Think of all the people you helped save from White Rock. Think of all the things you've helped with! Dammit, Hokura, you were the first to bear children in decades and helped the professor with the fertility project! Besides, Dorian is on this..." She watched as her friend shrugged and looked away and couldn't help but bristle in annoyance.

Adam had caught the fury in his wife's eyes as he placed a hand on her shoulder. "You're in a mood. We get it. Is there anything we can do to help?"

Tears came to Hokura's eyes as her lower lip trembled. "I just want somebody to save me..." it was true. She felt like she hadn't really been rescued from this nightmare yet, that even though she was back in Meridiana, she was still fighting for her life. "I'm tired of tests and never knowing what the next day is going to bring. I'm tired of feeling like everything is a race against time. That everyone is worried about me. I just want to go back to the way things used to be!" There. She had said it.

Adam sighed. "We all want that Hokura. We all have past regrets and wishes. Of course, we're all worried about you. We love you!"

"He's right," Amara piped in. "Thinking that people aren't going to worry about you is asinine! You're our family. We love you!"

Hokura couldn't help but feel defeated. She was being selfish and only thinking about herself. "I love you guys too." A smile cracked over her lips. "Even if you two were like crazy siblings in the beginning, you're also my best friends."

"Damn right!" Amara chimed. "And don't you forget it!"

"Amara's right," Adam smirked. "You're stuck with us through thick and thin. That's what you get for dragging us back here."

Hokura couldn't help but laugh. It had felt good to do so even though it no longer sounded like her. "Dragging you back here was the best thing I've ever done." She was glad the conversation had taken a turn and was a little lighter as the three of them reminisced over the past. It had felt refreshing and had been exactly what Hokura needed until her throat caught and the reminder of reality came crashing back as she stifled a cough. She had been quick enough to reach for a drink before it erupted from her as she struggled to clear her throat. She wasn't about to let this ruin her time.

Amara had noticed quickly. "You alright?"

Hokura quickly nodded as she took a big gulp. "Just caught a tickle in the back of my throat."

Adam nodded. "It's already been well over an hour. We don't want to overwhelm you. How about we help you pack up, and we can do this again soon."

The first child smiled. "Yeah, that sounds nice."

Hokura had told Adam and Amara to take home the leftovers as she entered her suite with her blanket in hand, as she raised an eyebrow to see Dorian sitting on her couch reading over a document. He casually took her in. "Your husband had to quickly see to something in the city. He didn't want to interrupt you, so he asked for me to be here."

"So, he sent you here to babysit me." She scowled.

The professor gave her a cool stare. "You've had a long and busy day. Between this morning and having your get-together this afternoon, he wanted to make sure you weren't feeling overwhelmed."

Hokura sighed, walked over to the couch, and sat beside him. "I know he's trying to make sure that I'm taking care of myself."

"He is. It wasn't meant to be a slight against you. It was

more so if you needed a hand to put things away and to make sure you were feeling alright," Dorian said.

"Fine," she huffed. She just wanted a few minutes to sit in peace. Her eyes wandered over to what Dorian was reading. It looked to be one of her files.

Dorian glanced at her on the couch and then noted the two novels sitting on her coffee table. He raised an eyebrow as Hokura tiredly looked up at him. "I want to finish those some-day... I want to find out who the heroine ends up with."

He pursed his lips and let out a sigh. "I didn't overly care for the ending."

Her brows furrowed. "Even you've read it?"

A small chuckle escaped him. "A very, very long time ago. I have no idea why I even picked the series up." He shrugged casually. "I must have been bored and tired of textbooks."

She tried to clear her throat as she struggled again. There was no fighting it this time as she began to cough. Her chest ached as she seemed to be losing the fight by catching her breath. Right away, the professor quickly retreated to her kitchen and handed her a cloth as she continued.

He watched helplessly as she gasped, coughing even harder into the towel as he gently placed his hand on her back and rubbed it. By the time she was done, there was a decent amount of blood splattered on the material. His eyes widened as he tried to remain calm. "I'll get you some water." He needed to move. Seeing her in such a state always made him feel on edge, as though he wasn't doing enough. That he was letting her down, he brought the glass to her as she hunched over and grasped her chest.

"I feel like I can't get enough air when that happens. My chest burns so badly. It's like my lungs are on fire."

He grimaced. The test he had done that morning had shown that she was getting worse. He knew from the original

CT scans that there was spotting on her lungs which he was sure was worse by now. "That's to be expected with how things are progressing."

Her hand gently touched his as her eyes looked up and bore into his soul. "Dorian, please, be honest. I want to hear it from you. Am I at the end? Am I going to die?"

He struggled to swallow as he took a breath. "No, you're not going to die." He steadied himself. Admitting such a thing would mean he had accepted he would fail.

Hokura nodded, but she didn't find comfort in his words. She took a sip of her water. She could taste the blood in her mouth as she swallowed and shuddered. How much had she coughed up? She had seen the towel. She had tried to suppress it because she didn't want to worry him. That's not what this visit was about. "I'm just about done your painting."

Dorian's eyebrows rose. "Oh?"

She rested her head comfortably on his shoulder. "It's kept me busy when I've felt inspired. I wish we could make some headway in the higher education program, though... that room is just sitting there..."

He couldn't help but roll his eyes. "We have all the time in the world to push that through, the eldest children in the city are yours, and they're merely thirteen. We could sit on that project for years, and it would be fine."

"I know, but I want to move forward." She sighed. "I think I might have overdone it today, I didn't mean to, but I know the others needed to see me."

His fingers tantrically worked over her arm as he felt her body relax. "Then you need to spend the rest of your evening relaxing." His voice was soft.

She took a deep breath. "I'm glad you're here..." Why did it seem so much easier to relax around him? Like she could be honest with him? "I've wanted to fall asleep beside you again..."

He looked down at her. Her eyes were already closed as her breathing evened out. He gently kissed the top of her head. "I'll always be here." His voice was a whisper. He would wait until Gavin returned and would make his way back to the labs. Today's tests didn't give him much to work with, but any new information he had was better than nothing.

Gavin had returned an hour later. He had run into Cassandra and Cyrus on his way up and checked that they would be joining them soon. As he opened the door to his suite, he saw Hokura passed out on the couch with a blanket wrapped around her. Dorian was sitting in the plush chair beside her as he looked up.

The governor sighed. "Thanks for keeping an eye on her."

The professor nodded. "She seems to have tired herself out today. She's been asleep for a while. Her body needs the rest." He rose quietly and looked down at her. "I'll be here for you both whenever you need me."

It was a sentiment Gavin took to heart. "Thank you for this, Dorian, thank you for everything."

He grimaced. He had wanted to tell the man not to thank him yet. He had yet to accomplish the task at hand. "If you need anything, page me." With that, he quietly walked to the door and let himself out.

Gavin took his place on the chair and simply stared at her. She had looked so peaceful, but he couldn't deny the physical changes as he took her in. "Sleep, my love... apparently, you need it."

Hokura had roused after the children had come home and had barely gotten through dinner before she made her way to the couch. She had picked up one of her books and found that simply holding it was exhausting as she put it on the coffee table and brought the blanket back over top of herself.

It had been a quiet night as Gavin's voice finally whispered its way into her subconscious. "Hokura, let's go to bed..."

She had made her way from the couch into their bedroom. Gavin gave her a wary look as she took her sleep aids. He wondered if she truly needed them tonight, considering how exhausted she was. "Have they been helping lately? I know you napped this afternoon and pretty much all evening," he asked as she swallowed them down hard.

She pursed her lips. "Today was a little overwhelming seeing everyone. I've been so tired lately, but it comes in waves." She didn't want to admit that she could feel her body shutting down as her throat caught and she started to cough again.

Right away, he was at her side. "Tell me what I can do!"

Hokura continued the fit as blood covered her palm. Gavin tried to soothe her by rubbing her back. "There's nothing you can do." She cleared her throat. "There's no stopping it or making it better. I just have to let it run its course."

Gavin looked at her hand in panic. "Let me grab you something."

She straightened. "No need, I can wash this off. By now, I should really just have something on me at all times."

"Has it been that bad?" Gavin asked in earnest.

"I had a bad fit while Dorian was visiting earlier today," Hokura stated as she went to the bathroom and washed her hand and face. As she gargled and spat the water out, she couldn't help but grimace at the amount of blood that was still in her mouth. Was it possible that she was just becoming used to the taste of it? The thought alone was horrifying as she returned to bed. The walk from the bathroom back to her mattress had been enough to exhaust her even further as she wrapped the blankets around herself.

Gavin lay down and outstretched his arm, bringing her into him as she rested against his chest. He just wanted to hold her. In moments, he could tell she was asleep. Good, at least she was getting rest. That's all he could ask for. However, his mind reeled. She was getting worse, and he knew there hadn't been much headway in the medical facility. Suddenly, the idea of being in bed was too much for him. He felt restless as his body needed to move. He slowly slipped from underneath her. She didn't even stir as he did so. He quietly dressed and made his way down the hallway. He didn't know where he was going as he aimlessly wandered.

As Gavin walked past the training facility, he saw the viewing room to the RTC simulator was ajar. He peeked in to see nobody was in it, and yet the simulator was running. He looked up at the screens to see the professor. He was pummeling a simulation to the ground as it disappeared, and another was on top of him. The professor flipped it with incredible grace and power as it crashed into the ground and was met with his fists. The way the man moved and fought with such extreme power and grace was exactly how a predator moved. He couldn't help but stare and feel envious.

Gavin shook his head. At least Dorian had an outlet other than destroying his labs now that he had his arm back. He truly wondered how the man functioned. He seemed to mentally exhaust himself in his labs and then spend his nights physically draining himself in the simulator. Yet he was sure he made his way up to his quarters to sleep every night. Gavin continued his way down the halls and made his way to the gardens. The sweetness hit him as there was a scent of the flowers blooming in the air. He breathed it in deeply.

He wished he could be beside her, but he couldn't keep his

mind in check. His worst fears were becoming a reality. Hokura was slipping further each day. How close was she to the edge? How much further would she slip until there was no bringing her back. He couldn't imagine his life without her, and suddenly there was a possibility of that happening. Fear and grief hit him just as it did when he had found out that she was ill.

Gavin's pace quickened. Maybe he could barter with the dead one last time as he hurried to the blueberry bush and sank to his knees in front of the plaque. "She came back... but she came different!" he cried. His rationale screamed at him that the rebel commander was in no way a deity, and yet the words came out. "If you loved her, you would find a way for her to continue on here!" No, that wasn't the way things worked. "Please, if there's any reminisce of you out there, I beg you. I know I failed her and that I failed you, but please give me one last chance! Let him save her!"

Why did he do this? Why did he always come back here to scream at a plaque when his body wasn't even here? When the rebel commander had never physically been here to begin with. When what was left of him was still in White Rock under a partially painted rock. Why did he think a man he never met was listening to his pleas? Because he had loved her too, and Gavin knew in his heart that James wouldn't have wanted this for her because the other man who had loved her was only hitting stalls in his race against time. Because Gavin knew... something deep opened up inside of him as it threatened to swallow him whole.

"I can't do it." Tears streamed down his face. "I'm not strong enough for this... how can life be so cruel?" He pounded the grass below him with his fist. "Dammit, why is life so unfair for her? Why does she have to suffer like this?" What would happen to the children? How would they grieve their mother when she was no longer of this world? How on earth would they carry on when she was no longer part of their life? And him... she was his everything. He clutched his chest. They needed to have this conversation. He needed to prepare as he hoped and wished it wouldn't come to that. How on earth was he going to tell them their mother was gone? He didn't know... How on earth could he say goodbye to the love of his life? What about her body? He couldn't... he wasn't that big of a man. His heart panged. There was a bigger man, someone he could ask. It would be the last thing he would ask of the professor if he couldn't save her. He could at least...

Gavin's insides rolled. What a cruel thing to ask of her creator, but he was the only person he could go to. As hard as Dorian was, he would understand. Gavin knew in his heart that he would do this for him. Even if it tore him apart, he would see to the task. "Forgive me, Dorian, I am going to ask you to do the hardest thing you'll ever do... and I apologize for the pain it'll cause... but you're the only one who's strong enough to shoulder it." He would page the professor in the morning. For now, he would allow the man to take out his physical aggression in the simulator. Gavin would make his way back to his bed, back to his love's side, and try to get some much-needed sleep.

Dorian walked wearily into the office with a cup of coffee in his hand. He found it strange that Gavin had requested a government office that wasn't his own. He looked up at the man who was already sitting at a large desk wearing a placid expression.

"You wanted to see me." The professor's voice was tired.

"I did."

He sat down across from the man, his thoughts a million miles away as he wondered what this was about.

"We need to have this talk. I know we've been avoiding it, but it has to happen," Gavin said in a listless tone.

Dorian closed his eyes as his heart wrenched.

"I know you don't want to talk about it, Dorian, but please, for me..."

"I can save her!" His voice was terse.

Gavin sighed as he tilted back in his chair. "And I believe you still can, however... if that isn't the case, there's something I am asking you to do."

The professor raised an eyebrow as he took in the man. He had looked disheveled and exhausted. "What is it?"

The governor couldn't meet his eyes. "Can you take care of things? Once... *If...* she passes. Her ashes are to be put in the blueberry bush..." His head slowly came forward as his brown eyes met Dorian's. "I can't deal with the loss. Please don't make me deal with processions of dealing with my dead wife's body."

The professor's mind reeled with the possibilities. If he were put in charge of the processions, Gavin would be none the wiser. It was as if the man was asking for this to happen. If he *did* fail... another secret... he could never tell Gavin. He doubted the man would ever allow for Hokura to be cryogenically suspended. "I will see to them." Dorian's voice was steady. He couldn't give anything away. Nothing was for certain just yet. However, if that's how things went, if he did fail, this solidified a second chance at things.

Gavin nodded sadly. "Thank you, Dorian, for what it's worth I've been incredibly grateful that you've been by our side through all of this."

"You can leave it all to me, governor. You have my word that I will take care of things." He watched as Gavin rose from his seat as he walked mechanically over to him, and placed a hand on his shoulder.

"I'm hoping it doesn't come to that."

"You and I both." He waited for Gavin to leave the room as he pondered. Why had the man suddenly brought this up? Maybe it was something weighing on him that he needed to make sure was dealt with. Dorian closed his eyes as he kneaded at his forehead and the pressure that seemed to be building in his skull. Another secret, another lie which would have many more to follow, but it ensured that Hokura's body would be under his watch, that even once things were over, he could still work on her system and bring her back. He wondered if he dared bring this up with her. Would she fight him in this? Of course, she would. He would stay mute about what he was doing until he was successful. He got up and walked idly down the compound hallways and to the area he had quartered off. He unlocked the door and walked in, taking in the slight blue glow emitting from the capsule. Walking up to it, he noted the cooling stats. They had all regulated, and the chamber was ready. The idea pained him. He would do everything possible to ensure he wouldn't have to view her from the glass above, that he could figure things out, and that he would save her. This was simply a backup plan, one he had sincerely hoped he wouldn't need to use.

It was early afternoon, right after Gavin had checked on her, that Hokura tiredly looked at the finished painting. It was perfect. It was everything that she wanted to say and more. It looked exactly like she had envisioned as a smile came to her lips. The emotions that she had poured into it, surely he could understand how she felt when he saw this.

"Dorian..." she whispered. "I've created a masterpiece. I hope it lives up to your expectations." Her heart swelled; it was easily the best piece of work she had ever done, and it was going to him. She pondered, how on earth was she going to present this to him? It was special... She recalled that night from so long ago and his words... *"Not the city... never the city."* That's when the idea struck her. She had the perfect plan of how she would give it to him. She would give the painting a little more time to dry and then take it to the library. She would wait him out, and when the time was right. Hokura beamed. It was perfect. She had been excited that she had felt more awake today, that possibly the rest from the day before had caught up to her. Maybe that's what she needed: more time spent resting her body and sleeping when she needed it. She nodded to herself. That's exactly what she would do then to ensure everything went perfectly for this.

After moving the canvas to the library, she had a leisurely afternoon. She relaxed on the couch and dozed for a few hours. She even had the energy to help Gavin prepare dinner after promising him that she wasn't overdoing it. After some light conversation with her children, she had showered. When it was time to sleep, she got up and told her husband that she was going to the library. There was no way she would have been able to sleep as her anticipation rose.

"Really? Are you sure?" Gavin asked, looking at her questioningly.

"I slept most of the day today and most of yesterday. I just want to read in there and relax in the moonlight. I promise I'll come back once I get tired," she pleaded.

He couldn't understand but knew pushing her to sleep

beside him would cause more of a rift. "Okay, come back to bed when you're ready."

She nodded as she bent over and kissed him on the cheek. "I shall. I love you."

"I love you too," Gavin responded. He just wanted to hold her but knew she still needed her freedom.

———————⚡———————

It was late, as Hokura stood in the library, taking in the city with a smile on her face. She left the curtains open so he would find her here. She would wait as long as it took as she couldn't quite explain why it had felt right to give it to him here... maybe to recreate the feeling she once felt... no... she had been uncertain back then. Her entire life had been in shambles. Since then, this place had held so much love and light for her. The library, which she had spent hours researching and reading. Her eyes gazed over the walls, to her paintings that Dorian had stored all those years after she disappeared until she came back and became pregnant. Dorian, who had brought them up and had hung them on the walls. She had added more over the years, yet it was the sentiment of having her art being enjoyed by others that warmed her. Reliving all those feelings of the paintings that hung on the wall, even if nobody else felt what she had, at least after tonight, maybe the professor would understand her a little better.

It had been half an hour later that she heard the familiar footsteps coming up behind her. "You're not sleeping again." His voice was tired.

She turned to him, he had looked exhausted and disheveled, but he was still beautiful. "I was waiting up for you to give you this."

He raised an eyebrow at her as he walked further into the library and stood beside her.

"For whatever reason, giving this to you in here, at night, it seemed right... fitting, I guess." She stepped to the side and revealed the large canvas beside her.

Dorian's eyes widened as he took it in, breathless as his fingers gently touched the canvas. "It's the city...."

"Yes..." Hokura answered.

"It's beautiful." His voice was hoarse. "The colors of the lights..." He silently stared, taking it all in, the brush strokes, the emotions behind them. "This is how you feel every time you look at it. This is what you see."

She nodded.

A sad smile came to his lips. "If only I could behold it in such a way." He looked at her. "It's the way I've always seen you."

Why was her heart feeling so heavy? "Dorian..."

"I understand now." But only partially. If anything, he was even more perplexed at how she felt things, how she felt about him, their relationship. How her heart and mind processed it, surely it was more profound than he could ever imagine. "This is so much more than I could ever ask for..." He stepped up to her. The moonlight cascaded off her making her look other-worldly. "May I kiss you?"

She was taken aback by the question. "You've never asked before..." He had always simply kissed her temple or her forehead.

"I know... but tonight I do..." He watched as she nodded slightly. He bent over, his lips gently meeting her cheek, lingering for a moment as he took in the warmth of her skin. "I will cherish this until the end of time, first child."

She wrapped her arms around him, burying her face in his chest when she noticed he was still in his lab clothes, that he hadn't been in the simulator. He had been exhausting himself again trying to figure this out. "I'll paint more. I'll paint you whatever you want!" she cried desperately.

His gentle hand came up behind her and cradled her head, simply enjoying being able to hold her. "Whatever you paint for me, I'll love."

Hokura didn't want to let go of him, as if time merely stopped for a moment as she gazed out the window. It had been raining again. The way the streetlights danced off puddles and shone off the windowpane looked magical. They stood for a while until she finally broke the silence. "The city looks especially beautiful in the rain tonight."

"It does tonight," Dorian stated, glancing out the window; somehow, it did, and he wondered if it was because he was holding her like this. That for a moment, they could just stand together enshrouded in darkness, merely holding one another, wishing for so much more. He would do anything for her, yet it seemed like the one task that was at his hand was eluding him day by day. His grip around her tightened. He couldn't lose her, not again, not like this, as he swallowed hard. He had made the choice long ago. He would rather love her from afar than live without her. It had been her confusion and feelings that still lingered for him, which allowed him to continue to be close to her. A love for one another that would never be anything more than what it was right now, lines drawn, and yet at times like this, he would take her hand and dance on those lines, allowing himself to feel so much more. "Gavin's most likely wondering where you are. You should get to bed." His voice was low.

"Is that what you want?" Hokura asked, still resting contently, breathing him in.

"No," he admitted, no more lies, he would be truthful. "But it's the right thing to say."

She couldn't help but smile. "Yeah... I guess I should get back... but... just give me one more selfish moment."

"Then it's selfish for the both of us."

"I love him." Hokura stirred. Why did she say it? Why did she feel like it was something she had to say when nobody else was listening?

"I know you do." Dorian's hand brushed through her hair. "You don't have to explain yourself."

"Maybe I feel like I do because most days I don't even know my own feelings. Maybe if I articulate them, I'll be able to make sense out of them." She looked up at him. "I love two people, and I can't be without either. That's not normal..."

A smile came to the professor's lips. "Maybe it's because you feel so deeply about others that you feel that way, Hokura. Maybe we're not meant to understand it, or..." He glanced at the canvas. "Maybe you need to paint a picture of it for others to finally understand."

"Have you ever heard of the red thread of fate? I feel like that, but mine wraps around myself, you, *and* Gavin, and we're all bound together back-to-back by it."

He raised his eyebrows. "That's an interesting way to see it. That puts some things into perspective, I guess. However, who is your thread actually connected to?" He shook his head gently. "None the matter. It's connected to Gavin."

"You're answering for me." Her voice was soft.

"Maybe it's mine that's connected to you, but yours is connected to Gavin," he answered. "In fiction, we call that a romantic tragedy." He nudged her gently. "Let's get you to bed. It's late."

Her brows furrowed. "I don't want to sleep. I don't want to close my eyes or waste the time that I have left sleeping." She looked up at him with desperation. "Why don't we stay up and watch the sunrise?"

He gently brought her chin up and smiled down at her. "I promise once you're better, we'll all stay up and watch the sunrise together, but until then, you do need your rest."

She pouted. Her mentor was instructing her to sleep because he knew she needed it. She did, even though she wanted to fight it.

"How are the nightmares?" he asked softly.

Hokura winced. "They've been changing because now I no longer fear Tobias or Richter. I fear the future."

"The future will be bright, Hokura. It's merely scary right now because you can't see the outcome." He gave her a squeeze. "It'll get better. Now let me take you back to your suite and then I can retrieve my painting and retire for the night myself."

After leading her to her door and bidding her goodnight, the professor went back to the library. He stared idly out the window and back at the painting. He had felt closer to her just now, more than he ever had before. He didn't want to lose ground, didn't want to lose *her* when he felt like this was the beginning. He shook his head. It wouldn't end. He would figure this out. Dorian picked up the painting. Indeed, he would cherish it forever. He would hang it in his bedroom so he could forever have a window from her soul that saw things so differently than the rest of them did. A small smile came to his lips. "Thank you, Hokura."

Hokura silently made her way to bed as Gavin stirred. "Hey," her husband said sleepily. "You alright?"

"I am." She sighed as she lay down, hoping if sleep would be kind to her that night.

"You were gone a bit. I was starting to question if I should check on you."

A meek smile came to her face. "No, I was just in the library..." She wondered if he could smell Dorian's cologne on her. "I'm feeling tired now, though... love you." With that, she rolled over and closed her eyes, her thoughts on the arms that were just around her, the promise of watching the sunrise together with everyone. She snuggled in and found herself fast asleep in a matter of minutes.

Gavin sighed... he knew who she had been with. There was only one person in the compound who had that signature cologne that seemed to waft from everything he touched... or held. He wanted to ask why she had felt compelled to seek him out, had wondered what they had spoken about. He let out a heavy breath. As much as she had loved him... as much as she had proven herself, Gavin couldn't help but wish he could take Dorian's place some days. He had noted that the painting she was working on was no longer in the closet that day. Perhaps she had taken it to him. He wondered if he could ask her to make him a piece of artwork. They had a few canvases of hers around their suite, but he had never asked her to commission him something. Then again, he felt odd asking. Dorian had asked for a painting to keep her busy. Would asking for one for himself make him seem jealous? Even if he was, he didn't want Hokura to know.

With that, Gavin rolled over. He didn't want to start over-thinking. That was the last thing he needed. All he wanted was to have a restful sleep as he tried to get comfortable again.

Hokura awoke to find Gavin at the kitchen table going over documents. "Good morning," she said groggily. She had slept well the night before. As if seeing Dorian had kept her nightmares at bay.

Gavin looked up at her. "Good morning. I made extra coffee if you want some." He was waiting for her to ask why he was home instead of being in his office.

"Thank you..." She walked over to the machine and poured herself a cup, stirring in some cream and sweetener before sitting across from him. She stared down at the documents. Adam's signature was scrolled over most of them. Obviously, he was overseeing more tasks to allow Gavin the opportunity to continuously check in with her. "Looks like there's been lots of work being done in the city."

"Yes," Gavin stated, turning a page. "The rainfall has caused some issues, but city maintenance has been on top of them."

"Looks like Adam's been putting his time in." She smiled. She didn't understand this solemn mood of his. If it was because he had figured out who she was with the night before or something else. Then again, if he had figured she had been with Dorian, then why was he acting this way? They had put this behind them long ago. Didn't he realize he had nothing to worry about? The thought ate at her.

"He has been and then some," her husband answered placidly.

Was she being insensitive to his feelings? She was having such a hard time gauging what to say to him. She didn't want him to feel like her time was ticking down, and yet it seemed that trying to do anything overly memorable was stating just that. She couldn't help but feel like she was reaching but needed to do so. "I was thinking," Hokura smiled lightly up at

Gavin. "Maybe we can go for a bike ride tonight?" She had been yearning to feel the wind again with her bike beneath her.

He grimaced, making a face at her. "I don't think that's exactly a good idea. It's been a while since your bike crash, but still... you're not getting any stronger."

"I know." She couldn't meet his eyes. "That's why I was hoping that you could drive, and I could hang onto you." It hurt to admit it, she knew she wasn't strong enough to be on her bike, but she could still ride with Gavin. If she was getting worse, this might be her last time to enjoy being on her bike, and she didn't want to allow the chance to slip from her before it was too late.

Gavin took her in as he came up from his spot and wrapped his arms around her. "Why don't we go at sunset then? Would you like that?" He could feel her nod as he closed his eyes. He just wanted to hold her for a bit. He knew she would rather be the one driving but knew that wasn't a possibility. He would do anything for her. The state she was in right now was causing his heart to bleed as every day she seemed a little weaker, her body becoming frailer by the day as the professor and his medical team exhausted themselves in the medical facility and the labs.

As Gavin held her, she closed her eyes and enjoyed his soft touch. Was this what he needed? To feel like she still needed *him*? The notion annoyed her. Of course, she needed him. He was her husband. "I don't want to keep you from your work."

"Work isn't important right now. Just let me hold you a little while longer..." His voice was soft. If she wanted to go riding, then he would oblige her. He would do anything that she wished; she simply needed to ask.

Hokura laid her head against him. Why did it never seem like it was enough? She wondered when the madness was going to end and when or if her life would ever resume to normal.

Gavin had spent the day doting on her, which Hokura had allowed. At this point, whatever he needed to do to bridge this emotional gap between them was something. She had read her book as he rubbed her feet. He had made her favorites for lunch, had even coaxed her into a warm bath, and massaged her shoulders. By the time the children came home, she was so relaxed that she almost opted out of the idea of being on her bike, but she knew she couldn't back out now. Cassandra and Cyrus had stepped up and helped with dinner even though Hokura had tried to wedge her way into helping with some meal prep.

"We're going to be out for a while this evening," Gavin stated at the dinner table.

The two nodded in unison and were helpful with clearing the table.

Hokura needed to excuse herself as she paced in her bedroom. Everyone was being so helpful. She had seen and felt the shift but couldn't deny the weight that she had felt because of it. Her heart felt heavy, as if no matter what she did, she wasn't doing the right thing by any of them. She sat on her bed; nobody was at fault. She couldn't allow herself to feel down and out about this. She was truly looking forward to riding that night. The thought lifted her morale. She hoped Gavin would enjoy it as well.

It was later in the evening as the two walked down to the garage hand in hand and up to Hokura's bike. She smiled slightly to see that Amara had apparently been on top of things and had repaired it since her accident. She felt grateful to have such a friend, yet her heart ached. Would she ever ride with the others again?

Gavin had noted her solemn expression since stating she wanted to go for a ride. He gently squeezed her hand. "You sure you want to do this? Why not wait until you're feeling better again?"

She didn't want to admit that she didn't know if she would *ever* feel better again. As much as Dorian had told her not to doubt him, as much as she believed he would save her, there was this nagging feeling in the back of her mind that told her differently. "I want this. I want to get out and feel the wind again. Besides, it might help my morale." She faked a smile.

He nodded and grabbed a helmet as he glanced over to Hokura, who seemed to be lost in her own little world as she was running her fingers over the bike. He would give her a minute.

Hokura's finger traced over the blue paint. It had been the side that had hit the cement. She had to hand it to Amara; she had done a flawless job of re-painting it. She couldn't even tell that it had been in an accident. An accident that seemed to be the start of all of this. She should have said something that night when she knew something was wrong. It had been a stupid mistake, and it had cost her. She had been lucky that it hadn't cost her more than some scrapes and bruises. Hokura rose and put on her helmet before turning to Gavin, who was staring at her. "Come on!" She smiled.

He walked over and got on the bike as she got onto the back and wrapped her arms around him. "Are you sure you're up for this?" he asked, his voice cracking. "You'll be able to hang on, right?"

She nodded "just go slow, this of this more as an easy joy ride tonight." She could feel the tears pricking her eyes. She wanted to be strong enough to do this herself, and yet the vehicle beneath her was now too much for her to control. Riding had always been a passion. There was something so freeing about it that she had yearned for. Even upon returning, riding her bike had held an unexplainable emotion as she commanded it underneath her.

Gavin revved the bike as they exited the garage. Her grip around him tightened as he promised he wouldn't go too fast. He was worried about her. He didn't think his reflexes would be fast enough to keep her on and keep the bike under control if she slipped. In a way, he had almost wished that she had asked one of the other peacekeepers to take her. Their speed and agility to move were incomparable to his when it came to riding. He wondered, too, why she hadn't asked Dorian to take her out. She had taught him to ride as well.

Nonetheless, he was happy to do it as they drove into the city. In fact, he had wished that she would ask him for more. It seemed lately like she had shied away from him when it came to her being so sick.

Hokura breathed deeply as she looked around her, at the city, which was basked in the warm light of the orange sky and setting sun. It was beautiful as always, everything from the greenery to the buildings. It wasn't the same with Gavin driving. She noticed his driving was especially stiff tonight as he was most likely concentrating on going at a slower speed and keeping her balanced. Something she never had to worry about in the past: she was content with this. If this was the last time she was ever on her bike, she was alright with it being a passenger with her arms wrapped around her husband. There was a calmness to the night as well, as if it were some kind of acceptance. No... they would never allow her to accept this, Gavin, Dorian, everyone... she needed to keep fighting. She needed to stay strong. She couldn't doubt her creator. Even as she was out here enjoying the evening, he was in the labs working.

Hokura shook her head. She was so selfish. Dorian had said he was a monster... he was wrong... it had been her. She had been the biggest, most despicable monster of them all. She had pushed her friends away, had pushed Gavin away, and then had the audacity at times to complain about feeling lonely. She had put up walls with everyone except the professor. Even now, he was on her mind. He was right about what he had said in the garden. His feelings weren't the complicated ones... again, it fell solely on her. Hokura chewed her bottom lip. She wasn't worthy of anyone's love with what she had put them through.

Gavin felt the faltering movement behind him as her forehead rested against his back. "You alright back there?"

"Yes..." She sighed. "Can we go to the memorial park? I'd like to see the garden."

He pursed his lips. He could only guess why she wanted to go there. She had frequented it. It had been a favorite place of hers because of the plaque erected in the central garden, which stood proudly in the middle of the park. He nodded and continued until they came to the area, and he parked in front.

Hokura silently got off the bike and walked towards the main garden.

Gavin stayed behind as he watched her. He crossed his arms and took in her mood. He had hoped it would lighten with the drive, but it seemed she was even more solemn now. After a few moments, he couldn't take it any longer as he strode up behind her and wrapped his arms around her. "Are you at least enjoying yourself?"

She nodded as she gazed at the flowers, they had been blooming beautifully, and she wanted to reach out and gently touch them. "I am... I just have a lot on my mind." She turned to face him. "I guess I'm trying to process things of the past." The problem with doing that was her mindset was that she was running out of time. She swallowed hard. "I've had a beautiful life."

"You will continue to have a beautiful life. This is merely one of those bumps in the road. We'll get you through this. You've come this far..."

Hokura glanced at the plaque. As if her following words were going to be a sacred vow to all of them. "You're right. I need to keep fighting. I need to stay positive" She was just so tired. The idea of continuing like this any longer seemed exhausting. "This was just what I needed. Thank you for doing this."

Gavin caught the tired undertone. Was she lying to him? Was there something more she had required of him that he hadn't delivered on? "Whatever you need, I'll be there to do it for you. You just need to tell me. I promise." It could be anything, and he would bend to her will to keep her happy.

She gripped him tightly. She needed him to believe that this was beyond him. "Gavin, you've done everything I've asked." Her eyes bore into his. "And everything you've done has meant so much, and I'm so sorry that this has been so hard on you. Please, my love, don't think you haven't."

"I just want to do more..." He felt powerless, helpless. He had wished he had some sort of higher understanding of what she was going through, that he had some sort of scientific or medical incline of how to help her. If only he had been Dorian.

"You've done everything you can." Her voice was soft. She could understand. Once again, this was a situation that was out of his hands. Just like when he didn't rescue her, in a way, she had been upset that it hadn't been him. Dorian's words hung in her mind. There was a reason why it had been him and not Gavin. She kissed her husband. It started gentle and then grew as he cupped the back of her head and brought her closer. He needed this. He needed her to stay with him more than anything. He needed *her*.

His lips came from hers. "I don't want this distance between us. I need you, Hokura. More than anything else, you are my world."

She didn't want that either. There needed to be some physical reconciliation between them. "Let's go home then, and you can have me." She smiled lightly, embracing him again. She would let him show her. As much as she had shied away from him, maybe this was exactly what he needed. She knew her body was grotesque and bruised, but he wouldn't falter.

Gavin squeezed her hand as they walked back towards the bike. He would remind her once again how much he loved her. He would entertain her through the night, kiss every inch of her battered body, and show her it didn't matter how bruised she was. None of that mattered as long as she was still physically with him.

Hokura lazily rose from her bed. Gavin had left a few hours before. He had told her to rest after their lovemaking session had gone later into the night. As she got up, her chest began to burn as she started a coughing fit. She didn't have a chance to reach for the towel beside her bed as she lifted the shirt she had been sleeping in to cover her mouth. Her fits were getting worse as this one lasted longer than she had ever experienced. By the time she was able to breathe, she had realized she had drenched the shirt in blood. "Dammit," she wheezed as she simply freed herself from the shirt. She couldn't just put it in the laundry. If Gavin saw this, he would surely worry even further.

Hokura put on another top as she walked to the bathroom to try and blot out as much of the blood from her nightshirt as possible. Her eyes gazed at herself in the mirror in shock. "Wha...?" She got closer to her reflection, her face almost unrecognizable. Her skin had a yellow tinge to it. The whites of her eyes also followed suit. She rubbed her face and then ran her fingers through her hair. They became tangled as he tried to comb them through it. To her horror, there were several strands of hair caught in her fingers as she brought them back. She grabbed her brush as she forgot entirely about the shirt as she gingerly and carefully brought it through her hair, tears forming in her eyes as she stared at herself. "No... no, no, no, no! This can't be it," she whispered in desperation, looking at her brush and the amount of hair it now held as she dropped it and rubbed her eyes, looking back into the mirror. "This can't be..." She took a deep breath. She needed to steady herself. Maybe she needed to be in the medical facility for a few days. Her throat caught again as the rising tickle was too much. She struggled to swallow it as she choked, and it erupted from her chest as she went to her knees. She had been thankful for the shirt as she hacked into it again, blood filling her mouth as she spat. Her head spun as she closed her eyes and fought for air.

"Is this the end of me?" she choked as her strength was sucked out of her. She lay on the floor in a fetal position as the fit continued. By the end of the fit, there was no way she could wash the shirt. She figured she would simply dispose of it as she wobbly got to her feet. "I just need a drink." Some warm coffee would surely help soothe her throat. Her chest was burning. She was tired.

As Hokura walked towards the kitchen, her body started to falter. Her head began spinning. What was happening to her?

Was it just an off morning, or had things gotten progressively worse? She knew the answer. As she entered the kitchen, she stumbled forward. Her reactions were quick, as her hand shot out to catch herself on the counter, but as it made contact, a sickening notion spread up her arm, and she heard a slight crack.

Hokura let out a stifled cry as she lowered herself, grabbing her hand, which was now pulsating. "How?" she cried as she braced it gingerly and stared at it. It hurt. It was a sensation she had never felt before as her hand began to swell. "No..." This wasn't normal... a peacekeeper's bones were hard as steel. They were created to withstand incredible impacts. How was this happening to her? She didn't want to admit it. She needed help. "Dorian..." She needed him... he would be in his labs... she needed to page him, but not until she disposed of her blood-stained shirt.

———✦———

He had gotten her page. After talking to her on the phone, he raced up to her suite. Upon opening the door, he gazed at her. Why did she appear to be so much worse? There were obvious bags under her eyes. Her face was starting to sink in. What on earth had changed so drastically over the past twenty-four hours? "Hokura?" He wrapped his arms around her as fear coursed through him. "You're looking..." He didn't want to say it. "Did you sleep at all last night?"

"I did. I slept in..." she replied. "Dorian... I can feel it... everything is starting to hurt, I'm becoming weak, I'm so tired..." She reached up for him as his eyes took in her hand.

"Wha..."

"I think I broke it..." Her voice was soft. "It hurts. It's throbbing."

He nodded. "We need to that X-rayed and set." He led her down the hallway towards the elevator and watched as she moved. Her once fluid motions now almost seemed to have a stiff, tired limp to them. "What else hurts? Where are you in pain?" He slowed his stride so she could keep up, something he had been doing for a while now, but now it seemed painstakingly slow.

"My chest, my hips..." She closed her eyes. This wasn't simply from the actions the night before. This was deeper. "Just everything... I feel like I just escaped again. My body feels like it's rotting."

He stopped. "Don't say that!" He could barely bear to look at her. Her perfect skin seemed to be discolored with a yellow tinge. Her cheeks were sunken in. Her body looked malnourished. Even her hair, which seemed to shine and reflect light, looked dry and dying. The elevator dinged as they got in. He couldn't take it as she sagged against the wall, barely able to keep herself upright. He didn't falter as he picked her up and pursed his lips in worry. She seemed so much lighter as she brought her head to his chest. She didn't fight him, didn't say anything. "We'll get you checked, get your hand looked after. Then maybe another CT scan would be best to see how things are progressing." His heart panged something horrible as his insides turned. This wasn't good. Their time was nearly up. His mind raced. What on earth could he do to buy more?

They exited the elevator as the professor continued carrying her. The whispers and stares continued to follow them as he brought her down to the medical facility. The halls had been barren as he got her to the X-ray lab and placed her hand properly on the machine as he turned it on. Indeed, she had broken it. He wondered if it would even heal in the state she was in. The peacekeeper's bones were incredibly tough. Even those of the compound had strong bones. To actually see the damage that she had done brought on a cold dread that washed over him. Was she already too far gone? "I'll wrap your hand and stabilize it as best as possible," he stated as he grabbed a splint and wrapped it. "After the CT scan, we'll get some ice on it as well," he instructed as he picked her up again.

"I can walk," she moaned.

"Do you want me to put you down and let you walk?"

Her eyes closed as she breathed deeply, her brows furrowed. "No... it just seemed right to say."

He could read the worry on her face and could only imagine the thoughts going through her head. "I'm going to call Gavin. He should be here."

"He didn't see me this morning... I was still sleeping when he left." Her voice was dry. "I know I look worse this morning."

That confirmed things. She was aware that she had gone downhill.

"It's okay. We're going to get you looked after." He tried to alleviate her worry as his own set in. Upon walking further down the medical facility hallway, he saw Dr. Spindler and Lucien walking towards him. "She requires a CT scan stat. We need to inform the governor to get down here right away and see what's happening to her. The deterioration of her system is progressing at a faster rate than we had hoped."

Dr. Spindler nodded. "I'll run ahead and get the machine started."

Dr. Lucien also nodded. "I'll retrieve the governor."

Dorian looked down at Hokura, so frail in his arms. "See, we're going to be on top of this. Everything will be alright." His voice was calm and soothing. His mind reeled. How on earth was it that she had her system deteriorated like this before his very eyes?

"It's bad, isn't it?" she asked, looking up at him tiredly.

He made a face. "We'll figure this out. The CT scan will help us and hopefully give us some answers with how we can proceed from here."

Hokura tugged at him. "Dorian, please... you just did an excellent job avoiding what I asked... I already know I'm not okay."

He stared down at her frail body. To admit so would be to admit that he was losing ground, but he couldn't lie to her when she already knew the truth. "No, you're not okay, Hokura... but I can still fix this."

Gavin ran down the hallway, Lucien following in his wake. He had gotten to the CT room to see Dr. Spindler standing outside it with a grim expression on his face. The governor's eyes widened. "Hokura..."

The doctor shook his head. "It's not looking good. The professor is in the room waiting for the scan to be done." Gavin was about to go in when Spindler placed a hand on his shoulder. "We're doing everything we can for her. I swear we are... but I don't know if there's enough time..."

Gavin took a deep breath. "I know, doctor..." He walked into the room to see Dorian pacing as the CT scanner was going through its motions. The professor gave him a grave expression, one that Gavin had seen before, one that spoke that he had lost everything.

Dorian's eyes met Gavin's. He licked his lips as his brows furrowed in sorrow. "At the moment, she's not doing well; it's spreading..." He couldn't finish the sentence as Gavin brought his hands to his face and covered his eyes.

"How much longer?"

Dorian couldn't look at the man. He didn't want to see how much this was tearing him apart as well. Still, he needed to stand firm. "We still have time... this isn't the end... she's getting weaker, but..."

The professor could see Gavin's eyes were beginning to water as he stared up at the ceiling. "Then you've done all you could."

"Don't think that this is the end!" Dorian stated in a harsh voice as he glared at him.

Tears escaped Gavin's eyes as he gently placed a hand on the professor's shoulder. "Dorian..." His voice was a soft quiver. "You've *done* all you can..."

"I can fix this!" His voice was stern.

Gavin shook his head. "Even I can see that she's gotten worse. She didn't look like this last night... it's time to accept..."

Dorian wrenched his shoulder from Gavin's grasp. "I will not accept anything, governor. I said I would save her and come hell or high water. I will stand by my word."

Why was he so stuck on this when it was so obvious that her time was running out? He couldn't fault the man. "I already asked if something happens... are you still okay with overseeing..."

He gave Gavin an irritated look. "Yes, I will see to it, but that's *not* going to happen. This is a misstep, another bump in the road..."

"Her road is ending! This isn't a bump... even I can see that... she doesn't have long. She's going to die!"

The professor took a deep breath. "Get out." His voice was soft.

"Dorian, please!" Gavin urged.

He closed his eyes; he couldn't face the man. His tone was even. "Get out... I can't have you questioning me like this, not when I've worked this hard... not when her life is on the line like this." He heard Gavin's footsteps as he walked away from him.

The scanner stopped after a few moments as it ejected Hokura, who brought herself into a sitting position, worry etched over her face. "He's right, isn't he?" Her tone was pleading.

Dorian's eyes held hers as he turned. "I will not allow you to lose hope, even if everything seems lost. I have made a promise to you," he said softly. "And I fully intend to keep it. Please, believe that I will not let you die."

She looked down solemnly. "Dorian... I..." she wanted to believe him, wanted to desperately hang onto his words and have them be her lifeline, but as much as she wanted to depend on him, she knew in her heart what was happening. "If something does happen...."

"I won't hear it, Hokura!" His voice was stern.

She flinched slightly, enough that he caught it. He kneaded his forehead. This was getting too much for him. "I'm sorry." He looked to see that Gavin had closed the door as he walked up to her. He fell to his knees and wrapped his arms around her. "I can't accept this... I won't... I can't lose you again."

The fingers of her good hand went through his hair as she gently soothed him. "I want you to hear this... please just listen to me and don't fight me. Let me say this one thing."

He silently waited as she commanded him to listen to her.

"Whatever happens, I will never fault you. I know you did everything in your power to save me." Her eyes were desperate as she brought her hand to his face and forced him to look at her as her eyes bore into his with an intensity he had never seen before. "You cannot blame yourself if I die."

His brows furrowed. How could she tell him such a thing? Yet... he lowered his eyes. He couldn't look at her. "If that's what you command of me, then I won't..." His mind reeled. If she died, then a new project would begin. He would suspend her only moments after death until he found a way to cure her. He would devote his days to making sure he succeeded in this. Didn't she realize that she was the only thing that kept him going? That a life without her wasn't a life at all? His eyes glanced at her broken hand. "Let me get you some painkillers for that."

"There's something you need to do first," Hokura stated. "You need to go find Gavin, and you need to talk to him. I can't have you two at odds right now. That won't solve or help any of this."

He grimaced. "If that's what you wish..." He obediently rose from his spot.

Hokura was taken aback but gave him a light smile and nodded. Why was he being so submissive? She was bracing herself for an argument.

"I'll go find Gavin and talk to him. I know Spindler and Lucien are close by. I'll have them see to you. I'll come back with your husband once I speak to him," Dorian said placidly. He didn't look at her as he left the room. As he did so, he found Spindler standing right outside the door. He instructed the doctor to oversee Hokura. "I need to find the governor." He was relieved he didn't have to go far. Gavin was sitting against the hallway wall, his head in his hands. The professor took a deep breath. "I'm sorry for being so rash with you."

Gavin's head rose. His voice was strained. "I know it's just as hard for you, but I feel like I need to start accepting what the reality of things might be. That there's a possibility that we're going to lose her."

This wasn't what he wanted to hear. Dorian took a breath. He needed to stay calm. He couldn't let his temper get the best of him. "If that is the process you need to go through, you are free to feel that way."

"What other avenues do you have left?" Gavin's voice rose. "How much further can she deteriorate, Dorian? Or is it that you're just in denial over what's happening?"

He couldn't let this break him. He couldn't allow Gavin's emotions to overtake him, or all would be lost. "I need to remain strong for her because the second everyone gives up hope is the second this project fails, and I swore to her and to myself that I would never fail her again."

The governor shook his head. "There's only so much you can do. You're not a miracle worker."

The comment hit him, and he bristled. "May I remind you that I am the father of science. I *created* the stem cell project that keeps every person in this sanctuary youthful. I aided in bringing back procreation among those here. Don't you *dare* think that this is beyond me!"

"I'm not blaming you." Gavin's voice was soft. "She won't blame you either. I can't keep pretending anymore, though."

The professor rolled his eyes. "You do whatever you deem necessary; I shall do the same, but we can't be at odds with one another about this. So, for that, I apologize."

A small smile cracked through Gavin's demeanor. "I wish I were as thick-headed as you. I wish I had it in me *not* to give up... but I need to accept this."

Dorian offered the man his hand. "Get up. She's waiting for us. I want to make sure she takes her pain medication for her hand. Then I need to see to her scans..."

Gavin took it and rose. "What did she do to her hand?"

"Broke it... which means her bones are weakening..."

"Then this had taken over her entire body if even her bones are becoming fragile..." Gavin commented solemnly.

Dorian pursed his lips. "I set her hand; it's wrapped... as for it healing..." He didn't know how to say it... "Her system is such a mess right now that it's possible that it's going to take quite some time. For the time being, I'm hoping I can find a way to isolate the healing process in her hand and speed it up... but as of this moment, that's..." He shook his head. "I have only some theories."

Gavin's hand came to his shoulder. "We'll do what we can."

They walked back into the room where Hokura had been waiting. Dr. Spindler had been checking her hand.

She smiled lightly as she watched the two walk in, Gavin's hand on the professor's shoulder. "I'm glad you two had a talk."

Gavin rushed over to her and locked his arms around her. "I'm taking some time off work, and I'm not going to hear any complaints from you."

Hokura wrapped her arm with her good hand around him.

Dr. Spindler looked up at the professor. "I've prescribed some pain medication and gave her an icepack. The swelling will go down in a bit."

Dorian's gaze followed towards Gavin and Hokura. "Thank you, doctor. Now, if you'll excuse me, I need to oversee these scans and get back to the drawing board." He noted the worried look on Hokura's face as he faked a smile. "Keep Gavin by your side and rest up. That hand isn't going to heal any quicker if you keep moving about."

Gavin nodded and turned to Hokura. "What on earth were you doing when this happened?"

She chewed her bottom lip. "I was going to make breakfast. I slipped and tried to catch myself. The impact of my hand hitting the counter is what must have caused the break."

Both Dorian and Gavin winced. The break had been caused by something so simple.

The professor could feel his insides churning. Possible balance issues, fatigue, the list was ongoing now. He glanced at the scans in his hand and felt like he was going to be sick. "Gavin will take care of you. If I come across anything further, I'll be in touch." He excused himself quickly and was down the hallway. Spindler quickly caught up to him.

"Dorian!" the man cried as caught up to the professor. "What would you have me do? I honestly am not sure on how to proceed with this any further. Her system has deteriorated to the point where..."

The professor stopped and hung his head. "I'm unsure myself, Spindler. I need you and Lucien to put your heads together. If there's anything you two can think of..." He knew the man was going to interrupt... "bounce a ball off the wall or something... go for coffee, and mull this over. I need some time to myself." With that, he continued on his way to his office.

Upon entering, he locked the door and crashed at his desk, his eyes watering. At least he was able to keep the front up. At least he was still able to be hard with Gavin. His hands trembled as he stared at the scans... "She's barely even there anymore." His voice hitched. Her bones had become so incredibly brittle. Her organs were spotted, and everything was crashing. He tried to keep his breathing in check as his vision blurred. He needed to hide the truth from the others; he needed them to believe in him, but at that moment, he had no idea what he was doing or how he was going to bring her back. He didn't know how long she had left. "I will hold myself to my promise." Dorian closed his eyes as the tears escaped. He tightened the grip on his emotional leash. He would have his time later this evening. Until then... he didn't need to continue to look at the scans. He knew her time was coming to an end.

Dorian got up from his desk and composed himself. He took a breath and cleared his throat. He needed to appear to be in control. He needed to appear to know exactly what he was doing. He couldn't let anyone know that he had hit a wall. He left his office and walked towards his labs. He had quartered off the one room specifically, but he would most likely add more rooms to continue his work if this continued. He unlocked the door and closed it directly after walking in as he stared at the pale blue light that illuminated the room. He didn't want this to be her resting place. He didn't want to see her body suspended and lifeless as it was encapsulated. "I don't know what else to do," he groaned. "I'm so bloody lost right now." It was a perplexing sensation, one he had never quite felt before. He had felt helpless before, but this was different. A man of stature and mindset, of his genius, should be able to figure this out, and yet there had setback after setback. "It's just like the damn stem cell project again." He walked over to the chamber and checked the temperature. It was right where it needed to be. The machine was also the reason why he had nothing else running to this room. He was sure the power that it had taken to stabilize had been astronomical.

The idea of her being dead inside of it hurt, but he needed to hold onto hope. There would be a way to save her. Surely there was. He had nothing but time on his hands. He could easily devote his years to bringing her back. He shrank to his knees as he sat beside the vat as he leaned against it. He didn't want to keep this secret. He didn't want to continue with the lies and deception. Would they see this as an act of betrayal? He promised Gavin to see to her body. The governor was expecting it to be cremated and for there to be some sort of ceremony... little did he know whatever ashes the professor came up with wouldn't be hers. Of course, it was an act of betrayal and trust. He scowled angrily. Certainly, once he cured her, everything would be forgiven. Gavin wouldn't be able to fault him.

"Get this last resort out of your damn head," he growled at himself. "You still have time. Don't you dare start faltering. I need to get up and get back to work." He didn't have time to sit and brood like this. He would go out tonight... the day was still young. He would take all his reports to Lucien and Spindler. They would spend the day combing over everything, from why the cloned blood was clotting to how they could possibly stabilize her system without causing it any further harm.

<hr />

Gavin had gotten Hokura settled as he mulled about the kitchen, making her breakfast. She had been quiet since leaving the medical facility. His mind was running a mile a minute. How was it possible that she had deteriorated overnight the way she had? He had made love to her the night before... had that been it? He had physically pushed, and therefore she had gotten weaker? He squeezed some oranges and made her some fresh juice. Maybe she needed more nutrients? No, he was reaching, and he knew it. He walked over to her on the couch and smiled lightly. "Freshly squeezed," he said, putting the glass down in front of her.

She raised an eyebrow. "Because what was in the fridge wasn't good enough?"

He gave an aggravated sigh. "You sure know how to keep kicking a guy once he's down, you know that, right?"

A laugh came from her, which surprised him. "Was that some dark sarcasm?" She chuckled.

Gavin rolled his eyes. He couldn't help but feel annoyed by her sudden shift in her mood as he sat down beside her. "You're taking this too well..."

Hokura looked up at her husband. "How do you want me to take this? I've felt upset, depressed, alone, I've shut everyone out... maybe I'm just at the point of accepting that whatever happens is going to happen."

His brow arched, he understood, and in a way, he hated it. He wanted her to keep her faith in the professor, the way he had sworn to her that he would succeed, but if she was now acting like this... did she know? Could she feel her time ticking away? "Whatever happens, I want to be by your side."

She leaned back on the couch. "Well, it's not like I'm physically going anywhere." She looked over at him. "How about we keep things light? Have some breakfast, relax, play some cards..."

This was unlike her. She seemed too at ease. Was this the calm before the storm? Or was it something different?

Hokura licked her lips as she took him in. "Gavin, I can't fight this, even if I wanted to. So, for now, let's just enjoy our time together." With that said, her stomach made a noise as she smirked. "I think my stomach is in agreeance."

He gave a meek smile. "Let's get you fed then. It's nearly done." He made his way to the kitchen. He had made her eggs benedict, something he had mastered years ago but only made on occasion. He quickly stirred the sauce as he made a pained expression, in a way he wished he had made it more often for her. All the times he could have indulged her, and now he wondered how many more opportunities he would have to do so.

Gavin plated her meal and walked it over to her. The way her eyes lit up as she ate panged at his heart. Something so simple that made her so happy. That was all he ever wanted was to see. Her happiness radiate off her like it was doing now.

"This is just what I needed!" She grinned as she ate.

At least she was eating... he needed something more... last night was a testament. She had been excited to be on her bike again, even if she hadn't been the one driving. Tonight, he would give her something special, another memory for her to look back to. Something they hadn't done in quite some time...

Cassandra threw a punch as she let out a heavy growl. She didn't know why she felt like she needed to overexceed herself today as it landed hard. She threw another and a third as she continued with her exercise.

Talon raised an eyebrow. "Something on your mind again?"

A smirk came to her face. "You know you're the best therapist around here, right Talon?"

The watch commander grunted as he crossed his arms. "Not exactly in my job title, but I can always tell when something is bugging you."

She didn't stop her sequence. "A while ago, my mom told me she's sick... I felt like I had to force it out of her even though I knew all along." She ducked, moved, countered, swung. "She's getting worse... I can physically see it, and yet she's said nothing."

"What do you want her to say, exactly?" Talon asked, taking the girl in. She was definitely working up a sweat today in order to tire herself out.

The girl scowled, swinging hard. "I don't know... I just want to be kept in the loop, and I feel like she's not going to say anything until..." Finally, Cassandra faltered as she turned towards Talon. "Until it's too late..."

The watch commander scratched his bald head. "Your mother is a fighter. It's in her nature. She might not recognize the same end that you do." He studied the girl. He had known her mother well enough to know what he was talking about. "Your mom sees and feels things differently. This isn't a slight

Cassandra. If you're feeling this way, maybe you should talk to her.

It was a simple enough solution, so why did it seem so hard to talk to her mother some days? Because last time her mother had said they would talk about things another day... then again, it hadn't been about this. "She's just so hard to talk to sometimes... I know she does it to protect me. I'm sure that's why she didn't tell me about this in the first place. She didn't want me to worry, but now it looks like things are going downhill."

Talon hmphed. "Communication be damned, kiddo, you're all family; you should be able to talk it out." He rubbed his head. "But I know your mom has a past..." He pursed his lips. It was a past that he could have been part of. He could have escaped along with her and the others but had stayed behind. Whereas Allen and Annette had perished, Talon had reaped the benefits of staying behind in the compound and had a prolonged life. "It's hard for her to talk about, so go easy on her too."

Cass gave him a smirk. "I can always count on complaining to you, Talon."

He matched her grin. "And I'll always be here to hear it, but don't expect me to go soft on you for it."

She let out a laugh. "I wouldn't want it any other way." She continued her circuit. Of course, Talon was right as always. She was glad she had him around to talk to. As much as she wanted to talk to the professor, the man seemed to be scarce lately. She understood. He was most likely working around the clock to see what he could come up with to stabilize her mother's system. Cassandra made a mental note. She would physically work out her frustrations today and stay later. She would talk to her mom in the next few days, maybe the rest day. She formulated a plan as she continued her training.

Cassandra made her way to the elevator when she saw Cyrus approaching it. She waved at him and called for him. "Wait up!" She quickened her pace as she went to his side. "You're coming home late."

Cyrus raised an eyebrow. "So are you... how was training?"

"I stayed late and worked on some extra drills today."

"Because you're avoiding something," Cyrus said, pushing the elevator button. "Or rather *someone*."

The girl made a face as she crossed her arms. "You're one to talk."

He shrugged casually. "I'm not denying it either." He gave his sister a look as the doors opened, and they walked into the elevator. Cyrus gave a sigh. "Mom will tell us what she needs to tell us when she deems the time is ready."

"Do you think her time is running out?" Cassandra idly kicked at the floor. "You think that's why she wanted to go out riding with Dad last night?"

Cyrus didn't meet his sister's look. "I have a hunch."

They exited the elevator and started down the hallway. Cassandra chewed at her thumbnail. "You think they're just avoiding another hard conversation?"

The boy shoved his hands in his pocket. "Nobody wants to have the kind of conversation you're thinking of... besides, the medical team and professor are working on things. There haven't even been any reports signed off from the professor for days. Usually, the botanists send him reviews to look over, and we've got nothing back."

Cassandra slowed her pace. She wasn't ready to be home just yet. "I'm sure he has enough to deal with."

Cyrus only nodded as the two had stopped completely and stood a few feet away from their door. "You know you can talk to me, Cass... maybe the professor was right. Maybe we should see some kind of counselor or something."

The girl's brow furrowed. "I have Talon. He listens pretty well... throwing some punches seems to help too."

He gave her a look. "We have each other. You know that."

His sister rolled her eyes at him. "And what about you? Why does it seem like you're the one bottling everything up and keeping everything in?"

Cyrus sighed. "I dunno. My logical rationale is that there's nothing I can do about this. I'm worried about things, but I have no idea what's going on. Worrying further won't solve anything."

She stepped back. As much as they were alike, they were also completely different. "For better terms, Cy, that sounds weird. Enough with your logical shit. How about you just get angry like every other person?"

He gave her a quizzical look. "Why? What good would that do?"

"Because it's not fair!" Cassandra shot back.

The boy took in his sister. She was driven by emotion, very much like her mother. There was nothing else he could do as he grabbed onto her and hugged her. "Sometimes that's just life, Cass."

She had felt perplexed since when did Cyrus have such a level head? Since when had he seemingly matured like this? "I'm going to talk to her again in a few days. Do you want to be part of my plan?"

He smiled as he didn't let go of her. "I'd like that... now how about we go have a nice evening with Mom and Dad?" With that, they continued the few feet to their suite. Upon opening the door, their eyes darted to their mother, who was sitting on the couch. A cold dread washed over them as they took her in. Cassandra stood frozen as she gazed at her. It was Cyrus's hand finding her's that snapped her out of it.

"Mom." His words echoed in her head. "What did you do to your hand?"

Cassandra's father answered. "She had a minor accident today and broke it. The professor had it X-rayed and set it. Hopefully, in time, it'll heal up."

The girl stood there in shock. Her mother looked worse than when they had rescued her. She remembered crying the words to Dorian that her mother was dead and how he had grunted that she was merely unconscious. The fear wrapped around her and gripped her chest as the world around her felt heavy. She needed to keep her breathing in check. Her mother was very much alive, sitting on the couch... her mouth moving. She was saying something. Her brows furrowed.

"Cassandra," Hokura said, giving her daughter a look.

"Mom..." The girl snapped out of it. She hadn't heard a word she had said as she shook her head.

Hokura gave her a sad smile. "I know it looks bad. I know that I look much worse today and that things are deteriorating, but you two need to stay positive. I don't want you worrying about me, alright?"

Cassandra could feel her anger rising. She wanted to yell at her, to scream and tell her, of course, she was worried! Did she not realize what she looked like? No, arguing and fighting wouldn't get her anywhere. It would merely upset her mother. That was something nobody needed right now. She put on a brave face. "Okay, Mom, whatever you say." She felt her throat catch as her father looked at her. "If you need Cyrus and me to do anything, just let us know." She shook her head. "I gotta shower. Drills went a bit longer than expected today."

Gavin licked his lips. "Freshen up. Then we'll have

dinner." He had seen the disdained look on his daughter. He wanted to tell her that things were getting worse... but he didn't have the words. Confirming it now and telling the children it was time to accept things was a conversation his heart still needed some time for.

It wasn't until Cassandra was in the safety of the shower that her tears flowed. How could Cyrus not feel the dread? Or was he that oblivious that their mother was dying? That she literally looked like she was already dead? How could they all act like everything was fine? She didn't want to face any of them, and yet she needed to be strong and put on a brave face for her mother. That's what she wanted. That's what Cassandra would do. She would talk to her mother again in the next few days. She yearned for that heart to heart with her.

Dinner was unusually quiet. Cassandra and Cyrus shared some clips about their day and how lessons were going. Cassandra couldn't help but stare at her mother whenever her eyes moved from her plate as she swallowed hard. She had lost her appetite. She didn't even think she was tasting her food.

It wasn't until after dinner, when the children had excused themselves to their rooms after helping tidy up, that Hokura gave Gavin a weary look. "I need to talk to them, to prepare them."

Something he didn't want to do as he pursed his lips. "Give it a day..." He had something planned for that night after the sun had set. "Why don't you let me help you wash up? You can't move your hands or get it wet."

Hokura nodded. Worry washed over her. She had picked up on Cassandra's mood all night. She knew her daughter was stressed about the situation. How on earth did one talk to their child about this? How did one tell their teenager to start preparing their heart for the possibility that their mother might die? She needed to think... she would talk to them both in the next day.

"Come on, let me help you to the bathroom and get you changed," Gavin offered.

At least she still had some time to think about it.

The evening had progressed into night as Dorian stumbled in the darkness and into the garden. He would have given anything to dull this pain. Any drug or substance that would keep his heart from breaking open and bleeding. He made his way to the blueberry bush. He needed to mourn in private. He was losing her again, and this time it would be permanent. No... there was the backup plan. There was the chamber. He had made sure it was ready... but still, it wouldn't be the same. Death... it was supposed to be something she never went through. Her body was supposed to stay young and healthy forever. He looked at the bush and fell to his knees, his memory going back to when they had so carefully dug it up all those years ago in the forest and had transplanted it here.

"I've failed," he choked. At least he could admit it here. "The only person I ever loved, and in the end, I couldn't even save her." He tried to hold back as a sob escaped him. He looked over to the blueberry bush and glared at the plaque. She had told him if he had jumped off the roof, she would have followed him because he was the only one who could save her. If he couldn't be with her in life... then... "Maybe it would be best..." No. He couldn't. He needed to come to the ugly terms and face the reality that there was nothing he could do right now. She was running out of time. She needed more time, and only cryogenic suspension would give her that, and for that to happen... He bit his bottom lip hard enough that he tasted blood. Thinking of her heart stopping was enough to drive him into madness.

"I will save you... I will bring you back... if it takes the rest of my damnable life, I will do it." He clutched his chest. The physical pain brought back so many memories. The day he decided to call off searching for her over fifty-three years ago, how he wanted to simply die back then. It had been that feeling all over again. He had let go of hope only to have her return forty years later. He knew there was a life beyond her, but now it seemed utterly pointless. What was living if she wasn't around? It was merely existing, and he had done that long enough. "I will still live for you. If not for you, then nothing." He breathed deep, his resolve slowly coming back. He would need to accept the reality as much as he didn't want to. She was going to die, and he would have to fall back on something that was possibly beyond him. He would not only have to suspend her, but he would also have to cure her and then find a way to bring her back to life.

His head pounded as though it was trying to break open his skull. Gavin had already asked for him to deal with the arrangements when it came to her body. It would be the perfect ruse. He would step down from his mantle of being the father of science and turn to finding a way to bring her back. There were enough scientists and doctors in the compound. With the system he had created and perfected, he was now expendable. The only person who would need him would be in his lab, waiting for him to reawaken her. He would. He could never fail her.

Dorian closed his eyes and kneaded his forehead; this was no time to break. He needed to remain calm and composed. He needed to accept the inevitable she was going to die. It needed to happen for him to suspend this process and buy time in order to bring her back. Should he tell her? Should he let her in on his plan, or would she say something to Gavin? He had known the man long enough to conclude that he wouldn't allow the project to move forward. He had already accepted things. After speaking with him that afternoon, he knew the man would never stand for Hokura to continue to be a science experiment even after her death. He could offer her no more comfort other than telling her he wouldn't give up. That hurt even worse. "I'm sorry, my love, I know I had said there would be no more secrets... but there will be one last thing that I can't tell you." It would be one kept out of love, out of his undying devotion to her.

It was late into the evening. Gavin had Hokura take a nap after helping her wash up. He hadn't wanted her to be over-tired for what he had planned. With Cyrus and Cassandra's help, he was able to set things up to how he had wanted. He had wanted to share more with them about their mother and what was happening but stayed tight-lipped. If they had brought it up, he would have. Perhaps it had been evident to them.

As the sky grew, dark Gavin took Hokura to the roof. He had wanted to surprise her as he led her up to the blankets and pillows he had set out. Upon Hokura seeing what he had done, she turned to him with a bright smile.

"What is all this?"

His heart ached. "Just something I wanted to do for us. It's been a while since we've really had a night together to enjoy ourselves up here." It hurt. They had wanted to leave Meridiana for some time so they could simply be together again. With everything that happened, it didn't seem like that was going to happen. "I know it's not the ocean, but it's private."

She knew he was worried. She was too. "Gavin... I know I said I've accepted things, but we still need to stay positive. Dorian's still working himself to the bone on this."

Gavin swallowed hard. She had been deteriorating right before his eyes. The coughing fits had been getting more frequent. She had been tiring and after today... It was heartbreaking to watch someone who had once had so much energy fade the way she had. He looked down at her broken hand sorrowfully. "I know he is... I guess this has merely reminded me that we should never take who and what we have for granted." They sat down on the blankets as he wrapped his arms around her. He couldn't help but stare down at the bruises on her arms from the multiple blood tests.

Hokura tilted her head back and stared up at the stars, idly wondering if her rebel commander was watching her as Gavin's warm arms held her tight. She was once again safe, comfortable, wiser, but it seemed the incident had shortened her time here. She wondered where Dorian was if he was still in his labs, wracking his mind to exhaustion trying to figure this out. Her heart panged. He deserved to rest too and not worry about her.

"You're being especially quiet," Gavin whispered in her ear.

She stared at the sky, hoping she could see a shooting star. She would wish it all away. Maybe whatever was out there would hear her plea and take pity on her. "Just thinking..." She took a breath. "I should have known better. I wish we were planning our trip right now... or on our trip."

"We'll plan it once you're better." Gavin gently stroked her arm. "We can go wherever you want. We can camp in the forest or on the ocean. We can go back to White Rock or beyond. We can do whatever it is you please." He yearned for that. To see her smile, to spend hours driving and talking about everything and nothing at all. To be close to her once again and repair whatever damage there possibly was between them.

A small, sad smile came to her lips. "There's one place I'd like to see again. One that nobody else knew about..." She'd give anything to be there again. Maybe if she did die and her spirit went wherever it was supposed to be, it would be there. Maybe James would be waiting there for her. She couldn't leave Gavin with what she had just said. "I promise once I'm better, we'll go there together."

"I'll go anywhere with you," he quietly mused. As much as she had shared about her past life, there had been things she had privately kept to herself. Maybe it's because she didn't see it as fair to him to delve too far into her past love. He wished he could understand her better. Even after over thirteen years, his darling wife was still a bit of a mystery to him. The two sat in silence for a bit. There was so much he wanted to say. He had wanted to beg her to be okay, to stay with him, to live by his side forever, or to simply stay with him in this moment for all of eternity. Finally, the silence was too thick as he cleared his throat. "Beautiful star scape tonight."

"Yes." Her voice became light. "You can actually see Venus and Mars from here." Her finger pointed upwards. "That bright light right there is Venus." Her finger moved slightly over. "That one is Mars."

Gavin chuckled. "After all these years, I still have problems with determining the stars from the far-off planets."

Hokura grinned. "Stars twinkle or appear to change color. Planets don't." She cocked her head to the side. "I spent hours studying old maps of the sky, learning about everything that's up there. When and where you could see certain constellations and planets. It always fascinated me."

He nodded at her. "Everything from the sky above to the ocean below, hmmm?"

"Even now, the vastness of it all is still astonishing to think about, and when you think about how much we had explored before the war happened. People had been to space and explored it. People had been into the depths of the ocean and were discovering new species. Now..." She licked her lips and wondered if they would ever recover from blowing the planet apart in such a way. "Now, I guess we just need to do the best that we can with what we have, but even now, we're always advancing."

There was still so much to accomplish. Even as a continuously growing and thriving civilization, they were still incredibly far beyond such feats. Gavin stared up at the sky. It was peculiar how he had lived under the sky for decades until she came into his life that he actually looked up at it and studied it at any length. There had been many things that he merely shrugged off until Hokura had brought them to life with such curiosity and knowledge. That's when he noticed her body went rigid.

Hokura tried to fight it as her body tensed, and she swallowed hard, trying to control her breathing. She fought to hold back as her lungs and throat began to burn and convulse as the coughs erupted from her as she lurched forward from Gavin's arms.

"Hokura!" he cried as he was at a loss at what to do and moved to sit in front of her as she grasped her chest and coughed harder.

She leaned forward as her head began to spin. She needed to close her eyes as she coughed all the harder, blood pooling in her mouth to the point she couldn't swallow it as it she hacked, and it covered the blanket below her. She heard Gavin crying out her name in worry as she tried to clear her throat, tried to choke out that she was okay, that she just needed a moment as her lungs continued with their heaves. The taste of plasma filled and coated her mouth and throat as she struggled to breathe.

"Hokura, here!" Gavin offered her a bottle of water, but the way she was going, there was no way she would be able to swallow it as she simply closed her eyes and shook her head.

"Give... me... a... moment," she wheezed as she spat out more blood. She needed a minute to get herself under control. After some deep breaths, the burning seemed to ease again as she was finally able to swallow, her head stopped spinning, but she was feeling incredibly exhausted from the fit. Her eyes finally came up to meet Gavin's, who had gone pale. "I'm okay." She rasped.

Gavin's eyes were wide in horror as he stared at her. She had blood trickling down her chin, her eyes had gone bloodshot from the heavy coughing, and the spray that was now soaked into the blanket. "You're not okay," he whispered in desperation as he took hold of her. "Tell me what I need to do. Do you need to go to the medical facility? I can get Dorian and Spindler on their way right this second!"

"No." Hokura's voice cracked. "Just some water, and I need some rest."

Gavin gently picked her up in his arms despite her protests that she was able to walk. "Just let me do this," he coaxed her gently. "Let me take care of you... you've barely allowed me to be by your side lately, and now with what I saw... I don't know what to think anymore."

"You shouldn't have to see this," she muttered tiredly against his chest. "This isn't anything new, Gavin..."

He let out a deep breath as they reached their suite. Upon depositing her in the bedroom, he rubbed his eyes. "Just rest for a bit... I need a few minutes."

Hokura nodded. "Can I at least clean myself up a bit?" There was a tone to her question that he purposely ignored.

"That's fine." He wanted to race to Dorian's suite, had wanted to get her into the medical facility as fast as possible... but for what? The night had turned into a disaster, and he didn't want to push. He wanted her to know that he was trying, that all he wanted was to be by her side and make her happy. Why had it become so damn hard?

Gavin walked out to the kitchen and took a breath. He grabbed her some iced tea as he grabbed himself a drink and waited for his racing heart to calm down. Seeing her like that had unnerved him, but she had stated this wasn't anything new. He realized that, but it still scared him. He wondered what was happening to her insides. They were shutting down. The amount of blood she had coughed up had unnerved him to the core. He was going to head back into the bedroom when his children walked into the suite.

Cassandra gave him a weary look. "Is everything okay?"

Gavin opened his mouth but thought about his answer. "Your mom just had a bit of a coughing fit, she's fine, but I think we're going to call it an earlier night than usual."

Cyrus nodded. "We'll be in for the night anyway."

His father was thankful for that. They were treading on the side of caution. He had known the conversation nobody wanted to have was looming over all of them. "Sleep well, both of you." He made his way back to the bedroom to see Hokura had tucked herself in. She looked tired as she lay with her arm resting on her forehead. His heart ached as he lay next to her. He had just wanted to have a nice evening together, reminiscing about how they had come to be. He swallowed hard. "I'm sorry if I overreacted."

Hokura shook her head. "No, I'm sorry. Nobody should have to watch this..." she grimaced. She had watched James' steady decline before he had passed. He had aged, which had horrified her. Something she would never do... or at least thought she would never do. She had felt these past months that she had aged a hundred years.

"You're my wife. The vows that I spoke on that day were ones that I took seriously... in sickness and in health..."

A small smile came across her lips. "Vows, words that were in place for a ceremony that hadn't existed in decades. Things are different now. People don't get sick in this life."

His brows furrowed as he shifted, bringing an arm around her. "I still took them seriously, every part of them." He kissed her forehead as he listened to her breathing. It seemed clearer. "I'll do whatever I can for you. Whatever you desire, you merely have to ask."

There was something she desired, more than anything else she could think of. She just wanted to live, but that wasn't something Gavin could offer her. "Right now, I just want you to hold me until I sleep." She sighed wistfully. Her body felt heavy. She didn't want to leave his arms as she breathed in his fresh scent.

"I love you," he said, wishing there was more to say, wishing he could pour everything out to her right now, but knew she would be fast asleep in minutes. He wondered if he should have her take her sleep aids but decided against it, considering how tired she was already.

"I love you." She came up and kissed him sweetly on the lips. "Goodnight, my love."

"Goodnight." Gavin turned off the light as she snuggled into his arms. He wanted to feel content with her being next to him as he held her, but he couldn't help but worry. He wondered how this would all come together, how she would survive, and what the aftereffects of all this were going to be. He couldn't help but worry.

Hokura puzzled over the scene. She was in White Rock, staring over an all too familiar grave. The sky was darkening as the breeze blew. The smell of rain was heavy in the air as she breathed it in. "Why am I here?" she asked lightly as she started to cough. She found herself on her knees, trying to catch her breath as her blood splattered the rock below her.

Heavy footsteps came up behind her. She turned quickly, trying to regain her composure as her eyes widened. "James!" She quickly rose and ran into his arms. "My love... I've missed you so much," she cried as his arms locked around her.

He cradled her deeply in his broad chest for a moment as he looked down at her. "You're sick..."

She shook her head. "I'll be fine."

James stepped back from her, scowling as he flicked her forehead. "You've never been one to lie to me, Hokura." His voice was gruff.

She pursed her lips as she rubbed the spot, making a face as her eyes met his. "I have to believe that I'm going to be okay." She shrank slightly. "But if I'm not... then I get to be with you again." Her hands reached his. "We'll be together."

He solemnly shook his head. "I never wanted this for you. I was always okay with the fact that you'd live forever, and I was merely a mortal man biding my time beside you."

Tears came to her eyes. "A mortal man that I would need for the rest of eternity."

He gave her that lazy, arrogant smile that she had so loved. "You shouldn't still need me. You should move on. Let me be a chapter in your book already."

She shook her head. "No, I obviously still need you. If not, then why would I be dreaming of you?"

"That's a good question... it's been a while... but at least you know now..."

"Can we take a walk?" she asked sheepishly.

He squeezed her hand. "It's your dream. We can do whatever you want."

She just wanted to be near him, to allow his memory to flood over her as they walked hand in hand. It felt so real, even his scent, which she could never explain. It was like the wind through the forest trees. "I don't know what's going to happen to me," she admitted.

"Neither do I..." His voice was husky as the rebel commander looked over at her. "I can't protect you, Hokura; I wish there was a way that I could... but I can't."

Her arm wrapped around his as she held it desperately. His muscles were so bulky. Then again, the commander she was seeing was the younger version of him. His hair was still long, and without grey hair, his face was still youthful. Her heart panged. If only he could have forever lived beside her. She would have never gone back to Meridiana if Allen could have figured out a way to keep him youthful. If there had been a way to take what was inside of her and put it in him. "Just be with me. You're here for a reason... this is enough."

They walked hand in hand from the cemetery to the main street and along the ocean. "This place wasn't built to last," James said as they continued. "It had a lifeline like the people who lived here. Its lifeline ran out... but you saved the civilians."

"I couldn't save you..." The reality was bleak as it broke her. "If I had gone back to Meridiana earlier, I could have..." The realization choked her as she stopped. Her eyes widened. "If I hadn't been such a coward and faced my fears, you could have..." It had been as if time around her had frozen. She spent forty years fearing Dorian and the compound, and yet upon returning, she had been so wrong.

"Don't," James warned, walking up to her. "Don't you dare start blaming yourself."

She trembled. "James... I could have gone back and sought out help. When people started getting sick and dying, I could have helped! We could have gone back together..." Tears filled her eyes as her heart broke. "You could have lived beside me in Meridiana! You could have spent your days being young at my side!" Everything around her started to break apart as the sky darkened and lightning flashed in the distance. Her heart pounded hard in her chest as the tears cascaded down her cheeks. "We could have been happy and lived without fear!"

He grabbed onto her and held her against him. "Stop it now!" he commanded.

"No!" she screamed into his chest. "We could have had the life we dreamed of! We could have had children! A family! A life without worry about food or clean water! We could have had it all, and instead, I robbed you of that! I'm living this wonderful life, and you're dead!"

"Stop it!" he yelled in command as thunder boomed.

She was crying, but her screaming had stopped. This realization was too much. Maybe this was karma coming back on her. The deaths of those she cared for had been on her hands because she had been a coward. She was a killer, a natural-born killer, not only because that's what she was created to be but because she was also fearful. Barrack, Annette, Allen, the rebel group... she could have saved them all. At that moment, the rain started as the skies opened up. She could hear his heart beating with her ear against his chest. The warmth radiated off of him as he held her tight, close...

"When are you going to get over it?" His voice was tired.

"When are you going to allow yourself to simply accept the way things happened and move on?"

"How can I?" she asked in a whisper.

His grip on her tightened. "It's not just this sickness that's killing you. It's your grief. It's how you hold onto your trauma so tightly without letting it go." His voice lightened as his hand came up under her chin. He looked down at her tenderly. "Hokura, I want you to let it go..."

Her tears were still falling. "I can never let you go, James, you were my everything... even with what I have... what I had with you was still so much more. I felt like you understood me better than anyone. That I could tell you anything."

The commander smirked. "Then tell me, tell me everything that you want to tell me." He leaned down and kissed her passionately.

As she broke from the kiss, the rain started to let up. "I feel like I was cheated from you, like I cheated you out of having a longer life. Like I'm being dishonest by being with Gavin..." she tensed. "Like I'm being even more so because of the relationship I have with Dorian."

There was a chuckle. His grip lightened, and he turned, grabbing her hand again as they started walking again. "Life is funny that way, isn't it? The reality we perceive one day can change in a second, so can our lives and our hearts. That's what it is to live, Hokura. That's why we can't take what we have for granted; it can be over in a second, even when you're supposedly immortal."

She hated this but... "you're right... you're always right. Why was that? Because you were mortal? Because knowing that your time would eventually be up, you became so much more of a critical thinker than I could ever be?" She couldn't help but feel he had such a different perspective of everything, something *she* always wanted to understand.

He shrugged. "I saw life differently. Maybe that's why. You had all the time in the world, I didn't, and I was reminded of that every day that I aged and had to look at you. I never took my days with you for granted because I knew they were limited, and *you* never wanted to talk about it."

Hokura smiled. "I'm here, so let's talk about it... let's talk about how much I hated that I loved you so much because you were mortal. Let's talk about how all I wanted was you... and how bitter I am about losing you. How bitter I am that it seems like chaos always follows me... that I'm an idiot, and that's why I am where I am right now." She shook her head. "Why do I always screw everything up?"

"You gonna start talking like that again? Is that what this is? Bantering and tough love? Is that what you need from me?" He shook his head. "I've never allowed you to talk down about yourself."

She licked her lips. "You were too kind to me on the best of days. I should have learned and still..."

"You need to get over this self-blame already..." He sighed.

She looked over the ocean. It seemed to be calming, as was the storm inside her heart. She was just glad to be here again. To be next to him and hear his voice. "Can I get out of blaming myself for the pot then?"

He laughed heartily. "Not on your life, sweetheart. You weren't watching it."

She laughed along with him. "I was busy with other things."

"When you were told to just watch the water boil." His eyes rolled. "You had one job. Shut up about the damn pot already."

She lightly shoved him. "I won't... because when you were alive, never let me hear the end of it."

James groaned. "Because woman, it was a good pot! It had

been my father's, and you burned a damn hole in it! That takes talent!"

When was the last time she had laughed like this? When she had felt so free, the rain had stopped. They were walking and holding hands. "I can cook eggs now..." she quipped.

"About damn time." He chuckled. "Set any kitchens in the compound on fire yet?"

A large smile came to her lips. "I'll have you know I've even helped with baking, and there haven't been any fires." Her heart panged. "I know you liked mucking about in the kitchen and cooking... we've actually perfected a lot of old-world cooking... I wish you could try it."

He made a noise. "I'll have you know true old-world cooking back before humanity started doing anything was over a fire..." He snickered. "And you couldn't even do that. How many things did I have to fish out of the ashes because you dropped them?"

"Hey!" Hokura cried. "Is this dream about you teasing me now?"

James made a face. "It's your dream, you tell me. This is my version of tough love, and you know it."

They found a bench and sat together as the skies started to clear to reveal the setting sun. "This dream feels different... deeper...," she confessed. "I've missed you..."

He looked over at her and wrapped an arm around her shoulder. "You've had a lot of shit to deal with lately, a lot of it that hit your plate all at once... and you've been wracked with nightmares again."

Her head tilted back. "Maybe this is why I'm dreaming of you again. It's been a nice change of pace..." She watched the sun as it started to dip... she knew what that meant as she snuggled closer to him; she wanted to feel closer to him before she woke up she took a deep breath and stared at her love, wishing she could bring him out of the dream with her. Wishing she could wake up and still feel his arm around her. The sun kissed the ocean in front of them as she turned and kissed him. The kiss grew heated as she wanted to pour everything she possibly could into him. Who knew when she would dream of her rebel commander again?

As the sun entirely set, her eyes opened, and she stared towards the ocean with a questioning look. "Something isn't right...." She whispered as she pulled away. "I never get to see the sun fully set in my dreams...."

James gave her a solemn look. "Yeah... about that." He shifted, comforting her. "You're going to be here a while..."

Gavin stirred the next morning. It was later than normal as he took a breath and rolled over to stare at her. "You must have been tired. You didn't move all night long." His brows furrowed, there was no response. "Hokura," he whispered, lightly brushing a stray hair from her face.

He could see she was still lightly breathing, so why wasn't she waking up? "Hokura..." He tried again, gently nudging her. When her eyes still didn't open, he flew in panic, screaming her name. "Hokura, Hokura wake up! Please, you have to wake up!" The desperate cries hadn't gone unnoticed as both Cassandra and Cyrus ran into their room.

Cassandra looked worriedly at her father, who was now clutching onto their mother. Gavin's eyes went up to her in desperation. "Get Dorian! Get him right away! I need him!"

With that, the girl's eyes widened as she raced out of the suite.

"Dad," Cyrus cried, running over to him. "She's still breathing... she's okay..." He tried to calm his father. "The professor will know what to do!"

Cassandra sprinted down the hallway and quickly banged on the professor's door. She put her ear up to it but didn't hear anything on the other side. Considering the time, her heart raced as she ran down the hallway. "He must be in the labs!" she cried, running as fast as she possibly could barefoot through the compound as desperation flooded through her. She needed to find him. She veered around the corner to see him making his way down to the medical facility when she called for him. "Dorian!" she yelled as she ran to him and crashed into his arms as she wrapped hers around him. "Dorian, please, we need you!"

Worry etched over his face. "Cassandra, what is it?" he asked quickly.

'It's Mom! She's not waking up! She's still breathing, Dad tried, but she won't wake up!" the girl cried.

His hands found her shoulders. "It'll be alright."

With that, the two were off, running up the hallway and towards the suite.

Dorian looked at the girl. She was doing a good job of keeping things together as she ran beside him. He couldn't imagine the fear that was coursing through the girl. "Was she ill last night? Was she seemingly worse last night?"

Cassandra shook her head. "It was a normal night as far as I know... nothing happened that was out of the norm!"

"Dammit," Dorian cursed. He had run out of time. It was most likely that Hokura was in a coma. Then again, there was the slight possibility that with being in a coma, her system would try to heal itself, that this is what it had needed. They came up the stairs instead of waiting on the elevator and raced to the suite. Upon entering it, Dorian ran into the bedroom, where he heard Gavin's manic sobs.

"Dorian!" he cried, looking up at the professor. "Please, help me... she's not waking up..."

He pursed his lips and walked into the room. He kneeled on the bed and placed his fingers gently on her wrist. "She's breathing, and she has a pulse. She's not gone yet."

"What is this? What do we do?" Gavin cried in panic. "This can't be it. There needs to be more that can be done! Please tell me that you have a plan and that you can save her."

Dorian's brows furrowed. "I swore to both of you that I would save her. There's still time. I can still do this. We need to get her down to the medical facility right away. We need to monitor her stats and make sure she doesn't slip any further from us."

Gavin nodded as he stood with her body in his arms. Her head drooped lifelessly in an unsettling way that made his stomach roll. He exited the room, following Dorian to see Cyrus and Cassandra standing idly by. "I need to take care of your mother. You don't need to worry. I'll be back in a bit, and then we can figure this out. Okay?"

Cassandra grabbed Cyrus's hand and nodded solemnly as the two watched their father and the professor leave the suite with their unconscious mother.

Cyrus squeezed his sister's hand. "This is the end, isn't it?" His voice was a whisper.

The girl shook her head. "No, Dorian won't let it end. Not like this." She gave him a comforting smile. "I trust him. I know he'll stop at nothing to make sure that she'll be okay. He'll cure her." It was a lie... but one that she needed to tell... one that she needed to believe because she didn't want to face the haunting reality that her chance to talk to her mother would possibly never come.

He gave her sister a questioning look. "How can you be so sure?"

"Because he loves her."

Dorian led Gavin into a hospital room and instructed him on how to place her. He then quickly went to work with grabbing monitors and placing them on her. "I want you to page Spindler and Lucien, get them down here right away," he stated, looking over towards the governor, who had gone pale as he stood over his wife. "Gavin!" Dorian spat.

The man breathed deeply, his eyes still wide as if he didn't know what to do. Panic still coursing through him.

The professor took a breath. He needed to be patient as he walked up to him. "Gavin, you need to listen to me. I need to get Lucien and Spindler. You need to keep a calm head about this. Now, if you would please."

"This is it..." Gavin trembled through tears. "Her time is up..."

Dorian furrowed. "Her time is up when I say it's up, and it's not over, dammit! Now, if you would please..."

Gavin nodded and quickly left the medical room leaving Dorian to set everything up.

The professor turned and helplessly stared at her. "Don't you do this to me. It is not your time. You will *not* leave me." He moved quickly, setting up the monitors. Upon attaching them and turning the machines on, they all lit up and beeped to life. He breathed a slight sigh of relief. Those precious beeps meant there was a heartbeat, there were brainwaves, she was breathing... but she was indeed in a coma.

He sat on his stool and rolled it beside her. "I thought we promised you wouldn't do this again. I thought we were both over comas..." He wished she would say something to him. That there would be a sarcastic comeback. Instead, there were the hollow mechanical sounds of her lifeline beeping away. He kneaded his forehead and pinched the bridge of his nose. If things had deteriorated to this state, would she survive any further tests? That's why he needed Spindler and Lucien. It all crashed down on him at that second. He couldn't allow it to impact him. He couldn't break just yet. He needed to remain calm and in control. He needed to fool the others because right now, he could feel the cracks forming, not now, not yet. Deep breaths... calmed breathing...

That's when Gavin walked through the door, followed by Dr. Lucien and Dr. Spindler.

Dr. Spindler stared over at her and took a breath. "It appears that her system has had enough. It's to the point where it's tiring and shut itself down."

The news didn't sit well with the professor. "Tell me something I don't know, doctor," he growled. "Tell me a medical deduction on how we're going to proceed from here."

Lucien stepped forward. "She's not gone yet. From what the monitors are showing, she's stable, which is something."

Gavin stood, pale, trembling as Dorian looked up at him. "Gavin..." His voice was soft. "She's stable, go and tell your children that... be with them... they need you right now. There's nothing more you can do here. If anything happens, then we'll alert you right away."

The man nodded automatically but still didn't move.

Dorian took a steady breath. "Dr. Lucien, it appears the governor is in shock. Will you please escort him to his suite and stay with him for a while."

The man nodded. "Of course, professor." He walked up to Gavin. "Governor, let's get you back to your suite and calmed down a bit. I can assure you that we're doing everything that we possibly can at the time, and she's in the best hands."

Gavin's eyes met and held Dorian's. "Save her."

"I will," he stated as he watched the man leave. After a few moments, he cursed loudly. "How could this have happened? She was down here just the other day, things weren't great, but they certainly weren't this bad!" he seethed as Dr. Spindler walked over and grabbed her charts.

"It's possible that whatever is attacking her system simply overwhelmed her. That it's taken over entirely." The doctor mulled over what he was reading. "Her oxygen levels seem to be low."

Dorian groaned. "Everything is low... everything is weak. We're running out of time." He looked over at Spindler. "What about a blood transfusion?"

The doctor grimaced. "We can try it, but everything that we've seen shows it would only slow what was happening to her system, but it also might overwhelm it past the tipping point," he pondered. It seemed like they were still running into walls. This had eluded them all at every corner, had defied the physics of their genetics, of Hokura's genetics. "Then again, it might buy us some time."

"Time is what we need." Dorian sighed.

Lucien had gotten the silent governor to his suite. He opened the door to see Cassandra and Cyrus tensely waiting for him on the couch. The doctor gave them a kind smile. "Your father is feeling a little overwhelmed at the moment. As I'm sure all of you are, let me make you all some tea, and we can sit down and talk about things." His voice was calm and smooth.

Gavin stiffly walked towards the couch as the kids both moved so he could sit between them. He buried his head in his hands.

"Dad, how's Mom?" Cassandra asked gently.

It was Lucien who spoke up as he moved towards the

kitchen. "She's in a coma right now. Her body needs more rest, so in a way, it's gone into a deeper sleep."

Cassandra shared a worried look with Cyrus as the three sat silently.

The doctor moved around the kitchen with grace as he heated some water and grabbed a few teabags. "With this happening, this may have bought your mother some more time. She's been in comas before and has come out of all of them. You three need to believe that the professor is doing all that he can to alleviate the situation."

Gavin still had his face buried. "I couldn't wake her up... what if she never wakes up again..." The thought drove him even further to the edge. What if the night before had been their very last night together? The last time she heard him say that he loved her. His breathing hitched. "What if this is it."

Cyrus took in his father's distress. "Dad... they're doing everything. We just need to believe."

Cassandra bit her bottom lip. She had seen it. She knew her mother wasn't getting any better. She knew she was trying to hide it and said nothing. She saw in Dorian's demeanor lately that this had been wearing on him as well. She had wanted to talk to her mother about it... but now it seemed like it was too late. Her heart broke, and yet there was someone else that needed her to remain strong. This is what the professor had meant about the survival of the fittest and doing what one deemed fit. Right now, there was someone else who needed that false hope, and she needed to supply it. "Dad, we gotta stay strong for her."

He didn't know how to be strong anymore. Didn't know how he would go on without her. The thoughts started to assault him even deeper.

Lucien walked over with three cups. "Some tea will help, and if you wish, Governor Gavin I can prescribe a sedative. I can understand that you're going through some deep emotions right now. It's fully understandable."

Gavin didn't want the tea or a sedative. He just wanted to go to bed and sleep. Maybe this was a bad dream... his worst nightmare come to life. Perhaps if he slept, he would awaken from it and find her sleeping next to him. He looked up as his eyes locked on the tea the doctor was pouring them. "Dorian loves her... he'll save her." His head started spinning as he turned pale again. Why did it feel so hard to breathe? He wilted slightly as he grasped his chest. Why did it physically hurt like this?

Lucien noted the man and placed a reassuring hand on his shoulder. "You need to steady your breathing, governor. You're having a panic attack. Close your eyes. Deep breaths, slowly, in through your nose and out of your mouth. Very good."

He had felt so helpless as he did what the doctor ordered. His children were watching him wide-eyed. He couldn't let this take him as well. He needed to be strong for all of them as he tried to steady himself. After a few moments, he tipped his head as he leaned back on the couch, stretching himself out. Maybe that would help as he struggled to fill his lungs.

"Very good," Lucien praised. "I understand this situation is stressful." The man's voice was as pleasant as always, without a hint of concern. He turned to Cassandra and Cyrus. "This is completely normal. You two have nothing to worry about with your father."

Cassandra nodded. "I just need a moment... if you'll excuse me." She walked mechanically to her bedroom. She counted the steps, trying to hold it in. The second she closed her door, she fell onto her bed and grabbed her pillow as she muffled a scream into it. Her tears flowed as she wondered how many times her mother had possibly done this, how many times she had hidden her true emotions from the others as she cried even harder. She had been too late. There were so many things she still wanted to say to her mother... so many questions she still had. "Please don't let this be the end," the girl whispered through her sobs. It hurt so bad, and yet she had this odd feeling that she needed to stay strong for her father and brother. Was this the burden her mother carried? After a few minutes, Cassandra took a deep breath and calmed herself. She would be strong. She quickly went to the bathroom and washed her face. If she needed more time to cry and scream, she could do so tonight. Until then, she would put up the front that she believed everything was going to be okay.

Dorian paced as he stared down at Hokura's body hooked up to the monitors. He licked his lips. They needed to make a decision as he looked over at Spindler. "Start set up for a whole blood transfusion."

The doctor's eyes widened. "We haven't had any overly successful tests from what we've seen, sir. I can't guarantee that we'll be at all successful in the live trial of what we're about to do."

"I know." The professor sighed. "But it's the only thing I have right now, and I can't sit idly by doing nothing. It'll either be a success... or..." He didn't want to think about it. "We'll monitor her closely."

Dr. Spindler nodded and left the room to get what was needed for the setup and to collect the cloned blood.

Dorian sat beside her as he rested his forehead on her bed. "Tell me what to do. Tell me how to save you... because right now..." He swallowed hard. "This has all become a science project again, and I can't bear the thought of losing you like I did all the others." He was exhausted; the past few months had been a spiral of nightmares for him, and now... he grasped onto her good hand. "All I want is to protect you and save you."

He wondered how Gavin was doing Dr. Lucien was able to snap him out of his shock or if they were sitting together. The man had a keen way of keeping his cool. His voice always had a soft, soothing lull to it. That's what Gavin needed at the moment. He wondered if he should alert Adam and have him make his way to the governor's suite as well. Dorian huffed. He didn't need Amara bursting in here and causing a stir. Right now, he needed his wits. He rose and cracked his neck as Dr. Spindler came through the door. The professor gave him a look. "Let's get this started."

Upon hooking everything up, the professor noted the time. If things were slow going, it could take up to four hours. "We need to monitor her at all times. We need to be prepared if things go awry. I'll be continuously taking samples to see if this slows things."

Dr. Spindler stood back, he didn't want to say anything, but he needed to know. "And what will we do if something happens?"

Dorian glanced up at the man. "Then we will have to be quick on our feet." He steadied her arm, searching for a vein. There was so much bruising. She had gotten so thin as he balanced her arm taking in the discoloration. Was this it? No, he couldn't allow her to slip any further as he gently set the line. He watched as the blood slowly made its way down. "Please... let this work..." he whispered. He didn't know who his pleas were going out to. Whatever entity there was left in this torn world he had created. Was there anything, anyone watching him? Playing the cards? Deciding her fate other than him?

"Stats are normal," Spindler stated.

"We'll continue to monitor them."

The professor had sat for an hour, his eyes going from the monitor to Hokura. The beeps had been steady as he lowered his head. The constant rhythm had made his eyes heavy as he tried to tap his foot to the beat to keep himself coherent. He was about to tell Spindler to grab him some coffee when there was an irregular beep, followed by another and another. His eyes darted up to see her breathing had become erratic. "Get her on oxygen!" Dorian rose to his feet in panic as the doctor sprang into action to get the oxygen mask on her. The professor's eyes widened. "She's breaking into a fever!" This wasn't going right. This wasn't going to work. He quickly moved to her side and pulled the line.

Doctor Spindler looked up at the man. "She seems to be having a reaction."

"Dammit," Dorian growled. "Most likely a hemolytic transfusion reaction. Her cells are fighting off the new ones at a higher pace." He rushed to the side and grabbed a syringe. Was it possible this had caused more damage? He watched her closely as he took the sample, hoping for a wince, a jolt... anything to show she could feel it... there was nothing as he sighed.

"We might just need to leave her be and monitor her. Maybe her body fell into the coma because it needed strength to heal," Spindler offered. He knew it was most likely false hope that he was going to have to watch the professor spiral into madness as he lost her.

"Possibly." Dorian's tone was flat. He needed to see how her cells were responding. He braced himself, knowing it wasn't going to be good. "I'm going to take this sample and check it over."

The doctor grimaced slightly. "Would you like me to oversee it so you can continue to monitor her?" he asked as he placed a cool, damp cloth on Hokura's forehead, hoping it would help with her fever.

The professor shook his head. "I won't be long. If anything happens, alert me." With that, he left the room with the blood sample. He had felt like the walls were about to close in on him. He needed to be out and away for a few moments to clear his head as he looked down at the syringe that held the answers he knew he didn't want.

He entered one of the generic labs. He didn't want to be in one of his own for this. If he went off the deep end, he wouldn't destroy what wasn't his. It had been a pathetic act, but he was desperate to keep it together. He grabbed a high-powered microscope and stared at the sample as his stomach tightened. He felt like his world had just crashed down upon him and wondered how it was possible that he was still standing. Every healthy cell... everything... had been destroyed by the toxin that was her blood. A cold wash went over him. What else was there? Maybe death was the only answer. It wasn't fair. He needed to hold it in... to hold it together, and so he made his way back to her.

Spindler looked up at him expectingly. "We need to report to the governor."

Dorian looked away. That was the last thing he had wanted.

"I'll do it for you," the doctor insisted. "I know the results weren't good, Dorian. I know she's dying. She's not coming back from this."

He licked his lips and took a deep breath. He didn't want to hear it. Didn't want to think about it, and yet it was the very stark reality. "Tell him she's stable for now... I can take it from here, Spindler. If Gavin wants to come in and sit with her tonight, he can... but the man needs his rest too."

The doctor nodded and took his leave.

Dorian slunk into the chair next to her body. "You were never one to do things the easy way." He glanced at her solemnly and gently wiped a stray water droplet from her cheek as he removed the cloth Spindler had placed on her forehead. Still feverish, he walked to the sink and refreshed the cloth. "I wish you could hear me... you're putting us through the wringer here, Hokura," he groaned as he walked back to her and replaced the cloth. "If you could hear us, we could at least say goodbye. Will you at least give everyone that?" His mind reeled... there was indeed a way... if this were the end, he would see to it that everyone got to say their final goodbyes to her. It had been over fifty-three years, but he would do it again. He needed the direct transcranial simulator.

The day had worn on as the sun began to dip. It wasn't until later that evening that Gavin left the suite. Spindler and Lucien had been so kind as to prescribe him something. It took the edge off slightly. He didn't feel physically ill anymore. In fact, he didn't know what he felt at the moment. He had asked the children if they were okay with him going. They had nodded solemnly as Cassandra hugged him and told him it would all be okay. He had wanted to confront her on what she was doing, had wanted to tell her it was okay to be upset, that she didn't need to pretend to be strong for them. He didn't say anything because perhaps that was what she needed.

Both children seemed as shocked as he had been. Cyrus barely said a word. He reverted to quietly sitting on the couch staring at nothing. His sister had been antsy and had helped Lucien with cleaning up from the tea. Spindler had come up a bit later and told everyone that Hokura had been in stable condition. That it was possible her body needed to go into rest mode to enable itself to heal.

Gavin didn't know whether that was true or not... he figured Dorian was somehow scrambling now, trying to buy whatever time he possibly could. He had wanted to go down and see her, but Spindler had specifically told him it would be best to wait until evening. He had left Dr. Lucien to see to Gavin and the children a little longer. Gavin had been grateful for the man. He seemed to have a calming effect on people, which was most likely why he had accompanied him and his family through the day. It wasn't until their dinner was on the table that Lucien gave him a warm smile.

"Make sure you all eat and take care of one another. If you need anything, you know how to reach me." His eyes went to Gavin's. "Know that we're all on top of this. We're doing everything that we possibly can."

Gavin noted that the compound was silent. He hadn't really noted the time. Apparently, it was later than he had thought as he walked to the medical facility and into the room that held Hokura. Upon opening the door, he eyed Dorian sitting beside her, working away at a laptop, furiously typing as he balanced the computer on his lap, a pen between his lips as he quickly wrote things down on a notepad beside him.

The governor cleared his throat, bringing the professor's attention to him.

Dorian's eyes went up and locked with his and then went to the clock on his computer. "I didn't realize the time. I'll let you sit with her for a while. I need to stretch my legs."

"She's not getting better, is she? This is the end," Gavin stated.

The professor rubbed his eyes. "I'm not having this conversation right now, Gavin." He rose and placed his computer on the counter, ignoring the man in front of him as Gavin gave him a pleading look. Dorian just wanted to grieve in his own way before doing this. He had held it all day, and if he held it for any longer, he was afraid he would crack. "Spend some time with her, talk to her...." His voice was soft. "I'll be back in a few hours. If anything happens, if the monitors start going off, page me right away." Without any more to say, he left the medical room.

Dorian couldn't dare face Gavin any longer at the moment. He couldn't tell him the reality of the situation as he blindly strode the garden in the darkness of the night, allowing his emotions to flow. The heavy rain was blurring his vision as it soaked his suit. He needed to yell. He needed to scream and fight and bleed as he pleaded. The professor stood in front of the blueberry bush. His fists clenched so tightly that his nails were cutting into his palms as his rage radiated off of him. "She's dying, you son of bitch! Is this what you want?" he screamed at the plaque. "Was this what you wanted? To have her no matter what? Is this her punishment for returning?" He bristled. "Is it because I said you couldn't have her?" Anger coursed through him as he grabbed the blueberry bush. "I hate you! You damn rebel! I've always hated you! Why can't you just let her go and be happy?" With that surge, he yanked part of the bush from the ground. His eyes widened in horror as some of the roots snapped.

Dorian crumbled in a heap of tears. "No!" What had he done? His hands shook; this bush... it had been sacred to her... "please, no!" he cried in desperation as he went to the earth and separated the dirt, trying to right what he had just done. "No, if I lose her... this plant..." Mud caked his hands as he clumsily tried to put the roots back into the ground. "Please... I'm so sorry. Don't take this from her." He dug further to see where he had snapped the roots as tears streamed desperately down his cheeks. Mud stained his hands and suit sleeves as the grass soaked into his pants, his hands working diligently. Only a monster would destroy something as innocent as a plant out of his rage and anger. Only he had the capability of being so despicable as to destroy one of their memories. "Hokura..." Her name escaped his lips. What would he do without her? What would she think if she saw this? Destroying his labs was one thing... this was something else. This was a living thing that they had been so careful to transplant. This was something special where she kept her fondest memory, where he was sure Gavin would want her memory preserved as well.

He righted the plant in the dirt and covered the roots as best as possible. The rain had made the task all the harder as he tried to assess the damage. He would have the botanists look into it in the morning. If she awoke, she would see this plant was still thriving. "It's not him... it's not anyone else... not fate... not anyone but me." His heart broke. "I'm the one who failed." The thought assaulted him as he pounded the grass beneath him. "I failed... there's nothing I can do... I don't know *what* to do!"

Dorian looked to the sky. "Tell me! Give me something! Don't take her from me! All those lives lost, they were all for her! Don't let them be in vain!" He clutched his chest. It always intrigued him how the emotional pain could become so physical. It felt as though his heart was bleeding and that it, too, was dying along with her. Death, it would be a sweet release. No, if this were it... he needed to prepare. Gavin, Cassandra, Cyrus, and the peacekeepers needed to say farewell to her. That was something he could do for them. They could say their final goodbyes. That's what he had been working on when Gavin had walked in. It wasn't over yet. This was why he had a backup plan. Still, the idea of failing her like this, it burrowed deep inside of him like the poison that was taking her away from him.

He looked up at the plaque with new resolve. "It wasn't you... it was me... I hate myself for it all. You were there to save her from me, and I *hate* that she needed saving. I hate that I am who I am, that I'm nothing but a monster with all the fucking answers, and yet I couldn't get this right!" He hunched as he sank into the grass, wishing the rain would wash it all away. His heart was bleeding because he understood her now... this was what it was like to watch someone die, to feel helpless, to wish it all away. To see life for what it was... precious and beautiful, even if it was full of heartache. Would he ever be able to tell her as much?

The silence in the garden became heavy. There was nothing but the sound of the rain hitting the plants, bouncing off the foliage. Whatever answer, whatever voice he was hoping to hear, didn't echo from the skies. It didn't impede his thoughts. That's when he knew for certain there wouldn't be one, that it needed to be his own, even if it trembled and shook. Even if he still didn't have an answer on how to save her, he knew how to suspend her and that he had all the time in the world to save her after the thought.

He stiffly rose. He would shower, eat, get a few hours of sleep, and continue setting up the TCDS so that others could interact with her. He would be able to integrate the same system from the RTCS to make it real-time as if they had entered her mind. Suddenly he was so tired. He knew Gavin would be with her for the night. He needed to rest... he needed to have his wits about him tomorrow because tomorrow was going to be another painful day.

Hokura smiled brightly as she walked hand in hand with James. "I never told anyone about this place. I always wanted to visit it again but never had the nerve."

He raised an eyebrow at her as he opened the cabin door. "Why not? It was just as much yours as it was mine... it was *ours*... and I'm no longer here."

She crossed her arms and gave him a meek look. "In a way, it was sacred. It was our little place away from everything." She shook her head. "Could you imagine me telling Amara that you and I got lost while driving and happened to stumble upon an old-world abandoned cabin in the heart of the woods in the middle of a storm while seeking shelter?"

James gave a grunt. "You're the most dangerous thing out here. What could have happened?" They stepped inside as Hokura's eyes gazed happily at it.

"If it hadn't been for the others, I would have liked to have lived here together." She sighed as she went over to the old wood stove and opened it. There had already been wood inside of it. Of course, there was. These were her recollections... why chop and gather wood while she was designing her own dreams?

"I would have done whatever you wanted." James came behind her and kissed her temple. He lit a match and tossed it into the stove. "It seems you have that effect on people."

Hokura made a face. "I didn't *want* to have that effect on people." She stood. "I didn't ask for the life I had... I was born into a destiny that I ran away from..." she grimaced. "And ran right back into."

He wrapped his arms around her and held her tight.

"Because you felt like Meridiana was home." His voice was soft in her ear.

"That's not true!" she countered, turning to him and shaking her head. "The truth is that nowhere felt like home once you were gone. *You* were home, James. When I lost you, I lost my place in this world, and when I thought about the compound."

"You needed to know... you were drawn back. Maybe it *was* your destiny."

She pushed him teasingly. "Don't talk to me about destiny. It's a stupid word, anyway. Was it my destiny to be a screw-up? To be a constant mess?"

He chuckled. "You were never a screw-up, so what if you were messy? That's part of being human. Believe me. I was messy, too, until I met you."

Hokura rolled her eyes. "Are you kidding me? You were perfect!"

He made a face and laughed as he flicked her forehead. "You know better. I acted hard because I was put into a role after my father's death. I didn't want to be a leader; the only reason I got as far as I did was because of Barack, and I'm sure there were days he wanted to smack me upside the head. There were days when he did. No twenty-five-year-old should have to fill their father's shoes and lead people to salvation."

"But you did it," she urged.

"Luck." James rolled his eyes. "Maybe it's because I had you that my luck changed." He gave a wicked grin. "Because we all know why no rebel in their right mind would bet against you."

Hokura gave him a look as she walked around the cabin. They had fixed it up after finding it. Had built shelves, put in a small wooden counter and sink. She ran her fingers over everything as she recalled the days spent here. "Yeah, well, it looks like my luck's run out."

James grabbed her hand and held it. "You're still here... you know what that means." He gently ran his hand over her cheek. "I'm sure the others will be coming eventually... I'm sure they're all watching over you right now."

She gave a pained expression. "I wish I could feel them, that I could tell them I love them all."

The rebel commander gave her the smirk she so loved. "They know how much you love them, now let's see if you can still kick my ass at Texas Hold Em' or if I have a fair chance against you."

Hokura chuckled. "In your dreams..." She was glad to have her mind occupied, but in the back of it, she wondered how long this would last. Was her time truly up? Everything was so hard to distinguish. She looked up at James, who was sitting at their makeshift table, cards already in hand, as he smiled at her. At least she got to be with him...

It was early in the morning as Dorian walked into the medical room. Gavin had been hunched over Hokura's bed sleeping. Her monitors were still beeping at a regular pace. He quietly walked over to his laptop and booted it up. He didn't want to disturb the governor if all he was going to do was sleep. He didn't think he had it in him to talk to him just yet about the reality of the situation.

Dorian scowled slightly. He wondered if he should bring up the possibilities of cryogenically suspending her after her death to the governor. There was still too much weighing on this. If he brought it up and Gavin said no, then it would be done. He knew the man would go above and beyond to make sure it didn't happen. He wouldn't trust Dorian to oversee her body once she had passed, and he would lose his chance to save her. He had already double-checked the chamber that morning. Everything was ready, even if she wasn't. He had yet to accept this as he went to work on the program he was creating. He didn't know if he could fully accept things until her heart stopped beating and the life had physically left her. He typed away. He would see about integrating the RTCS goggles into this so they could physically see her. Although they wouldn't be able to physically move about like in the simulator, it would be more like a dream landscape that they controlled mentally.

Dorian sighed. He would need to go down to the simulator and pull a few things. He was grateful he still had her TCDS from all those years ago and didn't have to worry about it properly syncing. If it wasn't one project, it was another. He felt the pit in his stomach growing with anticipation, and once this project had been settled, it would be an even bigger one. This was simple coding, something he could place into a machine and have it work properly. If there were an error with the code, it would show up simply enough. Her coding, on the other hand... if only he could find a way to erase it and start all over again, but that wasn't possible with human DNA.

Gavin stirred to the sounds of him clicking away at his keyboard as he groaned. "What time is it?" His voice was heavy with sleep.

Dorian didn't bother to raise his eyes to the governor. "It's five hundred hours," he stated, still working away.

"Five in the morning," Gavin mumbled.

"If you wish to keep sleeping, that's fine. I hope I'm not disturbing you," the professor said, adding a new line of code as he studied it for a moment.

Gavin let out a breath and looked at his wife. She seemed

to have been simply sleeping soundly in the hospital bed. His brows furrowed in sadness. "Dorian... we need to accept it..."

The professor cleared his throat. "I suggest you get some more sleep, it's still incredibly early, and I know that you've had a few stressful days. If you wish, I can pull another gurney in here for you so you can sleep more comfortably. I know from personal experience that being hunched over at the side of a bed is less than comfortable."

Gavin shook his head. The man was in denial. "I want to be like this, just for a while..."

"You can sleep next to her. There's enough room." Dorian typed away.

The governor didn't move. He merely laid his head back down and listened to the faint sound of typing and the mixtures of constant beeps. His fingers traced over Hokura's arm, it felt warm to the touch, but she didn't seem to have a fever anymore. He couldn't help but feel her time was coming to an end. He had left the children last night, telling them where he was going. He was wondering how they faired through the night. He had felt guilty about leaving them but told them they could call Olga if need be.

Olga... he should have given her a heads up. If it was only five, he would get about two more hours of sleep next to Hokura and would then make his way upstairs to tend to Cassandra and Cyrus. What on earth would he say to them? There had been no change, their mother was still in a coma, and he had absolutely no news for them. It seemed Dorian was at a stalemate as well. He was curious about what he was doing on his computer. What on earth could he be typing away at so vigorously? He didn't know, but the easy sounds helped him drift. It wasn't until he awoke to the door opening and closing an hour later that he realized he was once again alone with her.

"Dorian's working on something..." he whispered. "I hope he has a new theory." Again, he closed his eyes.

The professor strode down the hallway towards the training facility. He would leave Talon a note stating what he had done. The RTC simulator would still be functional. It would simply be without a few goggles. They were easy enough to recalibrate once he was done with them.

He entered the room and grabbed what he needed. He did a tally, everyone, all together. He needed to include Adam and Amara in this as well. Dread filled him with what he was doing, what he had been preparing for. It hurt. Not only was his pride broken, but his heart was slowly tearing apart as well. He walked to the viewing room and left Talon a note as he left with the equipment and walked towards the science facility, to where the transcranial direct simulator had been. He ran his fingers over it. This had been hers and hers alone. It had held and fed her all the education and information that she had learned as she slept and had been his lifeline to her the second time she had gone into a coma after the training facility incident. Now... now it would be used to connect her to those who deserved to tell her how much they loved her and say goodbye.

He studied the components. He could use his computer and set up the live feed again, and he could also calibrate the goggles. All he needed to do was make sure the program he created properly synced with everything. Never in his life did he imagine ever having to create such a thing. It had been a feat, a wild idea, and an accomplishment that deserved praise. Instead, he would forever regret why he had to generate such a program.

Dorian had put everything on a trolley and had brought it down to her room to see that Gavin was no longer there. He figured the man had gone up to his suite to check on his children. Fair enough, it meant he could work in peace. He didn't want to deal with Gavin telling him what he already knew. He didn't have it in him to argue with the man either. Upon bringing everything in, he couldn't help but stop and stare at her. He placed a hand on her forehead. At least the fever had gone down. Still, her system wasn't stabilizing. The professor bent down towards her ear. "Hokura... I wish you could hear me," he whispered. "I know you can't, but I want to let you know I will never give up on you... I swear it." He kissed her forehead tenderly. "I'm going to bring them to you. This isn't goodbye, my love. This is just until you see them again."

He set to work loading his new program and making sure everything would sync and work properly. If it would, someone would be able to put on the goggles and would be able to consciously see and interact with her as if transferred into her own subconscious. It needed to work. He had owed it to them, to her... because he had failed them all.

Gavin wearily entered his suite to see Cassandra and Cyrus at the kitchen table. They had been working together making breakfast. Right away, the girl was at her father's side, her arms wrapped around him, hugging him. "Dad!" Cassandra cried.

Cyrus gave a meek smile. "We figured if you didn't come up for breakfast that we'd take it down to you."

Their father nodded. "How did I get so lucky to have two amazing kids? Thank you." He straightened as Cassandra's grip on him tightened.

It was Cyrus who asked. "How's Mom?" That snapped Gavin to attention.

"No change, no news, I have no clue what the professor is working on right now. He was down there first thing this morning on his computer and working away and was on his way doing whatever he needed to do." He wanted to be back down in the medical facility at her side but knew the kids needed her. "Did you two get any sleep last night?"

Cassandra gave her father a look as she licked her lips. "We actually both slept in your bed last night..."

Gavin raised an eyebrow.

Cyrus gave a pained expression. "I know it's private, but we looked through Mom's box of stuff from White Rock and talked... we were on your bed and got tired..."

As the years went on, it seemed that the bond between the siblings had become a strong one. As much as Cyrus and Cassandra had fought when they were younger, they had become closer as they aged. Maybe it had to do with them being twins or that they were both the first children to be born in Meridiana. Perhaps it's because they were the oldest or that they had possessed the perfected peacekeeper genes, but there was something about them that even their father could never understand. It was likely that his wife would be able to better explain it, but she wasn't here. "It's alright. I was out all night anyway. I'm glad you two were able to find some comfort. I'm sorry I wasn't there." He was... he couldn't help but feel like a failure as a father.

Cassandra looked at him. "You needed to be there for Mom It's fine."

Cyrus spoke up. "Come on. Breakfast is nearly ready... maybe we'll get some good news today, especially if the professor is already on top of things."

Gavin could only hope.

After breakfast, he had paced. He knew Dorian was most likely working on something of importance and had fought with himself whether or not to go down to her room again. The professor had been accommodating that morning with his suggestions. Still, Gavin knew the man was struggling with his own internal battle of what was happening with Hokura. He hadn't blamed him, hadn't faulted him in any way. He wished Dorian would simply accept things because maybe then this wouldn't hurt as much when the time finally came.

Instead, Gavin had spent time with Cassandra and Cyrus. They sat on the couch in the family room as he told them stories about their mother.

"She literally picked this thing up and made a kissy face at it." Gavin scowled. "Of all the people I know and have ever met, only your mother would pick up a snake like that and coddle it." He shook his head. "She had a soft spot for animals, even ones you wouldn't exactly want to touch. She had a code that life was precious..." It was a strange sentiment, especially saying it out loud. She had been born and molded into being one of the strongest beings on the planet. Her fighting skills had been incomparable, she had taken out camps, armies... how many he didn't even want to think, and yet Hokura would hold onto a tarantula and place it somewhere "safer, where it wouldn't be seen by predators."

Cyrus smiled. "It would be amazing if we could have live specimens in the sanctuary... but I guess keeping them out in nature is best..."

His father nodded. "That was very much the professor's thoughts. Then again, I don't think he was one of those kids who ever had a pet growing up." A small smirk came and quickly left his face. The professor with a pet, the thought was amusing. He was sure Hokura knew if the man who was the father of science had a pet before the war happened and the world changed.

Cassandra giggled. "He doesn't seem to be one for animals. Maybe he had to test on lab rats when he was younger. I know I'd lose my love for them too if that's what I had to do."

The conversation had been kept light. This was precisely what they all needed. Recollecting their mother, sharing a few laughs, Gavin telling them things they were too young to remember. A tired, frazzled mother being the first in the compound, cooking experiments gone wrong, late-night talks about the constellations and what they had meant.

It had been mid-afternoon when the phone rang. Gavin excused himself and went to the bedroom.

"Gavin." Dorian's voice was soft.

"What's happening?" His voice was earnest. "Is there any news?"

"It's time that I accept what's happening..."

It hurt. It was a searing, breaking pain that he thought he had mentally prepared for, but the words still sliced through him. "This is it, isn't it? You can't save her, can you?"

"I cannot." This wasn't exactly a conversation he wanted to have over the phone, and yet to do it in person might be harder for both of them. "However... there's still time to say goodbye..."

Dorian stood in front of Gavin, giving the man a bleak expression. He asked him to meet in his office. "Have a seat... I wanted to tell you I've been able to hook her up to the TCDS. You can still talk to her... whatever might have been left unsaid you can still say to her. I don't know how long..." His voice hitched.

Gavin did as he said and gave him a sorrowful look. "How am I supposed to say goodbye?"

The professor shook his head as he sat across from him. "You and your children can go first, spend as much time with her as you can... then you can..."

"What about you?" Gavin looked up at the man. He could see that Dorian was breaking apart as he fought his emotions. That he was keeping his posture stiff, his fists were clenched, that his eyes were holding back tears. "I... I don't know if I can be there when she finally goes... it should be you..."

Dorian leaned back in surprise. "You're her husband, Gavin. You should be the one."

"No." Gavin trembled as he brought his hands up to the desk and buried his face inside of them. "I can't... I'm not even strong enough for this... I need you to do it for me, Dorian, and once it happens, I need you to..."

"You don't need to say it," the professor stated. He reached over, placing a hand on Gavin's shoulder. "I will see to the arrangements." He couldn't believe that it had come to this... no... this wasn't the end. He wouldn't allow himself to see this as the end. He still had his backup plan, he would cheat death, and he would bring her back. "Have you spoken to the children?"

"Yes." Gavin's voice was listless. "They're waiting in the hallway. I'll bring them in."

Dorian nodded as the governor rose from his seat and brought them in. Cyrus stood looking pale as he stood beside his father. Cassandra had caught him off guard as she ran into the room and dove into the professor's arm.

"Dorian," she cried. "Isn't there anything you can do?"

The man faltered under the girl's grasps. "Cass..." He wanted to tell her everything but couldn't. Not with her father and brother standing there... not when there was still a doubt that Gavin would pull the project before it even started. He leaned down in her grips. "I will tell you this once. You need to remember that whatever happens, not all is lost. I promise you." He would promise Hokura's daughter the world and try to deliver it. He didn't understand the relationship they had somehow formed. It was possible that it had become tightly knit during their rescue operation. The few times she had checked in with him. He walked them down to the medical facility, as Cyrus stayed at his father's side, Cass never left his.

The four entered the room as Cassandra gasped at the sight of her mother. She ran to her side and cried. "Mom! No..."

Dorian walked behind them as they gathered by Hokura's side. "I'm unsure if she can hear you, but with what I've been able to arrange with the TCDS machine along with the technology we used for the RTCS, you can put on these goggles, and in a way, you'll be transported into her subconscious. You'll be able to see her and talk to her, even interact with her."

Gavin's brows furrowed... "this technology...it's..."

"I started work on the program yesterday and finished it first thing this morning. It was a very long time ago, but I had used the TCDS to bring Hokura out of a coma before. Once you four start the process, I will alert the other two. They should be able to speak to her as well unless you have any objections," Dorian said as he took her in, the monitors that were hooked up to her forehead. He had never dreamed of her being in this state again. That once again, he would have to use this machine to communicate with her; it was no longer to wake her up... but to... he hated the thought as he closed his eyes and looked away. "You three can put the goggles on. I'll make sure everything syncs up."

With that, the three took a seat by the bed and grabbed the goggles. Before putting them on, Gavin gave Dorian a wary glance.

"Trust me," the professor said as Gavin nodded and slipped them on.

Immediately they were transported. They took a moment to get their grounds and take in their surroundings. They were on a beach staring at her as she looked out over the ocean.

"Mom?" Cassandra asked, taking in the scene as Hokura turned to her. Her mother's eyes and face lit up as she ran towards them.

Cassandra and Cyrus met her as they both wrapped their arms around her.

"How on earth?" Hokura asked as Gavin walked up to her.

"The Trans Cranial Direct Simulator..." he answered.

She gave a light laugh. "So Dorian is up to his old tricks again. I'm glad to see you three." She smiled at them.

Gavin's heart broke. How could she be so cruel? He almost expected to come into a dark room with her sobbing, but not this. How could she be smiling and laughing on a beach when she was in a coma and dying? He didn't understand it. This was bright, beautiful, warm, the crash of the waves, and the sand under his toes. This wasn't death. He needed to know. Did she know what was happening? He swallowed hard.

She looked at him and gave a sheepish smile. "We never got a chance to get out of the city. Let's spend the day together!" Hokura beamed as she turned. "There are some amazing tidal pools over this way!" She started moving as Cyrus and Cassandra followed in her wake.

Cyrus gave her a puzzled look. "Mom... you realize this is all in your subconscious, right? We're not really on the beach..."

Gavin sighed, leave it to his son to deduct things in a scientific matter.

Hokura took her son's hand. "I know," she stated lightly. "This place is a memory, one of my favorite places. I wanted to be here with all of you."

The boy nodded. He had no idea how to respond.

Cassandra looked around. "It's kind of like the RTC simulator..."

Hokura smiled "exactly! I'm guessing that's where the idea came from."

Gavin watched the three walk hand in hand, his brows furrowed. She had known... and yet it had been a while since he had seen her this happy. Before Tobias, they had wanted to get away from the city and spend some time together here, just them. He mourned that he had lost his chance to share in that time with her. He shook his head. He couldn't allow himself to waste this time as well. He needed to soak up as much time with her as he possibly could. He quickened his stride and met up with them as he smiled alongside his family.

———————————✦———————————

Dorian sighed as he raked his hand through his hair. Everything had synced up. He had watched everyone's facial expressions change and wondered exactly what was transpiring. No matter, he would have his time with her later. He had yet another duty to carry out as he rose from his place. He needed to alert the other two. Something he wasn't exactly looking forward to doing.

The professor made his way to the suites as he stood outside Adam and Amara's... he took a moment as he clenched his left hand in his pocket. He braced himself for the possible explosion of emotions that were going to come at him, possibly fists as well. He could take Amara, but he had hoped that Adam would be quick to subdue her if anything happened. He knocked on the door and was thankful Adam had answered.

"Dorian," Adam said, taking him in questioningly. "We weren't expecting you..."

The professor took a breath. "This isn't exactly something I would do over the phone. I needed to give you the news in person." He looked up to see he had caught Amara's attention as she walked over towards the door. He was relieved that Adam was acting as a physical buffer. Suddenly it was hard to articulate the words as he swallowed hard, fighting to keep his composure. "She doesn't have much time left. You need to come and say your goodbyes."

Amara's eyes widened as she walked up behind Adam. "What?" she cried as she walked past him and up to the professor. "What do you mean she doesn't have much time left?" she faltered as her hands came up to her mouth. "You mean..."

He closed his eyes and lowered his head. "I'm sorry you two... I've failed. All I can do now is see that she's comfortable, but there's nothing else I can do." His voice cracked. "Her system has become too weak. I can't save her."

Adam grabbed hold of Amara and held her tightly. "It's okay, professor, we understand."

"No, we don't!" Amara cried, pushing away from him, and staring hard at Dorian. "You said you were going to save her! I trusted you! *She* trusted you!"

Dorian looked away. "I know. And I failed." His fist shook as he couldn't bear it anymore as his eyes watered. "I failed her, dammit!" he cried as his tears escaped. "I would have given anything to keep her alive and to fix her, but I can't!" He trembled as everything around him slowly started to break. He took in Amara. "I'm sorry, Amara... I failed all of you."

Adam took a step forward. "You did all you could."

The professor hunched. "Did I? Maybe if I hadn't been so wrapped up in getting my arm back, I would have recognized the signs. Maybe if I had paid more attention to her, I would have realized something wasn't right."

Amara's tone softened. "Don't say that... this...," she sniffled. "This is just how it is."

Adam took her hand and squeezed it as his arm wrapped around her. "We need to contact Olga to make sure we have someone to watch the children. Then we'd like to see her."

"She's in the medical facility. Gavin and the children are spending some time with her. I'll take you down there, and you can join..." Dorian's voice cracked. "She's in a coma, but I was able to get her hooked up to the TCDS and created a program where you can still interact with her."

Adam quickly picked up the phone and made arrangements. He had been grateful as always that Olga was ready to be there at a moment's notice.

Adam and Amara followed Dorian down to the medical facility and to the room where Hokura was hooked up to. "There are two extra pairs of goggles. It's set up just like the RTC simulator; it'll transport you into her thoughts, and you'll be able to transverse with her. All you have to do is put them on."

Amara looked up at him, tears in her eyes. "What about you?"

"I'll be back later," Dorian stated. "I won't be too long." He watched the two enter the room. He then sprinted down the hallway and into his nearest lab, where he sank to his knees and wept, grasping his chest. He had tried to hold it in, tried to fight and deny it as long as he possibly could. This pain, he had never felt something like this before, even when he had given up hope for getting her back. This was a different loss. She was leaving him. He had tried so hard and yet met a wall at every turn. The only person he had ever loved was dying, and he couldn't fix this. This was beyond heartache, beyond knowing she hadn't chosen him, beyond the years he had devotedly stood by her side no matter her choice.

There was still his backup plan, but to be able to go through with that... she would have to be dead. The thoughts assaulted him in a sickening way as dread rolled through him. Once she was in that chamber, there would be a whole new set of experiments, the cooling and keeping her body suspended. Figuring out where he had gone wrong and then the process of bringing her back. He slumped. If she was gone, he would step back. Gavin would have to allow it. He had done his duty in perfecting those in Meridiana, had done so much over the decades. He would put all his time and effort into bringing her back, even if it took years since he would have nothing but time on his hands while the person he lived for was no longer physically in his life.

Hokura had been sitting by the surf with Gavin and her children by her side talking when she heard a familiar whistle. She turned excitedly to see Adam and Amara approaching them.

Amara looked over towards Adam. "This is weird..." she mumbled at her husband.

"This is definitely something... I don't know if weird is the word," Adam said as they walked hand in hand towards the rest. "Almost indescribable." He could feel the sand beneath his feet. The sea breeze felt amazingly refreshing against his skin. "Almost makes me want to come back."

Hokura smiled at them. "You guys came!"

Amara raised an eyebrow. "You were expecting us?"

She nodded. "In a way, yes... it's hard to explain. Everything that's happening is in my mind. It's like you've entered a dream that I control. You can talk to me and see the world that I'm imagining but can't go outside of it." She looked at Adam and gave him a wink. "I promise no crabs pinching your fingers."

He let out a strained chuckle as Amara squeezed his hand. How on earth was this meant to be goodbye?

Hokura rose. "Let's go further down the beach and see if we can find any starfish!"

Amara chewed her bottom lip. "If this is all controlled by you, don't you know if the starfish are already there?"

The first child beamed as she looked back at her friend. "Oh, I know they're there and in all different colors!"

Everyone followed in her wake as Gavin took Hokura's hand, and she led them all further down the beach. Cassandra walked at her mother's other side and grabbed her hand. Even if this wasn't real, she wanted the contact with her. Hokura glanced down and gave her a loving smile as she squeezed her daughter's hand.

Hokura looked into the distance. "I'm going to show you all some amazing sights, just you wait!"

Everyone had been astounded by the different tidal pools, the eels, the small fish that darted around. They had examined different seashells and, as Hokura had promised, starfish of every color they could imagine. Hokura's laughter echoed over the surf as the children chased gulls and ran through the waves.

Gavin looked over at her. "This is what you wanted..."

She nodded as he looked towards Adam and Amara. "This place serves as a fond memory for all of us."

"Hokura!" Amara's voice called as she, Adam, and the children were peering over a tidal pool. "C'mere, you gotta tell us what the hell this thing is called again!"

Gavin gave a solemn smile. "I'm glad we got to spend the day here all together."

She kissed him tenderly on the cheek. "Now, let's go see what they're asking about."

The hours had gone by. They had all shared in love and laughter as they had spent the day together reminiscing and enjoyed the beach. Hokura could feel things starting to dwindle, she didn't know how she knew, but she did.

Hokura noticed that the other two had broken away from the group as she walked up to Adam and Amara and hugged them both deeply. "This seems like a stupid time to apologize again."

Adam swallowed hard. "Apologize for what?"

"For not being around as much as I should have been. For not being a great leader or friend... for being me..."

Tears started down Amara's cheeks. "That's what we loved about you. You were you... even if we didn't understand it or understand *you*, we always loved you and saw you as one of us. You *were* one of us, Hokura... no matter what."

She smiled at her friends. "Thank you, both of you, for always being there for me."

Adam nodded, so this was what it was like to have to say goodbye to someone. This was the pain of losing someone that was special. He was sure she had felt it deeper because of how deeply she loved James. His grip tightened.

Hokura let out a sigh as she looked at him. "Take care of her, keep her in check." She winked at him.

Amara let out a sob. "Hey, I'm right here..."

Hokura gently wiped away one of Amara's tears. "You were like a sister to me, one of my best friends, and I love you. Keep going on for me. Help Cass out when she needs it." She took the two peacekeepers in. "Both of you be there for Gavin and

Cyrus. Make sure Dorian stays sane..." Her heart panged... he wasn't here...

Adam nodded. "We'll let you say goodbye to the others...."

Hokura nodded and gave them one last hug as they then disappeared from her arms.

Adam took off his goggles as Amara was doing the same, tears streaming down her cheeks.

"I can't believe it... just like that...," she cried.

Adam quickly hugged her.

Their attention rose to see Dorian standing near the door, taking in the scene with a solemn look. "You two got to say what you needed?" he asked in a mellow tone.

They both nodded quietly as Adam held his wife, who was still crying.

"We did," Adam said, giving the professor a sad look. "How much more time do you think she has?"

The man crossed his arms. His eyes couldn't meet the two... "I can't say for sure, but not long..." If anything, the blood transfusion may have sped up her deterioration. He didn't want to think about it. He glanced at the monitors. As long as they were beeping, he knew she was still alive.

Amara wiped away a few tears. "I'm sure she's waiting for you..."

He grimaced as his brows furrowed in a painful expression. "I'll see her in a bit."

She couldn't help it; her moves were automatic as she left Adam's arms and wrapped them around the professor. "She doesn't blame you. Nobody does. I know it hurts, I know it'll hurt more for you, but you did everything you could."

He looked down at her and awkwardly placed his arms around her. It felt strange to be comforted this way as Adam went to him placed a reassuring hand on his shoulder and embraced him as well. The notion was something he couldn't place, something he had never experienced before. Gavin had offered him consoling words, but it had always been Hokura who had physically consoled him. Having the other two do so was different in a way he couldn't quite explain. "Thank you both." Dorian sighed.

Adam could see that he was struggling. "You don't have to keep the façade up in front of us. It's been long enough, Dorian. You're allowed to show your emotions."

The professor sighed. "It's not a slight against you two or anyone Adam. It's simply who I am and who I'm sure I'll continue to be. Hokura was able to dig under the surface. Now that she's gone, I can't make any promises."

Amara glanced at her husband. This wasn't the time as she shook her head slightly. "Thank you for everything you've done." With that, her grips loosened as she wiped away some more tears.

Adam went to her side. "If you need anything, we're here as well."

"Thank you for the sentiment," Dorian said and watched as the two took their leave. He didn't have it in him yet to do this... he would sit and observe. Gavin asked him to go last... he wondered when the governor would want to switch off. Until then, he had nowhere else to be as he grabbed a stool and made himself comfortable.

Hokura walked back to Gavin, Cassandra, and Cyrus. She wanted them to forever remember this day, but not in a sorrowful way, more as a day where they got to see the ocean one last time with their mother. That's when she recalled the site from when she came back here after the war when she needed to find some solace from what had happened. "I want to show you something." She smiled as she looked at her family.

They got up and followed her as she walked further outwards past the tidal pools and towards the ocean edge. That's when they breached the water, a pod of orca whales swimming together.

Cassandra gasped as Cyrus's eyes widened.

The girl looked up at her mother. "You told us about this."

Hokura smiled as the whales swam happily in front of them. "Yes, this from that memory. Aren't they beautiful?"

Cyrus stepped forward. "There was always speculation about what ocean life survived... but to see it! Even if it's through a memory!" He was awestruck.

Gavin came up behind her and wrapped his arms around her as they all watched. "We've never been so lucky as to see them whenever we camped."

She tilted her head as she brought her arms around herself. "I had wished that you would have been here to see it when I did. There were so many emotions running through me that day... at that time. I don't know if they ever truly left me. In a way, I've always felt like parts of me have been scattered between these beaches, White Rock, the graveyard, and the compound." She watched as the whales dove and resurfaced.

Gavin's grip around her tightened. "Those pieces are all memories..."

"Yes," she sighed. "And I want you to share all the ones you have with me with Cass and Cy. Don't hold anything back from them." She looked lovingly at her two children as her heart ached. She was going to be leaving them.

Hokura walked out of Gavin's arms and to her children, grabbing each of them by the hand as they stood. "I love both of you so very much. You're going to do me proud and grow up to be amazing people." She turned to Cyrus and hugged him. "I remember how you kept me on my toes when you were younger, but even at a young age, you were curious about every-thing. You had a million questions about how things worked." She kissed him on the cheek. "Never lose that spark. Never stop asking questions or thirsting for knowledge."

The boy tried to hold back his tears. "Mom... you were also so happy and supportive..." He didn't want to think about a life without her.

She ran her hand through his hair as she comforted him. "You're going to do great things, my boy. Don't ever let anyone hold you back." She then looked at Cassandra with a smirk. "And you, my darling daughter." She chuckled. "You're just like me because you dive headfirst into things without checking the waters first." She held her arm out as Cassandra walked into her embrace beside her brother."

"Mom." She grabbed onto Hokura and sobbed quietly.

"Cass, you're always going to be a headstrong person, and it's going to cause trouble..." She chuckled. "It did for me, but always follow your heart. It'll never steer you wrong." She didn't want to let go of them yet as she held her children and accounted for the years. For the smiles and tears, for the joys and frustrations, for confiding in those around her as she wondered what on earth she was doing some days. Hokura glanced down at them. For a large portion of her life, she never dreamt of being a mother, but that had been one of her destinies all along. It was hard to think she wouldn't be able to see them grow any further. "I love you both so very much. I know whatever you do, you'll make me proud."

Gavin heard what she was saying as he walked over and put a gentle hand on both of them. "You'll make us both proud. I know it." They shared a last family hug together.

Hokura kissed both their heads. "I need to talk to your father for a bit."

Cassandra's tears started all the more as she grabbed onto her mother, all the more, and held onto her for dear life. This couldn't be the end!

"Cass," her voice was soft. "I know you have that strength inside of you. You need to call on it. You need to be strong."

The girl nodded as she looked at her brother as he gave her a sorrowful nod. They both hugged their mother one last time and kissed her on the cheeks.

Cyrus pursed his lips. "We love you, Mom... we'll never forget you."

As the twins took their goggles off, a gentle voice met them. "It's okay, you two."

Cassandra wiped her eyes to see Dorian standing in front of them as she crashed into him, sobbing. She had no words. She didn't know what to say to him as she cried.

The professor looked at Cyrus and raised his arm as the boy walked over to him, his eyes full of tears as Dorian put his arm around him. "Come, let's get you to Adam and Amara. They'll take care of you while your father spends some time with her." All he could do was what the other two had tried to do for him. He needed to offer them some comfort. He wanted to tell them, wanted to bow to her children and swear to them that this was now part of the process. That he knew it hurt but that he was going to bring her back somehow. Then again, would they truly believe him?

Cassandra sniffled into his shirt. "Thank you for taking care of us..."

He winced. He wasn't taking care of them... he was pawning them off on the peacekeepers because he had no idea how to help them right now. The support and sympathy he had felt forced and faked in a way no matter how genuine he tried to be. He wanted to tell them he'd always be there for them but didn't know if he could outright lie to them like that.

Once Hokura's heart stopped, he would be fully dedicated to the project of curing her. He escorted the twins out of the room and towards the living quarters as Cassandra hung off his arm, still crying, his hand still on Cyrus' shoulder guiding him.

Upon knocking on Adam and Amara's door, Amara rushed them and grabbed onto Cyrus, and hugged the boy. She noted that Cass was still clinging to the professor.

Dorian gently took the girl and bent down. Her eyes were red and puffy. Her face was a mess. It further broke his heart. "Cass." His voice was soft. "You're gonna get through this. I promise you that you will. You just need to remember what I told you..." His hand came to her head as he patted it.

Her eyes opened as they looked at him. His cold blue eyes held a sorrow to them, and yet there had been a light that flashed through them.

"I've never lied to you, Cass. I've always been forthright. Just remember what I said before." She nodded, trying to think about what he had told her. He had said everything would work out... how could he say that now?

Adam came up behind Amara and shared a look with the professor.

He straightened and took them in. "Gavin's saying his goodbyes now... I need to get back to her."

———————⟡———————

Hokura gently cupped Gavin's face. He had been avoiding her stare. "Look at me." Her voice was light. "No matter what, no matter what you think... what happened with Tobias wasn't your fault. All of this was nobody's fault, and you need to drill that into your head, Gavin."

His eyes finally came up to hers. "I was supposed to have a lifetime with you."

She pursed her lips in a sad smile. "Things didn't go that way, my love. I wish they had. I wish we could have watched the children grow to the age of majority. I'm sorry that I can't be there for it. I know Adam and Amara will be there... that Dorian will be there..."

"You don't get it..." Gavin's voice was hoarse. "You're the glue that holds us all together, what connects us."

Her lips met his gently and only for a moment. "Then let my memory connect you and hold you all together. Let the love that you all had for me keep you all strong."

Desperation came over his face. "I don't want you to go... I don't know how I'm going to go on... I don't know what I'm doing without you! What about the kids?"

Hokura took a breath. "Adam and Amara will be there. I want Cassandra to continue her training with Talon; it helps her. I'm sure Cyrus will continue his path with loving science. Let him do that... let them choose their own paths and support them. If the day comes when they want to be peacekeepers, let them. When the days get hard, lean on those who care about them."

He bit his bottom lip. "I never loved someone the way I did you. You showed me how it was to truly live..."

"Keep living!" she urged. "Do whatever you need to do Gavin, keep making this place a sanctuary. Keep helping your people."

Could he possibly admit that he didn't know what he was going to do? That he couldn't look into his future and tell her that he was going to be successful, that he wasn't going to be a shell of a man because his reason for living was no longer beside him. He said he had accepted things, but honestly, he hadn't imagined the reality of it as he locked his arms around her.

She lowered her head. "I love you, Gavin. The years that you've given me have been wonderful, and you gave me two beautiful children."

"They need you," he said. "They're just like you. You'll understand them in ways I'd never be able to!" Why did it sound like he was begging? Because he was... he knew it wouldn't do any good. "I'm sorry... we'll make it. I promise you we will."

"I know." Her voice was soft as she kissed him. "I'm sorry, my love, my time is growing near Gavin..."

His eyes widened. "There's still one last person..." Tears started spilling. He couldn't control them. "If you want... I can stay... but..." He faltered. He didn't know if he was strong enough for this...

Her lips were on his as they parted passionately. She would make him remember how much she loved him, that they were able to share one last kiss, and that she would never blame him for any of this. "I love you so much, Gavin. I know how you are... kiss me one last time, and let this be goodbye, my love."

He did, he didn't want the kiss to end, but when he pulled away, he knew he couldn't continue to stay by her side. "I love you..."

Gavin took the goggles off as he sobbed. A pair of hands found his shoulders as he wept.

"Gavin... Dr. Lucien is here. He'll take you to your suite. Adam and Amara are with Cassandra and Cyrus," Dorian said, his voice soothing.

"I don't know how I'm going to go on without her," he sobbed, grasping at his chest.

The professor gave him a sorrowful look. "One day at a time, that's all any of us can do."

Gavin stood and turned to her. She looked so peaceful other than the monitors hooked up to her. He bent over her form. "Goodbye, Hokura," he softly whispered and gently kissed her lips as his tears flowed.

"Come," Dorian said, gently putting his hand on Gavin's back. He looked at the monitors. She was getting weaker. "I'll let you know when it's done."

The governor nodded as he continued to cry. Upon opening the door, he saw everyone standing in front of it. Red-eyed, tears running down their cheeks as they embraced him. He needed this. They all did as Adam, Amara, Cyrus, and Cassandra went their way, followed by Doctor Lucien.

As the door shut, Dorian took a deep breath as he looked towards Hokura's form. He wasn't ready for this... would *never* be ready for this and yet his time with her was limited.

———————————

Hokura turned. She had been staring at the ocean, waiting for him. "You chose to be last..."

"Gavin asked me to be... and so... in a way, I guess I did..." he said, simply standing there, taking her in. She was the closest to heaven that he had ever experienced, and she was leaving him.

"Come, let's sit and take in the sunset together." She smiled lightly.

"How can you ask me, so light-heartedly, to do such a thing?" He was fighting to keep his composure.

"Is there something else you'd like to do?" She raised an eyebrow at him.

This was all an apparition... none of this was real... it was all in her subconscious. Yes, there was something else he wanted to do! He wanted to take her in his arms and kiss her, make love to her one last time on the beach before she faded away from him. He wanted to lay her down in all her glory and pour his passion into her so that even as she died, she wouldn't have any doubt of how much he truly loved her and how deeply that love for her ran and that there would never be anyone else. No, even in her passing moments, she still had her integrity. He shook his head. "Watch the sunset; how mundane." Tears filled his eyes. "That sounds wonderful."

The two sat. He held her as she leaned back against him. It was as if they were back in White Rock on that fateful day that she had run out of her apartment, stating she needed a walk, and he had followed after her. All the confusion and pain that was breaking her down, the regrets, the promises. Did he dare tell her that this wasn't it? "Hokura..." His voice was tight. "I promised I wouldn't fail you."

"You didn't fail me, Dorian. I don't want you to ever think you did." She shook her head. "Somethings just aren't in our hands. This was one of them."

"I'll bring you back," he choked. "Please trust me, believe me... this is not the end."

A sad smile came to her lips. "I believe you..." it was a lie, but it was all she could offer him. "There will never be an end to us, Dorian, because you'll live on, and so I'll forever live in your heart."

That wasn't it, dammit! "This isn't tongue and cheek, Hokura; I will bring you back from this."

She was silent. He wished he could prove it to her. He wanted to shake her, to tell her this wasn't the end. This wasn't death... that... he couldn't even put an explanation into words. Fear struck him. What if the cryogenic suspension didn't work, and this truly was it? What if this time was the last time they were ever together? His hand squeezed hers. "There's so much I want to say...."

"I know, and I think I know most of it... because I know you... because I know how you feel because you've always been honest with me." She looked towards the ocean. "Our time together was a gift." She turned and looked at him. "For what it's worth, I'm glad I came back to Meridiana. I'm glad I came back to face you..." She licked her lips as her brows furrowed. "It's so strange because..." A half sob escaped her. "I came back to fall in love with you all over again and experience feelings that I never thought existed."

Dorian took her words in. To hear it said out loud was an odd notion. She had feared him for so long, and although things had been complicated between them when she first arrived back, they had solidified a strong relationship. "I apologize for the confusion that I caused you, but you know as much as it hurt, I never stopped loving you."

"I know." Her voice was soft.

And that's why he couldn't, wouldn't let her go because she had been the only one he had ever loved or had ever loved him. Because what he felt for her ran deeper than anything he had ever felt, and he wasn't ready to allow it to leave him. The joy his heart felt whenever she was around, how she calmed the storm within him, it wasn't something he could lose. He needed her as he wrapped his arms around her.

Hokura leaned into him. This felt nice, it felt safe, but even the professor couldn't protect her from what was looming around her. She knew there was no escaping it.

Dorian's heart was shattering; the sun was getting closer to the ocean, and he knew what that meant; he wanted to hold her here forever... alas, he knew the time had come as she stood up and looked at him, turned, and helped him stand his heartbreaking. He suppressed a sob. "How am I supposed to go on without you?"

She smiled at him. "Just as everyone else will, Dorian. Be there for Gavin, continue training Cassie, and help Cyrus. As I told Gavin, if they decide to become the new peacekeepers of Meridiana, make sure they are successful, keep our city beautiful and thriving."

He couldn't take it as he dropped to his knees and hugged her legs. "No, not the city. The city was never beautiful; it was always you that held the beauty," he sobbed. He would beg on his hands and knees for her. "I was robbed of you for forty years, and then Gavin, now I have to spend the rest of my miserable life without you by my side. How is this fair, Hokura?"

She leaned down, grabbing his arms as she helped him up. This wasn't how she wanted their last minutes to be. "I'm so sorry. That's simply the way this life turned out for us. Maybe it was fate, maybe it was destiny or science, but there's nothing we can do now to go back."

"I can fix this! I'm *going* to fix this!" Dorian cried. His emotions and doubt flooded over him. "I just need more time! If I can find a way to suspend everything happening to your system, I will work on this for a hundred years until Meridiana is nothing but rubble and ash, but I can fix this!" He stopped. "I love you."

"I love you too, Dorian, but we can't fight what's coming."

"Then I'll hold you forever." His arms were wrapped around her. He wouldn't let go of her. As long as she was in his arms, that's all that mattered. The pain was too much. He would die here too. They embraced for a while, simply holding one another as Dorian broke over and over, his tears became manic sobs, and he trembled against her. He wanted to continue to beg her to stay with him... but if she had to go, death would be a sweet release for him. No... he couldn't think that way... there was still time, but his heart was bleeding so raw, the pain was devastating. The idea of her heart no longer beating crippled his very being.

There were light footsteps that came up behind them, followed by a clearing of a throat. Hokura turned and let out a small laugh of surprise.

Dorian looked up to see a man standing behind them. His heart broke further. The man before them had long, wavy brown hair and green eyes. There had been an air about him. Dorian knew right away that it had been the rebel commander...James.

Hokura looked back at the professor. "It's time for me to go." She smiled sweetly at him and kissed him gently on the cheek, allowing her lips to linger for a moment. "Please, Dorian, take care of everyone I love. Live on for them, for me." She walked away from his grasp and into James' arms as she smiled up at him sweetly. "I've missed you."

"Yeah, but you needed to say your goodbyes. I knew you would take your time getting back to me, but now it's for good." James smiled down at her, running his hand over her cheeks and taking her in.

"And now we can finally watch the sunset." She smiled up at him.

Dorian watched as the rebel commander bent down and kissed her as he wrapped her in his arms and held her. He didn't understand what he was seeing as the two embraced passionately and began to fade in front of his eyes. Had it been real? Had it been her one last memory of how she wanted to leave this world? With him, at her side, as she finally endured her last breath, and death overcame her? Pain engulfed him as he screamed her name, pounding at the sand below him.

"Damn you!" he screamed. "You promised me! All those

years ago, you said you weren't going anywhere! Come back to me!" His sobs raked through him as the screen turned black, and he was subconsciously pushed back to the hospital room.

"Hokura!" he screamed, moving to her body. The heart monitor had flatlined. "No! No! No!" he screamed as he pumped at her chest. "Not like this! Not yet!" He went over to her mouth and blew air into it, filling her lungs. "Breathe, damn it!" He went back to pumping at her chest. He knew it was futile. "Please!" he cried in desperation; her limp body showed no signs of her coming back to him. He let out a scream that sounded like a dying animal as it ripped through the medical vicinity, and he collapsed in sobs. He wasn't strong enough for this. How could she ask him to keep living when there would be nothing but pain filling his very being for the rest of his days.

The door opened as Gavin walked in. Spindler had heard the professor's screams and had alerted him. The governor was already heart broken as he placed a hand on Dorian's shoulder. "She's gone, Dorian," he cried, unable to keep his own composure. "There's no bringing her back. It's done."

"I failed," Dorian gasped through his pain. "I wasn't worthy of her."

"Come on, get up, let's go grieve elsewhere," Gavin said. "We're all meeting in my suite to be together."

"No... you asked me, and I have some obligations to see to first. I just need a bit to myself. I'll be there, but there are some things I need to see to..." Dorian said, rising from his knees. He didn't even look at the man but listened as Gavin walked out of the room before going to the transcranial direct simulator and inserted a chip. This was one last that the professor could collect from her. He had all her samples, all her original genetic coding. All that was left were her memories, which were now stored here in the TCDS. He waited listlessly for the download, everything that she ever experienced, ever felt, was now forever his, so in a way, she would always be with him. He looked at her body and the clock as he noted the time of death... time... yes, there was still time. Panic ceased within him. If there was still a chance, he couldn't afford to waste it. He still had something he needed to do, and he needed to work fast... his body moved. He needed to be swift. He made a promise, and dammit, he was going to keep it. He had never failed; he wouldn't fail her; he had promised her he would save her, and that's exactly what he was going to do, even if it took a hundred years. This was his second chance, and as much as he had dreaded this happening, he now needed to do what Hokura had done her entire life. He needed to plunge headfirst into the unknown because this was going to be the only other chance he had at bringing her back. She was still warm... his moves were automatic as he unhooked her from the monitors and wheeled her gurney down towards the science facility in new resolve. Down towards his quartered off lab. "I swear it on my being... this is not the end."

EPILOGUE

Two and a half years later

Cassandra stood in the garden solemnly. "Mom... we miss you; I miss you." The girl held back her tears. "Dad and Dorian are a mess; they won't even talk to one another anymore. Dad pretends he's okay, but I hear him crying every night on the couch. He won't sleep in your bed. He goes for walks some nights and doesn't come back until the morning. He said he doesn't want to be governor anymore." She wiped a stray tear escaping her eye. "He wants Cyrus to take over for him, I think that's what keeps him going these days, but I know Cyrus wants to be a scientist." She licked her lips as they started to tremble. "Professor Dorian has locked himself in his lab. He quartered off part of the compound for his own experiments. I think he thinks he's going to somehow bring you back. He doesn't even oversee my training anymore. When I asked him why he said it's too painful because I look too much like you, so he fully handed me off to Talon." She couldn't hold it back as she wept. "I wanted to know more about you. I wanted to spend more time with you! I wanted to hear more about the rebel commander and your life away from Meridiana, and now I'll never know! I was too late to ask you...." She looked at the plaque. "And I'll never understand why Dad had been so specific with where these plaques were supposed to be placed. I wish I knew the story behind the blueberry bush but Dad won't talk to me about it." She idly touched the raised words that paid tribute to her mother, the great super-soldier who had liberated the old city, who had saved the city from war, who had continued the line of peacekeepers. She then looked over at the plaque next to it, giving tribute to the rebel commander, that they were meant to be side by side for the rest of eternity. "I wish *he* could bring you back..." the girl cried. She bent down and placed the tiger lily at the bottom of the memorial. "I love you, Mom..."

Dorian stumbled around in his personal lab; it had been late, yet sleep eluded him once again as his mind wouldn't stop racing. He had a sector of the compound quarantined off to be his personal labs so nobody would disturb him. He had stepped down from his position as head of the scientist department after Hokura's death and released all files and projects he had been working on to the compound's lead scientists. Over the years, he had become a shadow of a man, barely leaving his laboratory as he slipped into darkness. He had spent the last hour in the RTC simulator trying to fight himself into exhaustion because the thoughts from his day simply wouldn't leave him. The professor walked over to the blue light that was emanating from the cryogenic suspension capsule and stared at her form lovingly. Why take to his suite when this was the only place he wanted to be? Close to her, watching her, talking to her, working on her system to perfect it once more. "Today was a slight setback, but I know I'm getting closer..." He slumped and sat next to the chamber, peering in as he placed his cheek on the cool glass. "If this takes the next hundred years, I swear to you, my love, I will bring you back."

ABOUT THE AUTHOR

Nicolette Fuller: Mother, wife, artist, lover of the arts, reptiles, and arachnids- not your average individual. Born and raised in the Okanagan region of Canada, she can be found enjoying an array of activities from gold panning to wine tasting. Her passion for reading fiction fuelled her love of writing, as she came up with her own series to follow alongside her author husband, James Fuller.

To learn more about Nicolette Fuller and discover more Next Chapter authors, visit our website at www.nextchapter.pub.

Malfunction
ISBN: 978-4-82419-835-8

Published by
Next Chapter
2-5-6 SANNO
SANNO BRIDGE
143-0023 Ota-Ku, Tokyo
+818035793528

28th September 2024